Driven by curiosity, Jess had opened the envelope ~~~~ the first red light on Route 1. It had been a mistake.

Now she sat frozen, staring at the sharply written words meant for her *personal* attention, meant, surely, to make her palms sweat, her pulse race, and her thoughts whir out of control.

Jessica Bates Randall, it read at the top of a sheet of blue paper that matched the envelope postmarked from the place called Vineyard Haven. The words that followed were few, but their impact was powerful.

I am your baby—the one you gave up. Isn't it time we met?

No name, no signature, nothing else. And no reference to the fact that Jess already knew her baby was dead.

Behind her a horn blasted. Jess pulled her eyes from the letter: the traffic light was green. She shoved the paper in her purse. Then she stepped on the gas and her car moved forward, steered by this woman who could no longer breathe or see past the pain in her heart and the mist in her eyes. . . .

Also by Jean Stone

Sins of Innocence

First Loves

Ivy Secrets

Places by the Sea

Birthday Girls

Tides
of the
Heart

Jean Stone

Bantam Books

NEW YORK   TORONTO   LONDON   SYDNEY   AUCKLAND

TIDES OF THE HEART
A Bantam Book / January 1999

ISBN 0-553-57786-7

Published simultaneously in the United States and Canada

Bantam Books are published by Bantam Books, a division of Random
House, Inc. Its trademark, consisting of the words "Bantam Books" and
the portrayal of a rooster, is Registered in U.S. Patent and Trademark
Office and in other countries. Marca Registrada. Bantam Books, 1540
Broadway, New York, New York 10036.

PRINTED IN THE UNITED STATES OF AMERICA

OPM   10 9 8 7 6 5 4 3 2 1

To everyone who has loved and lost
and grieved their grief,
then found the place to store the good
and the path to moving on.

ACKNOWLEDGMENTS

To Nancy Fitzpatrick for her friendship over the years, and for her courage to leave Manhattan for the other island she so loves; to Nancy's great friend, Scott True of The Black Dog Tavern, for sharing his stories of the pulse of the Vineyard; to Ann Nelson of Bunch of Grapes Bookstore for directing me to Vineyard Haven and West Chop; to Catherine Mayhew, genealogist and tour guide extraordinaire; and to Joe Mahoney of the Tuckerman House in Vineyard Haven. Thank you all.

And did I mention those folks at The Outermost Inn? Good grief, we cannot forget them. Carol would never allow that to happen! Thanks, gang. You are all truly special.

Tides of the Heart

PROLOGUE

From the tiny window of her attic bedroom at Mayfield House, she looked down over the steeple-topped landscape of Vineyard Haven, across the gray winter water to the land beyond: "the Mainland," some Vineyarders called it; "America," others said.

She turned to the left and studied the dots of the Elizabeth Islands silhouetted against the snow-threatening sky. Then her eyes dropped to the treetops and annoyance inched up her spine: It had always annoyed her that the tall pines blocked her view of West Chop. Of West Chop and the beach and his house. The house she had wasted so much time watching before she'd known the truth.

"It wasn't fair," she said in a whisper, though no one but her father was at the inn now, because it was February and the tourists had gone. No one could hear her lament but her father, and whatever ghosts lurked in the two-hundred-year-old, drafty halls. No one could hear her lament, feel her rage, see her tears.

She looked down at the papers that lay on the small oak chest and wondered what her father would think when he learned that she knew—that she found what she'd found in the secret compartment of the old rolltop desk; that she'd found out about the lies that he'd told. The lies they'd all told.

Then, from the pocket of her long black sarong, she extracted a handful of pebbles of smooth sea glass: blue, brown, rich bottle green—misshapen marbles, jewels from the sea. She rolled them between her fingers and wondered what would happen next.

Click-click, click-click.

And if they'd be sorry when they learned what she'd done.

Part One

Chapter 1

Jessica Bates Randall glanced up the chintz-covered wall to the clock over her sewing machine.

Damn, she thought. It was nearly six and she'd promised to drop off these draperies at Mrs. Boynton's in time to be hung for a seven-thirty dinner party. The Boyntons lived across town—in the elitest of the elite side of this southern Connecticut town—where Jess had once lived when she'd thought that it mattered.

It would take twenty minutes to get there. Longer, if the late February sky decided to storm, decided to actually do what the TV meteorologist had predicted.

Stomping on the pedal, she returned to her work, guiding the final hem of raw silk through the whirring machine, trying to remember when—before her divorce—this had been her hobby and it had been fun.

But now it was her business—*Designs by Jessica,* read the peach-scripted name on the window glass of the front door. It was her business and her responsibility.

She would not have been late if Maura hadn't called. But her daughter was plagued with yet another crisis—one in a never-ending, knotty string since going off to Skidmore two years ago. This time, it was about spring break.

"Mother!" Maura had shrieked. Maura seemed to have taken up shrieking since she'd been in college, as if it were a rite of passage, like keg parties and living off campus. "Liz thinks Costa Rica is cool, but Heather thinks we should go to Lauderdale, that there's something deeply spiritual about its tradition. But Liz says no way, and I don't know what to do. They're leaving it all up to me. . . ."

A muscle tightened, then tugged, at the base of Jess's neck. "What makes you so certain I'm going to allow you to go anywhere?" It was asked half in jest, half in earnest—a wounded reflection of a lingering fantasy that Jess could somehow hold on to the maternal control that weakened with each passing year as her children insisted on growing into adults.

"Mother! You can't be serious!"

"You're twenty years old, Maura," Jess replied, feeling more tired than guilty for challenging her daughter in the ongoing battle for her independence. "But I still pay the bills."

Silence smoldered over the line. Jess could almost see the pout on Maura's small face—the much-practiced pout that made the delicate, twenty-year-old face look no more than thirteen.

Then Maura spoke. "Daddy said he'd pay for it."

The lump that swelled in Jess's chest felt like a fur ball, a fur ball named Charles, that familiar, annoying fur ball that, no matter how hard she tried, simply wouldn't come out, apparently destined to remain forever lodged in her gullet.

She wanted to say, "It would be nice if he'd been so generous about child support," but Jess curbed her words, reminding herself to be grateful for her trust fund, for the fact that she'd not needed money from Charles to raise their three children in comfort, that it was only the principle that angered her. The principle, and her pride.

"Then why don't you pick somewhere different?" Jess asked. "If Heather wants spirituality and Liz wants to be cool, why don't you go to Sedona? You can bring back all kinds of stories to enlighten your friends." Years ago, when New Age was still new, Jess had gone to Sedona with Charles. While she'd marveled at the majesty of the red-rock, sculpted, Arizona mountains and soaked in the peace of the candlelit chapel vista, Charles had busied himself buying trinkets and T-shirts and souvenirs to prove to the country club set that he'd been there, to create the illusion there was a depth in his soul.

"Sedona!" Maura exclaimed with another shriek. "*Très* cool, Mom!"

So Jess had hung up, her daughter appeased for the moment, leaving Jess with an odd taste of lint still lining her throat and the feeling that she'd lost another round, that it was her own fault for spoiling the kids way-past-rotten in the years since the divorce.

She'd made a cup of tea, drank that, made another—all the while trying to focus on how lucky she was, lucky that Chuck had made it through Princeton, though he now worked alongside his father in the Wall Street firm; lucky that Maura had overcome her past traumas and was funneling them toward a degree in clinical psychology; lucky that Travis, her eighteen-year-old joy, had decided to go to Yale next year, so he would be closer to home. So he would be closer to her.

Distracted, was what she had been. Distracted from her work, distracted from her responsibilities, oblivious to the ticking clock that now said her assistants had left for the day and she was late with Mrs. Boynton's antique-rose-colored, ten-thousand-dollars-worth of overpriced drapes.

Flicking off the machine, she examined the stitches: amazingly, they were fine. She smoothed the lush fabric and moved to the steam table, pressing the edges.

Finally, she finished. She slid the drapes onto hangers

and sleeved them with plastic. Then she grabbed her coat with a quick prayer that the traffic would have thinned and it wouldn't start snowing.

As she pulled the blinds to lock up for the night, Jess spotted the stack of mail on her desk—four days' worth of bills, checks, and God-only-knew-what that she'd not had time to open. She buttoned her coat, slung the draperies over her arm, and gathered up the mail with a sigh. It would never get read if she did not bring it home.

Walking over to the alarm by the back door, she juggled the draperies to peek at the envelopes. A long blue envelope caught Jess's eye. Her name and address had been carefully hand-printed; in the lower left corner neat block letters underlined in red spelled out: PERSONAL. No return address appeared on the front or the back. But the postmark was clear: "Vineyard Haven, MA."

Vineyard Haven? She had no idea where that was. Was it on Martha's Vineyard, the island off Cape Cod? Jess knew no one there, knew little about it, aside from the fact that the president favored it for summer vacations and that Barbra Streisand, it was rumored, had once wanted to be married there.

Out of the corner of her eye she saw the red flashing light of the alarm.

Celia Boynton, she quickly remembered. *Damn.*

She finished setting the alarm and hurried out of the shop.

The note was from neither Clinton nor Streisand, or, at least, neither one was admitting to it.

Driven by curiosity, Jess had opened the envelope at the first red light on Route 1. It had been a mistake.

Now she sat frozen, staring at the sharply written words meant for her *personal* attention, meant, surely, to make her palms sweat, her pulse race, and her thoughts whir out of control.

Jessica Bates Randall, it read at the top of a sheet of blue paper that matched the envelope postmarked from the place called Vineyard Haven. The words that followed were few, but their impact was powerful.

> *I am your baby—the one you gave up. Isn't it time we met?*

No name, no signature, nothing else. And no reference to the fact that Jess already knew that her baby was dead.

Behind her a horn blasted. Jess pulled her eyes from the letter: the traffic light was green. She shoved the paper in her purse. Then she stepped on the gas, and her car moved forward, steered by this woman who could no longer breathe or see past the pain in her heart and the mist in her eyes.

She had no idea how she managed to hang the draperies with Celia Boynton hovering behind her and the blue-paper letter hovering in her thoughts. As she deftly maneuvered pleats and traverse cords, she wondered what kind of sick prankster would do such a thing. There was a knot in her stomach the size of the Boyntons' dining room table—not unlike the knot that had been there almost five years ago, when she'd been brave enough to try to meet the baby she'd given up, when she'd driven to the neighboring town of Stamford and walked on trembling legs up to a Georgian brick mansion, a mansion marked *Hawthorne*.

She'd rung the bell at the white wood door. And she'd waited, determined to find her daughter.

It had been twenty-five years since the adoption . . . twenty-five years since these people named Hawthorne had taken the infant she had never seen, never held, but always, always loved.

It was part of her plan for a reunion. With the help of Miss Taylor, their old housemother, Jess had already lo-

cated the children of the others: P.J., Susan, and Ginny—
"birth mothers," the world called them today—the girls
who had shared their lives and their pain together back in
1968 at the home called Larchwood Hall. Twenty-five years
later, Jess hoped that they would reunite and meet the children they had never known. Until the reunion, none of
them would know who would have the courage to attend:
not the children, not the mothers. It was a choice that had
once seemed so important.

She had saved her own child for last, deciding to find the
girl's parents first, to let them tell their daughter about the
reunion. Then, like the others, Jess would not know until
the designated day if her own baby would show up. If her
own daughter would want to meet her.

The plan had seemed foolproof. She had not expected
the result.

"May I help you?" The words were spoken by a gray-
haired, pleasant woman named Beverly Hawthorne.

"I've come about Amy," Jess had stammered out. "I am
her birth mother."

Mrs. Hawthorne put her hands to her face. "Oh, dear,"
she said, then began to weep. "Oh, my dear."

And then the woman told Jess that Amy was dead. That
she had been killed while riding her bike. That she'd only
been eleven and the driver had been drunk.

Jess jammed another pin into the last rose-colored pleat
and bit back her tears. It had taken her these past five years
to come to terms with her grief, to mourn the daughter she
had never known; it had taken every ounce of strength she
could find to walk through the anguish, to heal the heartache. And now, some sick prankster was trying to unearth
it again.

She could not let it happen. She would not let it happen.

If only she did not want so badly to believe that her baby
might still be alive. And was trying to reach out to her.

"Finished," she announced, climbing down from the
stool. It was 7:23, and Celia Boynton was pleased.

After accepting the check without examining the amount and repeating several "You're welcomes" to Celia's many "Thank-yous," Jess at last returned to her car.

There was only one place where she could go next.

"Jess," the elderly woman said with a warm smile of surprise. Though Jess always remembered to phone them at Christmas and on the anniversary of Amy's death, she had not seen the Hawthornes since they'd first met. "Come in, dear. Come in. It's so nice to see you."

Jess stepped past the woman and into the foyer of the Georgian brick mansion. "Mrs. Hawthorne," she said, "I wasn't sure you'd be home." She took off her gloves and nervously twisted the emerald and diamond ring on her finger—the ring that had once been her mother's, when her mother had lived and laughed and loved her no matter what. Mrs. Hawthorne, Jess guessed, was nearly as old as her mother would have been. She tried to picture her beautiful mother with white hair and a slight bend to her spine, with eyes from which the color had faded and lips that had grown thin.

"We got home from Florida last week," Mrs. Hawthorne was saying. "Please take off your coat. Come and sit down. And tell me what brings you here on such a cold night."

Jess followed the woman into a cozy sitting room, with soft easy chairs beside a glowing fireplace and walls lined with books. She remembered that Mrs. Hawthorne had been a history professor, her husband an attorney; she remembered she had been pleased to think her daughter had been raised by intelligent, educated people—people who would not have lied about Amy being dead. Of course they hadn't lied, Jess scolded herself. Jess had been to the cemetery, she had seen Amy's grave. . . .

She touched a hand to the pulse at her temple.

"Forgive me for not calling first," Jess said, settling into a chair across from Mrs. Hawthorne's. She noticed a young girl's picture framed in silver that sat on an end table. *Amy,* she thought, *sweet little Amy.* An ache of sorrow gnawed at her heart, and she forced her gaze away from the image of the smiling blond child. Clearing her throat, Jess pulled the blue envelope from her purse. "I received this in the mail." She handed the letter to Mrs. Hawthorne. "I don't know what to make of it, other than that it's very upsetting."

While the woman was reading, Jess's eyes drifted back to the picture, to the little girl she'd been told had been hers. She glanced around the room: Amy may have played here; she may have sat in this very chair.

"Oh, my," Mrs. Hawthorne said. "I'm afraid I don't understand." Her gray eyes clouded as her gaze moved from the paper to some faraway place perhaps filled with memories of the little girl in the silver frame, the child she'd raised as her own.

Jess leaned forward. "I'm so sorry, Mrs. Hawthorne. It seems as if all I ever do is intrude on your grief."

The woman wiped away a tear and attempted a smile. She shook her head. "It's all right, dear. Amy has been gone a long time now. But I don't see what I can do to help you."

"Well, I'd like to figure out who sent me that letter. And why."

"Do you think your baby was someone else? Not Amy?"

Yes, Jess thought. That was the answer.

Wasn't it?

"When you adopted Amy, you went through Larchwood Hall, is that right?"

"Oh, my, yes. Larchwood was private, you know. We never would have gone through one of those state agencies . . ."

"Did you deal directly with Miss Taylor?" It was Miss Taylor, the housemother, who had given Jess the Hawthornes' name.

Mrs. Hawthorne frowned. "I don't remember. I know we

had to talk with a social worker . . . someone who came out to the house."

"Would your husband remember?"

"Oh, my. Jonathan's worse at these things than I am." She folded her hands in her lap. "Would you like a cup of tea, dear? I made some delightful lemon cookies today. . . ."

"No," Jess said, shaking her head. "No, thank you. I'm afraid I'm too upset for anything."

"Well, dear, I don't know what else to tell you. I never had any idea who Amy's birth mother was until you came to our door. You're the one who told me. Perhaps there was a mix-up with your records."

A mix-up? "I suppose it's possible." But somehow Jess doubted it. She was not the kind of person who came out on the good side of mix-ups; she was not the kind of person to whom miracles happened.

"In which case," Mrs. Hawthorne added with a whisper of envy, "your baby might still be alive."

"Yes," Jess replied, "maybe she is." She took back the letter from Mrs. Hawthorne. "Or maybe it's someone's idea of a very sick joke."

Once home, Jess sat on the sofa of her vaulted-ceilinged, marble-fireplaced, "executive-style" condo overlooking Long Island Sound where she'd moved with the children after the divorce and tried to think of everyone who had known she'd had a baby back then, back when she was not much more than a child herself.

She tried to think of who would do this. And why.

She wrote on a white sheet of paper: *Father.* But Father had wanted nothing to do with Jess, nothing to do with the fact she had been pregnant, unmarried, and only fifteen. He had not wanted even to see her until "the ordeal was over." And of course, Father was dead now—had been dead several years. And Jess had no other family who could have found out about her shame, could have learned she'd become a disgrace to Gerald Bates's good name.

She thought about Larchwood Hall. She wrote down the name of Miss Taylor, the housemother, and beneath that added *P.J., Susan, Ginny:* the other girls who had been at the home the same time as Jess and who had given up their babies, too.

Then she wrote, *Dr. Larribee,* the doctor, and *Bud Wilson,* who was both the sheriff and the postmaster of the small town of Westwood where Larchwood Hall was. They had all known Jess Bates was there. They had all known Jess Bates was pregnant.

Staring at the paper, Jess let out a long sigh. It was ridiculous to think that any of them would have sent her the letter. They would have no reason to pretend to be the baby she'd given away. They would have nothing to lose.

Nothing to lose? She chewed on the end of her pen while another thought crept uneasily into her mind. There was someone else who knew. Someone who had lost a great deal already on account of her baby: his home and his family and his access to Jess's abundant trust fund. That someone was Charles, her ex-husband. Charles had known, and though he had been only too eager to leave when she'd opened the door, and he had quickly remarried a not surprisingly much younger woman, Jess often wondered how he managed to maintain his facade of grand wealth: she knew he was not the most brilliant investment banker ever born despite what he thought. Or let others think.

Charles, she wrote on the paper. Without thinking, she added *Chuck, Maura,* and *Travis.* She'd had to tell the children; she'd wanted them to know the truth. But surely her children would have had nothing to do with this.

She studied the list that had grown on the paper. But her eyes kept going back to one name, and only one name: *Charles.* She had no idea why he would do this, but it suddenly seemed obvious that it had to be him.

She balled her hands into fists. A sputter of curses flicked through her mind. Then she picked up the phone beside the sofa and dialed the number at his townhouse in Manhattan.

After two rings, the machine kicked in. "We're unavailable at present," his pompous voice said. "We won't be returning to the city until the tenth of March."

Beep.

Jess hung up. He wouldn't be home until March tenth? Where could he have gone? Then a sick feeling crawled through her stomach as she wondered if he and his new wife might be winter vacationing on an island—Martha's Vineyard, for instance.

Quickly, she picked up the receiver again and called Chuck's cell phone. If anyone would know the whereabouts of Charles, it would be his favorite son.

"Hello, honey," she said, after he'd answered.

"Mom? Hey, how's it going?"

"Fine. Are you keeping busy?"

Her son laughed. "Life was easier before I became an adult."

"I know the feeling."

"You want anything special, Mom?"

She winced at the reminder that she did not speak to him often, and that she never, ever called just to say hi. He had, after all, made it quite clear years ago that he did not want his mother keeping tabs on him. He was so much like Charles; he was so much like her own father had been. It all made her quite sad. "Actually," she said now, "I was trying to reach your father. I need to speak with him about some tax information." It was not true, of course, but Chuck would not know that.

"Dad's in the Caribbean."

The Caribbean? Not Martha's Vineyard. "What on earth is he doing there?" she asked before remembering it was none of her business. Four years of divorce apparently did not wash away every stain of twenty years of marriage.

"The last I heard, he was buying a boat."

Jess sighed, but did not comment that she wondered if her ex-husband would ever grow up. "Well, okay, honey. Thanks." Then she added, "I miss you, honey. When can you come out for dinner?"

"Not for a while, Mom. I'm not in the city right now. I'm at a seminar. In Boston."

"Boston?" she asked. "You're in Boston right now?"

"Yeah. The beauty of cell phones, huh?"

Boston? she wondered. Wasn't that awfully close to Martha's Vineyard?

She closed her eyes and tried not to think what she was thinking. Then she said something like yes, well, call me when you get back into town, then good-bye. But when she'd hung up the phone, Jess stared out the window and did everything in her power to convince herself that the fact Chuck was in Boston meant nothing at all, that just because he was so much like Charles did not mean he followed in every one of his footsteps. Besides, she reasoned, Chuck was her son. And he would never do anything to hurt his mother.

She turned back to her list to divert her thoughts.

Father.

Miss Taylor—the housemother.

P.J., Susan, Ginny—her long-ago friends.

She thought of her friends now and of how only Ginny—of all people—had had a happy ending. She smiled and wondered how Ginny would handle such an obscure letter, and if she would stoop to accusing her own child of the deed.

Chapter 2

 Ginny   Stevens-Rosen-Smith-Levesque-Edwards preferred to divorce husbands. Not bury them.

She stood in the front of the dim funeral home room in L.A. and stared into the oak casket framed in camellias, Jake's favorite flowers.

"You son of a bitch," she whispered at the satin-covered pillow that cushioned his motionless head. "You rotten, pig-fucking, son of a bitch."

He had no right to die. For five years, Ginny had been faithful to him. She had *loved* him, for chrissakes, if love was a word that anyone could define beyond saying it was a feeling that made you do bizarre things, like be faithful and give a shit when you wished that you didn't. But she *had* been faithful and had given a shit, at least for the past five years. And all it had gotten her was nowhere, except right here, staring into the box that held the bones of the man she had loved, and hoping she'd picked out the right kind of casket, and that he would have liked the pale blue satin lining.

Everyone but Ginny had been surprised that Jake had specified he did not want to be cremated in popular California style. True, Los Angeles was overcrowded and land was at a premium. But Jake had always been afraid of fire, and Ginny knew that. She knew that the same way she knew so much else about her husband—the fact that he harbored a secret longing to be a singer though he couldn't carry a tune, the fact that he had become a successful documentary film producer only because his alcoholic ex-wife, the mother of his two children, had not wanted him to, and the fact that he was the best goddamn thing that ever happened to Ginny.

And now where was he? Cold as a clam. Dead as a doornail. The rotten son of a bitch.

The touch of a cool hand at her elbow did not avert Ginny's eyes from the pillow under his head.

"Ginny?" The voice came from Lisa, Ginny's TV-star daughter, the only person left on earth now who gave a shit about *her.* "They want to begin the service, Ginny. Come and sit down."

Drawing in a breath, Ginny nearly gagged on the pungent aroma of hundreds of floral grotesqueries: pots and baskets and sprays and vases from studios and clients and actors and producers—everyone in the movie business who was shocked that Jake Edwards had dropped dead at sixty-four. Of course, many of the flowers were from Lisa's camp of ass-kissers: the herds of groupies who apparently felt it essential to send condolences to the girl they knew as Myrna the witch-bitch on *Devonshire Place,* the girl whose real-life sort-of-stepfather now lay in the box, which meant she must be devastated and they really must let her know that they cared.

"Ginny?" Lisa/Myrna repeated.

Ginny raised her chin and swallowed back a tear. Then she took a last look at the son of a bitch and let her daughter lead her to the bank of wing chairs reserved for the family that had been set apart from the white folding chairs and came complete with boxes of pop-up Kleenex at no extra charge.

• • •

She supposed she'd have to keep Consuelo on even though they'd never gotten along, even though the housekeeper/cook/laundress had never really liked Ginny, only tolerated her on account of Jake—the man she'd lie down and die for because if it weren't for him she'd never have her green card. Jake had un-alienated her in a world of illegals; he had made her someone, a Californian, an *American*. And aside from the fact it had most likely been Consuelo's cooking—her overindulgence of Jake by way of breakfast steaks and fried eggs—that had logjammed his arteries and crushed the life from his heart, the woman was probably entitled to some payback for her loyalty.

Shit, Ginny thought, surveying the heaping platters of postfuneral noshes spread out for the guests like barley for geese, she might as well keep her because she couldn't stand her own cooking and she'd never lifted a dust rag in her life. Besides, Jake would probably have wanted it that way. Consuelo, after all, had no one else: her revered Jake, his two totally fucked-up adult children, his unfortunate choice of a second wife, and the wife's illegitimate daughter had become the woman's family, like it or not.

Ginny plucked a stuffed artichoke leaf and wondered why those who serve ultimately are transformed into those who need to be served. It had been the same way with her mother: the woman who had once nurtured her little girl had ended up needing that same little girl to work her ass off to keep them in frozen dinners and booze, to keep bringing home tissues into which her mother hacked God-only-knew-what, until there was no more air left to come out of her lungs, until her liver was swollen beyond repair, until she was dead. Like Jake was now.

"Ginny," Lisa said, guiding a bald, bulky man toward her, "I'd like you to meet Harry Lyons, my director. Harry, this is my mother, Ginny Edwards." Ginny frowned at the daughter who oddly resembled Ginny's mother more than herself, then moved her gaze to Harry Lyons, the man who took credit for making Lisa a star. Ginny knew it had really only happened because of Jake. Jake, who had tirelessly bled his Hollywood connections until Lisa had screen tests secured from one end of town to the other. Jake had done it for Lisa, and he'd done it for Ginny, so she could be near the daughter she'd only just met.

But that had been almost five years ago, and it was Harry Lyons—a fat man with big teeth and jello-like jowls—who stood in front of her now, who had taken the credit for Lisa's fast rise to fame.

"Mrs. Edwards," the somber-face said perfunctorily, "I am so pleased to meet you. And I am so sorry about your husband."

Sucking the stuffing off the artichoke leaf, Ginny wondered why he cared. "Thank you," she said between the cream cheese and rosemary. "I'm sorry about him, too."

He cleared his fleshy throat and eyed the hors d'oeuvres. "Lisa tells me you were an actor, too. You must have trained your daughter well. Or you must have fantastically creative genes."

It came as no surprise that Harry Lyons was more interested in talking about Lisa—his abundant meal ticket—than in trading musings about dead Jake. But Ginny was too weary to explain that she'd never even laid eyes on Lisa until a few years ago. That she'd never planned to, that she'd never wanted to. "She's my daughter, all right," Ginny replied as expected, though a small part of her would have loved to watch his porky face fall if she told him that Lisa's "fantastically creative genes" were the product of Ginny's rape by her stepfather with a bit of her alcoholic mother thrown in for good measure. But that was cocktail party talk, and this was not a cocktail party. Not that any of the food-grabbing, drink-guzzling guests seemed to realize it.

"Lisa," Ginny asked as she bypassed the artichokes and

scooped up a pair of cheesy, gooey quiches, "have you seen Brad and Jodi?"

Rolling her camera-perfect, huge topaz eyes, Lisa gestured toward the patio. "Brad is sulking. Jodi is meditating."

"Excuse me," Ginny said to Harry Lyons, "but I really must check on Jake's children." The blank look on his face made her want to shout: "*Jake.* The man who is dead, the reason you're here." Instead, she drifted through the French doors to the patio, pulling the black widow's scarf from her throat as she went and tossing it onto the counter for Consuelo to pick up when the spirit moved her.

Brad, indeed, was sulking. He was slouched on a chaise, a beer in one hand, staring at Jodi, his white-robed sister. She was cross-legged on the concrete, eyes closed, arms folded, head raised toward the sky. Firmly planted atop her long, straight, flat hair was a wreath of daisies, the symbol of the New World Covenant to which Jodi had sold her soul several years ago. To Ginny, the girl merely looked like a leftover hippie who, but for the grace of three decades, might have taken up with Charles Manson instead.

"Mommie dearest," Brad chided as Ginny strolled into the scene, "why aren't you entertaining the guests? Too distraught over the loss of your dear departed?"

"Shut up, Brad," she said. She sat down, kicked off her sling-back heels and propped her feet on another chair. "We have to talk. Do you think you can coax your sister from her trance?"

"I'm not in a trance," Jodi's light voice drifted from her pale, thin lips. "I'm trying to connect with Daddy's aura."

"Daddy's aura is long gone," Ginny said. "Now open your eyes and listen to what I have to say."

Brad swigged his beer.

Jodi opened her eyes.

Ginny looked from one pathetic stepchild to the other,

and had no problem deciding where to begin. "I expect the reason you showed your faces here today is because of the money."

"Ginny!" Jodi squeaked in her overmeditated, mousy squeak. "That simply is not true! I have no need for material things. New World is my life force . . . my essence rises above it all."

Brad snickered.

"Well, whether you know it or not," Ginny said to Jodi, ignoring Brad, "your father sent a 'gift' to that life force every month. Five thousand dollars, to be exact. The price to keep you rising above it all." She shook a cigarette from a pack of Brad's Marlboros that lay on the table and lit it with an old match. "And as much as I hate the thought, I'll keep paying as long as you insist on staying there." The truth was, Ginny feared that Jake would come back to haunt her if she didn't. New World had been the only way to keep Jodi from relapsing into a drug-riddled hell.

Sucking in her breath and closing her eyes again, Jodi responded, "I do not *stay* there, Ginny. New World is my home. . . ."

"Whatever," Ginny said and blew out a sharp stream of smoke. It had been years since she'd smoked: the taste was dry and harsh, like a mouthful of sand mixed with warm camel shit. She picked a shard of tobacco from her lower lip and turned an eye to Brad. "I couldn't help but notice that you haven't said a word."

Brad shrugged, a slow, childish smirk creeping across his two-day-old beard growth and making him look like a cross between Tom Cruise and Don Johnson. "Whatever makes my sister happy . . ."

"Give it up, Brad. It's a little late to try and impress me with your familial caring." She narrowed her eyes at the errant son. "I am quite sure, however, that you are interested in the money."

He shifted his well-worked-out, taut little ass on the flowered cushion and flashed his winning, Kennedyesque smile. But the L.A.-speak that emerged from his mouth was just that: a phony, impossible-to-believe load of crap.

"In case no one's told you, my father has died. I'm here to grieve."

Ginny resisted the temptation to smack his cynical mouth, reminding herself that in a moment, Brad would have much more to grieve than the loss of his beloved father, whom he had done everything in his thirty-six-year-old power to humiliate, take advantage of, and otherwise suck off while the old man was still alive. She flicked her cigarette ashes on the ground. "I'd like to give you the benefit of the doubt, but experience warns me otherwise."

"And we all know, Mommie dearest, that you do have experience."

She disregarded the lash. "And *you* might as well know, Brad, that there's no money for you."

He did not answer, but steadied his eyes on his stepmother.

Studying the thin line of smoke as it rose from the orange-red cigarette tip and dissolved into the smoggy afternoon, Ginny felt grim satisfaction at her small contribution to polluting the air that Brad breathed. "A few years ago your father chose to put all his assets into my name, and my name alone," she said. "The house, his business, his investment portfolio—everything is mine."

Brad's expression revealed little, but a layer of pink tinted the flesh of his cheeks. "You don't expect me to believe that, do you?"

Ginny shrugged. "He gave you the restaurant. At least, he gave you the money for it. That was your inheritance. Sink or swim." The fact that Brad was sinking fast was not news to anyone. The once-popular restaurant he'd blackmailed out of Jake was in trouble with the IRS. Again.

Quickly, he stood. "I want to see the will. I'm going to call my lawyer."

"You're welcome to see Jake's will. It spells out his feelings in great detail. As for a lawyer, I think you'd better consider how you'll pay for it before you hire one." She stubbed out the foul cigarette and got up from her chair, moving her face to within inches of his, drilling her eyes directly into his. "You might consider joining the New World Covenant with your sister," she sneered. "It may be your only hope for redemption."

He bared his teeth. "Apparently I can't afford it."

Ginny allowed herself a small smile. Then she walked barefoot across the patio to return to her guests.

By seven o'clock the string of Bentleys and Mercedes and Jaguar convertibles had threaded their way down the canyon, leaving plenty of time for their occupants to change out of their mourning clothes for dinner. One party was over; another typically followed.

It was a lifestyle Ginny had always loathed, yet it was what had once held her together, what she had been good at. She sat on the edge of the king-size bed now—the bed that Jake would never share with her again—and listened to the muted, cleaning-up party sounds: clattering dishes, rumpling trash bags, one-line murmurs between thick-accented Consuelo, a nameless bevy of white-coated caterers, and deep-voiced Lisa, who had insisted on staying to help.

She supposed she should be able to find comfort in the familiarity of the sounds. She supposed she should pretend it was only the aftermath of any ordinary party—post-Oscar night, perhaps, like the one where she had worn the transparent dress and screwed not one but three megastars backstage, including the Best Actor himself.

But the truth was, those memorable nights had brought nothing but morning-after shame. And by the time she had fallen in love with the fourth man she'd married, Ginny had been ready, at last, to settle down. Lisa had come into her life at the same time: Lisa, who did not know what a whore her birth mother had been, who had seen, instead, a woman devoted to a good, kind man, a woman who had found far more happiness than she'd even come close to deserving.

"Ginny?" Lisa's voice called now from the doorway. "Are you okay?"

Ginny looked up. The room had grown dark while she'd been sitting there—daylight had turned to twilight, then dusk, during some moment when she'd not been paying attention.

"I'm fine," she lied, because even though her daughter was nearly thirty years old, Ginny's fractured maternal instincts told her it would be inappropriate for a child to think her parent was anything but.

Without invitation, Lisa entered the room, made her way through the darkness, and sat beside Ginny on the bed. "It was a nice funeral," she said. "Jake would have been amazed at all the people who came."

No, Ginny wanted to say, *he would have expected them.* For though Jake kept a low profile as a documentary producer, he had known the name Jake Edwards commanded respect in a town that had so little, just as he would have known that anyone who was anyone or who wanted to be anyone would have shown up at his funeral for the photo ops alone.

What was surprising was not the number of people who had been there, but that after nearly five years in L.A., Lisa was still so naive.

They sat for a few moments in the quiet of the darkness, because Ginny did not know what to say to her daughter and because she was fearful that if she opened her mouth, her hurt and her anger at Jake's death and at God would spew out, and then Lisa would feel she had to comfort her mother, and Ginny would hate that more than anything. What she wanted, instead, was simply for Lisa to leave her alone in the dark in her pain.

But when Lisa made no move to leave, Ginny finally found the courage to speak. "Don't you have an early call tomorrow?" she asked. It seemed the best way to tell her to go.

"I told Harry to shoot around me." Lisa grew silent again.

Ginny was suddenly aware of the sound of her breathing, aware of each inhale, aware of each exhale.

"I thought I'd spend the night here," Lisa added.

There it was, Ginny thought. The daughterly attempt at solace, the dutiful effort to comfort. Ginny stood up and snapped on the light beside the bed. "Thanks for the thought," she said, brushing the hair back from her forehead and raising her chin. "But I'm forty-seven years old, Lisa. I don't need a baby-sitter." Forty-seven, after all, was too young to play role reversal: too young for *this* daughter to start taking care of *this* mother.

"Tough," Lisa replied. "I'm staying."

Ginny took a long look at this person who was her daughter and wondered if she really was hers. Where Ginny's hair was dark, Lisa's was light, as light as Ginny's mother's had been; where Ginny's smile was small and tight, Lisa's was always warm and wide, again, the same too-friendly smile always worn by Ginny's mother. And even though Ginny and Lisa had the same perfect-size-six body, Lisa was tall, making her appear slimmer. And, God, Lisa had that annoying tendency to be nice . . . certainly not a genetic quality in this family. But there was the voice: If it weren't for the startling, husky voice that spoke not of too little estrogen but of too much testosterone, Lisa would definitely be someone else's.

Shaking her head, Ginny crossed the room to the sliding glass doors. She stared out at the hot tub that churned and bubbled within its dramatically lit deck, as if nothing had happened, as if nothing had changed. She stared at the bubbles and wondered if Lisa's hormones were as rampant as hers had always been, if sex for her daughter was as much a requirement as brushing one's teeth. She hoped Lisa was able to get her need for approval met in front of the camera, not in the bed or the hot tub or the backstage dressing room of any and every man who offered a hard-on.

Sex, Ginny thought. *Shit.* She turned back from the hot tub and wondered what she was supposed to do now that Jake was dead, now that the other side of the bed was cold and empty and no longer breathed. Quickly, she marched back to Lisa.

"Don't you have a date tonight or something?"

"No."

Ginny paced the carpet, wishing she still smoked. She'd always depended on smoking to fill in the blank spaces of conversation, to take up the time when she tried to hold back her words or didn't know what to say. But she'd quit years ago—right after Lisa had come into her life and Jake had asked her to, and he'd been so damn good to her that Ginny could in no way say no. She'd quit and had not missed it a minute. One drag on Brad's disgusting cigarette this afternoon had reminded her of that. Still, she wondered if she should—if she would—go back to smoking. Then she wondered what else would be different now that Jake was dead. Everything, she supposed. Every fucking thing.

"I haven't got time to date right now," Lisa was saying while Ginny was musing. "The show keeps me busy."

"As long as it's just the show."

Lisa shrugged. "Maybe I just haven't met anyone special."

"You have a zillion fans. Don't tell me there's no one 'special.'"

"Well, according to the tabloids, I've been seen with Lorenzo Lamas, I'm sleeping with Brad Pitt, and I'm the secret love child of Robert Redford and Jane Fonda."

Ginny laughed in spite of herself.

Lisa stood up and stretched her long, lean body. "The truth is, Mother," and Ginny braced herself, for Lisa only called her "Mother" when she was dead serious, "I think relationships are fairly scary."

Ginny did not mention that though she'd had more than her quota—and everyone else's—of men, there had only been one real relationship in her life—with Jake—and that had not happened until they'd been married for years and she'd finally broken down and let him know her true self. "Well," she said slowly, "relationships take time."

"I'll be thirty this year. Wouldn't you think that was time enough?" A slow crack splintered the husky, testosterone voice. Then quickly, Lisa shook her head and turned toward Ginny. "I don't believe I'm feeling sorry for myself when Jake has just died."

"Death has a way of scaring the shit out of us all," Ginny said. "It's pretty permanent."

"And pretty awful for those left behind," Lisa added.

Ginny wrapped her arms around herself. "Yeah. But I've buried enough people to know life goes on." She thought about her mother and her rat-bastard stepfather.

"What are you going to do now, Ginny?" Lisa asked. "What are you going to do now that Jake is . . . gone?"

The hollow pit that had bored into her gut two days ago when Jake had dropped dead now rolled like a cement mixer at a construction site. "I don't know," she replied. "Sell Jake's business, I suppose. Travel, maybe." She turned back to the glass doors and wondered what indeed she would do, and if it was possible to go back to a life of . . . nothing. Would she drown the pain in vodka? Would it even work? In these last few years, she'd even stopped drinking. Jake had never complained; it was a decision Ginny had made on her own. But part of her knew she was taking her cues from her husband, trying to please him— someone—for once in her life. She wondered where her cues would come from now.

Suddenly a voice came from across the room. "I was hoping I could interest Ginny in becoming a partner in a restaurant."

The irritation that rose whenever Brad entered a room climbed up her spine without missing a vertebra. "I thought you left."

Brad's grin was broad, catlike. "I deposited Jodi at that mausoleum like the good brother I am. I came back to fix you a drink."

Ginny's eyes darted from Brad to Lisa, then back to Brad again. "The last time I looked, the bar was not in the bedroom."

She let Brad make a pitcher of vodka martinis because it seemed easier than telling him to get out, safer than risking an argument in front of her daughter. But as she watched him move expertly behind the teakwood bar in the family room—the thick, clumsy bar that had been Jake's favorite piece of furniture, purchased when he and Ginny had honeymooned on the big island of Hawaii half a lifetime ago, at least one of Jake's—Ginny was struck by the discordance of Jake's son standing where his father should have been.

She leaned against the bar and took a glass from Brad. Thankfully, Lisa had sat down on the sofa across the room; typically, she had declined the vodka but accepted a glass of soda water instead.

"To Dad," Brad said, raising his glass in a toast.

Ginny raised her glass as well, but said nothing. She took a small sip, then set the glass on the bar. "Brad," she said, hoping to cut off any ideas he might have before he could spill them in front of Lisa, "whatever business you and I will or will not have I will not discuss tonight. We buried your father today, and that is all that matters to me right now."

He toyed with his glass and ignored what she said. "Speaking of business, what are you going to do with Lansing Productions?"

Jake had named his production company after the Michigan town in which he'd been raised, so he'd never forget his "humble beginning," he liked to explain. "I think I'll keep it," Ginny said. "I always wanted to be a Hollywood mogul." It was a lie, of course. She had no interest in running Jake's business, and had already received three offers to "talk." But Ginny had no intention of telling Brad anything even close to the truth. "But if you're here looking for a job," she continued, "I'm afraid I'm not hiring."

"I'm not here about a job, Ginny," he replied with the smooth coyness of a used car salesman from Podunk. "Actually, I came back because I thought you'd like a little post-funeral company."

Ginny picked up her glass again, but did not bring it to her lips. "As you can see, my daughter is here."

Brad nodded slowly, casting an up-and-down eye toward Lisa, then grinning back at her mother. "I noticed."

She cursed herself for not keeping up on current events, for not knowing if California had reinstated the death penalty for murder. "Brad," Ginny spit out, "I think it's time for you to leave."

Lisa was rigid on the sofa, as if just realizing there was tension around her, that mother and stepson were on the edge of a fight. "I can go outside," she said, "if you two want to talk."

Ginny blanched at Lisa's predictable innocence. But then, she supposed, Lisa had no reason to think there was anything wrong: She'd made it a point to keep them apart. She would not have been able to handle it if Lisa had learned about Ginny and Brad, the mistake she had made, and the way he held it over her head like raw meat outside a lion's cage.

"We have nothing to talk about," Ginny said flatly, then turned to Lisa. "And I really would appreciate it if you both left. It's been a very long day and I want to be alone."

"Poor Mommie dearest," Brad cooed, then set down his glass and moved away from the bar. "Don't worry, though. I'll be back. I can't stand to see you suffering so much." He spun on his heel and was gone.

Lisa stared at Ginny, but did not mention Brad, as if some part of her knew it was better that way. "Are you sure you don't want me to stay?"

"Positive." Her breathing had somehow returned to normal now that Brad was no longer in sight. She stepped close to her daughter and gave her a hug. "Call me in the morning. I'll be fine. Really I will."

But Ginny wasn't fine. She lay awake most of the night, eyes glued to the ceiling, praying for sleep that would not come, praying to rid herself of the emptiness that would not leave, praying that all these feelings would go away and never come back.

Chapter 3

 She wished that Maura weren't coming home for the weekend.

But it was Friday and Maura was coming and somehow Jess had made it through the day despite not having slept at all, despite not being able to keep her mind on her work but on the letter that was still in her purse.

She turned on the gas jet and watched the soft orange flames come to life in the fireplace. What she needed, Jess knew, was a peaceful weekend alone. She'd almost had one: Travis had gone skiing in Vermont with some friends, and Chuck—well, she reminded herself—Chuck was in *Boston*, and, anyway, he rarely appeared since he'd rented the loft in Manhattan. If Maura weren't coming, Jess could have had her peace. She could have wrapped up in her old chenille robe and spent Saturday and Sunday immersed in a book, shutting out the snow and the cold and allowing—or not allowing—herself to obsess about the letter, to feel her emotions swing from anger to hope, from anxiety to bliss, and to think about what, if anything, she could do.

But Maura was coming and there would be little time for emotion. Instead, there would be a trip into Manhattan to pick out a wardrobe for Maura to take to Sedona. A trip into Manhattan, endless chatter from Maura, and no time to ponder the past or fantasize about the future. Still, Jess realized as she moved from the fireplace and gazed out the window at the dark waters of the Sound, she was grateful that Maura wanted her mother as a shopping companion, that she still valued her mother's opinion as much as her credit cards.

Touching a finger to the cool glass, Jess wondered if she would have spent hours, days, caught up in the giddy fervor of shopping with her own mother, if her mother had lived, if her mother had not died when Jess was only fifteen.

They'd had their rituals, of course, when Jess had been a child . . . scooping up treasures at Bonwit's and Saks, toting their violet-painted and crinkly-brown bags to the Plaza for tea in the Palm Court, skipping across to F.A.O. Schwarz for a romp with the toy soldiers and musical dolls.

Those had been the moments of magic in Jess's young life; the magical moments when mother and daughter escaped into one of their dreamy flights, away from the sternness of Father, from the have-to-do things and the have-to-be ways that being the family of Gerald Bates had demanded.

But when Jess was fifteen, it had all changed in a heartbeat, a heartbeat that stopped.

She rubbed the chiseled stones of her mother's diamond and emerald ring now—the ring that Jess had worn since the day that the magic had been snuffed out forever.

"Pills," Jess had overheard one fur-draped lady whisper to another at the funeral on that grizzly New York morning in March.

"And booze," the other added.

Shock had ripped through her. *Suicide?* The idea had cut to Jess's heart like one of Father's icy stares when she'd done something of which he didn't approve.

Suicide. Her mother? It couldn't be possible. Not her mother. Not her light-spirited, happy-times mother.

But somehow, Jess had known it was true, as if she'd

always known her mother was fragile of soul as well as of body, as if she'd always known that light spirit was too perfect to last.

Shaking her head now, Jess moved her eyes to a string of faraway lights on a faraway barge and wished she weren't thinking of her mother. Thirty years had passed. Thirty years, many good times, many more heartaches. But nothing had ever quite equaled the magic—or the despair—her mother's life and her death had brought to Jess. Nothing, except maybe the hope, then the loss of the baby she'd given away.

She twisted the gold-banded ring on her finger once more, as if trying to lock in the past, as if trying to hold back the guilt and the emptiness and the memory of Richard that thoughts of her baby always evoked.

Richard—the one who had been there to comfort Jess at the funeral. Richard—the boyfriend Father had detested because his family did not measure up. Richard—who had quietly taken Jess's hand and led her to her father's limousine, where he had held her and kissed her tears. Where she had held him and kissed him back, and where, on that grizzly, drizzly, March afternoon, a baby had been conceived. The one who now was dead.

Or not.

I am your baby, the message had read.

She gripped her hands together, the stones of her ring pressing into her flesh. "What is going on?" she cried into the glass. "Why does this pain keep coming back?"

"Mom?" Maura's voice called from the foyer.

Jess blinked. She wiped her eyes, turned toward the sound, and tried to pull herself back to the present. "Maura," she said. "I didn't hear you come in."

"Who were you talking to? I thought someone was here."

Unlocking her fingers, Jess tried to smile. "No one. I wasn't talking. I was singing."

Her blond, petite daughter—a mirror image of Jess without the beveled edges of time—bounced into the room and tossed her backpack onto the sofa. Jess said a quick prayer of thanks that Maura had emerged into a confident young woman who had not had to endure the kind of pain Jess had known, who had been spared the wondering, the guilt, and the years—decades—of grief.

"It didn't sound like singing to me. Are you sure you're not going batty?"

Jess walked toward her daughter and gave her a hug. "I didn't realize that 'batty' was an acceptable term for a budding psychologist." She caught a scent of wet wool. "Did you have a good trip?" It had only been this year that Jess had succeeded in not succumbing to the second-by-second dread that something would happen on the route between Greenwich and upstate New York, that Maura would be horribly, tragically crushed on the interstate, her Jeep mashed to a heap of charred metal and shattered glass, her backpack and textbooks flattened under the wheels of a semi trailer that had been going too fast. It was a dread that Jess had for all her children, arising, no doubt, from hearing years before of the accident that had ended Amy's young life. But Jess's other children had, thus far, survived. Unlike Amy. If Amy had been hers at all.

"It's raining in New Haven," Maura commented, stepping away from her mother's hug and slipping off her coat. "What's for dinner?"

"Travis is skiing this weekend," Jess replied. "It's just the two of us, so I thought you might enjoy the new Thai place in town."

"Can we just order in pizza? I'm hoping that Eddie will call."

Eddie was Maura's new boyfriend, a Porsche-driving boy of "privilege," who, despite the fact he was working on his MBA at Yale, had yet to convince Jess that her daughter would not be better off with someone less impressed with his own credentials.

Jess realized that perhaps Maura's visit was due less to a

desire to go clothes shopping with her mother than to the geographic reality that Greenwich was closer to Yale than Skidmore was. She forced a smile and went into the kitchen, where she picked up the phone and ordered white pizza with extra broccoli—the way Maura liked it—consoling herself with the thought that she might have time this weekend for her chenille robe and a book after all.

Their shopping expedition was indeed cut short because Eddie had called the previous night, and Maura wanted to drive to the college to see him.

"You understand, don't you, Mom?" Maura pleaded over a quick lunch in a noisy sandwich shop on Fifty-seventh and Third. Yes, of course, Jess understood. She understood that this was the nineties and mothers and daughters were not like they once were and that the chicken sandwich parked on the plastic plate in front of her was not fresh seafood cocktail in the Palm Court at the Plaza.

"You're seeing a lot of Eddie these days," was all she could manage to say.

"Hardly a lot, Mom. We're a couple of hundred miles apart during the week."

Jess picked at her sandwich. "Is it getting serious?"

Maura laughed. "Serious? Mom, you sound like you just stepped out of a George Eliot novel. *Serious*," she repeated, rolling her blue eyes and pursing her lips. "Oh, Jessica, whatever will we do if the—*situation*—becomes serious?"

Despite her misgivings, Jess laughed in return, savoring her daughter's happy mood, wondering how many years it had been since she herself had felt carefree, invulnerable to despair. In this moment, Jess wondered if she should share the letter with Maura, share her feelings about it.

"Don't worry, Mom," Maura said, "Eddie and I are being careful about everything." Which, Jess knew, meant that yes, they were sleeping together, but they were using condoms to avoid pregnancy and, God help us, AIDS.

She swallowed a mouthful of tea and decided that now was the time to tell Maura about the letter. But Maura spoke first.

"I wish you liked Eddie better."

She set down her cup. "I never said I didn't like him."

"I know. But it's a feeling I get. Kind of like when I know you're pissed off at me even though you haven't said so."

Jess blinked at her daughter's language. She took another bite of her sandwich and realized that the moment for mentioning the letter had passed; that they were now re-entering the mother-daughter tug-of-war zone.

"I think it's because he reminds you of Daddy," Maura blurted out.

"Your father has nothing to do with this," Jess said quietly, although Eddie did seem to value the same things Charles always had: schmoozing with the right people, owning the right things.

"Well, he's not a bit like Daddy," her daughter continued. "Eddie is fun. Daddy's an insufferable, snotty stuffed shirt."

Jess burst into laughter. It was the perfect description of Charles. *Oh, yes,* she thought, holding a hand to her side, sometimes she underestimated her children's ability to think for themselves. "Hand me the check," she said, trying to stop laughing. "We still need to get to Saks before you have to get home."

Maura handed Jess the check: thirty-four dollars for two sandwiches and tea. Jess shook her head and opened her wallet. Even though she'd not had the chance to tell Maura about the letter, at least she'd had herself a good laugh.

As Jess helped Maura bring in the bags from Bloomingdale's and the one from Macy's with the "Mom, I *have* to have it" straw hat, she avoided asking if her daughter planned to spend the whole night in Eddie's dorm room. Instead, she counted her blessings that Maura was happy, and that it was neither snowing nor sleeting, though the late winter air had turned hard-bitten, New England frigid, and perhaps the roads would be slick from last night's rain.

Jess set the packages on the white tile floor of the two-story foyer and willed herself not to think about fast-moving trucks.

Maura breezed past her and went into the kitchen. "I'm going to check the phone . . ."

Jess opened the hall closet and squeezed her coat between ski parkas whose chair lift tickets clung to one another as if braced for the next storm.

Beep.

From the kitchen came the sound of the answering machine, but Jess was too weary to listen. She straightened the ski parkas and closed the closet door. Tonight she would have her night of peace. Tonight she would curl up in the old chenille robe. . . .

Maura appeared in the doorway. "Mom? There's a weird message on the machine."

This comment was not surprising: since the advent of Eddie, Maura seemed to feel that most of Jess's new friends were, indeed, "weird," that Jess's life must be weird without the country clubs and cocktail parties and dinner invitations that once had dominated her life. Jess hoped that someday Maura would see that for what it was, too. "Who is it?" she asked.

"I have no idea. I think you'd better listen."

Jess went into the kitchen. Her daughter stood back from the answering machine, staring at it as if it were a dead animal on the side of the road. Jess suddenly knew the message must have something to do with the letter.

"Well," she said, trying to sound in control, "let's have a listen." She leaned forward and pushed the button.

Beep.

"Why haven't I heard from you?" a hushed, garbled voice asked. "Why haven't I heard from my mother?" The caller hung up. The machine shut off.

Jess stood next to Maura, the two of them as still as the house when the children weren't home, like statues, like rocks.

"Mom?" Maura finally whispered. "Who was that?"

Wrapping her arms around herself to ward off the sudden chill that had entered the room, Jess thought for a moment. She could have told Maura that it was a client, one who enjoyed playing practical jokes. She could have said it was a friend, or a friend of a friend being silly. Jess could have said anything and Maura would have shrugged her "whatever" shrug and left to go see Eddie and do whatever it was she planned to do. But Jess remembered the pact they had made years ago, the decision made on their own, away from the offices of family therapy, from the easy chairs of the analysts' offices. It was a promise to always— no matter what—be honest with one another, a pledge to always tell one another the truth.

She had already lied to Chuck about the reason she wanted to reach Charles. She had lied to Chuck; she could not lie to Maura as well.

Jess pulled her stare from the answering machine and twisted her ring. "Do you have time for hot chocolate?"

Maura blinked quickly and pretended to smile. "Oh, God," she groaned. "I feel a mother-daughter talk coming on."

Maura had been Jess's greatest supporter, her us-against-him child, her buffer against Charles. She had once stood— albeit on legs that were only sixteen—resolutely beside Jess when she learned about Amy, when she learned that her mother had, in fact, become a mother long before she'd been a mother to Chuck and Travis and herself, long before the stigma of unwed and underage had ceased to matter to anyone but the right-wing moralists of the world.

Maura had stood beside her, helping Jess win the boys' acceptance of their mother's unsavory past. And though she had not succeeded in swaying Charles, she had made it a point to let Jess know that it was okay, that whatever her mother had done was okay, because she was their mother and they knew that she loved them.

Of course, that had all been five years ago, and the innocent high-school-girl-Maura of then was quite unlike the experienced, college-sophomore-Maura of now.

When Jess handed her daughter the letter on blue paper, she sipped her hot chocolate and waited for the look of disdain to appear on her daughter's face. It was there in an instant.

"Who sent it?" Maura asked.

"I don't know. But I expect it's the same person who left that message."

"It was hard to tell if that was a man or a woman."

"I know."

"But whoever it is, is saying your baby is still alive."

"I know."

"Mom? Is that possible?"

"I have no idea, honey."

"But I remember the picture of Amy that Mrs. Hawthorne brought you," Maura said flatly. "Amy must have been yours, Mom. She looked just like you."

"Maybe I only wanted her to look like me."

Maura picked up her mug, strode to the sink, and dumped the remaining contents down the drain. "But, Mom, you don't know who's doing this. It could be some wacko with a huge mental pathology."

Jess refrained from commenting that if Maura truly intended to become a psychologist, she'd better learn a few other terms besides "batty" and "wacko."

"No matter who it is," Jess replied, trying to soften the edge in her voice, "the person obviously knows I gave a baby up for adoption."

"So?"

"So someone is either trying to get me to connect with

my baby, or knows Amy is dead and is trying to drive me out of my mind."

"What are you going to do?"

"I don't know. There's not much I can do."

Suddenly her daughter turned around. "I think you should ignore it, Mother. For one thing, maybe it's time for you to let go of the past."

Jess blinked. "Excuse me? I didn't ask for this, Maura."

"Didn't you? It seems to me you opened the door when you decided to search for that baby."

Cellophane anger crinkled across Jess's shoulders. She reminded herself of what Maura's therapist had once said: that Maura suffered from guilt over having become pregnant herself at age sixteen. If not for that, Jess would never have searched for her own baby, would never have learned that Amy was dead, and would never have gone through with the divorce. Maura's miscarriage had possibly only deepened her distress. Still, Jess had hoped that several years and many thousands of therapy dollars later, her daughter would have dealt with it. Dealt with it and healed.

"To begin with, that was nearly five years ago," Jess said defensively—uncomfortably—now. "And I wanted to find my baby because it was unfinished business in my life."

"And now some psycho has come out of the woodwork and is probably going to try and get money out of you."

"What does money have to do with this? I don't hide anything anymore."

"No, Mom," Maura said brusquely. "I guess you don't. But maybe the rest of this family would prefer it if you did." She plunked her mug in the sink. "I'm going to Eddie's," she said, stalking out of the room.

Jess stayed in her chair, silent in her anguish. Certainly, she had not expected this to be Maura's reaction. She had not expected her to be so judgmental. She wondered if this had anything to do with Eddie's country club influence. Then she took another sip of lukewarm hot chocolate and wondered if Travis would feel the same way as Maura, and if Chuck, the eldest, would follow suit. If Chuck ever returned from Boston, and if she could ever be sure he was in no way involved.

Why did this have to happen now, just when her life seemed to be coming together, just when it had settled into a level of comfort, of routine days and predictable nights?

Jess closed her eyes. Surely it would be better to ignore the whole thing than to upset her family like this, or to give in to the risky hope that her baby might still be alive. She knew, in her heart, that Amy Hawthorne had been her's— didn't she? And that Amy was gone, Amy was dead.

Quietly, Jess rose from her chair, went to the answering machine, and erased the garbled message.

Just after midnight the telephone rang. Jess's eyes sprang open. She lay there, staring at the dark ceiling of her bedroom. Her pulse was racing, her hands shaking.

The phone rang again.

She turned onto her side and flicked on the light. She stared at the receiver that rested in its cradle.

It rang again.

It must be her, she said to herself. Or whoever this person was who was determined to drive her mad. *Well,* she thought defiantly, *whoever it is, is not going to get to me or my family. Even if it is my family. Even if it is Chuck.*

She grabbed the phone.

"Mom?" the voice on the other end asked. "Did I wake you?"

Maura.

"Yes, honey," she said, her pulse easing back, her heart slowing. "What is it?"

"I decided to stay at Eddie's tonight," she said. "It started snowing and I know you hate it when I drive in the snow."

"Okay, honey," Jess said, even though she knew she was

condoning something she didn't want to condone. "I'll see you tomorrow."

There was a pause, then Maura added, "Mom? I'm sorry about our fight this afternoon. I love you."

"Me too, honey."

Afterward, Jess couldn't sleep. Mixed with her anxieties about Maura and Eddie was the certainty that the blue-papered letter and the phone message were going to make her and everyone around her crazy if she didn't do something. If she didn't learn the truth.

She could not exactly go to Martha's Vineyard, stand in the middle of the island, and demand to know who had sent her the letter. But there was somewhere else she could start. Someone else who might be able to help.

Mary Frances Taylor had retired to Falmouth after a career steeped in unwed mothers and other women's babies. As for herself, she was an unhappy old maid, or at least that's what the girls at Larchwood Hall had presumed until the night Bud Wilson emerged from her bedroom, zipping his pants, hair all askew. The night that had turned so . . . hideous.

But Jess could not allow herself to remember that night now. She needed to stay focused on her mission.

After a night of broken sleep, she dressed warmly and left a brief note for Maura saying only that she'd gone out of town. She hoped to return before Maura went back to Skidmore: maybe there would be news to tell her—news that would settle this once and for all.

The four-hour ride helped Jess put things into perspective, or at least into a perspective that she could accept. She decided that Charles could not have done this; he would not be this inventive. If he needed money, he would find a more direct route. Even more important was Jess's realization that Chuck would not do this. He might take after

Charles, but he was her son, too. And though they weren't terribly close, they rarely argued; they rarely took the time.

No, she reasoned as she steered the car off Route 28, neither Charles nor Chuck could be behind this. Then she wondered if Maura would call this denial.

Winding her way through narrow side streets lined with Cape Cod–style houses and canvas-covered boats in snow-crusted yards, Jess finally located the driveway of the cottage Miss Taylor shared year-round with her sister, Loretta. She turned off the engine and studied the small house in front of her: the cozy, many-paned bungalow that her old housemother called home. The shingles were grayer than Jess remembered, weathered in the salt air to a soft, faded silver; the white picket fence, which had been dotted with beach roses when she was last here, now stood unsteadily in the late afternoon light, decidedly in need of a coat of fresh paint. Edging the lawn were clusters of withered hydrangea bushes, whose once fat blue blossoms were brown now, brittle-looking and barren. But even more disturbing was the stillness—the vacant feel of the tourist-free street, the ghost-town numbness of desolation, the wintertime loneliness of a summertime haven.

She wondered if it was the same way on Martha's Vineyard.

Uncertain what she would say to Miss Taylor, suddenly weighted with dread, Jess reluctantly emerged from the car and stepped into the stillness.

She took a deep breath of damp sea air and tried to convince herself that Miss Taylor would know if the letter and the phone call were anything more than a prank—or if there was a chance there had been some mix-up, that Amy had not been hers, that her baby was still alive.

Jess walked along the ice-dotted flagstone path, regretting not having worn boots.

At the front door, she rubbed her hands together, then rang the bell. "Please be home," she whispered at the wooden door.

After a moment, she heard the shuffle of feet from within. Jess wondered how old Miss Taylor would be now—nearly eighty, perhaps. Loretta would be even older from what she remembered about the only time she'd seen the woman five years before.

At last the door opened. It was Loretta, a bit more bent over, her bluish skin more translucent than before.

"Loretta Taylor?" Jess asked.

The woman scowled. "What is it? What do you want?"

Jess cleared her throat. "I met you several years ago," she said loudly, as if the woman were deaf as well as old. "My name is Jessica Randall. I've come to see your sister?" She wondered why the last sentence had come out like a question.

"You're wasting your time," Loretta Taylor grumbled. "My sister is dead."

The door started to close. Jess raised her hand to stop it from shutting. Quickly, she said, "Wait. Tell me what happened."

"Last summer. The damn cigarettes finally got her."

Jess closed her eyes and pictured Miss Taylor, a bright slash of red painted on her lips, a nonfilter cigarette dangling from her hand, staining her fingers in brown-yellow tinge. "Oh, I'm so sorry," she managed to say. "I didn't know . . ."

"Well, you do now." Loretta abruptly closed the door, leaving Jess alone on the stoop.

Jess slipped her hands into her coat pockets and stared at the door, as if waiting for it to open again, as if expecting Miss Taylor would be there this time, saying what a terrible tease her sister was and always had been, and why didn't Jess please come in and sit down.

She stared at the door, but it did not open. Slowly, Jess realized that it would not. She stood there, feeling a dull pull on her heart, the pull of yet another loss, another thread torn from the fabric of her life.

Miss Taylor was gone.

Miss Taylor was dead.

As the blunt knife of reality carved a new hollow inside her, Jess also realized that without Miss Taylor, she might now never know the truth. Miss Taylor, the one person Jess had been able to trust.

The sky grew darker. A sudden spray of sleet began to pelt her face.

Chapter 4

 Maybe she was just a little bit horny. Ginny sat on the edge of her bed and laughed, knowing that being a little bit horny was probably like being a little bit pregnant.

She touched her hand between her legs; she slowly rubbed the warm, dry spot within.

Nothing.

Not the tiniest tingle nor the dewiest drop of moisture hinted that her hormones needed tending to.

She flopped her naked body back on the bed where she'd been for nearly forty-eight hours and flung her hand over her head. *God,* she thought, *I'm not even freaking horny.*

She closed her eyes. Why was she feeling so uncomfortable, so damned displaced, as if her mind had left her body and was floating around in outer space, looking for another ride? Looking for a better place to live?

She wondered if this was grief: the kind of shit those mindless people on those mindless talk shows went on and on about, as if they were the only ones who'd ever been screwed by life.

Somehow, Ginny doubted if her problem was simply grief. She'd been there. She'd done that. But grief for her had always meant a time of living, a time of screwing, a time to reaffirm the fact that she was still alive, that she was still a person. Grief was party time. Grief was not the time to lie across the bed naked and alone, touching herself to see if she had any desire left at all. Touching herself and coming up with a sad, pathetic nothing.

No, this couldn't be grief. She shuddered at the thought that maybe Jake had had the last of Ginny's sex, that he'd had the last of her predictable, gushable, wondrous orgasms. As a lover, he hadn't even been that good, with a smaller-than-average uncircumcised penis that spent more time drooping toward his balls than pointing up at her. It had been, she knew, the reason he'd tolerated her escapades with all the others—the tight-assed, washboard-stomached others whose dicks knew where to go and how to make her beg for more.

But something had happened after Ginny found Lisa. Something weird and strange. For finally she'd stopped running; she'd stopped needing more. She had her husband; she had a daughter. They both wanted to be a part of Ginny's life, though who the hell knew why.

She rolled onto her side now and ran her hand across her flesh, over the humps of her firm, silicone-implanted breasts, bought and paid for with Jake's money, like everything else in her life.

It had been a miracle that he'd never learned about Brad.

Pinching her nipple, waiting for the spark between her legs that did not come, Ginny thought about the night she'd fucked Jake's son.

She'd been dressed in one of her hottest dresses, the white trapeze, unbuttoned nearly to her navel, the hem grazing her suntanned thighs. Jake was gone. Out of town again, leaving her alone. She'd hit Club LeMonde, in search of action. But the guy who picked her up turned out to be a virgin and thought she was his mother.

So she'd come home. Drunk. She'd poured herself another stiff one and downed it in one gulp.

And then Brad was there, standing in the family room, his big hands strong and eager, the muscles of his chest straining through his shirt, his dick so huge and ready, she could see it pulsating through his jeans.

She let him slide the fabric of her dress off her shoulder. She let him gently rub the skin. And then she let him kiss it, making tiny circles with the tip of his warm, wet tongue. And then he lowered his head and found her breast.

"God, how I want you," Brad said. "How I've wanted you from the first day I saw you."

She thought that she protested. But once his mouth was on her nipple, his tongue teasing, licking, sucking, firm, firmer, firmer . . .

Ginny moaned and parted her legs. "Bite me," she commanded.

His teeth sank into her.

"Harder!" she screamed. "Hurt me!"

He bit her again.

Her body throbbed. And then he was between her legs, ramming and slamming that great big juicy dick over and over until she cried and shrieked and only wanted more.

And now, the memory of that night was too damn clouded to even make her want to cum.

"Screw it," she said, hauling herself from the bed and stalking to her closet.

She jerked open the door and stared inside, remembering that after that night with Brad, she'd burned her clothes. Every last bit of sexy, white-hot clothes.

Somehow, she'd replaced them. She'd replaced the clothes but not the feeling. And now when she reached in, she wanted only sweatpants and a big, snuggly shirt. One of Jake's shirts. One of dead Jake's shirts.

Ginny was standing in the family room in sweatpants and Jake's shirt, staring out the window, stuffing baked-not-fried Tostitos into her mouth when the doorbell rang.

It was probably another flower delivery from Lisa's well-wishers. Or worse, it might be Lisa herself, the nice-nice daughter that Ginny really didn't need right now. Not that she had any idea exactly what—or whom—she needed. She brushed some crumbs from her shirt and hoped Consuelo would quickly send whoever it was away.

"Ginny," a small voice came from across the room. "It's me. Jess."

Ginny blinked at the nothingness outside. Jess? *No,* she thought. And yet she knew. It would not be out of character for Jess to come all the way across the country when she'd seen the media reports about Jake's death. Like Lisa, Jess was nice. *God help me,* Ginny thought, then slowly turned around. And there was Jess. That whisper of a woman from another place in time.

"Jesus," Ginny said, "what the hell are you doing here?" It hadn't been that long ago—had it?—since Jess had shown up with the idea of a reunion. With the idea of meeting Lisa. She'd come unannounced that time, too. Unannounced, and most decidedly unwanted. And though they hadn't seen one another since the reunion, they had stayed in touch—if phone calls once every few months and Christmas cards with kids' pictures tucked inside was considered staying in touch.

Jess walked toward her now, a thin smile on her pale, New York–winter face. "Ginny, I think I need your help."

Ginny looked back at the window, but there was no escape. She turned reluctantly to give Jess a kiss-kiss-hug. "I guess it's ludicrous to say you weren't expected."

"If this isn't a good time, I'll leave."

As Jess slipped from Ginny's hug, Ginny noticed the pink that rimmed her eyes. It seemed a little odd—Jess had barely known Jake. Then again, as a kid she'd been prone to tears—she had spent many weepy days and nights at Larchwood, waiting for her boyfriend who'd never written. Yeah, Ginny decided, news of Jake's death might be enough to touch off a torrent of Jess's ready tears. "Did you cry the whole flight out?"

Jess tossed her small, boxy handbag on the leather sofa, dead center on the cushion where Ginny had fucked Brad's brains out so very long ago, back when she had a libido, back before Jake was dead. Ginny shoved another Tostito into her mouth and waited for Jess to say how sorry she was that Jake was dead and ask what she could do to help.

Instead, Jess said, "It's been a long time, Ginny. You look . . . good."

"What I look like is a piece of shit," Ginny replied and held the bag toward Jess. "Chips?"

Jess shook her head.

Ginny plunged her hand into the corn chips again and pulled out one, then two. She examined each carefully as if looking for the words she was supposed to say, as if they'd be imprinted between the flaky bits of brown stuff and the little flecks of salt. She knew she should thank Jess for coming. She knew she should say that Jess looked good, too, or that at least she looked the same, which, of course, was true. Ginny popped the chips into her mouth and wondered if teeny, tiny people ever aged, or if they one day simply folded up into an osteoporosislike, embryonic position and wrapped themselves in hand-knit afghans. "Have a seat," she said. "I guess."

Jess had a seat beside her handbag. "Ginny," she said, "the strangest thing has happened."

And then, while Ginny remained standing, eating, numb and motionless in the middle of her family room, Jess went on and on about some letter from her baby and a phone message and that Miss Taylor was dead and Jess's kid might still be alive and she really didn't think anyone would do this to her if it wasn't true and God, what should she do.

She never even mentioned Jake.

"You're the only one I have to turn to," Jess continued. "You're the only one who understands."

She was wrong, of course, because Ginny didn't understand. She didn't understand what the hell Jess was talking about or why she was here. "All I know is that you're telling me Miss T. is dead."

Jess nodded. "She died last summer."

"Christ. I can't believe that she's dead, too." The woman had kept tabs on Ginny like a hunter tracking deer, had seemed to know each thought she had and every move she made.

"Miss Taylor was old, Ginny. Not like Amy."

Ginny turned back to the window. "Or Jake," she said.

Behind her there was only silence—that bracing, dead-air kind of silence that happens just before someone cries. Or screams.

Then Jess found her words and her tiny voice asked, "What?"

Folding her arms around her waist, Ginny steeled herself and faced her friend once more. There was a look of shock on Jess's face. "I thought that's why you came. I thought you heard it on the news. Now that Lisa's so damn popular . . ."

Jess rose and went to Ginny, putting her hand on Ginny's arm. "Jake?" she asked.

"Yeah. Dead. Gonzo. Can you imagine?" She wasn't sure, but Ginny thought she felt a big, fat lump of tears harden in her throat.

"I . . . I've been so immersed in my own problems I haven't watched the news . . . or read the paper. . . ."

She swallowed down the tears. "Forget it, kid." Quickly she glanced around the room. "I'm going to find that worthless Consuelo and have her get us some coffee. And maybe some of those little quiche things left over from the funeral."

Jess stared at the floor, twisting that ring of hers the way she always had whenever she was upset, whenever she was thinking. "Ginny," she said, "I have a better idea. Let me take you out for dinner. Then you can tell me everything that happened."

Ginny looked down at her sweatpants. At Jake's shirt. "I haven't exactly had my beauty treatment for the day." She did not mention that she had not showered in two—or was it three?—days now.

Jess shrugged. "I'll wait."

The restaurant was overcrowded, with tables crammed together, downtown Manhattan–style. The waiters, however, were California-tanned and blond and wore tightly fitting muscle shirts that Ginny didn't seem to notice.

"I'm so sorry about Jake," Jess said, watching Ginny nibble on another sparerib between bites of butter-slathered fresh dill bread. She was glad she'd come. Ginny, of course, would never have asked her to. She would never have called and said "Jess, I need a friend."

"Yeah, well, that's life. We had a good few years."

"And Lisa," Jess said. "You got to share Lisa."

Ginny nodded and kept eating while Jess tried not to stare. She couldn't believe how ghastly Ginny looked. Even with makeup, Ginny's face had a pasty pallor, as if the lifeblood had been sucked from her, as if she'd died along with Jake. And the baggy brown dress she was wearing was so . . . sexless. Not like Ginny at all.

"Ginny?" she asked quietly. "What are you going to do now?"

As if the pendulum of her clock began losing time, Ginny slowed her chewing, slowed her breathing. She lowered her eyelids. "Luckily, Jake was between film projects, so I don't have to worry about his business right now. But don't worry about me. I'll be fine."

Right. Jess sipped her wine. "Change is scary," she said. "We've both had a lot."

Ginny didn't respond. Jess sensed that Ginny didn't want to talk about it, and it wasn't the time to try and force her.

"So what do you think?" Jess asked. "Should I try to find

out if there's anything to this letter? If my baby is still alive?"

"Shit. Don't ask me."

"But it's worked out so well with you and Lisa. . . ."

"Yeah, well . . ." Ginny began, and then a smile crossed her mouth. "Lisa's a good kid."

"I'm not sure Maura will speak to me again if I do. I think she'd be pretty upset."

"She'll get over it. Kids are resilient." Ginny polished off the last bit of her dinner.

"But how can I find out anything? With Miss Taylor gone . . ."

"You said her sister is still alive."

"Alive, yes. But she's not very friendly. Besides, how would she know?"

"Maybe Miss T. told her. Or maybe she has some old records or something. I remember Miss T. always was writing stuff down in those leather journals. God knows what she put in there. She probably recorded all the times we were bad."

"Like when you took off for the Dew Drop Inn?"

Ginny laughed. "I still can't believe the old bitch caught me."

"She had friends in high places."

"Old Sheriff Wilson—the mailman with a badge. God. I can't believe Miss T. was sleeping with him. Hey—do you suppose she wrote about him in her journals?"

Jess was pleased to see that a small sparkle had returned to Ginny's eyes. Not the same hell-raising, screw-the-world sparkle that had been the trademark of her youth, but a sparkle nonetheless. "I doubt it," Jess replied. "But it would be fun to find out, wouldn't it?"

Reaching for a last remnant of dill bread that lingered in the basket, Ginny proclaimed, "Then here's what you're going to do. You're going back to see Miss T.'s sister. You're going to win her over with your charm, and you're going to ask her if Miss T. left her journals behind."

"Oh, Ginny, I don't know. . . ."

"Hey." Ginny's eyes were dancing, her face brightening. "If you want to find out about your baby, it's probably your best shot. You can do it, kid. Just think about all the devious things I taught you."

Jess laughed. "That was a long time ago, Ginny."

Ginny shrugged. "Like I said, I think it's your best shot." She glanced around the restaurant and added, "I wonder if this place has anything decent for dessert."

Chapter 5

 Two days later Jess found herself back on the other side of the continent, standing once more at the front door of the weathered Cape Cod cottage, wondering if she was out of her mind. She was not, after all, Ginny, who had been born with a gene called "brazen" and baptized into a life that necessitated its use for survival. And as Jess held her breath and rang the bell, she reminded herself that Ginny had nothing to lose. Ginny was not the one who had spent five years thinking her daughter was dead. She was not the one who had Maura, who would have to face Maura no matter what the outcome of this search.

She fixed her eyes on the door. Maybe this was wrong. Maybe she should leave. But then she heard the shuffle-shuffle of feet from within and the door opened.

"What do you want now?" barked Miss Taylor's sister, Loretta.

"Please," Jess said. And suddenly the words came out in a rush as she told the woman there might have been a mix-up with her baby. "I'm sure it's a mistake," she continued. "I was hoping you might have some old records of Miss—of your sister's. Something to help me find out the truth."

The old lady grumbled and wiped her gnarled hands on a faded, cross-stitched apron.

"Please," Jess begged again, "I was so fond of your sister. She meant so much to me. . . ."

The woman scowled. "I never did understand why Mary Frances wasted her life with young girls who got themselves into trouble."

Into trouble? Jess winced at the old-fashioned attitude. "My mother died," she said quietly. "My mother died and I was a scared little girl. I don't know what I would have done without Miss Taylor. She was so kind . . . so kind to all us girls."

"Kind?" The woman laughed, a laugh that bordered on a cackle. "Mary Frances?"

A small heat rose in Jess's cheeks—a combination of the humiliation she was feeling and a need to defend poor Miss Taylor. "Perhaps we never see our families through the eyes of the strangers who they touch. I don't expect you to understand, but your sister was like a guardian angel to many, many girls."

"A guardian angel?" The woman laughed again. "Mary Frances?"

Jess doubted that even Ginny would bother to continue wasting her time on this woman. "Never mind," she said and began to turn away. "I'm sorry to have bothered you."

"Wait a minute," Loretta Taylor called. "If you're so fired up to find something, you might as well come in. My sainted sister might never forgive me if I let you get away."

The cackle was still there, but did not seem as threatening. Jess hesitated, then turned around. "Do you mean it?"

"There are some old boxes in the spare room," the woman said with a sigh. "But I think it's just a bunch of junk."

Jess braved a step forward.

"You'll have to move them yourself. I'm not lifting a finger."

"Thank you," Jess replied. "Thank you very much." She took a last breath of salt air and went into the house.

The smell of must was choking. Must and mildew and mold spores clung to the unwashed muslin, ball-fringed curtains that hung on the small-paned windows, laced the yellowed quilt that covered a narrow twin bed, and coated the stacks of boxes and tilting piles of magazines that Loretta announced were *Saturday Evening Post*s, her favorites. She proudly told Jess she had saved every single copy since 1942, even though she'd canceled her subscription twenty years ago when the people changed the format and she didn't like it anymore.

"Mary Frances used to tell me the magazines were worth something, but that was Mary Frances, always thinking about money. I used to figure that was why she stayed in that business, on account of there was so much money in taking care of rich girls who got into trouble."

There was that phrase again. Jess hauled the first accessible box onto the creaking bed. She did not say that she doubted there had been much money in "taking care of rich girls who got *into trouble*"; she could not afford to alienate Miss Taylor's sister until she found what she was looking for, if there was anything to be found at all.

A corner of old masking tape was curled; Jess easily peeled it back and opened up the box. More dust, more mustiness. Her sinuses throbbed. "Do you think we could have some tea, Loretta?" she asked.

"Tea? Mary Frances loved tea. I, for one, never had much use for it. . . . Give me a stiff bourbon any day. . . ."

"Never mind." Jess looked into the carton, maybe a stiff bourbon was exactly what she needed.

She pulled out a stack of file folders—file folders, but no leather-bound journals. She smiled and hoped Ginny would not be too disappointed. The first folder was marked *1974*, the second, *1975*. Jess opened the first.

On top lay a yellow lined pad with a handwritten list, divided into five neat columns. *Date entered,* the title of one column read. *Name. Due Date. Birth. Released.* She scanned the sheet, her eyes grazing the dozen or more names, including Sally Hankins, Beatrice Willoughby, Janelle Pritchard. A small catch came into Jess's throat as she realized she was reading the names of other girls, girls who had followed the group she'd been with, girls who, like Jess, Ginny, P.J., and Susan, had become pregnant out of wedlock, had had their babies and given them up to other people, people like Jonathan and Beverly Hawthorne.

Then the page was blurry, and she realized tears had risen in her eyes. "Oh my," she whispered. "There were so many others."

"Maybe I'll go make you that tea after all," Loretta said. "Never was much for digging up the past."

Jess was barely aware when Loretta left the room. Instead, she turned the pages of 1974, studying the entries of the girls. Separate small files were included for each: medical records, financial transactions, notes of whom to call in case of emergency. Jess wondered if her father's name had been included in her file as the emergency contact. Probably not, she thought. Probably it had been his secretary. Not him. For he had not wanted any knowledge of what transpired at Larchwood Hall. He had only wanted it over and done with. He had only wanted it out of his sight, out of his mind.

She sighed and closed the file. Then she dug deeper into the box. The records were for later years, not 1968.

Returning to the closet, Jess pulled out another box. As before, it was packed with files. The first read *1973.* She held her breath and lifted it out. Below it lay one marked *1972.* Half closing her eyes, Jess reached deeper. And then she pulled it out. The one marked *1968,* the one at the bottom of the box, the one from the first year that Larchwood Hall had opened.

"Oh." The small moan escaped from her throat. Holding

the file in her hand, she hesitated. She could not open it. And then she remembered when she had done a similar thing: sitting in her own sewing room at the home she had once shared with Charles, she had unsealed the box of her treasured memories, the box filled with bits and pieces of 1968—her own 1968—bits like the bracelet from the maternity ward, and . . . and Richard's Bible. No matter that he'd abandoned her, no matter that he'd broken her heart, Jess had never been able to throw away his Bible.

She took a deep breath and slowly opened the file. And there it was. The list of names: Jessica Bates. Susan Levin. Pamela Jane Davies. Ginny Stevens.

"Oh, my," Jess cried again. "Oh, my." It had been so many years, and yet it seemed so real again. So real, and yet so unreal. As if she were reading other people's names, not theirs, as if she were delving into other people's lives, not theirs, not the lives of poor-little-rich-girl Jess; gorgeous, brilliant P.J.; scholarly, hippieish Susan; and . . . well . . . Ginny. Streetwise, frightened Ginny. She took another deep breath and carefully turned back the page.

Red and blue notations littered the yellow paper, scribbles of memories now born again: the time Ginny had tumbled down Larchwood's tall, wide staircase; the time Jess nearly miscarried after the girls had sneaked into town to the Dew Drop Inn and Jess had become so sick from the Scotch.

Staring at the words that evoked so many images, Jess wondered if a miscarriage might have been better; if there had been no baby, she would not be sitting here now, trying to learn if her child was dead or alive, trying to figure out if she had been deceived by a woman she had trusted with her life and with the life of her baby.

She turned over the paper. Her eyes fell on another yellow lined sheet, this one a list, with names and addresses neatly aligned. She scanned the sheet: *Jessica Bates,* read one line. *Baby girl. To Jonathan and Beverly Hawthorne.* The address was the Georgian brick mansion in Stamford. The house where Amy—*her baby*—had lived and died.

"Tea's ready."

The sharp sound of Loretta's voice made Jess jump. The contents of the file spilled onto the floor.

"You'll have to drink it at the kitchen table," Loretta said, "I'm not going to carry it in there."

Jess closed her eyes. "I'll be right out." She quickly gathered up the papers as if they were on fire.

As she stood to return the file to the box, a small envelope slid from the folder and dropped to the floor. Jess picked it up and tucked it inside. Then she hesitated. There had been something different about it. Everything else had been written in the housemother's fine penmanship, but the envelope had been marked in heavy black ink, scrawled with Miss Taylor's name and address.

Jess took it out and studied the handwriting. It was bold and unfamiliar. Carefully, Jess opened the unglued flap and removed the small note that was inside. "Enclosed," read the same bold handwriting, "$50,000. Thank you." There was no signature.

"Tea's getting cold," Loretta barked from the kitchen.

Quickly, Jess tucked the note back into the envelope and returned it to the file. "Coming," she yelled, and left the musty room.

Loretta plunked a mug on the small oak table. "Find what you're looking for?"

Jess hesitated. "No," she replied. "It's only some business papers about the girls at Larchwood. And medical records, things like that."

"I knew it was a bunch of junk. Don't know what you expected to find."

Raising the hot tea to her lips, Jess felt her head pound, her sinuses twinge. "I was hoping to come across your sister's journals." She did not want Loretta to know she was trying to find out if Miss Taylor had lied. She did not want to give the unpleasant sister reason to think Jess was prying too much.

"Those old things? She burned them. Guess she didn't want anyone to find out about her old boyfriend."

Jess nodded. She suspected Loretta was talking about Bud Wilson. The image of the small-eyed man who doubled as the sheriff and the postmaster crept into her mind. Maybe the journals had detailed memories of Miss Taylor's affair with him. Maybe they had also contained other private information, such as who Jess's baby really was and what had happened to her. *Maybe. Maybe. Maybe.* But the journals had been burned. And with their ashes, perhaps Jess's answers had been charred into oblivion. Unless there was another way to find out.

Jess looked around the unkempt kitchen, trying to act indifferent. "Loretta," she asked, "I've been thinking about buying property on Martha's Vineyard. Do you know anyone who lives there?"

"The Vineyard? No. Who the hell wants to live on an island, anyway?"

Someone who wants privacy, Jess thought, but said, "I suppose you're right."

"Only people like Mabel Adams like it there." Loretta chuckled. "Served her right, too. Not long after she went her husband up and died. Left her with a huge headache, I heard."

Jess sipped her tea.

Loretta frowned. "Guess I do know someone there. But that was a long time ago and she was old then. She's probably dead now, too."

Jess did not feel the need to agree that, indeed, an old, dead woman named Mabel Adams would probably be of no help. Any more than Loretta Taylor would. She checked her watch and wondered how soon would be polite enough to leave. "How long have you been living on Cape Cod?" she asked in a halfhearted attempt at small talk.

"Hmm. Let's see. Since right after the war. When was that? Nineteen forty-five? Forty-six?" Loretta leaned across the table and surprised Jess with a wink. "Was the best place to meet all those sailors coming back from overseas."

Jess sat back. "Sailors?"

"Sure. Me and Mary Frances. We were on our own. But Mary Frances took a different road from me. I married one of them, then found out the bastard already had another family. Men. Damn men."

"And you've lived here ever since?"

"Well, I left for a while, trying to get work. They gave all the jobs to the boys coming home."

Jess nodded and sipped her tea again, the pressure finally beginning to ease from her cheeks.

"Had a few rough years. Until the late sixties. That's when Mary Frances bought this house."

Jess paused. She glanced around the kitchen again. "Did you say your sister bought this house?"

Loretta laughed. "Said she was tired of supporting me. Bought this house for me to live in and take care of for her until she retired."

"My goodness," Jess said, "I didn't realize your sister owned this house." She had assumed it had been Loretta's. She had assumed Miss Taylor had been the less fortunate sister, the one who needed Loretta's generosity to survive her retirement years.

"Like I said, there was money in taking care of you girls. Big money, if you ask me."

Jess did not ask. Her thoughts, however, drifted back to the note she'd seen. Fifty thousand dollars seemed like a great deal of money back in 1968. Even for taking care of those "girls." She stared into her mug. Who would have paid Miss Taylor that much money? Was fifty thousand dollars what it cost to go to Larchwood Hall? And was that why Miss Taylor could afford this house?

Then another memory gushed to the surface, a memory

of another exorbitant amount of money Jess had learned about so long ago. It hadn't been fifty thousand dollars. It had been two hundred thousand.

Two hundred thousand dollars. It was the amount her father had paid Richard's family. Paid the father of her baby's family to have no contact with Jess, to pretend that this had never happened, to disappear from sight.

She closed her eyes to the sight of Loretta Taylor's kitchen and remembered how she'd felt the day she learned about the payoff. She'd been so scared, so lonely. She'd sneaked from Larchwood Hall into the city; she'd risked her father's wrath by going to his office, needing only to see him, to feel if there was any love there for her anymore.

He had not been in his office, yet Jess could smell the scent of his pipe tobacco and knew that he was near. She sat in the big leather chair behind his desk and waited, opening one drawer, then another, looking for something, anything, some clue that he still loved her, that he, unlike Richard, had not abandoned her.

That's when she saw the checkbook. That's when she opened it and ran her finger down the entries.

LH. One thousand dollars, one entry read. The one below it read the same. Jess realized *LH* must have stood for Larchwood Hall. She was struck by a sick feeling that Father had not even been able to spell out the name, as if he was afraid someone, at some time, might come across it, as if someone would find out his only child, his fifteen-year-old daughter, had gotten herself "in trouble" and purposely shamed his name.

Then she saw the next entry: *Bryant,* it read. *Two hundred thousand dollars.*

That was when he came into the room.

"What the hell are you doing here?" he shouted. The checkbook fell to the floor.

"Why?" Jess managed to ask, her voice cracking. "Why did you pay Richard's family this money?"

He smiled an I-told-you-so smile. "As I suspected," her father said, "he was only after you for your money."

She protested.

He laughed. "He's gone, Jessica. He and his lowlife family took the money and ran."

Took the money and ran. His words echoed in her mind now. She opened her eyes and looked around the house that Miss Taylor had bought.

Fifty thousand dollars was a long way from two hundred. Yet something about it now seemed very, very strange. She wondered if there was a connection.

Or was she imagining things? The handwriting, after all, had not been her father's. Nor was it his secretary's, which she knew so well—the secretary who had been responsible for sending Jess her money, the one person, after her mother's death, who corresponded with Jess at all.

The handwriting certainly bore no resemblance to what was on the anonymous letter she'd received. There was no real reason to think there was a connection.

Still, it nagged at her. And as she politely finished her tea, Jess became anxious to return home, to call Ginny, and learn if the sum fifty thousand dollars meant anything to her or not.

But before leaving, Jess gave Loretta her telephone number, asking her to call if she thought of anything that might help. Loretta grumbled, then retreated to the mustiness of the house that her sister had bought.

"Are you crazy?" Ginny asked later that night when Jess finally reached her. "The fee for that place was a thousand a month, plus medical expenses. Believe me, I remember. I stole just enough from my stepfather to go there. Ten thousand total."

"Oh, God, Ginny," Jess said with a moan. "What should I do now? There was nothing else there. . . ."

"I'd say fifty grand is enough to prove something weird

went on. It was thirty years ago, Jess. That was a shitload of money . . . for most of us."

"Do you remember when we were at Larchwood—and I told you that I found out my father paid off Richard's family?"

Ginny laughed. "I wasn't real shocked, Jess."

"I was. Father paid them two hundred thousand dollars."

"Two hundred grand?" Ginny shrieked over the line. "That was a freaking fortune back then! Well, I guess some of us had it. Some of us didn't."

"Apparently Miss Taylor did," Jess said, then added with a sigh, "Or she got it. Fifty thousand, anyway."

"Maybe your father gave it to her."

"But I remember seeing the entries in his checkbook. He paid a thousand dollars every month, too. Why would he give her more?"

"Who knows. Maybe she was sleeping with him, too."

"Ginny . . ."

"Sorry. My mistake."

Jess tried to ignore Ginny's comment. "Well," she said, "there was no mistake about one thing. Miss Taylor's records said my baby went to the Hawthornes."

"And mine went to the Andrews," Ginny said. "And P.J.'s to the Archambaults, and Susan's to—oh, Christ, I can't remember who got her kid."

"The Radnors."

"Right. From New Jersey."

Jess laughed. "I'm surprised you remember."

"You might say your little reunion was rather a significant event in my life. Hey—I wonder if Susan's kid ever tried to find her."

"I don't think so. I had a note from her at Christmas. She married some college professor named Bert and they were going to England to teach at Oxford."

"Yuck. All that tweed and wool. I'm sure she'll be quite happy."

Jess did not bother to agree that Susan Levin had not been one of their favorite people: older, wiser, sedate Susan Levin, who had never quite fit in with the immature, fantasy-driven teenagers. Susan, who had been so stiff-upper-lipped when she learned her son had not wanted to meet his birth mother, that he was content to know only his adoptive parents. Jess once again remembered the reunion, and how ironic it had been that Ginny's story had turned out best.

"Ginny . . . Should I forget about this?"

"And do what? Go crazy every time you get another letter or another phone call?"

"But what if it's just a prank?"

"Look, kid, maybe it is. But why? It makes no sense why someone would do this, unless it's for real."

Jess did not mention Charles, or the fact that Chuck had been in Boston. She did not want to bring her own family under suspicion, even to Ginny, who would never be shocked.

"Here's what there is," Ginny continued. "You've got a letter from Martha's Vineyard that says it's from your baby. Followed by a weird phone call. Now you tell me there's a note saying Miss T. was paid fifty grand for who knows what." Jess listened quietly, trying to absorb Ginny's words. "They may not be connected, but if I were you, I'd want to know. Fifty grand—thirty years ago—reeks of something shady."

Part of Jess had hoped that Ginny would not react the same way that she had. "But what should I do? I can go to the Vineyard, but where would I begin?" She heard the tap-tapping of Ginny's fingernails on some surface.

"Hire someone," she finally said. "Somebody who'd care."

"Like a private investigator? How do I do that? Look through the phone book?"

There was another long pause over the phone line, then

Ginny asked, "Hey—what about P.J.'s son? Wasn't he in law school?"

"Phillip?" She had a quick-flash memory of a handsome boy. "Yes . . . he's probably a lawyer by now."

"Then as they say in the courtrooms—I rest my case."

Chapter 6

 Phillip Archambault despised playing racquetball. Running was his favorite sport; he preferred to compete against himself rather than others, which was probably not the appropriate attitude for an up-and-coming corporate attorney. Then again, it wasn't Phillip who had wanted to be a corporate attorney, but his brother Joseph. It was Joseph who had bought him a desk and a briefcase and a health club membership long before Phillip had taken his boards.

They had kept the same storefront office on the Lower East Side that their father had worked out of for nearly thirty years, though Joseph—more inclined toward dollars than sense—was determined to take it uptown, or, at the very least, midtown. Which was why Phillip was at the Manhattan Health and Racquet Club now, playing a game that he despised, trying to win over the thirty-something CEO of McGinnis and Smith—computer gurus on the fast track to global software greatness. Joseph dreamed that Archambault and Archambault would be along for the ride. And Phillip felt destined to help his brother's dream come true.

"Game!" Ron McGinnis roared with a crack of his

racquet and a slam of the ball against the wall. A victorious grin broke through the sweat that trickled down his face. "Good match, Phillip," he said. "You're getting better."

Wiping his brow, the young attorney returned the smile. "Apparently not good enough."

"You put up a fight. Which is just what McGinnis and Smith needs." He grabbed a towel from the floor and headed for the door. "Wish I could catch another game, but there's a board meeting at three."

It was not news to Phillip: Ron's partner, Ed Smith, had already told Joseph that they would be presenting the Archambault and Archambault credentials to the board today, that today the decision about the next legal counsel for the firm would be made. Until recently, McGinnis had seemed unwavering in his choice of Brad Eckerman—a hotshot Wall Street type who had been an instrumental force in the Microsoft-Apple deal. But Ed Smith wanted to throw their business to Joseph and Phillip: Joseph, after all, had been a frat brother, and frat brothers trusted frat brothers no matter what the odds.

Phillip tipped his hand in a semisalute. "Then we'll talk later," he said, walking to the corner where the racquetball lay silent, its energy depleted, its duty done.

McGinnis waved and went out the small door, leaving Phillip alone in the tall-ceilinged, wood-walled cell. He stood for a moment and listened to the muted echoes of other balls against other walls, other deals being banged out in the macho-sweat rhythm of the prestigious club that Joseph had insisted they join.

"Fifty thousand dollars a year?" Phillip had moaned. "Are you out of your mind?"

"Look at it this way," Joseph had rationalized over pastrami sandwiches at the deli next to the office. "If we lived in the burbs we'd have to join a golf club. How much do you think that would cost?"

"But we could hire a real secretary for fifty thousand!

God, Joseph, can't we just get clients on our merits? Not on our athletic performance?"

"Little brother, you have much to learn," Joseph said, sinking his teeth into his pastrami and dismissing further talk.

Phillip picked up the ball now and slipped it into his leather bag. Joseph probably would have wanted him to follow Ron into the locker room, to continue the back-and-forth banter of bullshit so seemingly crucial to winning a client. But Phillip's arms ached, his head ached, and he'd done the best he could.

After all, he reminded himself as he left the room, he'd really rather be running.

Back at the office, Phillip arranged and rearranged the pens in his desk drawer, pretending not to notice the clock that said 3:07, pretending that he didn't care about the outcome of the McGinnis and Smith board meeting.

But damn it, he did care. For all the differences of opinion he had with his brother, Phillip knew that Joseph had their best interests at heart, as he always had, as he always would. Phillip had still been an undergraduate when their father died; Joseph, two years out of law school. It was Joseph who had worked while Phillip finished law school; Joseph who had told their mother she needn't worry, that he had a plan in which he and Phillip could save their father's law firm and take care of her forever. Phillip, of course, had agreed.

He glanced at the clock again and wondered how long the board meeting would last. And if Joseph's tie to Ed Smith would carry any weight at all.

He would rather it didn't. He wanted their success to be based on his hard work alone. Phillip had spent the past eighteen months researching the firm, researching other software companies, studying copyright and the new Internet laws that hadn't even existed a decade ago when

Joseph graduated from Columbia. It was dull, tedious work, but Joseph expected him to do it, and do it well. And he had. Now he wanted to make his brother—and mother—proud. Even if it meant playing racquetball for the rest of his natural life.

Joseph stuck his head into Phillip's office. "Don't forget that Mom's expecting us for dinner." He glanced at his watch. "Maybe we'll be able to bring her good news."

Phillip continued to straighten his pens. He wished that just once he could stay in the city on a Wednesday night, maybe go to bed in his loft apartment early, maybe even watch some mindless TV. "When do you think we'll hear?"

"I expect by four."

Phillip nodded.

"It's a shoo-in, little brother. Don't sweat it."

"Hey, I'm not sweating," he lied.

But a few minutes later, when the receptionist-for-a-day buzzed the phone on Phillip's desk, he could feel the sweat on his forehead and his heart began to race. Dropping the pens, he reached over and lifted the receiver.

"Yes, Marilyn."

"I'm not Marilyn. She's the girl you had last week. I'm Sandy, remember?"

Phillip closed his eyes. "Right. Sandy. What is it?" But he knew by the flashing red light on line one that there was a phone call, and it was for him. A short burst of pride that McGinnis and Smith would call him—not Joseph—was quickly replaced by a moment of dread: maybe they didn't want to call Joseph because it was bad news; maybe Ed didn't have the guts to tell a frat brother he was out before he was in.

"You have a call on line one."

"Did they say who it was?"

Her pause was unnerving. "Well, no, did you want me to ask?"

"That would have been nice."

"Well, sorry. Do you want me to find out?"

"No, no, Sandy, it's all right. I'll take it."

But before he cut her off, the receptionist added, "I didn't want to pry. On account of it's some woman."

A woman? What woman would be calling him? It must be his mother. God knew he'd been too busy to date in, well, too long. But as he reached for the button to access line one, Phillip had another thought. Maybe it was Ron McGinnis's assistant. Maybe Ron was too chicken to be the bearer of bad news. *God,* Phillip groaned as he punched in the button, *I hate being a lawyer.*

"Is this Phillip?" asked a female voice. "Phillip Archambault?"

"Yes. What can I do for you?"

"Phillip. I don't know if you remember me. We met a few years ago. . . ."

A filmstrip of faces clicked through his mind of girls he had dated and women he'd known. But none in his memory matched the soft voice he heard now. "Go on," he said.

"It's Jess Randall, Phillip. I was a friend of . . . of P.J.'s. Remember?"

The filmstrip stopped, the faces dissolved. And in their place came the clear vision of a beautiful woman, her head wrapped in a turban, her emerald green eyes locking onto his own. *P.J.* The beautiful woman who had at last taken his hand and held it in her own. The woman who had been his birth mother, whom he never would have known had it not been for Jess Randall.

It was Jess who had found Phillip, Jess who had brought him to meet her, Jess who had been responsible for those months of special love that Phillip had found before P.J. died.

"Jess," he said quietly. "Gosh. It's so good to hear from you. How are you?" He quickly brushed something away from his cheek; he was not surprised that it was a tear.

"I'm fine, thanks. And you're doing well. A law firm in Manhattan?"

"Well," he laughed, then glanced up at the wall again,

suddenly remembering that his future was in the hands of the clock. "It was my father's. We're struggling, but it's going okay."

"I know. I got your number from your . . . mother. She's very proud of her boys."

"Yeah, well, mothers are like that." And, he reminded himself, Jeanine Archambault *was* his mother. It had been Jeanine Archambault who had raised Phillip, sacrificed for him, loved him every day. Loved him as much as she did his brother, Joseph, who had also been adopted, who was also "special," a chosen child. He was glad he'd never told Jeanine that he'd met P.J. He would not hurt her for anything in the world. Besides, telling Joseph had been stupid enough. "So what can I do for you, Jess?"

"I need to see you, Phillip. Are you free for lunch, maybe next week?"

"Sounds serious."

"It is. It's business, I'm afraid. Though I'd love to see you even if it weren't."

He remembered the small, gentle woman who had been so kind when he had been so scared. Looking at his calendar, Phillip said, "I can't make it until Thursday. Is that okay?"

She paused a moment, then said, "Thursday is fine. I'll come into the city. Shall I meet you at your office?"

"No," Phillip said abruptly, not wanting to take the chance that Joseph would be there, that Joseph would demand to know why Jess had come and what trouble she intended to stir up this time. "Let's meet at Tavern on the Green. Say, one o'clock?"

"I'll see you then, Phillip. And thank you."

After hanging up, he wondered what Jess wanted. Surely she had a bevy of attorneys at her disposal: people with the kind of old money Jess had inherited needed lawyers the way sick people needed doctors—a lot of them and often. No, he could not imagine what business Jess Randall would have with him. He did, however, know why he'd chosen to meet her at Tavern on the Green: The restaurant was on the west side, close to where P.J. had lived. And sometimes just walking by the building where Phillip had first met his birth mother comforted him, made him feel more at peace, even though P.J. was gone, even though he'd never see her again.

He sighed and glanced at the clock again. It was 3:42. Maybe he should get out of the office, stop waiting for the phone to ring. Maybe he should go uptown and walk by P.J.'s apartment now. Maybe it would make him feel better again.

McGinnis and Smith be damned.

The building looked the same. It had been nearly five years since he'd stood there with Jess; five years, and yet it looked the same: brown brick with beige trim, in the style of the 1930s, when only the very fortunate were allowed to look out over Central Park West, when women in furs and men in top hats had stepped into limos stretched along the curb. Today there were BMWs and cabs waiting, and yuppies who moved in and out of real estate, rich for a time, perhaps, then downsized or outsized and credit-carded to the max.

Turning up his collar against the early March wind, Phillip counted the windows from the ground floor up to the twelfth: P.J.'s floor.

It had been fall when he'd come here, the late afternoon sun losing itself to the Hudson, as it was now. A dim yellow light already glowed in the twelfth-floor living room window—light from a lamp that was no longer P.J.'s. Phillip closed his eyes and pictured the inside the way it had been—the high, ornately carved ceilings so perfectly preserved; the plush, curved, celery-colored sofa and matching soft-tinted walls; the sleek marble-topped tables; the classic paintings and sculptures that accented the rooms. It had been a sharp, inviting contrast to the dark mahogany tables with lace-crocheted doilies, the upholstered recliners, and the braided oval wool rugs of the house in which Phillip had been raised—the house of Donald and Jeanine Archambault, upper middle class for the era in which they lived, meaning there was always enough to pay the bills and a little extra for such things as college educations for their two adopted sons. There was always enough, but there were no paintings, no sculptures. So as Phillip stood in P.J.'s living room on Central Park West surrounded by the elegance, the grace, and the glamour, he had shifted from one foot to the other, waiting to see if P.J. would welcome him and wondering if she would be disappointed in him.

It had been difficult.

"No!" she had screamed when Phillip and Jess entered the bedroom, P.J.'s sickroom domain. She pulled the comforter over her turbaned head.

"I wanted to see you," Phillip answered, his voice trembling, his legs jellylike. "I wanted to meet my mother."

Slowly, she pulled the comforter from her face. "Well, take a look," she'd hissed. "If you want to look closer, I'll take off this rag and you can see the bald freak that's your mother."

He did not know where his courage had come from. Maybe from years of wondering who his birth mother was, maybe from hours he'd spent drawing and painting and wondering if his mother, too, was an artist, if his creative genes had come from her. Whatever it was, it had definitely been courage that helped him move toward her bed, helped him sit on the edge and move closer to her. "Your eyes," he said. "I've got your eyes."

And he did have her eyes, her clear emerald eyes that had not been faded by the cancer.

Then he handed her the rose, the one he had bought many hours earlier, when he'd hoped she would come to Larchwood Hall. "It's a little droopy," he apologized. "I'm sorry."

"Oh, God," P.J. cried, taking the flower. She shivered

and started to cry. She reached out and touched his face. "You are so handsome," she said. "My God, you are so handsome."

A light mist of snow sprinkled against Phillip's face now. He let it moisten his cheeks, his brow, the lashes of his emerald eyes. He was so grateful to have met her, to have known her, if only for those few months before she died, before the breast cancer took her too fast, too soon.

And now, on Thursday he was going to see Jess again— the woman who had enabled him to feel so much joy, joy that had culminated in such deep sorrow. Phillip put his gloved hands in his pockets. It seemed that life was merely a string of good times and bad, held together by spaces of nothingness in between—hours, days, weeks, years of doing things like practicing law while waiting for the next good time or bad time to come along.

He turned from the building and walked slowly toward the subway that would take him downtown to the train bound for Fairfield. It was Wednesday night, after all, when dinner was shared at the mahogany table that stood on the braided wool rug.

"Call your brother on his cellular telephone and let him know you're here," Jeanine Archambault said as soon as Phillip stepped inside the house. "He's been frantic trying to find you."

Phillip hung up his coat in the back hall off the kitchen, smiling at the stilted way his mother referred to the "cellular telephone" as if it was an important invention that necessitated a respectable proper name, like "automobile" or "mathematics." At least she hadn't chosen tonight to include a guest for dinner, some eligible young woman who would make Phillip a nice wife. Nor had his mother fussed over him with her usual questions—how was the train ride out from the city, had he had anything decent to eat all day, and why hadn't he brought his laundry—she really wouldn't mind doing his laundry because he must be so busy and she had plenty of time. Perhaps things weren't typical tonight because Phillip had been "bad" and big brother was angry.

He loosened his tie and walked past the stove on his way to the phone, stopping to lift the lid of the black enamel pot that simmered deliciously with the promise of dinner. "Hmm," he said. "Beef stew."

"And rolls." His mother took the lid from his hand and stirred the stew. "Now call your brother. Ask him what time he and Camille will be over."

Joseph and Camille, Phillip knew, would be there at seven-fifteen, the same way they were every Wednesday night. Seven-fifteen on Wednesdays, two-thirty on Sunday afternoons. Phillip's brother and his wife were as predictable as Jeanine's making whole wheat rolls for dinner tonight to go with the beef stew that she would put in the dark blue tureen and serve in the matching blue bowls. Phillip wondered what had ever made him suggest a few years ago that Jeanine sell the house and move to a condo. His mother would no more leave this rambling old place than she would play bridge on Wednesdays instead of cook for her grown-up sons.

The tinny voice of a recording told Phillip that the Bell Atlantic customer he was calling was not available at this time. He glanced at his watch: 7:06.

"They must be on their way," he said, then pictured the Bell Atlantic customer behind the wheel of his BMW, his wife by his side, as he explained to her that the reason he was not answering his phone was because Phillip had taken off for God only knew where this afternoon and had totally pissed him off. "The biggest goddamn deal of our lives at stake," Phillip could almost hear his brother sputter, "and he leaves the office without so much as a good-bye."

Camille would listen and nod but not interfere. The two had been married long enough for her to know not to wedge her opinions between the two brothers. And she was probably too preoccupied with awaiting the results of their third attempt at in vitro fertilization to care about the latest rift between the brothers.

Still, the phone would keep ringing and Joseph would not move to answer it. "Well, little brother," he'd bark at the black plastic rectangle, "you can just sweat it out. I'll be damned if I'm going to let you know what happened any too soon."

That, Phillip assured himself, was what Joseph was saying right now. And to make matters worse, Phillip couldn't blame him. He should have stuck around for the McGinnis-Smith verdict. He should have pulled his head out of those go-nowhere clouds and not let himself get so . . . sentimental. Sentimental and stupid. Like the little kid he sometimes still felt that he was.

"Want me to set the table?" he asked his mother, the same as every Wednesday night.

"If you want," she answered the same answer, then added, "I think we'll use blue bowls tonight. The ones that match the tureen."

Phillip nodded and went into the dining room to get the dishes from the china closet.

"I can't believe you bailed out," Joseph said, his voice low so their mother and Camille would not hear. "You just up and bailed out when we were waiting for the biggest break of our career."

Phillip leaned against the china closet, feeling small and naughty, trying not to look at the snarl on Joseph's otherwise chiseled, fair-skinned face, the face that could have come from Irish heritage or Polish—Joseph had never cared to find out.

"Sorry. It was business."

"Business? You didn't even tell Marilyn you were leaving."

Phillip moved past his brother and straightened the soup

spoons beside the knives. "It's Sandy, not Marilyn. If we had a decent secretary instead of those temp girls, you might keep the name straight."

"Well, not that you care," Joseph said haughtily, "but we can afford one now." He turned and began to leave the room.

Phillip blinked and went after him. He grabbed his arm. "We got them?"

The anger on his brother's Irish-Polish-whatever face melted into a smile. "We're going uptown, little brother," he said. "We're in with the big guys."

Phillip's hands flew to his face. He had done it. *They* had done it. He let out a whoop and smacked Joseph's high five. "McGinnis and Smith," he hollered. "Unbelievable!"

"Un-*friggin*'-believable!" Joseph exclaimed, then threw his arms around his wayward little brother and together they laughed and hugged and danced around the braided rug like two little boys who had won their first Little League game.

Chapter 7

As the yellow cab barreled up Sixth Avenue, dodging people and bicycles and other yellow cabs, Jess stared out the dirt-filmed window and thanked God that the week had finally passed. It had been one of those weeks when most things that could go wrong did, and when things one never dreamed would happen had.

It started when she arrived home from the Cape. Wendell, the dining and banquet room manager of the country club—*the* country club, Fox Hills of Greenwich—had called asking her to quote on new draperies and decor for the ballroom.

At first she was flattered.

"Celia Boynton's dining room is the talk of the club," Wendell had said. "I need someone I can trust, and I know you'll come through."

Of course he did. Wendell had watched Jess come through for function after function over the years, volunteering her time because she had so much of it, doing whatever was asked, making Charles look good.

But that was then and this was now, and Jess didn't think she was ready to deal with the people she'd once courted. It had not escaped Jess that Celia had probably only hired her so she could spread the word about what Jess was doing and, of course, how she looked. Dealing with Celia Boynton was one thing, but the whole club? Where Jess's work would be visible for all to see and critique? Where her name would be bandied about like locker-room gossip, where the men in Jess Randall's life—or lack thereof—would become as talked-about as her drapes?

"As far as I know, she's not seeing anyone."

"She hasn't, you know. Not since the divorce."

"And she must have financial problems—why else would she work?"

The tut-tuts and whispers would be difficult to take: She'd heard them before about other former club members like KiKi Larson and Maggie Brown who had leaped—or had been thrown—into the outré black hole of divorce. But behind the gossip-monger facades, Jess always suspected that more than one woman kept her hideous marriage intact simply to avoid being served as verbal fodder at lunch.

So she had wanted to say "no thank you" to Wendell with a noble excuse that she was much too busy to devote the kind of detailed attention the club so deserved. It would have played well on the grapevine, if not on her profit statement. But the fact was that a job as large as the club's would keep her assistants busy for several weeks and would look impressive as hell on her "Designs by Jessica" résumé.

So Jess had sent Grace, her most dependable assistant, to the club to take measurements, then had given Wendell an exorbitant price, half hoping the club's officers would not accept her bid. Three days later, they did, just as Grace announced she was moving to Tucson because her husband had been transferred.

Then Maura had phoned to tell Jess the spring break trip was off: Liz had decided to go home with her boyfriend, and Heather did not want to go without her. What should Maura do? Jess did not know what to say, so she said, "Why don't you come home and work on your paper for psychology?" which, of course, was the wrong thing to say to a college sophomore. "*Mother,* you just don't understand" was her reply, followed by an abrupt hanging up of the phone.

Even Travis had been in an uncharacteristically foul mood the past week, having bombed his math midterm because he'd come down with the flu.

The only positive thing about the week was what had *not* happened: There had been no more ominous, anonymous letters, no more nebulous, garbled phone messages.

As the cab screeched to a stop at Tavern on the Green, Jess clutched the armrest and wondered if Maura had been right—maybe it would be better to put out of her mind the remote possibility that her baby might still be alive. Then she thought about Ginny and about the note for fifty thousand dollars, and she knew that it was too late to turn back.

Grateful for having survived the ride, and promising herself—not for the first time—that she would never take a death-defying taxi again, Jess paid the driver and stepped out of the cab. Her head was aching and her heart was heavy. But then, as if whisked by a feather in a light summer breeze, her anxiety disappeared as she spotted Phillip Archambault waiting by the door.

He had not changed. His cheeks were still round and rosy, his smile warm and happy, his eyes the same vibrant emerald as P.J.'s had been. Jess felt a small ache of longing for her long-ago friend. She hugged Phillip gently, trying once more to process the fact that this tall, handsome *man* had been one of their own, one of their *babies,* who had grown into an adult.

"Jess," Phillip said. "Gosh, you still look so young."

Jess laughed and stood on her tiptoes to kiss his cheek. "Flattery, young man, will get you everywhere."

Inside the restaurant they were escorted past long brass rails bordering richly paneled walls, past finely stenciled glass partitions and pots of thick, green plants to a small corner table set away from the lunch crowd.

"I hope this is okay," Phillip said after they had been seated and the maitre d' left. "I asked for something private."

"It's fine." Jess sipped from a thin crystal water glass, her pleasure in seeing him slowly giving way to the disquiet over the reason they were there. She so hoped that P.J.'s son would be supportive; she so hoped he would understand why she needed to do this. She did not need another reaction like Maura's; if that happened, surely she would give up. And then she would never know.

"What's going on, Jess?" he asked.

She shook her head. "No. Tell me about you first. Tell me how you've been and if you're happy . . . tell me everything."

He laughed. "Well, for starters, I'd be a lot happier if you hadn't said this was business. If there's one thing I've learned, it's that when anyone asks for a lawyer, it means there's some kind of trouble."

"There's no trouble, dear, only a minor complication." She twisted her ring and realized that, along with the eyes, Phillip had apparently also inherited his mother's nononsense directness. "I really want to hear about you. You're working in Manhattan, but are you still living in Fairfield?" Fairfield, Connecticut, had been where she'd located Phillip's mother when she was tracking down the children for the reunion; it was not very far from where Jess had lived in Greenwich, where she had raised her three children and pretended to be happy as Charles's wife.

"Nope," he replied. "I hated the commute. I see Mom every week, though, on Wednesday nights. Sometimes on weekends, unless I'm stuffed in the law library, looking up cases."

"You work hard. Your mother—I mean, P.J. did, too."

A boyish grin crept across his round, sunny face. "It gets confusing, doesn't it? That I have—had—two mothers?"

Jess felt her face flush. "Did you ever tell your . . . mother . . . about P.J.?"

He shook his head. "It would only have hurt her, Jess. It was probably wrong, but I just couldn't do it."

Sensitive, Jess thought, *and kind. If P.J. had lived, she would be so proud of her son.* Then a mother-instinct darted through her mind: Why couldn't Maura find someone like Phillip instead of the arrogant, spoiled boys she latched on to? Quickly, she pushed away these thoughts and asked, "Any girlfriends?"

"They come, they go," he replied with a nonchalance Jess was not convinced that he felt. "My life is too busy these days for anything more."

The waiter appeared and asked for their orders. Without looking at the menu, Phillip recommended the grilled salmon to Jess. "It sounds wonderful," she said.

After the waiter left, Jess toyed with her water glass; Phillip's eyes held steady on her face. "So," he said firmly, "enough of this small talk. What's your 'minor complication'?"

There was apparently no use in stalling. She sipped her water again and cleared her throat. Then she told him about the mysterious letter, the phone call, and the fact that Miss Taylor was dead. He listened with the patience of a veteran attorney, nodding at intervals, his expression revealing neither a glimmer of surprise nor the least hint of judgment.

She told him about the note in Miss Taylor's things for fifty thousand dollars. She even mentioned the payoff her father had given Richard's family. Throughout it all, Jess felt oddly detached again, as if she were speaking of other people and other people's lives.

"So what I need," she said, "is your help. I need to know if Amy was my daughter, or if my daughter is still alive."

He loosened the knot of his tie and fixed his emerald eyes on her. "I don't see how I can help, Jess. I'm a lawyer, not a private investigator."

"I don't want a private investigator, Phillip. I don't want to pick someone out of the yellow pages. I need someone I can trust. I can trust you."

"But I'm a corporate attorney, Jess. I deal in takeovers and mergers and that kind of stuff."

"Not in lost babies?"

His expression was apologetic and sincere. "I'm sorry."

Their lunches arrived. Jess stared at the delicate presentation of the orange-pink salmon and willed herself not to cry. She was so tired of thinking about this, so tired of wondering what to do and what not to do. Closing her eyes, she decided maybe it was for the best, that maybe this was one of those clues from the universe the kids today spoke of—a clear, God-ordered message to drop the whole thing. If Phillip couldn't help her, she would not look elsewhere. Then she felt his warm hand rest on hers.

"It isn't that I wouldn't like to, Jess. But I wouldn't know where to start."

Her eyelids lifted along with her spirits. At least he didn't seem to think she was foolish. Or wrong. "I don't know either. That's why I called you."

"But even if things were different, well, we're so busy at the office . . . we just landed a big account. . . ."

"A corporate account," Jess commented.

Phillip nodded. Jess looked down at her wilted spinach salad. It was hopeless, she thought. The message was clear.

"Other than the housemother, who else might have known the truth?" he asked quietly.

"I made a list," she said. "There was the doctor, of course. Dr. Larribee." She tried not to get her hopes up when she noticed that Phillip had produced a small pad and was now making notes.

"Do you remember his first name?"

"William. William Larribee. I only remember that because I used to stare at his name badge rather than look him in the eyes. It was so embarrassing. . . ." She looked away again, scanning the other luncheon customers, wondering if their lives were as complex and painful as hers had been. "But I have no idea where Dr. Larribee is, or even if he's still alive." She turned back to Phillip and tried to smile, reminding herself that none of this was his fault. "In fact, Dr. Larribee brought you into this world, too."

"I'll be sure to thank him," Phillip said with a grin. "Who else?"

Jess recalled her list. "Bud Wilson. The town sheriff and postmaster. Apparently Miss Taylor and he . . . well, they were good friends. I don't know what happened to him either."

"What about the other girls?"

"I've spoken with Ginny. She has no idea. Susan is off to England. And P.J. . . . well, it was just the four of us."

Phillip took a bite of his salmon and slowly chewed. "What about people not connected to that place? Who else knew that you were . . ." He hesitated a bit.

"Pregnant?" Jess asked. "Only my father knew. And Richard, of course. The boy who . . ." her words trailed off, as if it were her turn to feel awkward.

But Phillip nodded. He understood.

"This is difficult for me," Jess said. "Thank you for being so kind."

His brow wrinkled into a frown. Jess noted that there were far too many frown lines for someone so young. "And that's it?" he asked. "No one else?"

She bit her lip. "Well, my ex-husband, of course. And my children. I told the children just before the reunion. And the Hawthornes, Amy's parents. No one else."

He ate more of his lunch, the frown lines growing deeper with every mouthful. "What's the deal with your ex-husband?"

"The deal?" Jess asked. A small touch of that too-familiar fur ball tickled her throat.

Phillip set down his fork. "I'm not trying to pry, Jess. But often when, well, when hostilities erupt in a family, it comes from within. Especially when divorce is involved."

He took a long drink of water. "But I'm sure you know that."

Allowing her gaze to drift among the other diners again, Jess said, "I've been divorced four years, Phillip. There's been no problem so far—and I have no reason to believe there is now." She blinked and looked back at him. "I think our best clue is the postmark from Martha's Vineyard. At least it's something concrete."

"Does anyone you know have ties to the island?"

"I only know that Miss Taylor lived on Cape Cod. I can't imagine that's any more than a coincidence." Jess suddenly felt exhausted. It felt as if she'd told her life story to a boy too young to hear it.

"Tell me, Jess," Phillip asked slowly. "What will you do if I can't help?"

"Drop it. Leave well enough alone."

"Well, I can't let you do that, now can I?"

She held her breath. "But, Phillip . . ."

"I owe you, Jess. I had some wonderful months with P.J., but I never even would have known her if it hadn't been for you."

A layer of tears rose in Jess's eyes.

"No guarantees," P.J.'s son continued. "But I'll at least try and find out if your baby was Amy Hawthorne or not. Beyond that," he added with a quirky half grin, "well, like I said, I have a business to run and a brother who might kill me if I don't hold up my end."

"If you can find out if my baby was Amy," Jess said, smiling and wiping her tears, "I won't bother you with anything else. That's a promise."

Later that evening, Jess stared into her huge walk-in closet, trying to decide between pressing the navy faille suit or the cocoa silk dress—or slugging half a bottle of antacid instead.

She had butterflies in her stomach. As a little girl Jess had once pictured yellow and orange and blue and green wings fluttering against her pink insides, delicately tickling the walls of her tummy. What she hadn't understood was if it was tickling, why didn't it make her laugh? Why did it make her feel upset instead? And why did it always happen before she had to do something really important, like reciting a poem in front of the class at Miss Winslow's, or later, trying to impress the unimpressionable housemother at Larchwood Hall?

By the time she'd reached Larchwood, of course, Jess had known there were no pretty butterflies dancing within. She knew it was merely a symptom of nerves: rock-hard, unquietable, someone's-out-to-get-me nerves.

The someones out to get her now, she knew, were the ladies of the country club, the Celia Boyntons and Dorothy Sanderses and Louise Kimballs of the world, women who had once been friends. Now Jess lived on the other side of the social tracks—divorced, out of touch, a working woman, for God's sake, who no longer did lunch between tennis and golf, who no longer shopped for the sheer need to kill time.

Instead she made drapes for other people's grand homes and the places they partied, and wasted emotional energy looking for a long-lost baby who was a grown-up adult. Who was *maybe* a grown-up adult.

She stood in the middle of the densely packed closet of her working-woman condominium and wondered why she cared what she would wear tomorrow—why she cared what she looked like for her return to *the* country club of Greenwich—where she once had been a member and had since been voluntarily downgraded to subcontracted employee.

Not that there was any need to care: Celia Boynton, Dorothy Sanders, Louise Kimball, and the rest of them would not be there for another month or six weeks, until the greens became green again and the clubhouse wine cellar had been properly restocked for another season, another year.

She yanked the navy faille off the hanger and decided it was good enough. It didn't matter anyway who would be there, who would be witness to her measuring and note-taking and the awkward juggling of her sample books on her too-petite frame. It didn't matter, anyway, because they were not—had never really been—her friends. They were country club friends, not the real thing. Not the stick-by-her-through-thick-and-thin friends like P.J. and Ginny and once perhaps even Susan.

She moved back into her bedroom and spotted the telephone, reminding herself that she still had at least one real friend in the world, one true, stick-by-her friend. She tossed the suit on the bed, pulled the address book from her nightstand, then picked up the receiver and dialed L.A. She had been far too neglectful of her one, true friend—far too self-centered when her friend was now suffering real pain, real, life-altering pain.

"This is Ginny," the voice on the other end said. "Leave a message, and don't forget your number. I hate looking them up, and I can't remember anything these days."

Beep.

Jess felt a sad smile cross her face. "Ginny," she said into the phone, "this is Jess. I wanted to see how you're do-ing . . . and I wanted to tell you that Phillip has agreed to take my case. Call me when you can."

Then she went to press her dress, amazed at how just the sound of Ginny's voice had made her feel better, made her feel not so alone.

Ginny clicked the remote from *Wheel of Fortune* to *Inside Edition* to *CNN Headline News* then back again.

"I'm doing just fine, Miss Jessica," she mumbled to the television screen. "Thanks for asking."

As good as could be expected, was what she'd overheard Consuelo tell one of the lechers who was hot to buy Jake's business when he stopped by inquiring about Ginny's mental and physical health.

She ran her hand through her stringy hair and rubbed her palms across the thighs of her old gray flannel sweats, wondering what, exactly, was *expected* after one's husband had dropped dead.

Then she reached for the nachos, crunched a few in her mouth, and flicked the remote to the Discovery Channel, where there was a fascinating look at the mating habits of the weasels of North America.

If she could get her work done and slip out the door before the lunch crowd arrived, Jess would be able to avoid seeing anyone she knew. Anyone, of course, except Wendell, the dining and banquet room manager, the person responsible for giving her the job, the middle-aged gay man who had always liked Jess, who had probably thought Charles—like most of the men of the club—was an overinflated, self-centered ass.

Wendell would certainly have been right about that.

Hunter green with touches of butter yellow, Jess decided, scanning the empty banquet room, where she had spent so many dull evenings sitting on the dais next to her overinflated, self-centered ass of a husband. She had smiled stiffly and acted as if she were having a good time. Until, of course, that last night, when Maura had pretended to try to kill herself, when Jess and Charles had raced from the golf banquet to the hospital, when Maura had lost the baby, when the walls of Jess's marriage had come tumbling down, which hadn't been difficult because they were cracked anyway. Cracked, flawed, as they always had been. The difference was that after that night Jess no longer bothered patching and repatching, trying to hold the facade together.

"What's it going to be?" Wendell asked her now.

Jess blinked back the past and showed him the sample of fabric she'd selected. "Hunter green to please the masculinity of the men, butter yellow to appeal to the ladies' soft touch."

"Ha!" Wendell laughed. " 'The ladies' *soft* touch'? I thought you knew them better than that."

She bit back a small smile. "I'm thinking about the green with the yellow hydrangea blossoms for the draperies and border; the coordinating stripe for the wainscoting and seat covers."

Wendell chuckled and nodded. "I have faith in you, my dear. Just let me know what color to order the napkins and tablecloths and send samples to the florist. We can't have our centerpieces clashing, now, can we?"

No, Jess thought. *We definitely cannot have that at Fox Hills of Greenwich.*

"The same for the dining room?" Wendell asked.

Voices outside the banquet hall distracted her. She glanced at her watch: 10:20. Surely it couldn't be one of the ladies.

"Jess?" Wendell asked.

"Right," she answered. "I mean no. Not the same for the dining room. I think butter yellow as the main color— accented by navy and powder blue."

"Wonderful."

The voices ceased, the sound of footsteps seemed to diminish. *Probably suppliers,* Jess told herself. *Suppliers, like me.*

"Well," she continued, trying to ignore those damn metamorphosing, unquietable butterflies. "Blue is a cool color, so it's not something I'd ordinarily choose for a dining room. But there are so many lovely shades today . . ."

"I'm sure it will be superb," Wendell said. "Now, I really must go, my dear. Do you need help with the measuring?"

"No, thanks, Wendell. I have Grace's preliminary figures. I only want to double-check before I order the fabrics."

He nodded again, waved, and swept from the room. Jess was grateful he did not say, "It was so wonderful to see you again," or "You look fabulous, darling," or any of those false phrases that seemed to come with club membership.

She checked her watch again, hoping to be out by eleven, long before she could possibly run into anyone else. Taking her measuring tape and small notebook, she scratched down "B. Room, Main wall," and moved toward the window to measure.

The tape had barely stretched from her hand when she heard the footsteps of someone entering the room.

"Jessica?" It was a female voice.

Jess turned around. The butterflies resumed their flight.

"You look fabulous, darling," said Dorothy Sanders. "What ever are you doing here?"

She considered pretending she was not who she was, that Dorothy Sanders, so sorry, had confused her with someone else. She considered telling the woman the truth: that she was trying to give her children a sense of the work ethic they never would get from their father; that she was being a productive member of society because she had wasted too many years as a woman like Dorothy. And she considered saying she was there killing time until she learned if the baby she gave up for adoption was dead or alive, or if her other daughter would ever speak to her again if she found out.

But Jess did not do these things. Instead, she called up that old plastic smile reserved for such occasions. "Dorothy," she said quietly. "How nice to see you." She gripped the tape measure in her hand, the steel threatening to slice into her palm.

Dorothy's amazon body glided across the parquet floor on square, sensible shoes. When she reached Jess, she leaned forward and gave the inevitable kiss-kiss on Jess's cheeks. She smelled like Elizabeth Taylor must, if Miss Taylor actually wore the perfume she promoted.

"Celia's drapes are *divine*," Dorothy said in her tight-lipped way that made Jess feel like a small child who had just won a spelling bee. The woman fingered the triple strand of pearls around her neck as her gaze fell to the swatch book at Jess's feet. "And you're re-doing the club? Well, that's wonderful. The mauve has become so tiring."

Tiring. Yes, Jess thought, now *that's* an appropriate word.

"I'm only measuring today," she said in a quiet voice. There was no way she wanted to involve Dorothy Sanders or anyone else in her decision of color, of fabric, of look. It was her job. Not Dorothy's.

Quickly, Jess scooped up the book.

"Well," Dorothy said with a sigh that raised the pearls on her plastic-surgeried, tight throat. "It's nice that you have your work to keep you busy."

Which was her way, Jess knew, of patronizing her about the divorce. About the fact it had been final for four years and, unlike Charles, Jess had not remarried.

"My work, my children, my life," Jess said with a smile. "You're right, Dorothy. It all keeps me quite busy. And I love every minute of it."

"Oh, Jess," she cooed, "we do miss you here, darling. You were always such a help with the charity events . . . you know, that witch of a woman Charles is married to now can't give us the time of day."

The butterflies flapped their wings.

"Last month I phoned to ask if she could make half a dozen calls for me. Half a dozen! But no, she was too busy. They were off to the Caribbean to buy a boat for their cruise. They're actually going to live on a catamaran. Can you stand it?"

No, Jess could not stand it. "Well," she said quickly, snapping the tape measure closed, "we all have our priorities. Which reminds me, I have another appointment across town, and I'm running late."

She slipped from the banquet room without acknowledging Dorothy's cheerio or ta-ta or whatever trendy form of good-bye the woman was using these days. Out in the parking lot, she dumped the fabric books in the back of her car, knowing she'd have to go with Grace's preliminary measurements. The only way she'd return to the club was if she was guarded by assistants, armed with distractions.

And she would only come back after hours.

On the way back to her shop, Jess made a detour, deciding to go home and change from her country club suit, to slide into pants and a sweater more conducive to work. She also admitted she did not want to face her employees right now—it always took time to stop the sting that formed in her eyes each time she was forced to think about Charles, each time she was faced with the reality that his life, indeed, had moved on, was now spent with a woman who loved being what he so wanted—the eager-to-please young beauty, the long-legged lovely with the wide smile and blond mane, the perfect woman, the trophy wife.

Sometimes it was difficult to remember that it was a life she would have detested; it was especially difficult when she realized her life had become just what she said: her work, her children. Nothing more. There was no love of her life, no special man. At forty-five, Jess wondered if love would always elude her, and then she wondered why it mattered anyway. One Charles in her life had been quite enough.

She parked the car in the garage and made her way into the kitchen, grateful for the neatness and the order that surrounded her, glad she did not have to share her space with any self-centered man.

Jess walked to the counter where she set down her purse and slid out of her coat. The red flashing light on the answering machine caught her eye. She was tempted to ignore it. What if it was another of those calls? But then she remembered it might be Phillip.

She pushed the button.

"Mom?"

Oh, she thought. *Maura.*

"I wanted you to know everything's fine about spring break. Eddie's going to spend it with me."

Maura's giggle did little to ease the trepidation that formed in Jess's heart.

"Before you go getting all nervous and everything, I wanted to tell you we're spending it with Dad. Cruising on a catamaran in the Caribbean! Eddie is so excited. Catch you later, Mom. Bye!"

Jess stood there staring at the answering machine, feeling as if her life were draining from every vein in her body and was being sucked out the bottoms of her feet.

Chapter 8

Phillip slid his foot out of his loafer and rubbed his aching toes. It was two-fifteen, and the waiting room at the Long Island Geriatric Home presented the first opportunity he'd had to sit down today. With luck, he'd get this over with in time to meet Joseph back in the city, in time to look at the office space Joseph wanted to lease on Park Avenue and Seventy-third.

He glanced around the ivory-painted walls, the seascape prints of the Atlantic, the blue plastic chairs that lined the perimeter of the small room. He wondered if the man inside would have the answers that Jess needed.

At last, he'd been lucky. A phone call to the Westwood town offices on Friday had established that the old sheriff-postmaster, Bud Wilson, was as dead as Miss Taylor. Phillip had crossed one name off the list of those who had known of Jess's secret.

But then, at the library on Sunday—when he should have been doing dinner at Mom's—Phillip had hit pay dirt: William Larribee, the long-ago retired doctor, had kept his membership current with the AMA. On Monday—yesterday—Phillip had proved to himself that even this lowly corporate attorney was capable of finding an AMA doctor's last known address, which, in this case, turned out to be the Long Island Geriatric Home with the blue plastic waiting room chairs—one of which he sat on now.

Still, finding Dr. Larribee was one thing; obtaining any helpful information from him might be quite another. But Phillip would do his best for Jess. And he would do it before Joseph found out what his little brother was up to when he should have been tending to business.

But, God, it was already Tuesday. He hoped Jess was as patient as she was nice.

According to the round, white-faced clock on the wall, it was already two-twenty. He'd have to leave by three to make the meeting with the real estate agent who was going to make it official that they at last could move uptown.

Phillip aimlessly flipped through a *People* magazine. What would his father have thought of the move? Donald Archambault had not been one for pretenses. He'd been a dedicated worker whose specialty was probate, where Joseph said there was no big money now—in fact, there never had been.

But Phillip had liked, respected, and, yes, loved their father. In his quiet, steady way, the elder Archambault had guided his two young sons toward manhood. On weekends he'd taught the boys to fish in the stream behind their house; several times he'd taken them to the great museums in Manhattan and Washington, D.C., because, he said, "You can never learn enough"; and he was always there in his recliner after dinner, cigarette in hand, ready to explain the evening news or offer homework help.

Phillip had never expected that one day his father would not be in that recliner. When Donald Archambault died suddenly and Phillip went home from college for the funeral, he walked to his father's chair and looked at it for a long time, too afraid to sit in it himself. To this day, he never had. But dealing with his father's death had in some ways prepared him to deal with P.J.'s later on; he'd learned how difficult death was on the people left behind. And that it could be a blissful release for those, like P.J., who had been in so much pain.

He returned the magazine to the table for the next visitor. He thought about how to introduce himself to Dr. Larribee. Maybe he should say: "My name is Phillip Archambault. I'm one of the babies you delivered in 1968."

Could be good. Might endear the doctor to him, and make him think this was a social call, not an inquest about the past.

He couldn't help feeling a little odd, though, about meeting the doctor who had delivered him, the man who'd slapped his bottom or whatever doctors did to help him give his first cry and take his first breath of this thing called life. He wondered if the doctor would remember P.J., if her auburn hair and emerald eyes would have remained in memory.

For Jess's sake, he wanted this to go smoothly. And quickly. He doubted there was any truth behind the letter or phone call she'd received. The world, after all, was filled with weirdos.

But for Jess, he needed to be sure.

Suddenly the door to the off-limits-beyond opened, and a woman entered the waiting room. It was not the receptionist; it was a stern-looking woman in a white coat with a rectangular blue name badge—not nondescript white like the other badges he'd seen there. The blue-badged woman walked toward him. Phillip slipped his foot back into his loafer and stood. He had fifteen minutes left to find out all the answers.

"Mr. Archambault?" the woman asked in a voice that was, indeed, stern. "You asked to see William Larribee?"

Phillip's eyes fell to the badge: *Marjorie Banks, M.D.*, it read.

"Yes, Dr. Banks."

"Visiting hours are not until seven P.M."

He dug into his pocket and handed her his card. "I'm an

attorney, Dr. Banks. I need to see Dr. Larribee on business."

"This is a retirement home, not a prison. The fact that you're an attorney makes no difference." Her eyes narrowed behind her wire frame glasses. "Visiting hours are at seven." She handed him back his card and turned from the room.

"Tonight?" Phillip asked. "Can I see him tonight?"

"Seven to nine," Dr. Banks replied and disappeared through the door.

"Location, location, location," Joseph said smugly, folding his arms and looking out the huge office window directly onto Park Avenue. "We've made it, little brother."

Phillip was unsure if the flush he felt in his cheeks was from his public-transportation sprint back into town, from knowing he'd have to repeat the frenzied trek to make the seven o'clock visiting hours, or from the excitement about where he now stood.

The brownstone was impressive: The stenciled, frosted glass on the oak front door created a dramatic entrance, and the first-floor access would certainly be convenient. The interior was polished and inviting: Its gleaming wood floors and turn-of-the-century mahogany woodwork had been carefully restored; its high ceilings and tall windows were stately and . . . lawyerly. It was a place where they could be proud to bring clients. For some reason, Phillip thought of Jess. He would be proud to bring Jess here. He would have been proud to bring P.J.

"Can we really afford it?" he asked his older and presumably wiser brother.

"We can't afford *not* to afford it," Joseph replied. "This is our turning point."

He wondered if Donald Archambault had had a turning point or if he'd been content with what he had built: stability, not great wealth. "I wonder what Dad would think," Phillip heard himself say.

"Dad would be stunned. Maybe even a little envious."

Walking to the white marble fireplace, Phillip closely examined the detail of the intricately carved mantel. "Can we still have a secretary? A real one?"

Joseph laughed. "With health insurance and personal days? You ask for a lot, little brother."

Irritated, Phillip loosened his tie and thought about Joseph's slightly skewed motto: *It doesn't matter what's in the checkbook, it's what other people think is there that counts.* "We have to have a secretary," Phillip said.

His brother laughed. "Only kidding. I've already contacted a placement service. We'll have not only one secretary, but two. One for me. One for you. And a receptionist. Full-time."

Phillip looked into Joseph's Irish-Polish-whatever eyes. "Are you sure?"

"Quite. And so is Jim Crowley."

Jim Crowley was their overworked accountant, a nervous little man who had so far managed to keep Joseph's extravagances within the confines of their budget. Phillip had no reason not to trust him.

He relaxed, nodded, and looked around thoughtfully. It was not difficult to picture a grand cherry desk, comfortable wing chairs, an Oriental rug. He could not deny it would be pleasant to come here each day. The richly paneled walls symbolized the success and confidence that even Phillip longed to feel.

"So is it a go?" Joseph asked.

Phillip smiled. "Remind me to thank McGinnis and Smith for their business."

"You can do it tonight. We're having dinner." Joseph picked up his briefcase. "Seven-thirty. At the club."

"Tonight?" he asked, an image of blue plastic chairs and a faceless Dr. Larribee coming into his mind.

"Don't tell me you have other plans."

"I wish I'd known earlier. . . ."

Joseph set down his briefcase, the leather slapping the wood floor and echoing in the empty room. "Do you finally have a social life?"

"It's not social, Joseph. I'm doing a favor for a friend. . . ."

His brother's eyebrows raised.

"Not a favor, exactly," he said. "Possibly a paying client." Jess, after all, had said that she'd pay him, though he had no intention of accepting anything from her. He flicked his eyes away from Joseph's, so his brother would not detect the white lie he'd just told.

"Are you holding out on me, little brother?"

Phillip did not respond. He wasn't trying to be evasive, shrewd, or manipulative. He simply did not know what to say.

"Come on, Phillip. I'm not just your partner. I'm your brother, remember?"

The old radiators hissed, warming the room. "Forget it, okay? Seven-thirty at the club is fine. What I planned I can change to tomorrow."

"No you can't. Tomorrow's Wednesday. Dinner with Mother."

"Oh. Wednesday. Right." Would his life ever be his own?

"And you'd better wear your Sunday best. Camille hinted that Mother's found another girl for you to inspect." He leaned toward Phillip and winked. "Unless, of course, these secret plans you have would interfere with meeting another hot-to-trot female."

Phillip groaned. "Hot-to-trot? I'd settle for one who was just decent to look at." He knew he was exaggerating, the way guys needed to exaggerate in order to sound like men.

"Mother worries about you, Phillip. She wants you to settle down."

No one seemed to care that Phillip was not ready to settle down, to buy a house in the suburbs like Joseph and Camille, to pick out china and silver and have someone else in his space who would surely not appreciate his socks on the floor. No one seemed to care because Phillip was almost thirty and it had been decided that it was time.

Joseph plunked a well-intentioned hand on Phillip's shoulder. "Humor her, little brother. Now let's go sign these papers before those vulture real estate people sell this place out from under us."

"Right. Okay." He buttoned his coat and tucked his wool scarf around his throat, resigning himself to the fact that William Larribee would have to wait until after McGinnis and Smith. Until after dinner with Mom and the latest of her dream girls. Phillip's priorities, after all, were about to move uptown. Surely Jess could wait another couple of days.

Jess tried to act normal as she watched Maura pack for the Caribbean, tried not to let her anger, her hurt, her frustration show. It had been nearly five years ago that Maura had come to Jess: sixteen, pregnant, and scared. That was when Charles had called his daughter a whore; had tried to insist she have an abortion she did not want; had accused her of trying to destroy his reputation, his business, his life. Apparently, Maura had forgiven her father, had forgotten her tears and her pain.

Jess had not. Nor did she doubt that if Maura had not had a miscarriage—if she instead now toted a four-year-old illegitimate child whom Charles's business associates would discreetly not ask about over lunch—she would not have been invited on this catamaran junket.

Jess also wondered if Maura would have ever considered spending spring break with her father if he had not agreed to let Eddie go with them.

"Mom," Maura said, folding a tank top and tossing it into her bag, "I know you're probably not thrilled about me going with Daddy, but it'll be fine. Besides, it's time I tried to get to know my stepmother. Family units have changed today. We have to adapt."

Jess wondered if this philosophy was straight from one of Maura's human development courses or if she'd come to that realization on her own. "Well," she said quietly, "I can't argue with that."

"Why don't you ever go out, Mom?" Maura asked so quickly it startled Jess.

Jess laughed. "And just where would I go?"

"Have dinner. Go to the theater. Travel."

"On a catamaran in the Caribbean?"

"Mom, one of these days you should start having some fun and stop being a martyr."

"A martyr? Is that what you think of me?"

"Well, no. I don't know. You work so hard at your business. You still cook dinner for Travis every night. God, you still do his laundry."

"Travis is still in high school, Maura. He's a child."

"In a few months he'll be on his own. You've babied him, Mom. You babied all of us."

Staring into Maura's suitcase, Jess tried to digest what she had just heard. "You are my children," she said, not undefensively. "You are my responsibility. I did not baby you. I took care of you." At this moment, Jess hated it that Maura had come home from college with all this psychobabble.

Maura sat next to Jess on the bed, the puffy-pink-comforter-covered bed that Jess had always made sure was just so for her little girl. The little girl she had raised.

"I'm not criticizing you, Mom. But it really is time for you to let go. After Travis goes to college, what will you do? Work twenty-four hours a day? There's more to life than that, Mom."

"For your information, after Travis leaves I am going to curl up at night and read wonderful books. I am going to cook microwave dinners and enjoy the peace." In her mind, the idea had once sounded blissful. Now that she said it aloud, it sounded isolatingly lonely.

"Why don't you ever call KiKi Larson? You used to be friends, and she's divorced, too."

Jess laughed. "Oh, my, yes. KiKi is divorced, all right." She did not mention that she had seen KiKi one night last fall, when the woman had hounded Jess into attending a singles social at the Grand Oaks Hotel. "You *must* get out, Jessica," KiKi had whined. "A new man isn't going to come marching into your living room. You have to *mingle*." So Jess had tried. But KiKi's concept of "mingling" meant dancing with every man who asked her and asking those who did not. Feeling both absurd and embarrassed, Jess had left early and vowed never to mingle again. She looked at her daughter now and smiled. "I'm afraid KiKi's only interest is in men."

"That doesn't make her wrong," Maura replied, as she stood up and shook her head. "I don't know what you're afraid of, Mom. Not every man is like Daddy." Maura returned to rifling through her closet.

Jess remained on the bed and thought about what her daughter had said. There was some consolation in Maura's acknowledgment that Charles was not perfect. But, of course, she was right. Once Travis left in the fall, Jess would be alone, her job as a seven-days-a-week mother eliminated for the first time in twenty-three years. Her thoughts drifted to her other daughter, who might or might not still exist, who would turn thirty this year, who might even be a mother herself, who might have a family to care for. She wondered if she was a good mother, if she would care as much as Jess had. Too much, according to Maura.

Of course, first of all, she would have to have found a man. Hopefully, one of the ones who, as Maura said, wasn't like Charles.

She rose from the bed. "I'm going to get the sunblock," she told Maura. "You'll need plenty of it down there." As she headed down the hall, Jess wondered if providing sunblock was babying her daughter. Then she wondered if she had been overprotective in an effort to make up for Charles being so insensitive. Or maybe she had needed to keep her children close so she would not lose them the way she'd lost Amy. Amy, or whoever her first child had been.

Her name was Nicole, and her father was a Chicago defense attorney who played in the big leagues and had tried—and won—huge settlements for weeping, diamond-clad women whose wealthy husbands had scorned them. Jeanine Archambault played bridge with a friend of a friend of one of Nicole's father's much-satisfied clients. Nicole was a first-year law student at Columbia, so naturally she must be in need of a friend like Phillip, someone to show her the ropes in Manhattan, legal and otherwise.

Nicole was attractive in a law-student sort of way, with plain chestnut hair cropped just under her ears, a black cashmere turtleneck and black pleated pants hugging her too-thin frame, and wide brown eyes bloodshot, no doubt, from reading too many books. It was a look that Phillip certainly could relate to.

But Nicole's smile seemed genuine as she accepted the platter of pot roast from Phillip's mother now and commented how wonderful it was going to be to taste home-cooked food.

Jeanine smiled at Phillip. Camille smiled at Joseph. Joseph looked at his mother and winked. And everyone seemed to agree that Nicole was a quite suitable girl for the young attorney whose time had come.

Scooping mashed potatoes onto his plate, Phillip hated himself for wondering if P.J. would have tried to fix him up, if P.J. had raised him, if P.J. had not died. Nicole was one more in the long, poor-Phillip-has-no-time-to-meet-anyone string of potential mates handpicked by Jeanine, Camille, and, on one occasion, Joseph himself. To date, they had resulted in a series of rather dull evenings at

Mom's, followed by Phillip's obligatory invitation to dinner in the city, which had only heightened the dullness. Except, of course, with Suzanne Devine, who had hung up the proper gray sheath she'd worn to Jeanine's table and showed up in the city in a red spandex minidress and four-inch stilettos. Phillip suppressed a grin now as he remembered the night he shared with Suzanne—the outrageous way she'd flirted with him all through their obligatory date, the even more outrageous way she'd spent the rest of the night slathering him with whipped cream and giving him head.

He shifted uncomfortably on the tapestry-upholstered dining room chair now, sorry that Suzanne had returned to San Antonio the following day, where she told him she had a fiancé waiting and that it most definitely was her loss.

Jeanine interrupted his thoughts. "Nicole's specializing in children's rights," she said.

"Labor laws, mostly," Nicole said. "More and more children are working today. It's a shame. The world is moving so quickly they barely have time to be kids. We have to protect them."

Handing the guest the bowl of potatoes, Phillip half-smiled. "Children's rights is a long way from divorce court."

A rebellious twinkle came into the bloodshot brown eyes. "If you're speaking about my father, you're right. I'm sure he'd rather see me in a gray suit and heels, following in his high-profile footsteps."

Phillip wondered if it would be appropriate to ask if she owned any red spandex dresses. Instead, he decided he'd invite her to dinner—maybe this weekend—not tomorrow, of course. Tomorrow night was reserved for William Larribee. Tomorrow night was reserved for helping Jess. Then, once he learned what had happened to her baby, he would make time for Nicole. It would please his mother, and it might not be such a bad idea for himself.

• • • •

The man in the wheelchair had thick white eyebrows that stuck straight out from his forehead as if they'd been glued on. His face was liver-spotted, his eyes filmy from cataracts, and he was completely bald. All in all, he resembled a Mr. Potato Head, one who, perhaps, had spent too many years at the bottom of a bottle of gin. In a court of law, he would not be the picture of a credible witness.

"Dr. Larribee," Phillip said, extending his hand. "You brought me into the world."

"Don't hold it against me," the old man said, planting a dry, gnarled hand into Phillip's.

It was not the welcoming response Phillip would have expected from a doctor. He withdrew his hand from the dry one and sat down on the blue plastic chair in the "activities room" where he'd been escorted by the receptionist moments ago when the clock had struck seven.

"I'm an attorney," he said, handing his card to the doctor.

The old man shook his head and averted his eyes. "Can't read anything with these damn eyes," he said. "Don't need a damn lawyer, either, if that's why you're here."

Just how bad was his eyesight? Too faulty to have written the letter that Jess had received? Phillip slipped his card back into his pocket. "No, Dr. Larribee, I'm not looking for business. I'm looking for answers." The old man was surly, the old man was curt. Phillip decided to be direct. It might be his only chance to find out the truth.

"Depends on the questions."

"My mother was P.J. Davies," Phillip began. "She was a resident at Larchwood Hall." He had wanted to mention her distinct auburn hair; he had wanted to share with the doctor that P.J. had died, but that he'd been there beside her, reunited at last. He'd wanted to share these things with this man, but he could not. Instead, he watched Larribee rub his palms on the rubber wheels of his chair.

"Don't remember her."

Phillip wondered if the old man was lying, or if he himself would be able to remember a client thirty years from now—even one as strikingly beautiful as P.J. had been. "What about Jess Bates?" he asked. "She was very young. Only fifteen. You delivered her daughter in 1968, the same year as me."

"Never heard of her."

"Ginny Stevens?"

Phillip would have sworn that a hint of a smile passed over the old man's pale lips.

"Nope," he said, then his yellowed eyes closed. "Can't help you." With a harrumph, he opened his eyes and began to wheel his chair away.

Phillip jumped up. "Just a minute, Dr. Larribee. You may be an old man, but I can still subpoena you." He really had no idea what he was saying; he only knew he had come all the way out here—twice—and that Jess was counting on him. If the doctor would not talk to him, Phillip would not know where to turn next. And no matter how old or cranky the guy was, Phillip did not believe for a minute he hadn't recognized at least one of the three names.

The wheelchair stopped. "Subpoena me? For what?"

"You tell me. And you can start by telling me what you know about Jess Bates. And the baby that was adopted by the Hawthornes."

The activities room grew quiet. Over by the window, an elderly woman muttered to herself. At a shiny round table, a man knocked over a tower of wood blocks he had built. Phillip blinked back the stale air and the faint odor of urine that permeated the room and wondered if he'd be thrown out for harassing an old man for no justifiable reason.

"Christ," Dr. Larribee grumbled. "Why don't you ask that Taylor woman? She was the one in charge."

Caramba, Phillip thought, trying to remain calm, steady, trying not to let his excitement show. "Miss Taylor is dead," he said evenly. "Tell me what you know. Do it here or in the courtroom."

"It wasn't malpractice," Larribee said. "You can't pull my license."

The idea that the dotty old man was worried about losing his medical license was absurd. But what struck Phillip even more profoundly was the doctor's use of the word *malpractice.* Phillip loosened his tie. He decided to go out on a limb just to watch Larribee's reaction. "Switching babies is a felony," he said, with an authority he did not feel.

A mutter or a sputter or something like that blubbered from the doctor's lips. "Christ, it's been nearly thirty years."

"Doesn't matter," Phillip commented, unsure if that were true, but sure that corporate law never made his adrenaline pump the way it was pumping now. "You could spend your last days in a six-by-eight cell unless you cooperate."

The old man's eyes drifted toward the window. "I had a lawyer once," he said. "But he's dead. Everybody's dead. The only people left alive aren't worth their salt."

"What happened, Dr. Larribee?"

He closed his eyes again and let out a shallow sigh. "Frances Taylor," he said, "God, she was a greedy woman."

Greedy? Phillip listened.

"She threatened to turn me in. She knew I liked my gin, maybe a little too much. She blackmailed me into signing those forms." His voice drifted away, as if his thoughts were sliding back to a painful place.

Phillip leaned forward to hear him more clearly. "What forms?"

The doctor shook his head. "She said no one would ever know."

Phillip rested his hand on Dr. Larribee's arm. "What happened to Jess's baby?"

He did not answer at first, then raised his head and wiped a trickle of drool from his mouth. "It was supposed to go to the Hawthornes. Another girl's did instead. A girl from Bridgeport."

"Who was she?"

The old man's thin shoulders shrugged. "Can't remember her name. A charity case. I told her her baby died."

Phillip held back the rage he felt begin to boil beneath his skin. "What about Jess Bates's baby?"

"I don't know what happened to it."

"Was it born . . . did it live?"

"Yes," he responded. "It was small, but it lived." He slumped a little in the chair, growing older with each tired heartbeat.

Phillip's anger gave way to a prickly tingle that raced from his forehead straight down to his toes. *Jess's baby was alive. And it had not been Amy Hawthorne.* He resisted the urge to run from the room, rush to a pay phone, and get Jess on the line. He resisted because there was too much left to learn. Phillip squared his jaw.

"Who took Jess's baby?" he repeated.

"I told you. I don't know."

He stood up straight and moved to the front of the doctor's chair. He paced three steps to one side, three back again, a practiced performance of cross-examination he'd seen on *L.A. Law* reruns. Then, ever so slowly, the pieces began to fall together, a jigsaw puzzle taking shape. He abruptly stopped and turned to his defendant.

"What about the fifty thousand dollars, Doctor? How much of that did Miss Taylor pay you?"

Dr. Larribee became alert once more. He sat up in the chair. His eyebrows danced. "I didn't see any of it. I swear. Why don't you ask Bud Wilson?"

"Wilson's dead, too."

Larribee snorted. "See? Everybody's dead."

Phillip slipped his hands in his pockets and took another stab. "Who paid her the fifty thousand, Doctor?"

"I don't know," he answered, shaking his head. "I swear I don't know."

Phillip had another idea. "How many others were there, Doctor? How many other babies did you . . . switch?"

The big eyebrows danced. "None! It was just hers . . . just that Bates girl."

"Are you certain?"

"Yes. Not that Frances Taylor would have objected." He puffed at the air and again rubbed his hands on the wheels. "Now, please. Leave me alone." He wheeled from the room, his chair creaking and groaning with each turn of the spokes.

This time, Phillip did not stop him. He knew where to find him if he needed more. For now, he had what he wanted: confirmation that Jess's baby had not been Amy Hawthorne and that the fifty thousand dollars was somehow connected. And, thankfully, it did not appear as if this had been a big business: it was a small-time, one-time scam that happened only because the opportunity had been there and a greedy old woman had grabbed it.

As Phillip walked down the corridor toward the nursing home exit, he realized that he had done what he'd promised for Jess. But he could not stop now. He had to help Jess find her real daughter, even if it meant risking his brother's wrath.

Chapter 9

 It was one of those warm, March-leading-to-April mornings that held the promise of sunshine and pastels and spring. Jess gazed out the window of the shop across to the park and wondered how long it would be before the crocuses poked their purple heads above the ground, before the daffodils shared their yellow beauty with the world. It was easier to think of these things than to count the days it had been since she'd seen Phillip (seven), to obsess on the prospect that Amy might not have been hers, or to wonder why, if her baby still lived and knew who Jess was, she had not come forward and let herself be known.

Jess also knew it was easier to think about flowers than to imagine Charles and his new wife playing congenial hosts to his daughter and her boyfriend.

As the sewing machines whirred in the background, her assistants working diligently on the country club draperies, Jess realized that Maura was right. Life had to be more than working and worrying about other people. Working, worrying, and curling up in an old chenille robe, no matter how cozy that was. Her thoughts drifted to the remote possibility that there might ever be another man in her life, a man not like Charles, but rather someone able to share her pleasures and her pain, someone who loved her and whom she could love back. Someone who would accept her past as well as her present and embrace her right to welcome any child that was—or was not—part of her life.

She was thinking these things so deeply, she did not notice Phillip coming up the walk until his green eyes met hers and he gave a big wave. Jess blinked and opened the door.

"Phillip," she said with a smile, stretching up on her toes to kiss his soft cheek. "I didn't expect you."

"The way you were standing in the window, I thought you were watching for me."

Jess laughed. "I was watching for the crocus to bloom."

He frowned.

She laughed again. "Only kidding. What brings you out here?"

He studied her face.

"Oh, my God," she said quickly, her thoughts suddenly gelling, suddenly springing back to her real world, where catamarans and lovers did not exist. "You've learned something."

"Can we talk somewhere private?"

Her eyes darted around the shop. Her workers were busy, but not deaf, despite the noise from the machines. She glanced out the window again. "The park," she said hurriedly. "Let me get my jacket."

The park bench was damp with the remnants of morning dew, but Jess did not mind. She sat perfectly still, her hands in the pockets of her light canvas coat, listening as Phillip told her that Bud Wilson was dead, listening as he told her of his conversation with Dr. Larribee. She listened and was aware of her own gentle breathing; with each inhale and each exhale she tried to assimilate his words, tried to sort their meaning.

When Phillip had finished, Jess did not move; Jess did not speak.

"So, based on Dr. Larribee's story," Phillip concluded, "I think we can be certain that Amy was not yours."

Jess watched a pigeon alight by her feet, his small black eyes staring up at her, sizing her up as if trying to determine if she had any bread crusts.

And then the butterflies took wing in her stomach. She twisted the emerald and diamond ring on her hand, the ring that had been there for thirty years, her mother's ring, her mother's love.

"My daughter is still living," she whispered.

Next to her, Phillip crossed his legs. "Well, we don't know that for certain, Jess. But I think we can assume she's probably out there. Somewhere."

"On Martha's Vineyard?"

"Maybe. We don't know that, either. I'd have to do some fairly deep digging."

Jess lifted her eyes to the tall trees, to the bright green buds that would soon be full leaves, that would soon be thick and shady and lovely. She thought about Maura, about her daughter's newfound independence. She would be a strong woman, Jess decided. Not perfect, but strong, strong enough to handle what Jess needed to do, strong enough to, someday, understand.

"I need to find her." Her words floated into the air, past the pigeon, up into the trees.

Phillip nodded. "I will help."

"But your brother . . ." Jess said, "Your practice . . ."

"They'll survive." He smiled and lightly touched her arm. "Besides, I think P.J. would want me to help, don't you?"

Jess remembered the bright, auburn-haired woman with the wide smile and the unstoppable drive. Unlike reluctant Susan and "no way, never, not in my lifetime" Ginny, P.J. had agreed to the idea when Jess had gone to her condo, suggesting the reunion. "Yes," P.J. had said, "I would like to meet my son." Jess smiled now and gently patted Phillip's hand. "You're right," she said clearly, "I think P.J. would like it a lot."

"Amy was not mine." Jess's small voice came from the answering machine that was perched on the bar across from the sofa where Ginny was sprawled, sipping a Coke, watching Regis and Kathie Lee, and eating her third egg-and-cheese croissant of the morning. "Phillip is going to help find my baby."

Consuelo waddled into the room, stared at the machine, then moved to pick up the phone.

"Don't," Ginny commanded. "Leave. Vamoose."

The housekeeper shook her head. "Why you no talk to your friend?"

Ginny pulled herself up. The machine beeped, then clicked off. "None of your business, señora. Now, vamoose. Leave me alone."

The woman, whose white-streaked dark hair was pulled back into a bun, planted her hands on her wide, wide hips. "Mr. Jake, he'd be so ashamed."

Ginny brushed crumbs from her lap onto the white carpet on the floor.

"Look at you," Consuelo continued. "You're a god-awful mess."

"What I am is your employer. Which means you need to shut the hell up and leave me alone."

"Alone? You want alone? So you can keep hanging around stuffing your face like a little piglet?"

"Little" came out sounding like "leetle." Ginny did not understand why when these Mexicans learned English they couldn't at least learn to speak it right.

"No one want to be around you anyway," Consuelo huffed. "Not even your own daughter."

"Leave my daughter out of this."

"Lisa is a nice girl. I bet her other mother is nicer to

her." The housekeeper huffed again and walked from the room.

Ginny stared at the TV where Regis was sticking a red-headed straight pin into some place on the map of the country, somewhere near Dubuque. She supposed there were people out there who had had a husband or two drop dead. She wondered if that was why they were sitting watching Regis and Kathie Lee in the middle of the day. She wondered if they were eating egg-and-cheese croissants.

"Sheet," Ginny said, mocking Consuelo. She flicked off the remote and decided the housekeeper was right about one thing: She was a mess.

Hauling herself to a sitting position, Ginny thought about Lisa. The last time she'd seen her had been on the weekend—not last weekend, the weekend before. Or the one before that; it was hard to remember. Lisa had shown up without warning. Ginny had been lounging outside in the hot tub, naked.

On another day, at another time, it would not have fazed Ginny for her daughter to see her without any clothes. But as she looked down at her white, rounded belly and jiggly, puckery thighs, Ginny was embarrassed at the weight she was gaining, the visible result of the fact she could not seem to stop eating everything she could see, smell, or touch.

So instead of greeting Lisa with a smile and a hello, Ginny tried unsuccessfully to cover her bulges by turning her back on her daughter.

"What the hell are you doing here?" she muttered.

"I came to see you," Lisa answered. "I wanted to see how you're doing."

"Well, now you've seen me. All of me. Go home, Lisa. I want to be alone."

Lisa crouched down on the deck of the tub. "Ginny," she said, "I want to help you. I loved Jake, too."

Ginny slipped her head under the water, letting it steam into her hair and sink into her scalp, wishing it would saturate her brain and wash away all the memories that lurked inside. Then she broke through the surface but did not open her eyes. "Go home, Lisa," she repeated. "I need to do this alone."

For a moment, Lisa remained silent. Then Ginny felt her daughter's cool hand on her bare, wet shoulder. "You're not the only one who's hurting. I need you, too, you know."

She left, and since then, they'd not spoken. Ginny had not wanted to talk to Lisa or anyone: she had not wanted to be reminded that life was happening outside the walls of her house. Life—where people worked and laughed and loved and . . . breathed. Where people like Lisa were at the top of their game, churning out successful careers that helped buffer the pain; where people like Jess were drowning in their day-to-day crap, like sewing, for God's sake, and trying to find old babies, as if those things were the most important in the world. Well, as far as Ginny was concerned, her world had stopped several weeks ago when Jake dropped dead, not that she would expect Jess or Lisa to understand.

I bet her other mother is nicer to her, Consuelo had said.

"Yeah," Ginny muttered now, "I bet you're right."

She stared at the TV screen and thought about Regis, Kathie Lee, and the widow in Dubuque. Suddenly—perhaps it was the croissant slathered with butter churning inside her—Ginny knew she had to shape up. She had to emerge from this self-induced prison or she would go out of her fucking mind.

Lisa was probably where she should start. Her daughter was most likely pissed off that Ginny had shut her out—or maybe Lisa really was upset that Jake had died and really did need Ginny, too.

"Yeah, fat chance," Ginny mumbled. She knew a con when she saw one, and she figured Lisa would do or say anything to get Ginny out of her funk. She was, after all, nice.

But Ginny stood up and decided to go. Con or no con,

Lisa was the one person in the world who might be able to stand being with her, no matter what the señora said. Lisa was Ginny's daughter, and Ginny was her mother, and Lisa understood her moods. Understood them as if she had known her all her life. Only to herself would Ginny ever admit that there was something soothing about Lisa, something grounding about being in the same room with the one creature on the face of the earth who had sprung from her womb, no matter how tainted that womb had been.

Yes, she thought now with a small smile. She would go and see Lisa. Maybe they could do lunch.

All her pants were too tight, so Ginny had thrown on the same shapeless dress she'd worn when Jess had been there. With a long white sweater that was older than Consuelo, she tried to cover the creases across her swollen lap that hadn't been there the last time she'd put on real clothes. But when Ginny stepped outside into the infernal California sunshine, she quickly realized it was too hot for a sweater: It was nearly April, and it was L.A., where women did not need to hide under sweaters. They ate alfalfa sprouts instead of egg-and-cheese sandwiches, and did not let themselves become a god-awful mess.

Hopefully, Lisa would be so glad to see her that she wouldn't care.

Pulling off the sweater, she flung it into the backseat of her Mercedes, started the ignition, and headed down the canyon road. She longed for a cigarette, for the sharp, soothing taste of self-destructive tobacco. If she had a cigarette she could suck in a deep breath and blow out her thoughts on a thick cloud of smoke. If she had a cigarette she could die of lung cancer instead of obesity.

But she had no cigarettes, and she had no food. So she snapped on the radio.

James Taylor was on one station; LeAnn Rimes on another and a loudmouthed deejay spouting off about a feared big earthquake on another. Ginny played the buttons as she had the TV remote, with nervous, angry twitches and disbelief that she could not land on something that would take away the battle that raged inside her.

Adjusting her oversized sunglasses, she tried to relax, which she knew would be much easier if the elastic of her underpants didn't feel like a girdle around her gut.

Girdles, she thought with a laugh. "Now there's something I haven't thought about for a while."

Of course, Ginny had never worn one. Not even in the sixties, when everyone else did. Girdles were so . . . restrictive. And you never knew when you'd need to take one off quickly, when a man would desire to touch your flesh and not want to come up with a handful of rubber, even if the rubber had been hand-edged with lace.

Her thoughts drifted to Jess, who had been too tiny to need a girdle, then to Susan, whose broad ass could most definitely have benefited from one, but who probably felt her long tunics, love beads, and caftans compensated for the enormous shimmy of her enormous butt. P.J. was probably the only one of the girls at Larchwood who had worn one: not that she needed to, but a mother as uptight and prissy as P.J.'s probably had insisted. After all, what would the church ladies think if she didn't?

None of them, of course, could have squeezed into girdles at Larchwood Hall, where their stomachs were bloated with unexpected babies, where their mountainlike mounds hid their adolescent ages.

With a twinge of unexpected feelings, Ginny realized she was glad that Jess's baby was not dead. She had been so cruel to Jess when they were kids: stealing her money, then stealing her ring—even though she gave it back in the end—she'd been cruel to her and had not cared that Jess was such a scared little girl. "Hell, we were all scared little girls," Ginny said aloud.

She turned onto the road toward town and resolved to call Jess this afternoon, after she had had her emotional fix from Lisa, after she'd pulled up her bootstraps one more time for the world.

Maybe she'd even have a diet special for lunch: a watercress salad with endive and sprouts and balsamic vinegar. Puke.

The soundstage was quiet, an unusual event for a hit like *Devonshire Place.*

Ginny's heels clicked against the wood floor as she picked her way in the darkness amid cables and cameras and lights and booms. Stopping in the center of the stage, she let the hollow sound envelop her, return her to those days so long ago when she had tried so hard to be a star, when all she wanted in the world was her name up in lights and people kissing her ass. A small memory struggled to come to the surface: a memory from Larchwood Hall days, when she lay on her bed devouring movie magazines, dreaming of capri pants and high heels and standing on the corner of Hollywood and Vine, Ginny Stevens, the star, the sought-after box office sensation waiting for her pink Cadillac to come and collect her and whisk her off to another cocktail party, another premiere.

Her dreams, of course, had been just that. Oh, there had been a few small parts—damn few and damn small—when she'd first dragged her mother from Boston to L.A. once her stepfather was dead, once Lisa had been born, born and permanently (she thought) ensconced with the family who had signed the appropriate papers and come up with the appropriate bucks.

There had been a few small parts, long before her dress creased across her middle. A few parts and many husbands—three before Jake: the cigar-stinking agent who died and left her his floundering business and beat-up car; the studly young Texan whose heart-stopping face and her fifteen percent of it landed him enough roles to put Ginny back on her feet and not give a shit when he announced he was gay; the soft-porn writer with the hard-core imagination who prodded his wife into cavorting with other women until he found religion and traded his life with Ginny for one of the cloth.

Bit parts, bit husbands, until Jake. Until Jake Edwards, the documentary producer, who had given Ginny some decent roles, then a decent home, a respectable life.

God, she thought, the ghosts of the fantasy moviemakers swirling around her in echoes of missed lines and lost opportunities, *I was such a bitch to Jake.* Until she met Lisa, it had been true. Ginny had been an insufferable, ungrateful bitch, a tough, hardened woman who'd spent her whole life on guard because she'd not had much choice if she wanted to survive.

"You looking for something, lady?" someone called from across the stage.

Ginny began to speak, then cleared her throat. She quickly dabbed the small tears that had found their way down her swollen, puffed cheeks. "Lisa," she said. "I'm looking for Lisa Andrews."

The man stepped into the dimness. "You and half the world." He carried a clipboard and wore a tired-out look on his face. "How'd you get in here?"

He thinks I'm a fan, Ginny thought. *He thinks I'm a crazed, obsessed fan, maybe even a woman from Dubuque.* "You don't understand," she said, "I'm Ginny Edwards. I got 'in here' because Jake Edwards was my husband." If there was any recognition on his part, he did not respond. "Lisa Andrews is my daughter."

He lifted a curious eyebrow. "Your daughter?"

Ginny wasn't sure whether he couldn't believe Lisa would have a mother so young or a mother who was such a god-awful mess. "What is your name?" she demanded.

"O'Brien. I'm a grip."

"Well, O'Brien, I suggest you tell me where Lisa is," she said firmly, "or I'll find Harry Lyons and ask him myself." She was pleased—and surprised—she'd remembered the name of Lisa's director, the porker who had sucked down her food after Jake's funeral.

"They finished blocking for the day," the grip said. "If she's still on the lot, she's probably in her dressing room." He pointed to a corridor off to the left. "Third door on the left. The one just before Harry's office. Better knock, though. Her boyfriend's with her."

Boyfriend?

Ginny stared at him a moment, then decided he must be joking. If Lisa had a boyfriend, surely Ginny would have been the first to know. Then again, how long had it really been since they'd talked?

A boyfriend? Was it possible?

She left the stage, heading in the direction of the dressing rooms.

The door did not have a red wooden star on the front, merely a metal slot into which a plastic nameplate had been slid. *Andrews,* the nameplate read in neat, disposable print. *Star today, gone tomorrow,* Ginny thought. Life molded by the ratings. Not like the old studio days, when stars were stars. Guaranteed by their contracts. Not that Ginny had ever seen one.

She reached for the doorknob then suddenly stopped.

Boyfriend?

Glancing over her shoulder, Ginny saw no one. She pressed her ear to the door and listened. No laughter, no conversation. And definitely, she thought again, no boyfriend.

Still, she raised her hand and knocked. There was no answer. *Shit,* she thought. *Sheet.* So much for emotional support. So much for the daughter who would want to see her anytime, anywhere.

Turning on her heel to leave the studio, she suddenly heard a sound from inside the dressing room. She stepped back and knocked again.

"Go away, O'Brien," Lisa's voice said from the other side of the door. "I'll be out in a minute."

So Lisa was there. Ginny smoothed the crease from her dress and turned the knob. "Lisa," she said, opening the door and entering the small room, "it's Ginny." But as soon as the words were out of her mouth, she stopped. She froze. Her body went cold. Solid as a marble statue on a museum pedestal. Stiff as the dick that pointed at her from across the room. The big ramrod dick with the too-familiar head. Brad's dick.

The scream that shot from Ginny's lips fired down the hall and reverberated onto the soundstage.

"You bastard!" she shrieked, pushing past her half-naked daughter and lunging for her stepson.

"Ginny!" Lisa shouted. She grabbed Ginny's waist and pulled her back. "Leave him alone."

Ginny fought to grab his dick, to rip it off, to make him pay. "You bastard! You filthy bastard!"

Brad stepped back. And grinned. "Mommie dearest," he said, "what an unpleasant surprise."

Her arms flailed toward him. Lisa held her back.

"O'Brien!" Lisa yelled. "Help!"

Slowly, Brad leaned over and removed his jeans from the back of a chair. He slipped into them as Ginny still struggled with her daughter, his eyes and his grin fixed on Ginny. He stuffed his still-hard dick into his pants, and just as he began zipping the fly, O'Brien bolted into the room.

"Christ," he said, wrangling Ginny from Lisa's grasp. "Do you want the police?"

"No," Lisa said, "just get her out of here. Please."

The grip tightened Ginny's hands behind her back. "I knew she couldn't be your mother. Any mother of yours would have a lot more class."

Her anger went . limp. "Bastards," she muttered, as O'Brien pushed her from the studio. "All of you."

• • •

She wasn't wearing red spandex, but the promise of sex was there, just because they were a male and a female and adults, for the most part, and because there certainly seemed no reason to hold back.

Phillip had taken her to a small Italian restaurant on West Fifty-fourth not far from her apartment. He tried to enchant her with first-date enthusiasm. He knew, of course, that she could not be enchanted. There was nothing enchanting about corporate law, especially to a do-gooder children's rights advocate who probably detested the white-collar world in which she was raised. Still, she appeared interested, and for that he was grateful. Phillip never missed being with a woman until he was with one.

Toying with his rigatoni and sun-dried tomatoes he finally said, "Stop. Enough about me. Tell me about yourself. Do you like the law?"

She sipped her Chianti, her deep red lipstick not leaving a mark on the glass. "Not at all. I'm only getting my law degree to spite my father." Her words were matter-of-fact. Phillip mentally groaned, *Oh, no. Not another weirdo.*

"To . . ." he stuttered a bit, sipped from his own glass. "To spite your father?" He couldn't imagine doing anything to spite his father, his mother, or even Joseph.

Nicole smiled. "Daddy wanted me to be a teacher. Or a doctor. Anything but a lawyer. He says it's become such a despised field."

"Oh." Phillip took a mouthful of rigatoni, grateful that Nicole wasn't weird, after all, but not sure if her comment meant he was despised too. "Well, I guess there are rotten apples in every bushel." He wondered if he had his cliché right, and if Nicole was too bright for clichés. "So to speak," he added.

"But let's face it," she continued, "lawyering is where the money is. Especially with the kinds of contacts Daddy has made."

Phillip was getting confused. "But your father does big divorces. If you're getting into children's rights . . ."

Nicole grinned. "I'm no liberal, Phillip. Divorced people have children. And who could despise someone who fights for kids?"

Phillip nodded. He couldn't.

"Your mother's nice," Nicole said suddenly.

He smiled.

"I think Daddy secretly hoped that I'd be like your mother. You know, domestic." She said the word as if it were sour.

Phillip laughed. "You don't seem anything like my mother."

"Oh, believe me," Nicole said, her wide lips curling into a smile. "I'm not."

"You're an independent woman."

"Very."

"And smart."

"Extremely."

"And you know what you want."

She leaned back in her chair and sipped her wine again. "You know what law school is like, Phillip. You work and work and hardly have time for a life. Well, I want a life. *Part* of a life anyway. I want dinners like this, and I want a man to share them with. I want a man who understands the demands I have and who can adapt. I want him to be my lover." She swirled the ruby liquid in her glass. "Are you interested?"

At least she didn't say she had a fiancé in San Antonio.

Chapter 10

 The sheets on her bed were not satin: they were rumpled and soft, with the familiar feel of a bed that was probably not changed often enough.

Phillip lay on his back, smiling, watching the early-morning sunlight that played above him stir dust specks in the air and suspend them like stars. He wondered why it was that dust specks always seemed so evenly spaced, why they were never clumped all together or spread too far apart. Then he wondered why he was wondering about such trivia; it was Saturday, a day when he was out from under the inquisitive eyes of his brother, a day he should be using to plan his next move to find Jess's baby.

But he didn't think Jess would mind.

He stared up at the high ceiling in Nicole's brick-walled loft, listening to the gentle sleep-breathing of the young woman beside him. The sex had been—well, phenomenal. Fast, heated, Oh-God-I'm-losing-it sex. There had been no time for bells or fireworks: it was sex for sex's sake; direct, need-based sex that provided release if not passion. It had certainly not been unpleasant.

His eyes moved around the big, open room, which, for all its potential, was in need of a decorator. The tall, arched windows were adorned only by iron bars; there were no pictures, no sculptures, no *textures* scattered about, merely a litter of law books stacked on plain, open bookshelves, strewn across a metal computer workstation and heaped on a single tattered rug that covered the stone floor. Nicole had been right about one thing: She certainly was not domestic.

Phillip smiled again. For all his mess and all his clutter, he was pleased that at least his apartment had warmth, with its living, if not thriving, trio of plants; his large framed photos of marathons in which he had run; and his favorite pictures: two of P.J.'s original watercolors, scenes from the Hamptons. P.J. had enjoyed so many years there with Bob Jaffee, the man who had been her lover, the man who had wanted to marry her, the man who had moved to Australia after P.J. died.

He looked off toward the windows again and wondered what miracles Jess could create there with fabric and color and feeling. He was wondering this as, next to him, Nicole began to stir.

She gently rubbed her eyes, her hair. Phillip had a quick desire to touch her, to make love in the morning. Maybe they could take their time this time, maybe the frenzy of first-time sex could give way to tenderness.

But before he could touch her, Nicole pulled herself up and sat on the edge of the bed.

"I guess this is the part where I'm supposed to offer to fix breakfast," she said.

Phillip laughed. "I know. You're not domestic."

She pulled a T-shirt over her small, delectable breasts and stood up. "Not entirely true. I have some blueberry muffins. And orange juice."

If he couldn't have sex he would prefer coffee.

"No coffee," she said, as if reading his mind. "I don't drink it."

"Orange juice is fine. And a muffin would be great."

He waited until she had disappeared into the bathroom

before sitting on the edge of the bed and pulling on his clothes. He knew his modesty was ridiculous, as if the intimacy of being naked was only acceptable when sex was involved.

Tucking in his shirt, Phillip regretted that they had not had morning sex. Had Nicole's previous lovers always let her call the shots in the relationship, always let her have her own way? Last night she'd said she wanted a man who could adapt; the message was clear that if he couldn't, she'd find someone who would. Love, apparently, did not enter into it—law school left little time or energy for the entanglements of emotions.

It's no wonder attorneys are so despised, he mused then wondered how Jeanine Archambault would feel if she knew she'd selected a girl who had no intention of falling in love with her bachelor son.

Phillip looked around the room for a mirror, so he could check whether his light brown hair was, as usual, sticking up in the back. But there was no mirror, just the iron-barred window that offered little reflection.

"It's all yours," Nicole said, emerging from the bathroom.

In the closet-sized room was an old-fashioned toilet with the water tank on top. Phillip studied it a moment, used it, then hoped that pulling the chain would make it flush. It did. He glanced at the narrow shower stall and wished he could take one: but there was only one towel draped on a hook on the door. Apparently, Nicole had not intended for her guest to stay very long. He splashed cold water on his face, looked in the small oval mirror over the round pedestal sink and tried to wet down the cowlick that was indeed standing up on the crown of his head.

"I have an early class," Nicole said when he came out of the bathroom. She pulled an oversized sweatshirt over her head, stepped into jeans, and pinned back her hair with a large silver clip. She pointed to the counter by what would be the kitchen sink if there were a kitchen, if this were more than a one-room loft. "Breakfast is on the counter," she said. "Sorry it's not more."

Phillip went over to the counter. A lone muffin sat on a square of paper napkin. Next to it was a cardboard container of orange juice, individual-size. He smiled as he saw she had removed the plastic straw from the side of the box and inserted it in the hole for him. *Who says you're not domestic?* he thought.

Then she was next to him, her arms loaded with books. "I hate to rush you," she said, "but I've got Ethics this morning. I don't want to be late." She stood waiting.

Phillip grabbed the muffin in one hand, the juice in another. "Lead the way," he said.

When they were out of the apartment and getting onto the elevator, he asked, "Can I see you again?"

"Well," Nicole replied, her mind clearly now on her studies, "tomorrow I'll be in the law library."

"Perfect," he said. "I'll meet you there." He had planned to go to the law library at some point; he intended to start there to find Jess's baby. He and Nicole could do their own work but be together. Then maybe after, they could have Chinese food. Chinese food and sex. *Not a bad idea,* he thought with a smile on his face and a tingle in his groin.

It wasn't until they were out on the street and gone in different directions that Phillip realized Nicole hadn't given him a chance to kiss her good-bye.

"I could kiss you for letting me come, Mom." Maura's voice crackled over the line that had reached all the way from some place called Cat Island and into the phone in the kitchen of Jess's condo.

Jess was not aware that she'd let her daughter go to the Caribbean; as she recalled, she'd been given little chance to even voice an opinion. But she'd learned long ago that sometimes it was easier not to point out the truth to her children. "I'm glad you're having fun, honey," she responded. "Has Eddie enjoyed himself, too?" She did not want to ask about Charles. She did not want to know—or care—if he and his new wife were partying it up, showing Maura and Eddie the time of their lives.

"He got burned, Mom. God, he was so red!"

"The sun is hotter down there."

"He's okay now. Kelly had some really great ointment."

It took Jess a moment to remember that Kelly was Charles's wife, that in addition to the youth and the body, the trophy wife had a name. "That's good," she said, trying to sound motherly.

"So are you working hard back there where it's cold?"

Jess laughed. "It's not so cold now. Spring is coming. But yes, I am working hard. I'm re-doing Fox Hills."

"The club? Hey, cool, Mom. Maybe you'll meet some new people."

She did not tell her daughter that few new people had been granted membership there for at least two decades— and only then if they were connected to someone Jess already knew.

"Have you heard anything else about . . . Amy?"

Maura's words came so quickly, they caught Jess unprepared. "Amy?"

"You know, Mom . . ."

Well, yes, of course she knew. She also knew that now was not the time and this was not the way she planned to tell Maura the news. "We'll talk about it when you get back, okay, honey?"

Silence drifted across the Caribbean, up the Gulf Stream, and over the Atlantic until it hit land. "You know something, don't you?" Maura asked accusingly.

"Honey . . ."

"Has there been another phone call?"

"No."

The line crackled again.

"A letter?"

"No. Honey, this is foolish. We'll talk when you get home."

"I'm not going home, Mom. I'm going right back to school. And stop treating me like a child. I want to know what's going on. I have a right to know."

Jess was unsure exactly what Maura's rights were in this situation, especially since Charles—the enemy—was probably standing nearby. But Jess did not want to spar anymore with her daughter. *She'll get over it,* Ginny had said. She hoped Ginny was right.

"Amy was not mine, Maura," Jess finally said.

Static gave way to dead calm.

"So your baby is still alive."

"Well, I don't know that for sure."

"Not yet?"

She knew Maura was asking if Jess was going to pursue this, if Jess was going to be persistent in finding her daughter, her *other* daughter, the one she gave away.

"Not yet, honey. We may never know."

She did not want to tell Maura that Phillip was looking. She did not want to say that yes, she was persisting. Not until she knew something. Not until she could sit down and discuss this with Maura intelligently, maturely, not over the wire of a long-distance call.

"Well," Maura said flippantly, "I guess that's your business. I've got to go now. Daddy's taking us to dinner and a show at one of the casinos tonight. Our last fling before we leave tomorrow."

Jess wanted to ask Maura to change her plans, to fly into New York. She wanted to spend some time with her daughter; she wanted to make sure that she was okay.

Then again, hearing the details of Maura's wonderful vacation was probably not what Jess needed right now.

"Okay, honey," she said. "Call me when you get back to school."

After she hung up, Jess wondered if the gap between her and Maura would ever be bridged.

• • •

Ginny decided that Jess had to be out of her mind to try and find her daughter, alive or not. There was definitely something to be said for leaving well enough the hell alone, for not trying to have a relationship with a kid you gave up thirty years ago who you could never hope to get to know, not really, no matter how close you might think you were.

Damn Lisa.

Damn her. Damn her.

Of all the men in the world, of all the stupid things she could do, why was she screwing Brad?

The apple doesn't fall too far from the tree, she remembered hearing somewhere. Her stomach was hurting again.

She pushed aside the unopened bag of Tostitos. Seeing Brad's dick in the same room with her daughter—her *naked* daughter—had shut off her appetite, replacing her need for Tostitos with a bowling ball in her gut.

Damn Lisa.

Damn Brad.

She clenched her fists and sputtered.

Then a white-hot thought flashed into her mind: How long had it been going on? How long had it been, and how much did Lisa know?

Had Lisa lied the night of Jake's funeral, lied when she'd said there was no man in her life? Or had Brad stepped in at that moment and smothered her with his . . . charm?

The bowling ball careened down the alley of her intestines. Ginny gripped her stomach. Was Brad using Lisa to get to her?

Was this about the money from Jake's estate . . . the money Brad would never see?

Did he think he could get to Ginny by screwing her daughter?

Was she losing her mind?

Since the incident, Lisa had not called, not even left a message saying she was sorry, that they needed to talk, *anything*. She had not even called. And suddenly Ginny knew that the longer she waited to face her daughter, the more time Brad would have to get his claws into her, let alone his dick, which he knew how to maneuver with much-practiced skill.

"Oh, God," Ginny moaned, then got up from the sofa, knowing she had to straighten this out once and for all. Maybe it wasn't too late. Maybe he hadn't yet told Lisa about the night that Ginny had screwed his brains out when his father was still very much alive.

Lisa lived in a condominium in Westwood, in a neighborhood overpopulated with UCLA students and too many boom boxes. With the success of *Devonshire Place,* she could well afford to live elsewhere, but Lisa was not only nice but also practical, and had told Ginny she would rather put money away than squander it on a lavish house she might not be able to afford if anything happened and her contract was not renewed.

Brad, Ginny thought now, scanning the parking lot for a red Porsche, might be that "anything" that would ruin Lisa's career.

Ginny had spent years toughing things out, acting as if she didn't care about things. How had she done it, and why couldn't she do it now when it mattered? But as she gritted her teeth, took a deep breath, and knocked on Lisa's door, she knew the answer: She really *hadn't* cared before; she had never let herself care.

"Ginny," Lisa said when she opened the door. Her vacant expression did not reveal whether she was still angry or not.

"We need to talk," Ginny said, stepping past her and marching into the living room. "I hope you're alone."

"It's just Ernestine and me." Lisa closed the door and followed Ginny into the room. "And Ernestine is asleep in the sun." Ernestine was the huge calico cat that Lisa had adopted from the animal shelter—adopted, as she herself had been.

Ginny sat in a high-backed, plump-cushioned rattan chair by the window in which Ernestine lazed. She folded her hands across her lap and tried not to be distracted by the fact that Lisa—even though it was a weekend—was gorgeously attired in designer pants and a silk blouse, while Ginny wore an oversized sweatshirt that covered the straining zipper of her jeans and the unbuttoned metal button that was currently gouging the soft flesh above her navel.

"He wants your money," Ginny said.

Lisa, sitting across from Ginny, straightened. "You don't know anything about it. You've never given Brad a chance."

"A chance? Is that what he told you?" She wondered once again if Brad had told Lisa about their one-night fling.

"He's caring. And he's kind."

Ginny put her thumb in her mouth to stifle a laugh. "You don't know him, Lisa. It's your hormones talking, nothing more. I know Brad. I've known him for years. He is not caring. And he is not kind. He is a lazy man who uses women for whatever he can get. Then he dumps them."

"He is not going to dump me."

"No? Would it help if I gave you a list of the other women who said that? Let's see . . . there was Betty, the one who owned the restaurant. He dumped her after the papers were signed over to him." Despite her best intentions, Ginny's hands started to shake. "And then there was Denise. And Lori. And—"

"Stop it," Lisa said.

Ginny shut her mouth and averted her eyes to the cat, who purred softly in its sleep, undisturbed. "How long has it been going on?"

Lisa did not answer.

Ginny turned back to her daughter. "How long, Lisa?"

"A while," she said vaguely. "Not long."

"Since Jake's death? Because if that's true, then surely you can see it's all about the money."

Again, Lisa did not answer.

"Are you in love with him?"

Lisa stood up and crossed the room. She bent down and scratched the cat behind its ears. "I don't know why you mistrust Brad, Ginny, nor do I know if I am in love with him. But I do know he makes me feel like no other man has been able to. He makes me feel wanted, and he makes me feel complete. And he's been there for me in my sadness about losing Jake. The way I've been there for him."

"Oh, Christ," Ginny said.

For a long time, neither of them spoke in that small, neat living room, with the cushions and rattans and glass-topped end tables that did not show the teeniest speck of dust. Ginny considered telling Lisa about Brad—about them. But Lisa might think it had been Ginny's own fault, that she had asked for it, that she was a slut. If she told Lisa, Ginny might have to accept that about herself.

So instead of telling her, Ginny said, "You're not from the streets, Lisa. You don't know Brad's kind."

"I know I'm almost thirty years old and I've never felt about anyone the way I feel about him."

Ginny mentally fast-forwarded to a wedding of daughter and stepson, with Brad smiling his snakelike smile at Ginny, toasting her in mock respect; a child or two born soon after, grandchildren to whom she would not be able to say no; then his desertion, stripping Lisa of her self-esteem along with the money she'd worked so hard to earn and probably a chunk of Ginny's, too.

If she told Lisa about them, it might make a difference. Or it might not.

"When you first moved to L.A.," Ginny said quietly, "I vowed to do everything in my power to help you have a wonderful life."

"And you have, Ginny. And I appreciate it."

"If it means anything, Lisa, Jake would not be pleased about this match. He knew what his son was. Which is why he cut him out of his will."

"Because you convinced him to?"

An odd sense of warmth rose in Ginny's cheeks. "Is that what Brad told you?"

"He said that you had turned Jake against him. Against Jodi, too."

"Brad and Jodi are the only ones who 'turned Jake against' them. I had nothing to do with it."

"You have all his money."

Clearly, Brad had gotten to Lisa. And if Ginny knew anything, it was that arguing with hormones was a damn waste of time. "That's right," she said, standing up. "I do have all of Jake's money. And you can tell your boyfriend that's not going to change until I'm dead." With a weighted heart, Ginny walked to the door.

"Ginny," Lisa said, following her. "I can't believe you're going to let this come between us. Can't you be happy for me? Can't you see how much Brad means to me?"

"No," Ginny said flatly, and left.

She barely remembered the drive home, her eyes aching with unshed tears, her thoughts a jumble of loss: first Jake, now Lisa. The two people who had meant more to Ginny than she'd ever before allowed—the only two people who meant anything to her—were gone from her life.

Pulling into the driveway, Ginny was overcome by a loneliness like she had not even known when her mother died, when she'd thought there was nothing left for her in the world, when she'd known her life was only going to go on if she forced it. But she had been young then; she still had her dreams. Now it was different.

As she entered the foyer, the telephone began to ring.

Lisa, she thought. Lisa had come to her senses; Lisa had realized that scum Brad was not worth the loss of her mother.

"I'll get it," Ginny screeched to Consuelo, who might or

might not even be in the house. She bolted into the family room and grabbed the phone. It was not Lisa. It was Jess.

"Ginny," came the sweet voice of that distant friend. "I've been trying to reach you."

She wanted to hang up; she wanted to pretend she wasn't herself, that her voice was the prerecorded message on the answering machine. She wondered if Jess would believe it if she made the sound of a beep. Instead, she sighed heavily. "Jess," she said, "yeah, well, I've been busy."

"Good," Jess replied. "Staying busy is good."

"Yeah, well, what's on your mind?"

"Did you get my message? That Phillip met Dr. Larribee and that Amy was not mine?"

"Yeah. I got it."

"Phillip is going to start looking for her," Jess said.

Ginny flopped onto the sofa. "Don't expect any miracles."

Jess did not respond right away, then she asked, "Ginny? What's wrong?"

"Wrong? Nothing." *My husband is dead and my daughter is fucking my stepson*, she wanted to say. *What's wrong with that?*

"Ginny, it's me. Jess. I know when something's wrong. Besides, I thought you'd be pleased that my daughter is still alive. Well, we assume she's still alive."

"Sure. Whatever. But like I said, don't expect miracles. If you're lucky, she won't want to meet you."

"What are you talking about?"

Ginny snorted. "Children," she said, "are highly overrated."

"Did something happen with Lisa?"

Her throat constricted, the way it might if someone had encircled it with a very fat rope and was pulling it very tightly. "Oh, God, Jess," she said, "I've made so many mistakes."

"We all have, Ginny."

"But this is the worst," she said quietly. "Lisa is screwing my stepson. Or I should say, he's screwing her. In order to get to me. In order to fuck up my head because Jake left me his entire estate." As usual, Jess had reached under her skin and somehow had gotten her to talk. As usual, Jess had made her *feel.* Damn.

"Good grief, Ginny."

She gave up holding back. "Yeah, well, it might be tolerable if he weren't such a waste of a human being."

"Surely Lisa will see that."

"Not while her hormones are raging." Ginny stopped short of adding that, given the size and expertise of Brad's dick, it might be a very long time.

"If it will make you feel better, I'm having some problems with Maura, too." Jess told Ginny about the sailing trip to the Caribbean, about how Maura disapproved of Jess's looking for her other daughter.

"And you want another one?" Ginny asked.

"I need to know, Ginny. I at least need to know what happened to her."

Ginny closed her eyes. And then she remembered. She remembered how Jake had encouraged her. She remembered his gentle prodding, his unwavering support the day they went to Larchwood Hall, the day Lisa was there for the first time, the day Ginny at last got to meet the daughter she had given up.

"Yeah, well, keep me posted, okay? I gotta go now." She hung up, lowered her head, and stared at the floor, the ache in her eyes finally giving way to tears.

Chapter 11

 "I need to find the statutes on adoption," Phillip said quietly to Nicole as they stood among the racks of leather-bound volumes in the Columbia law library. He had been waiting for her for nearly an hour: "Slept late" had been her excuse. He tried not to think that meant she wasn't as eager to see him again as he was to see her.

"Adoption?" she asked. "I thought you did corporate law."

"I do," he stammered. He was not ready to tell her about his efforts for Jess. It would mean telling her that he'd been adopted, which would lead him to admit that he'd met P.J., that his brother had been incensed, and that, no, he'd never had the courage to tell his mother. Telling Nicole the truth would have turned into a lengthy confession, and that did not seem appropriate for a girl he'd only just met, no matter how great the sex had been. "This is a special part of a case," he added vaguely.

She leaned close to him; the scent of something musky lifting from her skin. He resisted the urge to slide his arm around her slight waist, to bury his face in her neck and inhale her fragrance. *Later*, he commanded the warm tingle that returned quickly to his loins.

"Adoptions are state issues," she said, sliding out a book. "This section is federal law."

"Right," Phillip said with a half smile. "I knew that."

"State books are in the gallery. Is your client trying to adopt?"

He was confused a moment. "No. They're trying to find the child they gave up for adoption." Just because the Larchwood Hall records had been altered didn't mean the state ones did not hold the truth. And it might be the fastest way to get Jess her answer.

"Wow," Nicole said with a hint of sarcasm, "corporate law gets more complicated every day."

Phillip shrugged and reluctantly moved away from her and her musk scent.

"Phillip?"

He stopped and turned.

"If they're looking for the child they gave up, they're not going to find it legally."

Just what he needed. A children's rights specialist who was going to give him a hundred reasons why he shouldn't be doing this, why his "client" had no right to interfere in the child's life. He squared his jaw. "I know that," he said, trying to soften the bristle that had come into his voice. "But I told my client I'd make an effort."

Nicole eyed him slowly, as if sizing him up. "Well," she said, matter-of-factly, "there are services that do searches. Most are private. Very discreet."

Private. Discreet. It sounded exactly what Jess would want.

"You're not going to find them in the library, though," she added. "But I have a friend who knows someone . . ."

Phillip shifted on one foot. A friend-of-a-friend was often the safest way to gain gray-area information. He suspected that with the type of law Nicole's father practiced, there were many friends-of-friends in the family.

"That would be a big help," he replied, not wanting her to know she had just saved his life, for the sooner he could wrap this up, the less chance there would be for Joseph to find out.

"I'll call her tonight. After I'm finished with my own research."

"Oh," he said. "Right. Terrific." He had no idea what to do now. Nicole had a lot of work to do. He could tell her he might as well leave, that he had nothing to look up if that was the case. But her scent filled his nostrils again. "Guess I'll go look up some precedents on a merger I'm working on," he said lamely, though there was no such deal in the works. Later, he would smell her musk more deeply. Later. After her work was done and her friend was contacted, and he'd felt he'd accomplished something on Jess's behalf.

They picked up a vegetarian pizza on their way back to Nicole's. Phillip would have preferred to go to his place—where they could sit at a real table, drink wine from real glasses instead of plastic cups, and eat off real plates instead of paper towels. But his apartment was thirty blocks from Columbia, and if it meant he could spend the night with Nicole again, it was worth the inconvenience. Besides, he thought now as he sat on the edge of the bed juggling a pizza slice while Nicole phoned her friend, it was apparent that she'd changed the sheets.

"Got it," she said, after hanging up. She walked toward him, holding out a scrap of paper towel on which she'd written a phone number. "It's a woman named Marsha Brown. She does adoption searches."

Phillip took the paper and looked at the number, noting the absence of an area code. "Where is she?"

"Right here in Manhattan."

With a small disappointment, Phillip realized the woman probably only did searches for New York State. He had not, after all, told Nicole that he needed Connecticut. "Perfect," he lied. "Now sit down and eat your pizza," he said, patting the mattress.

"Gulp it might be a better term," Nicole said, picking a slice from the box. "I have to study tonight."

He got the message. "Oh," he answered, folding the paper towel scrap and slipping it into his jeans. "I understand."

"I knew you would," Nicole responded. "Dating someone who's been through law school has its advantages."

He took another slice of pizza, pleased that at least she'd described them as dating, yet unhappy that it meant he'd be sleeping alone tonight.

Jess had decided that she really needed to get a life. Waiting for Maura to come out of her snit, waiting for Phillip to find her other daughter, waiting to finish the country club job while worrying about who she would run into next—it was all making her miserable.

So Jess had done the unthinkable: She'd called Kiki Larson, the grande dame divorcée. That was how she'd ended up sitting on a hard chair in a cappuccino café, sipping a mocha latte and listening to a bearded man read poetry.

It was awful.

"This is fun," KiKi said to Jess, sweeping her black-fringed shawl over one shoulder.

Jess wondered how soon she could tactfully leave. Thank God she'd brought her own car.

The man finished one poem, then started another. Maybe KiKi had heard he was single, and that was the real reason they were here.

KiKi leaned toward her. "You have to admit it's better than listening to those horticulture speakers Louise Kimball was always digging up."

Jess had always found the occasional gardening lectures at the monthly club meetings interesting—a welcome change from the who's-doing-what-to-whom gossip that had become mainstay entertainment among the ladies.

"Speaking of the club," Jess whispered, "I'm afraid I have to go shortly."

"Go? But darling, we just got here. You have to give it a chance."

She smiled. "I have to be at the club early to install the new drapes. And I'm really exhausted."

KiKi rolled her eyes.

Jess stood up and picked up her purse. "It's been . . . great," she lied. "I'll be in touch."

As she left the café, she decided that if this was a "life," maybe she'd rather not get one.

Monday morning Jess met her assistants at the club at eight o'clock—an hour at which she'd be assured of not running into any of her old friends. Though it was now April, the grounds were still too wet for golf, so she should be safe from interruptions—at least long enough to have the draperies hung before the arrival of the lunch crowd.

Standing back, she surveyed the floor-length drapes as her assistants adjusted the coordinating scarf across the top of the traverse rod. They had done a good job, even though Grace was now gone. Jess was especially impressed with Carlo's perseverance and attention to detail: perhaps his work had been overshadowed by Grace's. Jess made a mental note that Carlo could become her second-in-command and could nicely take some of the workload off her.

Smiling at this revelation and at the work now finished before her, Jess felt more satisfied than she had in a long, long time. The butter yellow and hunter green had been a perfect choice for the room; the new wallpaper was up, the carpet had been installed, and it looked like a new room in a new place. *If only it were a new place*, she thought. If it were a new place it might be somewhere she might enjoy going, where she might enjoy being escorted by . . . whom?

She stopped herself from laughing out loud. Last night had confirmed what she'd always suspected: Life spent alone was far preferable to the struggle of trying to fill it with a man—any man—just because everyone else was doing it. For now, the only man in her life would be Carlo, and the only relationship they would have would be on opposite sides of the sewing machine.

"A little to the right," she instructed him now, making sure the fall of the scarf was loose and lovely, looking as if it were not rigid, but casual.

From the ladder, Carlo nodded, then looked past Jess at something that had caught his eye. He tugged the scarf slowly to the right. "Is this okay?" he asked.

"Looks good to me," said someone behind her.

Jess stared at the drapery, her good mood dissolving like sugar in hot tea. She did not want to turn around. She knew the voice and did not want to be feeling the way she was feeling. "It's perfect," she said. "Now let's do the same in the dining room." She was surprised that her words came out so evenly. She was not surprised that her feet were pinned to the floor, unable to move.

"You've done a wonderful job," the voice said again.

Jess did not reply.

"Jess?"

She sighed and slowly turned. "What is it, Charles?"

He was tanned and healthy-looking, his light brown hair made blond by the Caribbean sun, the whites of his eyes looking whiter, the teeth that showed with his smile looking brighter. "I heard you were re-doing the place. It looks great."

"Only the banquet and dining rooms." She picked up her bag and headed toward the dining room. "And we have work to do, so if you'll excuse me . . ."

He stepped forward and touched her arm. "Have you talked with our daughter?"

Jess's mouth went dry; spiny needles prickled up her back. "She called to say she was back safely at college." She did not want to meet his eyes. She did not want to talk with him. And more than anything, she wished he'd get his hand off her arm.

"She told me what you're doing," he said.

"Everyone at the club knows I'm redecorating."

"I meant about that other thing. That baby."

From across the room the ladder snapped shut. Jess jumped at the noise. "It's none of your business, Charles."

"It's my business when it affects my daughter."

"Excuse me?"

"Maura is upset about this, Jess. Haven't you put her through enough? Is finding that baby worth more to you than Maura's peace of mind?"

Heat flamed in her cheeks. She wanted to kick him. She wanted to slap him. She wanted to shove him out of her way. Instead, she said, "I repeat, Charles, it's none of your business." She turned to her assistant. "I'll meet you in the dining room," she said, then brushed past Charles without looking back at him, without saying another word, and without letting him see the tears that had formed in her eyes.

"It will take three to four weeks," Marsha Brown told Phillip when he'd given her the information about Jess's baby. It apparently did not matter that she was from New York, that the baby had been adopted in Connecticut. "I'll contact the right people, but it will take that long."

"And you'll find her?" he asked. "Just like that?"

"Just like that," she replied.

He did not ask how she would find her. He did not want to know the illegal methods needed to break through the sealed records to locate the children who had been meant to disappear. Children as he himself had once been.

"Thank you," was all Phillip said, then he gave her his office number and told her to call when she knew.

As soon as he hung up, he called Jess's house. "We'll know in three or four weeks," was the message he left on her machine. "Keep your fingers crossed."

He sat back in his chair, looked around the sparse office, and realized that in three to four weeks he and Joseph would be ensconced in their new headquarters on Seventy-third and Park, and that maybe Nicole was going to bring him good luck.

Devonshire Place was probably done shooting for the season. Ginny stared at the television screen, watching her daughter, in the role of Myrna, plot to steal her best friend's husband. As Lisa/Myrna strutted around the room of the penthouse set, Ginny studied her movements—determined, gutsy, unafraid. They were moves that had once defined Ginny—never Lisa. Never sweet, nice Lisa. Sweet, nice Lisa who had clearly lost her mind, who desperately needed to be saved by someone other than Ginny, who needed to be told she was making a big, fat mistake to have fallen in love with Brad. She was, after all, too sweet. Too nice.

Then again, Ginny thought, maybe she hadn't really known Lisa at all.

She knew Lisa had been raised by the Andrewses—a middle-aged, middle-class, middle-everything couple from New Jersey who, after Lisa, had adopted twin girls. Ginny had met them three—no, four—times, when they'd flown to the East Coast to spend a few days with Lisa each year. It was then that Jake had taken them all to dinner: a few hours, once a year, were all Ginny had as reference on Lisa's upbringing. And they had been pleasant enough. Pleasant, certainly, to Ginny, who probably didn't deserve their congeniality, although they told her many times how grateful they were that she had brought Lisa into the world, that she had allowed them to raise her.

Allowed. As if she'd had a choice. As if she could have considered anything else. For one thing, she couldn't very well have brought home a baby whose father was Ginny's stepfather—a baby who'd been conceived in one of his drunken, groping moments. Nor could she have brought herself to have an abortion: in 1968, those that could be found were the back-alley, coat-hanger kind.

So much for *allowing* the middle-class Andrewses to have Lisa.

But Lisa's life could have been worse. Mr. Andrews was an insurance salesman; the missus worked in the school cafeteria where Lisa and the twins had gone. Pictures of their home revealed a three-bedroom, one-and-a-half-bath ranch, with a carport "done over" into a family room, an aboveground swimming pool in the backyard, and a small vegetable garden where tomatoes were staked and zucchini sprawled. It was the kind of home that sent shudders of entrapment through Ginny—an image of a place like she had only ever imagined, never experienced.

She had also not been able to imagine any child of hers being raised in such a house. But the photos of Lisa on her eighth birthday, laughing, seated at a Formica kitchen table, an angel food cake with candles in front of her, told the story, as did the shot of her standing before a black marble tiled fireplace, wearing a pretty pink organdy prom dress, a white corsage on her slender wrist, and a big smile across her happy face. Lisa had been a happy child, she had told Ginny so. But that had been in New Jersey, a century ago.

"You've come a long way from the tomato patch," Ginny said to Lisa's image on the television now.

Then she realized that maybe the Andrewses could talk some sense into Lisa about Brad. They'd take one look at him and, in their middle-class way, they'd know he was not right for their daughter. She wondered when they'd be coming for their annual visit; soon, she thought. They were usually here in the spring.

Eyeing the phone, Ginny decided there would be nothing wrong in hurrying things along. She hadn't called to thank them for the flowers they'd sent when Jake died—the too-large bundle of red and white carnations. The flowers were ugly, but the Andrewses had meant well.

Ginny pulled her address book from the drawer of the end table, looked up the number, and placed a call to the opposite coast. Surely they could talk some sense into Lisa.

Mrs. Andrews was so glad to hear Ginny's voice! "It's been so long, Ginny . . . we were devastated for you about your husband . . . I'm sure Lisa's been a big help to you . . . we're all peachy-keen, the twins graduate from the university this year so, no, we hadn't planned on coming west. We were hoping Lisa would come here for their graduation, do you think there's a chance? And, of course, we'd love to have you, too . . . we could put you in the basement . . . we've done that over and it's a rec room now. . . ."

Ginny regretted that she'd called. She said good-bye without mentioning Brad, without a hint that Lisa was not speaking to her, nor she to Lisa, without the slightest innuendo that everything was not just peachy-keen, too, out here in L.A.

She hung up the phone, flicked off the TV, and knew there was only one other person capable of talking sense into Lisa. Only one person whom Lisa would dare not cross: Harry Lyons, her director.

Slinging her feet to the floor, Ginny decided to pay a call on Harry and have him haul out his big guns of persuasion. But first, she had to bring out hers.

• • •

At forty-seven, Ginny supposed her legs weren't exactly what they used to be. Then again, she figured, pulling onto the studio lot where only days before she had been evicted, Harry Lyons was far from the catch of the century. She supposed, however, that he believed otherwise. After all, he was a man.

Glancing around nervously in case she needed to dodge that grip named O'Brien, Ginny got out of the car and checked her reflection in a glass door. Thankfully, she'd found a minidress that was loose and flowing and did not reveal her newly added pounds. It would be easier to convince Harry she needed his help if she had any interest in sex—specifically, his. It would not be the first time Ginny had had to fake it, but that, she reminded herself, had been back in the days when she could count on her libido to make up for her apathy.

But she had to give this a shot. It was her only chance.

With her chin held high and her eyes fixed straight ahead, she stepped inside the cavernous building and strutted toward the director's office as if she belonged there, as if she came there every day. She marched toward the dressing rooms, past several closed doors until she reached the door just past the one where she'd last seen her stepson screwing with Lisa's mind.

She held her stomach to stop it from rolling. Then she took a deep breath, raised her hand, and bravely knocked.

"Yeah?" came a voice from within.

Ginny sucked in her gut, undid another button at the neckline of her dress, tossed back her hair, and strolled into the room.

Harry was there, seated at a desk, as bald and bulky as Ginny remembered. On the edge of the desk perched a fat woman smoking a cigarette.

"What d'ya want?" Harry asked.

Ginny stepped forward and extended her hand. "Harry,"

she said smoothly, "it's so nice to see you again. I'm Ginny Edwards, Lisa Andrews's mother."

"Shit," he said standing up quickly and taking her hand into his sweaty one. "Ertha, leave us alone, will you?"

Ertha—whoever she was—gave Ginny the once-over, then left the office.

"I'm glad you found me." Harry motioned for Ginny to sit in an overstuffed vinyl chair. "Two more minutes and I'd have been outta here."

"I'm glad, too," Ginny said, swallowing her pride—if she'd ever had any at all. She glanced around the photo-lined walls. "So this is where Harry Lyons hangs out."

He chuckled, the many folds of his neck rippling in response. "This is only my studio office. My real office is across the lot."

Ginny smiled and crossed her legs. She let her dress inch upward, silently grateful for the fat woman who had preceded her. No matter how puckery Ginny's thighs had become, she had a long, long way to go to match Ertha. "I need to talk to you, Harry."

He grinned, sat back in his chair, and lit a plump cigar. "If you're looking for work, have your agent contact me," he said in a directorish sort of way.

She laughed in return. "I don't need work, Harry. Though I'm sure you're the best to work for, if I were so inclined."

He blew out a stinky cloud of smoke. "Well, then, this is a first. Beautiful women only come calling when they're looking for a job."

Ginny smiled through her clenched teeth. "I'm looking for help, Harry, but not a job."

"Help with what?"

"Lisa."

"Lisa Andrews hardly needs help. She's doing a great job."

"It's not her job, Harry. It's her personal life I'm concerned about."

He narrowed his already squinty eyes. "Is she in some kind of trouble?"

"Not yet. But she might be." Ginny stood up and slowly ran her hands down the front of her dress, over her breasts, down to her thighs. Harry's eyeballs predictably, idiotically, followed each move she made. "Even though Lisa isn't a child, she is an innocent." She hoped he was not going to tell her otherwise.

"She's a good kid . . . is it Ginny?"

Ginny flashed another smile. "Yeah. Ginny." She liked the way his eyes were locked down on her breasts. She only wished she could feel . . . something. Without her dependable flash of heat inside, she wasn't sure she could pull this off. "Harry," she continued, her voice as low and throaty as she could muster, "I'm sure you're a man who's had a lot of experience with women." She couldn't believe she'd just said that and kept a straight face.

"Well," he stammered, "well, of course . . ."

"Which is why I need you. I need you to explain to Lisa that the young man who she's seeing is not good for her career."

"He's not?"

"Oh, believe me, Harry, he's not. I've known him many years. But that's not the point. She won't listen to me, Harry." Ginny laughed again. "You know how daughters can be with their mothers. Anyway, this guy she's seeing is bad news. Very bad news. I think he's out to damage her career. I think he means to ruin her."

"Why would he do that?"

"Envy. Greed. All those things that people like you and I know about. Things that Lisa is naive to."

"So you want me to tell her to dump him."

Harry Lyons was definitely not as dumb as he looked. "Precisely. But she can't know I've come to see you. She can't know it's my idea." She sat on the edge of the desk where the fat woman had been, then leaned toward Harry, the neckline of her dress, she knew, parting slightly, revealing more than a hint of a large, round breast. "After you've talked to her, maybe you could come out to my house and tell me how it went. I have a wonderful wine cellar. We could toast your success."

His eyes returned to her breast. He blinked, then looked back at her. "Sounds inviting. There's only one problem."

She pulled back. "What problem?"

"Lisa's not here. We wrapped for the season this morning, and she took off. Said she was driving across country or something."

"Driving? Across the country?"

"Yeah. Something about her sisters' graduation. And I don't know how to tell you this, but she also said her boyfriend was going with her."

Ginny blew out of his office so fast he must have choked on his cigar. She steered her Mercedes toward Rodeo Drive with revenge pumping through her veins. *Fourteenth Street,* she said to herself. Fourteenth and Rodeo Drive was the home of Fresco's—Brad's sink-or-swim restaurant. The place she prayed he'd be right now.

She stepped on the accelerator as she rounded the curve, then sharply turned down Fourteenth. With a squeal of tires, Ginny double-parked, got out, and ran to the front door of the restaurant. Hopefully, they hadn't left yet. Hopefully, there was still time to kill him.

The door was locked. She peered inside. There were no tables within view, no chairs. Only an empty, vacant restaurant abandoned and alone.

"Fuck!" Ginny screeched into the air. She kicked the door and pounded on the glass. "Fuck, fuck, fuck!" Then her screech turned to a mutter, and her fucks turned into sobs, and she knew that she had lost Lisa again, this time, most likely, forever.

Part Two

Chapter 12

The three or four weeks Phillip's message had promised evolved into five. As Jess tried to busy herself with work, the crocuses turned to daffodils, the daffodils to lilacs. It was May—precariously close to Maura's return from school for the summer. Jess would have preferred to have learned the information without her daughter anywhere around. Then again, she reminded herself on her more realistic days, there might not be any information.

She had not spoken with Ginny; Ginny seemed to have enough of her own problems right now. Besides, there was nothing to say.

She thought about calling Phillip, but each time she lifted the receiver, she quickly hung up. And waited.

There was little Jess could do except wait impatiently for the mail delivery every day, then carefully examine each envelope, searching in vain for another blue envelope postmarked Martha's Vineyard. At night she went directly to the answering machine at home, but there had been no more calls, no more contact to make her believe that this had been anything but a dream.

She wondered. She waited. And slowly, on the calendar

on the wall over the small desk at her shop, Jess marked off
the days in thick black X's.

Lisa hadn't called. Damn her, she hadn't even called. Not
that Ginny wanted her to. Not that she wanted to learn
anything more than she already knew from the covers of
the tabloids at the supermarket checkouts, that with every
mile and every stop, Lisa became more hooked to Brad's
hip.

The headlines said it all:

Witchy, Bitchy Myrna on Cross-Country Fling
Lisa Andrews Lands a Hunk
Lisa/Myrna's New Starring Role in a Red, Red Porsche

It was enough to make her gag. Ginny flung the latest
issue onto the seat of the car, her twice-weekly vigil to the
market complete. As in the past few weeks, she was determined not to read the crap printed inside, determined not
to look at the photos of Lisa and Brad vamping in Vegas,
dancing in Denver, and ogling one another in Oklahoma.
As in the past few weeks, however, she would break down
and do it.

She would read the articles recounting the couple's over-
land escapade that was "better than flying"; she would
learn about the shops they visited ("could the trinkets they
purchased be to furnish an impending home?"); she would
study the speculations that they might soon be married
("Brad was seen spending a very long time at a jeweler's in
Baltimore"). And with each word and each photo, Ginny
felt increasingly ill.

Not that it mattered. Because Lisa Andrews was out of
her life, gonzo, kaput.

Besides, who needed her, anyway?

• • •

Phillip removed the poster of the New York City Marathon from the wall of his cubicle office and wrapped it in brown paper for the movers. He could not believe the day had finally arrived: Archambault and Archambault was going uptown, this time for more than a racquetball game.

He looked around the room and decided he was grateful for his brother, Joseph, who had pushed them to change along with the times, and had probably saved them from the ambulance-chasing, no-fees-unless-you-collect gutter. The world, after all, was different from when their father had practiced law: faster, bloodier, different.

Joseph's wife, Camille, poked her head into the cubicle. "Phillip, is Nicole all set for tonight?"

Camille's short hair was off her face in a headband, her denim shirt large and out of character for the usually tailored, conservative woman. But Camille was pregnant now—the last in vitro had worked—and in a burst of prenatal energy, she'd taken on the responsibility of the moving details, right down to making certain the post office would begin delivering their mail to Seventy-third and Park today, right down to badgering the telephone company into switching the lines by noon. Included in her plans was dinner for four at the White Rose, a small, neighborhood Italian restaurant—in their *new* neighborhood—Camille and Joseph, Nicole and Phillip. A celebration for the new address of success.

Phillip smiled. "She has a late class, but she promised to be there by eight." *Nicole,* he thought, her musk scent coming to mind. Nicole signified one more example of the importance of moving ahead: No woman like her would be content with a man who spent his days out of the loop.

Camille nodded just as the phone rang. She raised her eyes to the ceiling in exasperation. "Doesn't anyone know this is moving day?"

"I'll get it." Phillip laughed, stepped over a carton and reached for the phone, because their new receptionist—

their full-time-with-benefits receptionist—would not begin work until tomorrow.

"Phillip Archambault, please," a woman's voice asked.

"Speaking."

"Phillip, this is Marsha Brown. About your adoption search."

Brown. Marsha Brown. *Oh, God,* he thought, shoving aside a box and sitting in his chair. It wasn't as if he'd forgotten about Jess or about Amy. But he'd been so busy . . . "Yes, Marsha," he said into the phone, "how are you making out?"

"I have an answer for you. Do you have a pen and paper?"

Phillip scanned the mess of papers and files strewn across his desk. He rifled through the drawer, but came up empty. It had already been packed. "Ah," he said, "could you hold on a minute?" He set down the receiver. "Joseph?" he called, walking from his desk, gingerly stepping over cartons. "Hey. Does anybody have a pen?"

Joseph emerged from the hall, a Mont Blanc in hand. "Always ready for business, little brother," he said with a smile.

Not without guilt, Phillip grabbed the pen and returned to the phone, wishing that Joseph would go away. Instead, his brother leaned against the woodwork of the doorway and folded his arms. Phillip tried to turn his head as he said into the phone, "Okay, Marsha. Go ahead." He plucked an old notepad from the trash and scrawled *Marsha Brown* in a corner.

"The infant daughter of Jessica Bates was adopted by a family in Stamford. A Jonathan and Beverly Hawthorne."

Hawthorne. *Shit.* "That's not right," Phillip said, conscious of Joseph watching and listening. "There was some sort of mix-up. . . ." Joseph scowled. Phillip turned his back on his brother. "Can you keep searching?"

"I'm sorry. This is what we learned. The child's name

was Amy. I have her social security number if you'd like that. . . ."

"No. That won't be necessary. I'll be in touch if I need anything else."

He hung up the phone, trying to mask his disappointment.

"What's up?" Joseph asked.

"Nothing important."

"You don't seem too pleased for something so unimportant."

"Look, I said it's nothing." He tossed the notepad back into the trash and handed Joseph the pen without meeting his brother's eyes. So the state records had confirmed Miss Taylor's file, which meant that she and Dr. Larribee had indeed covered their tracks, their crime, and their lying asses well. The letter and call to Jess might have been hoaxes, but Dr. Larribee would not have made it up: He'd admitted that they'd switched the newborns; what he claimed he didn't know was why. Or who had paid Miss Taylor fifty thousand dollars. Or where Jess's baby was today.

"Sorry I'm late," Nicole said as she swept into the White Rose, slid her backpack from her shoulders and sat on the chair beside Phillip. "You guys look exhausted."

She was right; she was late. Forty minutes late, to be exact, an irritating habit that seemed to happen more often than not. Phillip had decided it must have something to do with the fact that Nicole had been raised in California, where being late must be as expected as being on time in the East. She was also right in saying that Phillip was exhausted, but he was not too tired to be pleased that she had at least shown up. He had only been seeing her once a week as she geared up for finals, and he was finding it difficult to build a relationship based solely on time confined to the law library or spent between the rumpled sheets of her bed.

But as glad as he was to see her, Phillip found himself wondering if she owned anything that wasn't black. Tonight it was a black jersey and jeans, an outfit he'd seen so often it could be a uniform. She also, as usual, wore no makeup. But, damn, there was that smile. That so-sexy smile and that man-teasing scent.

"We're so glad you could join us," Camille said, bypassing the Chianti for mineral water. This was the first she and Joseph had seen of Nicole since that night at Mom's, and Phillip sensed that Camille was excited about the "match." "Phillip was just telling us how busy you are with final exams."

Nicole smiled that smile. "Boring, boring," she said. "Not nearly as exciting as the big move. How did everything go?"

Joseph took over the conversation, telling her about the computer consultant who was still at the new office wiring the system, about the movers who dropped the old oak credenza that had been their father's and taken a chunk out of the side, and about how, thanks to his wife, the phone lines were switched, no problem. Then he added that Smith had not only sent over a huge ficus tree for the foyer, but that Ron McGinnis himself had stopped by to wish them well. Phillip couldn't tell whether Nicole's look of interest was sincere or not—even after all these weeks, he didn't know her well enough.

"Best of all," Joseph continued, as the waiter arrived to take their order, "the mail arrived on time, so Archambault and Archambault will not be considered missing in action. Thanks to the about-to-be-new mother," he added, brushing a discreet kiss across Camille's glowing cheek.

They ordered antipasti and fusilli with basil and fresh mozzarella.

"Speaking of mothers," Nicole said, watching the waiter pour Chianti into her glass, "have you heard anything, Phillip? About that adoption search case you're working on?"

Phillip gulped down a swift drink of wine. His eyes flickered around the room, at the soft fresco paintings that lined the walls, at the plaster statues of children who held bowls of plastic grapes. He sensed Joseph's eyes boring into him. "Ah, well," he said quietly. "It was a dead end. No problem." Hopefully Joseph would let it go. Hopefully . . .

"What adoption search?" The question did not come from his brother, but from well-meaning Camille, whose antennae quivered lately around any conversation remotely connected to babies.

The flush of wine crept into his cheeks. "Just part of a case I was working on. No big deal." He reached for the basket of garlic bread. "Try some," he said, handing it to Nicole, "it's really terrific."

"What case?" Joseph asked.

Phillip shrugged. "Nothing. Forget it, okay?" He ripped off a chunk of bread for himself, and took a large bite. Strains of mandolins and violins drifted across the room.

"I thought we went through this a few years ago," Joseph said flatly, not forgetting it, not caring that Nicole was there and that perhaps Phillip might not want to discuss this in front of her.

"It's not about me," he said. "It was for a friend."

The sigh that Joseph emitted must have been heard all the way downtown, down to their old office, to the place where Phillip probably belonged instead of uptown with the racquetball players. "Why can't people just leave well enough alone." It was a statement, not a question.

Nicole decided to speak up. "Children have rights. They are entitled to know about their history if it's something they choose to do."

Phillip wanted to lean over and kiss her smack on her unlipsticked lips. He neither knew nor asked if her opinion extended to birth parents as well.

"I disagree," Joseph said. "It opens up too large a can of worms. It invades privacy, and our privacy is invaded enough these days. It also invites pain and distress and too much emotional blackmail."

Nicole laughed. "I doubt if Phillip's friend is interested in blackmail."

Blackmail. Jess would never blackmail anyone. Her father, of course, had been different. The man apparently had been cold enough, unfeeling enough, to pay off the family of the father of Jess's baby so they would leave town and not contact Jess again. *That,* Phillip reflected, *was blackmail.* He broke off another piece of bread.

Two hundred thousand dollars, he thought, half listening to the civilized quarrel now taking place between Joseph and Nicole. Two hundred thousand dollars was what Jess's father had paid Richard's family; and someone had paid Miss Taylor fifty thousand for who-knew-what. An enormous amount of money for back then.

"I'm not saying anyone is to blame," Joseph was saying, his voice growing louder. "But it seems to me no good can come out of a child meeting his or her parents—people who never wanted to raise him or her in the first place."

Raise them? Suddenly, Phillip sat up straight in his chair. *Blackmail?* he wondered again.

And then, he had an idea. An idea so outrageous, yet so clear, he could not stop it from forming. "We can find anyone's social security number," Marsha Brown had said. "Believe it or not, that's the easy part."

He stood up quickly. "Excuse me," he said. "I have to make a phone call."

"Jess," he said breathlessly into the phone. "What was the name of your baby's father?"

On the other end of the line, Jess paused a moment. "Richard," she replied. "Richard Bryant."

"What was his father's first name? Do you remember?"

There was quiet a moment. Phillip could hear his heart

beating softly, could feel his adrenaline pumping through his runner's veins.

"I'm not sure," she said finally. "I think maybe Richard was a Junior. It's so hard to remember."

He squeezed his eyes. "Perfect," he said. "I'll be in touch."

He fumbled in his pocket and came up with a fistful of more change. His next call was to Marsha Brown.

Jess stared out the window, wondering what Phillip had meant. Why did he care about Richard or his father? What did that have to do with her baby?

"Mom?"

She jumped a little, startled by the sound of Travis's voice, sheepishly grateful that it wasn't Maura's. "Yes, honey?" She turned around in her kitchen to see Travis standing there, covered with mud. He had taken a job with the condo association helping out with the groundskeeping: a job that he said would give him extra money for college, money he'd earned, not been given by Jess. "What happened to you?" Jess asked, stifling a chuckle at the sight of her eighteen-year-old, redheaded son, looking as if he'd just come in off the elementary school playground.

"Had a little slip into the pond."

"A *little* slip?" She stepped forward and held out her arms. "Off with your clothes. I'll throw them right in the wash."

He unbuttoned his shirt and stepped out of his jeans.

"What are you doing by the pond, anyway? It's after dark."

"It wasn't when we started."

"God, Travis," came Maura's voice from the doorway. "Do you have to walk around in your underwear? Eddie's on his way over."

Jess scooped up her son's muddy clothes and headed for

the laundry room. "He had an accident," she said in his defense. "Leave him alone."

She opened the lid of the washing machine and dropped in the clothes. Since Maura had arrived home for summer vacation, the tension between them had remained thick. So far Jess had refrained from confronting her daughter about spilling the beans to Charles. However, Jess thought as she dumped in the soap powder and snapped on the machine, maybe it would be better to just talk to Maura and get it over with. Talk to her, listen to her shouting, get it out in the open once and for all.

She returned to the kitchen where Maura stood, the refrigerator door open, looking inside. Travis was nowhere to be seen. He must have, as usual, deferred to his big sister's wishes.

"Maura," Jess said softly, "Can we talk for a minute?"

"Don't we have anything good to eat? What am I supposed to feed Eddie?"

Jess did not ask why Eddie was not capable of bringing his own food. He had decided to stay at Yale for the summer, and it appeared as though Jess was going to be expected to keep him in nourishment. "There's chicken in there. Make him a sandwich."

Maura shut the refrigerator door. "In the Caribbean there was snapper and mahi-mahi and conch chowder every night."

"And in Connecticut there is chicken," Jess replied, rubbing the back of her neck.

Maura gazed around the room as if conch chowder would suddenly materialize on the stove. "He'll be here any minute."

"Order pizza," Jess said. "Or Chinese."

"Gross."

"It didn't used to be." She did not add that a lot of things seemed gross to Maura lately, including her brother, including her mother. There was no doubt how she would react if Jess tried to talk with her once again about the baby, about her renewed search.

"What did you want to talk to me about?" Maura asked, opening the refrigerator door again just as the doorbell rang. "Oh, God, there's Eddie," she said, slamming the door and racing to the front hall.

"Nothing important," Jess said under her breath. "You'd think it was gross, anyway."

Two days later, as Phillip sat in his new chair at his new desk, his new receptionist buzzed him from the waiting room. "There's a Marsha Brown on the phone."

He grabbed the receiver. "Yes, Marsha?"

"I've found them," she said.

"Them?"

"Father and son. Both named Richard. But their last name is different now. It's no longer Bryant. It's Bradley."

"Bradley?" Phillip asked, quickly jotting it down on a pad.

"The son lives in a town called Edgartown."

Edgartown, he wrote beside *Bradley*. "Is that in New York?"

"No," Marsha replied. "In Massachusetts. On Martha's Vineyard."

Martha's Vineyard? The air he sucked in whistled through his teeth. He jumped from his chair and started to pace as far as the phone cord could take him, then back again. "Martha's Vineyard," he said. "Unbelievable."

"The father lives in Vineyard Haven," Marsha continued. "He owns an inn there, from what I can gather. A place called Mayfield House."

"Well," Phillip said, writing down *Vineyard Haven*, then underlining the name of the postmark on the note Jess received, "nice place to retire."

"Oh, I doubt that's what he's done," Marsha said. "The

family moved to the island when they changed their name. Back in 1968."

1968. The year it all had happened. The year his world began and so many others' changed.

Phillip closed his eyes and hated to think what this information implied . . . and what it would do to Jess.

"So Richard's family changed their name, took the money my father gave them, and moved to Martha's Vineyard," Jess said quietly, a little too quietly.

"That's how it seems," Phillip said. They were standing on the deck of Jess's condo, overlooking the lazy water of Long Island Sound, out of earshot of Maura and Travis.

"How nice for them."

"There's something else," Phillip continued. "Before I came out here I checked with the registry of deeds in Dukes County on the Vineyard. The Bryants—or the Bradleys—didn't buy Mayfield House right away. Richard's father apparently went to work there."

"As what? A caretaker? With two hundred thousand dollars?"

Phillip shook his head. "I don't know. I only know the inn was owned by a woman named Mabel Adams. When she died, the deed was transferred to Richard's father. She left it to him in her will."

Jess nodded. "So he turned out to be a frugal Yankee and socked his money under his mattress. None of this explains why I received that phone call or that letter. None of it explains . . ." She abruptly spun around and stared at Phillip. "*Oh, my God,*" she cried. "*Who did you say owned the inn?*"

"Someone named Mabel Adams."

The trembling began inside her heart and quickly spread throughout her limbs. "Phillip," she said. "Mabel Adams knew Miss Taylor."

He blinked. "Shit. I knew someone paid her off to get your baby."

"Was it Mabel Adams?"

"Maybe," Phillip said slowly, "or it could have been Richard's family."

"Richard's family? What are you saying?"

"That I think Richard's parents took some of the money your father gave them and paid Miss Taylor for your baby."

Jess stood silent. "What?" she repeated.

"I think you have to be prepared, Jess. I think if your baby's not on Martha's Vineyard, then someone there knows where she is."

A seagull flapped its wings near the shore. "Richard's family," Jess said aloud. "My God."

The gull cried out then flew away. She watched as it grew small and distant, then disappeared from sight.

"What do you want to do, Jess?"

"They have my baby," she said, her eyes fixed across the water. "They have my baby and I'm going to find her."

She had phoned the Steamship Authority and secured passage for her car the next day. Now Jess sat on the edge of her bed and placed a call to the one person who might care about what she was doing.

Surprisingly, Ginny answered the phone. Jess quickly told her what had happened.

"So you're going to the Vineyard," Ginny said slowly. "Is Phillip going along?"

"No. He offered. But he has a business to run."

"Where are you going to stay?"

Jess took a deep breath. "I made reservations at the Mayfield House."

"Are you nuts?"

"Probably."

"Did you use your real name?"

"Of course. If anyone there sent me the letter, I want them to know I'm coming."

"Even if it's some crackpot?"

"Yes." Silence hung over the line. "Ginny, I have to do this."

"I know you do, kid. And I think you're insane. Which is why I'm going to meet you there."

"What?"

"Call back those folks at the Mayfield House and reserve me a room. There's no way I can let you do this alone. You're far too nice. Besides," she added with an odd-sounding chuckle, "I need to get the hell out of L.A., and I was thinking it might be fun to head east."

Chapter 13

She called him Brit and he called her Yank and she fell in love with him the first time she saw him at Mayfield House, when he'd come to the Vineyard looking for a summer place and ended up renting one in West Chop.

He was older than she was—quite a bit, actually—but it was, after all, 1969, and she reasoned that if we could put a man on the moon, for God's sake, a few years' age difference shouldn't matter.

For twelve years, it didn't.

The Brit/Yank thing began the day she went out to West Chop because he needed a girl to keep the house—cook his meals when he was there, do his laundry, dust, and vacuum when he wasn't. He said he'd been given her name by someone in town. He said his name was Harold. Harold Dixon.

"Oh," she said with surprise when he first spoke to her. "I thought you'd have an English accent." He wore a navy blazer with brass buttons, light gray flannels, and an ascot loosely tucked inside his open-necked white shirt. Leaning against the white railing of the wide veranda that overlooked the sea, holding a carved teak pipe that smelled like cherries simmering, he looked a bit like Cary Grant.

He laughed. "Sorry to disappoint you."

She shrugged and flipped her long dark hair over her shoulder. "What do I know? I'm just a Yankee who lives on an island in New England."

"A Brit and a Yank," he said. "Well, Yank, do you think you can take care of things around here without creating a revolution?"

She smiled, glad that Harold Dixon wasn't nearly as proper as he looked, not like so many rich people who came each summer to rent the houses on the beach and act as if they owned the island. "I'll do my best, Brit," she replied, setting off to start her chores, the fantasy of the nineteen-year-old island girl being swept away by the handsome tourist beginning to root itself inside her heart.

That first summer, though, she saw little of him. She spent her mornings at Mayfield House, changing beds and cleaning guest rooms, and helping Mabel Adams check new faces in and others out. After lunch she rode her bicycle to West Chop to start this second job—grateful for the extra money that her parents would need this winter when the tourists weren't around.

In the afternoons when she was there he went down to the beach; she did her job in the quiet of the sea breeze that danced in through the big screened windows of this huge house that this man lived in all season by himself.

"Hey, Yank," he said, startling her one afternoon, coming into the kitchen, dragging sand in on his shoes.

She stirred the chowder in the pot that cooked slowly on the stove and tried not to shout that she'd just vacuumed and could he please wipe his feet outside.

"Look at this, Yank," he said, holding out his hand to her. "I do believe I've found a sapphire."

She looked at the nickel-sized deep blue stone that rested on his uncallused city palm. "Sea glass," she said. "Did you find it on the beach?"

He looked a little disappointed. "Glass?"

"Special glass," she said, attempting to cheer him up. "Shards and chunks from ancient bottles—remnants off ships that capsized in the strong currents that swirl around this corner of the island. West Chop's the best place for sea glass." She looked more closely at it. "Cobalt," she said. "A beautiful specimen. That piece has been smoothed and smoothed for generations by the tides."

"And finally tossed onto the shore," he said, and for a moment, one brief moment, their eyes met, the Brit and the Yank.

She turned off the flame under the gas burner and stirred the chowder. "It would make a lovely pendant," she said.

He closed his hand and slipped it into the pocket of his neatly pressed chinos. "Yes, well," he replied, "I think I'll go into the study and do some paperwork. Are you almost finished for the day?"

"Yes," she answered, "I only need to take the rolls out of the oven."

He nodded and left the kitchen.

She did not know what he did with so much time alone: he seemed to have no friends or family—no one came to visit, not even long-forgotten relatives who seemed to have a way of finding out when so-and-so had rented an island summer house, especially one as big as this.

Sometimes, though, in the evening, she saw him walking.

She'd be sitting on the porch of their weathered Cape Cod house just past the center of Vineyard Haven, playing with Mellie, her baby sister. It was just the two of them— she and Mellie—while Mom cleaned the kitchen after supper, and Dad was napping from another long day keeping the grounds at Mayfield House, and Richard was off working as he did every day and every night at the ferry docks earning money to go to college.

"Evening, Yank," Brit would say as he strolled along the sidewalk that cut through their small front yard. He'd often stop and say a few words of idle chitchat, playing a moment with the baby, never staying long enough for lemonade or iced tea, or to meet Mom or Dad or Richard. As quickly as he'd come, he'd be off again, bidding Mellie and her good night and continuing his walk, leaving her to fantasize that when summer ended, he would take her with him.

But when summer ended, he, of course, did not.

The following year he came back. Again, he was alone. She decided he must be a writer—one of those independent, solitary types who could not stand interruption while he was hard at work. He wrote in the summer; perhaps in the winter he went to cocktail parties in the city where important people talked about his books and he told them that all his inspiration came while he was away on Martha's Vineyard.

"I brought you something, Yank," he said one day while she sat in an Adirondack chair on the porch, snapping green beans to go with his dinner.

She brushed the long hair from her eyes and looked up from her work.

He handed her a small white box.

Setting down the old tin colander, she crossed her bare feet and wiped her hands on the apron that covered her blue-flowered sarong. She looked into his eyes—for another brief moment, they locked on hers. Then she took the box and slowly lifted the lid. Inside was the beautiful cobalt piece of sea glass, rimmed with a pure silver border and strung from a fine silver chain. "Oh," she said, because she did not know what else to say, because she did not know if this was meant for her or if he was showing it to her to see if she thought it was good enough for someone else.

"It's yours," Brit said. "I had it made for you."

"Oh," she repeated.

The next day he asked if she played tennis. Well, of course, she hadn't since they'd moved here to the island;

there was no time for tennis in the summer and no place to play in winter. But here in West Chop private tennis courts were set among the pine trees, exclusively tended for the summer people, for people who had nothing else to do unless you counted playing golf.

"Can you have dinner with me tonight?" he asked while she was folding linens. "After dinner we can play a game or two. I've come across some old racquets in the closet in the hall."

For the next few weeks, they played tennis nearly every evening before the sun went down. She darted around the court, her dark hair flying, the sea glass pendant bouncing lightly between her breasts. When they finished they said good night and she rode off on her bicycle, back to Mom and Dad and Richard and Mellie and the life she really led, not the one in West Chop in the big house on the beach.

Then one night there was a thunderstorm that crept up unexpectedly, the way island storms so often did. He urged her to stay until the rain and lightning stopped, and before she knew what or how or why, the thing that she'd been craving finally happened.

He said he didn't know she was a virgin. And yet he took her clothes off with all the tenderness she needed; he caressed her breasts and kissed her throat and grazed his hands there and there and there with all the patience she had ever imagined a lover would—should—have.

And in the fall Harold left again, hinting that, perhaps next year when she was twenty-one, she might go with him.

He gave her his address, a post office box in New York City, where she could write and send him pictures, and say how much she missed him, which was exactly what she did. She had not expected that in one of those letters, she'd be telling him that her mother had a sudden aneurysm and died on New Year's Eve.

• • •

When he returned that summer it was clear that she would not go with him.

"I can't leave Mellie with my father," she tried to explain. "He would not know how to raise a little girl."

But then he took her in his arms and told her that he loved her. He said he would be hers for every summer, if that was how it had to be, that they would have their summers until Mellie was a little older, until she could be on her own.

And that was how it was. For twelve summers they played tennis and had picnics with Mellie. They combed the beach for sea glass, but none they found was as beautiful as the one set in the pendant that hung from her neck. And with each autumn he was gone again, leaving her with memories and hopes and dreams and fantasies of the life they would have someday.

The day, however, never happened.

In the year that she turned thirty-one, and Mellie just thirteen, he did not come back to Martha's Vineyard. He did not call, he did not come. And her letters to Harold Dixon at his post office box were returned to her unopened. She'd wanted to track him down, but she didn't know how to find someone with only a post office box number. She supposed she could trace him through the people he rented the West Chop house from, but in the end she did not, for she was too embarrassed: the island girl used by the tourist man—a tired, old story that had been told too many times.

She'd cried a million tears since then; she'd walked a million miles back and forth to West Chop, hoping he'd come back to her.

He never did.

And yet she smiled now. She'd come down to the beach this morning to walk and smile and congratulate herself on a job well done. Because after what they'd done to her, the others now would suffer, too.

At first, she hadn't thought her plan would work. But now it had. She'd been afraid that Jessica Bates Randall would not receive her message. Or care about it if she did.

But Jess had.

And Jess did.

And now Jess was coming. Here to the Vineyard.

She watched the sand filter through her toes and wondered how life as she knew it—as she had been *tricked* into knowing it—would change. And if they'd all be sorry that they'd destroyed hers . . . her one chance at happiness sucked out with the tide.

A sparkling glimmer caught her eye. She bent down and scraped a few grains of damp, low-tide sand. Beneath the grains—just waiting for her to find it—was a perfect amber specimen of precious, smooth sea glass. She picked it up, slipped it into her pocket, and smiled again.

Chapter 14

Boston Harbor murked below, a bowl of gunmetal water rimmed on one side by the blue Atlantic, on the other by the gray landscape of tall city buildings that stood too close together.

Ginny looked out the small window of the plane, down to the place she had not seen in thirty years, the town she had once called home. As the plane descended, an invisible cord tied itself around her neck. With each breath, it tightened. Her heart began to softly pound; her chest began to sweat. Inside her head, a low buzz droned; her ears closed up; the seat in front of her grew fuzzy, out of focus. Her knees grew weak and watery, as if the blood and bones within had somehow turned to liquid—cold, numbing liquid.

She gripped the tray table and closed her eyes. *Jesus Christ,* she thought. *Jesus H. Christ.* She did not know how long it had been since she'd had one of these attacks. Not since she'd been living in L.A., not since she'd put the past behind her.

"Please close all tray tables and return your seat to the upright position."

The words came from overhead, from somewhere in the

ceiling that spun above her now, that swayed and swirled with each slow-motion of the air around her, the air she fought to breathe.

"Miss?" Another fuzzy voice. This one closer, louder, with a hollow, gurgled echo as if spoken through a microphone submerged in a tub of water. "Miss? You have to put up your tray table."

Ginny's eyes followed the sound and landed on a young woman dressed in navy blue with a neat white collar and small golden wings pinned to her lapel. She was standing in the aisle smiling down at Ginny. "Are you all right?" she asked.

"How much longer until we land?" Ginny somehow found the strength to ask.

"Only a few minutes now." She smiled again.

Ginny did not return the smile, but stared out the window once again and wondered what she'd have to do to get the pilot to turn back.

Then she remembered he was dead. Not the pilot. Shit, she hoped the pilot wasn't dead. No. It was her stepfather who was dead. That filthy piece of crap who had forced himself upon her so many, many times—that rat bastard Ginny dared not push away, for if she had, he would have beat her mother. Again and again, he would have beat her. Not that he hadn't anyway. But only when Ginny was not around, only when she could not give him what he wanted.

He is dead, he is dead, she repeated over and over to herself in a twisted, manic mantra. *Dead, dead, dead.*

And then she remembered the night it happened.

She'd been asleep, awakened by a sense of something pressing on her mouth. Her eyes flew open.

"One sound and you're dead," he'd whispered in the darkness.

Her head began to ache; her heart began to bleed. She'd thought she was safe at Larchwood Hall. She'd thought he'd never find her there, that he would never learn about the baby.

He stretched a wide piece of tape across her mouth; he tightly wound more around her wrists.

"Is it my kid in there?" he laughed, his penis waving in her face—his hard, straight penis, poking at her mouth, then pushing at her swollen abdomen.

And then he ripped her nightgown off and shoved his dick between her legs.

"It's mine, isn't it?" he growled with acrid, foul breath.

Suddenly, all Ginny could think of was the baby inside her. The living little person who had not asked to be conceived, who had not asked to be a product of Ginny's stepfather and his drunken, abusive trysts.

With more might than she knew she possessed, Ginny heaved her legs together, crushing his tight and throbbing balls.

He screamed.

He rolled from the bed to the floor, dragging her along.

She kicked.

He screamed again.

And then Ginny saw a figure standing in the shadows, hands raised above its head. Swiftly the hands came down, aimed directly at his back.

The light in the room was snapped on.

And there stood pregnant, fifteen-year-old Jess, one hand on the light switch, looking at the blood that spurted from his back, from the deep thrust that she'd made with the pair of sewing shears.

Her stepfather was dead.

Jess had killed him.

And thanks to the dickhead sheriff, Bud Wilson—who'd been downstairs screwing Miss Taylor while Ginny was fighting for her measly life—no charges were ever filed.

And Ginny—and her mother—at last had been set free.

Her breathing slowed now; her heart eased. She opened her eyes as the feeling returned to her knees; her eyesight came back into focus. She looked out the window again; the big plane floated lower toward the city: the Prudential

Center, Fenway Park, the lazy Charles River. Places she had never wanted to see again as long as she lived. Now she was back. Because Jess needed her. And because, thanks to Jess, that filthy piece of crap was dead, had been dead for nearly thirty years. For that, Ginny owed her.

As the runway rose to meet them, Ginny also knew she owed Jess for bringing Lisa back into her life: the once-unwanted baby who had become the only family Ginny had left, the only remaining part of her that walked the earth, would ever walk the earth. Whether or not she chose to walk it next to that creep of all time, Brad, was Lisa's choice. In the meantime, maybe there was a way to salvage what might be left of the birth mother–daughter relationship. Jake would have wanted it that way.

The wheels screeched on the asphalt; Ginny had made it home. And as they taxied to the gate, she wondered if the real reason she'd come back east was not for Jess at all, but because Lisa was in New Jersey—a do-able drive from the island, should the opportunity arise.

Jake used to say "Opportunity has no way of knocking if it doesn't know you're home."

Ginny had never been certain exactly what the hell that meant, but Jake had built a great production company, so it must have worked for him.

With that in mind, and a convenient hour to kill before the shuttle left for the Vineyard, she found herself standing at a phone booth in the far end of the concourse, dialing New Jersey information.

"Mrs. Andrews," Ginny said moments later, "this is Ginny Edwards. Did Lisa make it there yet?"

"Oh, my. Can you imagine? They drove clear across the country for the twins' graduation. . . ."

"Yes, I know. Is she there now?"

"No. She went for a drive. With Brad."

The mention of his name made Ginny's heart began to

pound again. *No,* she commanded herself. *He cannot hurt you.* After all, it was only Brad. He was not her dead stepfather, and he had no power over her no matter how hard he tried. "Well," she said, carefully forming each word, "please tell Lisa I'll be on Martha's Vineyard for a few days." She gave Mrs. Andrews the name of Mayfield House in Vineyard Haven "in case she needs to find me."

Feeling satisfied at what she'd done, Ginny said goodbye, checked her watch, then went to find a Mrs. Fields concession to celebrate her return to Massachusetts with a half dozen chocolate–macadamia nut cookies.

Jess leaned against the rail of the ferry from Woods Hole, a kaleidoscope of thoughts turning through her mind like the sun's sparkling prisms dancing on the churning water.

There were so many questions that funneled into these few: Did Richard have her—*their*—baby? Who had tried to contact her? And would she have the courage to confront whatever awaited on the other shore?

Holding tightly to the rail, she tried to tell herself that no matter what happened, she was lucky. She had her three children, she would always have them, despite the speed bumps along the road of their lives. If Maura chose to distance herself from her over this, there was little Jess could do except pray that someday Maura might understand. Or at least forgive her for what she had to do.

She had lied about this trip. Well, not lied, exactly, but she had not quite told the truth. "I'm meeting my friend Ginny on Martha's Vineyard," Jess had told Maura and Travis. "Ginny's husband died recently, and we're going to spend a few days together."

Travis had told her to have a great time.

Maura—who knew quite clearly who Ginny was and how she had come to be her mother's friend—had not exactly helped her pack, but neither had she begun another fight. Jess wondered if her daughter had forgotten that the obscure note had been postmarked Vineyard Haven, or if Maura had simply—gratefully—not made the connection.

Jess tilted her face up to the warm spring sun now with a silent prayer of thanks that Chuck had not been involved in this; that Charles hadn't, either. She did not know how she could have handled such betrayal. Then she felt a twinge of guilt that she'd accused them in the first place.

Maybe they deserved it, a small voice inside her said.

She shook her head and looked off toward the coastline that grew larger as the engines chugged ahead—a curving, sculpted coastline, where a fleet of mismatched sailboats bobbed in lazy waves and huge, timeworn homes stood up on bluffs above the dunes and peered across the water with big, foreboding window-eyes.

She wondered if one of them was Mayfield House, the home once owned by Mabel Adams, whoever she once had been; if Richard had lived there, if their daughter had played along the beach and watched the ferry come across and wondered what the world was like beyond.

The engines slowed and she gripped the rail, reminding herself that there were many things she did not know, but that she was moving closer, closer to the truth.

Then the purser announced it was time for passengers to return to their vehicles. It was also, Jess knew, time to return to the past.

Mayfield House did not hug the coastline but sat atop a hill above the densely packed center of Vineyard Haven. It was not far from the pier, though it took Jess several minutes to traverse the narrow, hilly, one-way streets that rose up from the ocean, a land mass swollen by the gods. At last she found the sign. She took a small, short breath and steered into a driveway made of broken shells that crunched beneath her wheels. She stopped and stared at what she saw.

Mayfield House was not the small, quaint inn Jess had

expected. Instead it was a sprawling, stately, huge white house with buttercup yellow shutters and a sweeping wrap-around veranda. The lawn was lush and manicured; the entire place was protected by a tall, thick border of privacy hedges. It clearly appeared to be the estate of a wealthy family—a *very* wealthy family. She wondered if Phillip had been wrong, and if perhaps it had been her father's money, after all, that had secured this place for Richard's family thirty years ago, when two hundred thousand dollars was—as Ginny had so aptly put it—a freaking fortune.

She parked her car and slowly turned off the ignition. She sat for a moment, gazing at the gardens that bordered the house—wide, well-tended gardens thick with yellow tulips. Stepping out of the car, Jess inhaled the scent of the nearby sea, the salt and the seaweed, the lobsters and the driftwood, grown damp and pungent with the tides. She wondered if her daughter had been raised here, to know these scents as if her own, to know the spray of salt upon her cheeks, the island wet within her bones.

"Jessica Randall?"

The voice came from the veranda. Jess looked up and saw a tall, thin woman whose long, dark hair was streaked with white, who was oddly clothed in a plain white T-shirt and a sarong of orange flowers that hugged her hips and snaked down her long legs to touch the porch floor. She also wore a crooked smile that looked almost like a smirk.

"Yes," Jess answered. "Hello."

"Do you need help with your bags?"

Jess looked back to her car. "Oh," she said, "well, yes, if it's not too much trouble."

The woman did not reply, but padded across the porch and ambled down the stairs. Jess noted she was barefoot. "Karin Bradley," the woman said, brushing a long string of hair from her face and extending a hand to Jess.

Karin, Jess thought. *Richard's older sister.* She had never met her when they were young, had only heard about her, had only heard that she was smart and pretty, the apple of her father's eye. But Karin Bradley now looked neither smart nor pretty. She looked plain and tired, an aging woman who'd had a hard, unhappy life—or maybe that was what Jess imagined, what she hoped had happened to this woman who must have played some role in stealing Jess's child. Jess blinked back her thoughts and shook the woman's hand: it was cool and dry, not like her own, which she was sure was too warm and perspiring.

Karin did not say it was nice to meet her or welcome to the Vineyard or any such pleasantries. Instead, she grinned that Cheshire cat grin and headed toward Jess's car.

"It's a beautiful day," Jess said, following close behind, determined to act as if nothing were wrong. There would be plenty of time to give herself away later; plenty of time, once all the facts—and all the people—had come to light.

"Almost summer," Karin replied, not revealing whether or not she found that pleasing. She opened the car door and slung a suitcase onto her shoulder, leaving the other one for Jess.

Jess grabbed the bag and trekked after Karin toward the porch and up the wide wooden stairs. "The house is magnificent," she said, but Karin didn't answer.

Inside the huge foyer, Jess marveled at the polished woodwork, the long marble-topped side table, and the crystal chandelier that shimmered in the light that filtered through sheer curtains hanging from tall windows. She did not know for certain, but guessed that the Oriental rug that ran the length of the massive hall was very old and had been quite expensive. She wondered if her father's money had bought that, too.

"I'll take your bag up to your room," Karin said. "Wait here for my father. He'll check you in." She disappeared up the steep staircase, her bare feet slapping the oak stairs.

Jess stood in the foyer alone, wondering how to calm her growing trepidation or stop the nagging disbelief that she actually was there. She set down her suitcase and walked toward a set of French doors. Peeking in, she saw an enormous living room that spanned the depth of the house. A large brick fireplace was at the opposite wall of the room; a grand piano sat at one end; a trio of sofas was clustered around dark-wood tables; and all the walls were lined with antique clocks, all reading 4:43.

"Jessica Randall?"

Jess turned to see a man of seventyish, dressed in a flannel shirt and jeans, with snow white hair and blue, blue eyes. The same blue, blue eyes she remembered Richard had. She touched her stomach to quiet the turmoil bubbling inside and wondered how long she could pretend to be just another tourist, a casual vacationer. "Yes," she said unsteadily. "I'm Jessica Randall."

The man did not seem to recognize her. Then again, he had no reason to. She'd only met him once, more than thirty years ago, the night after her mother's funeral when he'd come to pick up Richard at the townhouse in the city. She didn't remember what he'd looked like either, only that he drove an old DeSoto with rust on both front fenders.

"Welcome to Martha's Vineyard," that man said now, handing Jess a thick brass key and a small brochure with a picture of Mayfield House on the front. His smile seemed genuine; he did not seem unhappy like his daughter. Nor did he seem to be the kind of man who would take two hundred thousand dollars, then steal a baby, too.

"Thank you," Jess replied.

"We've put you in room seven. Up the stairs to the left. Breakfast is at nine. The dining room's across the hall." He gestured to her bag. "Would you like me to carry that up?"

"No, thanks." The sooner she got away from him . . . well . . . perhaps the ache inside her head would stop and she'd be able to think straight once again.

He nodded. "If you need anything, just give a holler." He started to walk away then stopped. "Oh, I almost forgot. Name's Bradley. Richard Bradley."

No it's not, she wanted to shout. *Your name is Richard BRYANT and you—or Mabel Adams or someone here—kid-*

napped my child. Instead, she nodded and said, "Mr. Bradley. Thank you."

He tipped a hat that wasn't there and left her in the foyer, alone again, standing in the house where her firstborn may have walked, may have been raised, may have spent the first three decades of her life . . . and might, at any moment, step into the room.

"It's about damn time you got here."

The voice inside room number seven startled Jess. She dropped her bag and held her hand up to her throat. "Ginny," she cried. "You scared me half to death."

"Which must account for the fact your face is as white as Miss Taylor's without her rouge."

Jess laughed and went to hug her friend. "No one told me you were here. How was your flight?"

Ginny broke away from the hug and moved to sit on Jess's bed—a very high four-poster bed with a George Washington bedspread and ivory lace canopy. "Long. Uneventful." Her eyes moved around the room. "They put me down the hall in number three. I don't have a canopy bed. I'm thinking of complaining to the management."

"No complaints!" Jess whispered. "I don't want to call any more attention to us than necessary, okay?"

Ginny scowled. "Why don't you just come out and ask the old man to tell you the truth?"

Jess unzipped her bag, took out some clothes, and hung them in the small closet. "I have to go slow, Ginny. I have to be sure."

"And you don't want to blow your chance to meet her if she's here."

"Right."

"But how will you know if you see her?"

"I'll know."

Ginny rolled her dark-lined eyes. "Well, don't count on Morticia to introduce you."

"Morticia?"

"The welcoming party in the sarong and the bare feet."

Jess laughed again. "That's Richard's sister. She is a bit strange. I don't think she was like that when we were kids."

"A century ago."

"Yes. I guess people change." She removed her cosmetics and set them on the broad rim of a marble pedestal sink. "Have you . . . have you seen anyone else?"

"Only Dad. No twenty-nine-year-old girl and no guy who looked like he might have been the father to your kid."

A tiny need to defend Richard swelled in Jess's heart; she walked to the curtained window and looked down across the town, the way she had once watched for Richard from her room at Larchwood Hall, where she had waited for him to come for her and had never understood why he had not.

"Come on," Ginny said, interrupting her thoughts. "Let's go see if there's a decent place to eat in this backwater town."

Jess sighed and tried to smile. There would be plenty of time to think about Richard later.

Main Street in Vineyard Haven was alive with pickup trucks and the sounds of summer approaching: saws buzzing, hammers banging, painters painting wide white strokes across small clapboard shops.

"What a charming town," Jess commented as they maneuvered their way along the sidewalk, dodging ladders and canvas drop cloths. "I've never been to the island before."

"You're kidding," Ginny said. "I would have thought people with your kind of money came here the way my mother and I hung out by the hot dog stand at Revere Beach."

"No. Before my mother died, Father traveled a lot for his business. I spent summers at the swim club. That was where I met Richard. He was a towel boy." She heard her words trail off into memory. Quickly, she cleared her throat. "Anyway, after Larchwood Hall, well, I stayed in England at school all year."

"So you never saw your old man?"

"Once a year at Christmas. A little more often after Charles and I were married, but not much."

They stopped in front of a store and watched a girl hang T-shirts in the window.

"Well, believe it or not," Ginny said, "I was here on the Vineyard once. I was six or seven, I guess. One of my mother's boyfriends brought us here for two days."

"Do you remember much about it?"

"We stayed in Oak Bluffs," she said with a snort. "Probably because they could drink there. Most of the island is dry." She raised her hand and shook a finger like a stern schoolteacher trying to give instruction. "If the name of a town doesn't have an *O*, you can't buy liquor there." She laughed. "It's amazing the important stuff I've retained inside this brain."

"Vineyard Haven doesn't have an *O*."

"Right. But Oak Bluffs . . . well, that was why we stayed there. Anyway, I remember the carousel. And saltwater taffy. You could watch them make it in the shops."

"Did you have a fun?"

"Yeah, sure. It was a blast." She turned to Jess and curled her lip, then continued strolling down the sidewalk.

Quickly, Jess caught up. "I wonder if this is a good place for children. An island is so . . . isolated."

"I suppose it's like anywhere else. It mostly depends on the people you're with."

They passed a bookstore and an art gallery and an upscale jewelry store. Jess stopped and looked at the velvet-draped display of gold charms: Nantucket baskets, lighthouses, and small triangular maps of the Vineyard.

"Don't look now," Ginny whispered beside her, "but we're being followed."

Jess fixed her gaze on the glass. "Followed?"

"Morticia's right behind us."

Jess looked up. "Karin?" There, two doors down, stood Richard's sister, her orange sarong bright against the new white paint of the Tisbury Inn. Their eyes met briefly, then Karin averted hers before Jess could wave.

"Don't be so melodramatic, Ginny. I'm sure she wasn't following us." Jess watched as the woman walked through a line of sidewalk café tables and ducked inside the inn.

"I'm not," Ginny replied. "Let's go down the hill. Old Man Bradley said the Black Dog has good burgers."

"Old Man Bradley?"

"Richard's father. Before you arrived, he and I had a nice little chat."

"You didn't . . ."

"Don't worry, kid. I didn't blow our cover."

But as they headed down the hill, Jess quickly looked back in time to see Karin emerge from the inn and watch their progress. It left her with an unsettled, upset feeling that things might not be as easy as she'd hoped.

There was nothing to do on the island in the evening— an evening that preceded Memorial Day weekend, when apparently the whole place would come to life.

Until then, there was nothing for Jess and Ginny to do but sit and watch the ferry glide back and forth across Vineyard Sound and plot their best approach to uncovering what had happened.

By the time the sun had set they had a plan: Ginny would be the one to ask the questions, and they would start at breakfast the next morning.

The dining room of Mayfield House was eerily like the one at Larchwood Hall had been: a long cherry table and matching sideboard, silver candlesticks and tea sets, gilt-framed oil paintings of stern-looking New England ancestors of someone, but no one knew who.

Jess and Ginny were alone at the big table: Jess had not slept well, but had lain awake most of the night, listening to the many clocks downstairs chime two, then three, then four. Now, they chimed nine times, and through the door, as if on a rigid schedule, came Karin with a coffeepot. Today she wore a sarong of blue. Again, she wore no shoes.

Right behind her was Richard's father, smiling and bearing a basket of what smelled like warm muffins. Tucked under his arm was a newspaper. "Good morning," he said.

"Good morning," Jess replied. Ginny did not speak, but sized up Morticia/Karin instead.

"Tide's up, the sun's shining, and it's going to be a perfect island day," he said.

"Tell that to my sinuses," Ginny commented, watching Karin pour coffee into her cup.

"So what brings you ladies to our fair island?" he asked.

The silence that fell between Jess and Ginny dropped with all the ease of a guillotine.

"Well . . ." Jess began, hoping that their plan would work, that they could pull this off.

"Vacation," Ginny blurted out. "It's the only reason why anyone comes here, isn't it?"

Mr. Bradley smiled. Jess noticed that when he smiled he looked much younger than what his years must be. Richard would be forty-seven now; she wondered if he was aging as well as his father. She also wondered why Ginny had said they were on vacation when that was not what they'd decided.

"If it weren't for folks taking vacations," he answered Ginny, "we'd be a deserted island."

Karin padded across the floor toward Jess and tipped the coffeepot above her cup. Jess noticed the woman wore a large silver pendant with a flat, smooth, deep blue stone. "What a lovely necklace," she commented.

Karin's gaze dropped to her chest as if she'd never seen it; then she stared back at Jess without uttering a word.

"Sea glass," Mr. Bradley said. "Karin collects it on the beach in West Chop. I keep telling her she should make it into jewelry like that and sell it in the shops."

"Oh, you should," Jess said. "It's really quite extraordinary."

Karin left the room.

"Have you lived on the Vineyard long?" Ginny asked.

Jess sipped from her cup, then averted her eyes to the newspaper Richard's father had set down.

"Almost thirty years."

We know that, she wanted to say. *Now where's my daughter?* Instead, she picked up the *Vineyard Gazette* and scanned the front page news. *Let me do the talking,* Ginny had said, and so Jess tried now to comply.

"I could never go back to the mainland," Mr. Bradley continued, as he took a seat at the table and watched Ginny dive into a large muffin. "My kids grew up here, my wife died here. Nope," he said, scratching a weathered, clean-shaven chin, "I could never go back."

"How many kids do you have?" Ginny asked.

Jess almost choked. She feigned interest in the newspaper, but she could not focus on the words.

"Well," he replied. "Karin, you've met. Then there's my son, Richard, who works there." He pointed at Jess, at the paper in her hands.

She blinked and looked at the inky headlines. The main article was about the renovated fishing docks in a village called Menemsha. "Your son works in Menemsha?" Jess asked.

Mr. Bradley laughed. "No. At the *Gazette.* He's a reporter. Best one they've got, if you ask me."

They hadn't asked, although they'd planned to. But the open flow of information hardly seemed as if it would be coming from a man who had sneaked his family out of town and changed their name. Jess gripped the paper, suddenly realizing he had just said that Richard worked there. Richard was a newspaper reporter. Richard really was alive and well and living on the island. Now it was official.

"Does he live here?" Ginny asked. "In this house?"

Jess could not unglue her gaze from the newspaper. Every muscle in her body tensed, became immobile.

"No. He has a place over in Edgartown. That's where the paper is."

Edgartown. Yes. Phillip had learned that Richard lived in Edgartown.

"Is he married?" Ginny fired the questions without hesitation, without the slightest hint of guilt that she was prying into his life.

"Divorced," Mr. Bradley said with a slight frown. "Has two kids who live with their mother on the mainland. Boston. She was a tourist. She liked coming here, but not living here. Damn shame, too."

Jess glanced up at Ginny and saw her reach for another muffin. "Any other kids?" she asked nonchalantly.

Jess set the paper down and took a gulp of coffee. She did not know how much longer she could sit there, acting as if she didn't care.

"Oh, yes," Richard's father answered, his frown turning to a beaming smile. "My daughter Melanie. Mellie, we call her. She's an elementary school teacher."

Melanie, Jess thought. *Mellie. Could it be . . .* Nervously, she sat up, broke off a small piece of muffin, and popped it into her mouth. It was warm and crumbly, and made her mouth go dry.

"How old is she?" Ginny blurted out.

Richard's father laughed and stood up. "Most guests ask twenty questions about the island. They couldn't care less about us."

The piece of muffin lodged itself inside her throat. *We're not most guests,* Jess wanted to respond. She took another drink of coffee and washed the muffin down.

"Sorry," Ginny said. "Just curious. I'm a sociologist at

Southern Cal, and I'm doing a study on people who live on islands. You know. Why they like it. Why they stay."

Jess turned back to the newspaper, afraid that if she caught Ginny's eye, she would laugh.

"So you're not exactly here on vacation, then?" Mr. Bradley leaned back in his chair.

Not exactly, Jess wanted to say.

"Well . . . call it a working vacation," Ginny replied.

"Don't know that we've had a sociologist ever stay here." Ginny smiled. "Good. I enjoy being first at what I do."

"Well," Mr. Bradley said, "I'll leave you two to your breakfast. You're the only ones here today. That'll change this weekend, though. Memorial Day. The end of our sanity before the tourists come." He started to turn away, then looked back with a chuckle. "You might want to do your research on that. How the people change once tourist season starts." He nodded as if he liked that idea, than added, "Enjoy your breakfast," and disappeared from the room.

Jess looked at Ginny. "Finish your muffin," she said quietly. "We have somewhere to go."

Ginny's eyebrows raised. "And where might that be?"

"Edgartown," Jess said, pointing to the newspaper. "We're going to start at the *Gazette*."

"It's her," Ginny said moments later as they walked down the stairs and headed for the car. "Melanie. She's yours."

"We don't know that, Ginny. We don't even know how old she is."

Ginny took another bite from the last muffin she'd taken from the basket. "It has to be."

"We'll start with Richard," Jess replied. "And then we'll see." Her words sounded much more patient, much more calm than she felt inside her heart.

•   •   •

From the window of the upstairs landing, Karin watched Jess and Ginny cross the driveway and climb into the shiny Jaguar. From beyond the door into the dining room, she'd listened to the bullshit questions the dark-haired one had asked. She'd listened, and she'd smiled, for she'd known that they must be tormented wondering what they should do next.

As she watched the Jaguar leave the driveway and turn right, Karin would have bet the ladies were headed to Edgartown in search of Richard.

God, she thought with a seed of envy, how she'd love to be a witness to that unexpected meeting.

Chapter 15

 Ginny scanned the onslaught of road-rage traffic and wondered if they'd get there in one piece. She juggled the island map she'd lifted off the marble table in the hall at Mayfield House and determined that they'd reached the spiderweb, five-cornered intersection in the center of Vineyard Haven: Cars and trucks converged from all directions, paused, then moved, in some secret bumper-car performance known only to the islanders. "Take a right," Ginny said.

"Easy for you to say," Jess replied.

"Well, you're the one who wanted this freaking adventure."

Jess stepped on the gas. The car lurched forward, then Jess braked again, stalled behind a string of vehicles that were going nowhere fast.

"We'd get there faster if we walked."

"I'm in no hurry," Jess said. "I've waited thirty years to see him. A few more minutes probably won't kill me."

Ginny looked at Jess and wondered if she could possibly be as calm as she pretended. If she once had truly loved this guy named Richard, wouldn't she be jumping out of her pampered skin?

Until Jake, Ginny couldn't have understood what love was all about. She had never understood why tiny, quiet Jess had pined away at Larchwood Hall for some dumb boy she'd let sleep with her, wondering why he didn't come and rescue her. She'd never understood why Jess had written letter after letter on scented sheets of paper, only to have them go unanswered, then, the last ones, returned. She'd never understood the power love could have. Now she did. But she also knew that if she were Jess, she'd be having a major panic attack right now, right here, stuck in traffic on the beach road to Edgartown.

Shit, she thought, hating herself for these damn . . . *feelings* that always seemed to surface whenever she was with Jess. An unexpected thought of Lisa drifted into her mind. She wondered if, unlike Jake, Lisa would ever come around again, would ever come back to her, or if Ginny would remain alone forever until, like Jake, she dropped dead.

"Would you like to sleep with him again?" she suddenly asked Jess.

Jess flinched. "What?"

"Richard. Would you like to sleep with him again? Was he good in bed?"

"Good grief, Ginny, what a question. I haven't seen the man since we were . . . children."

"Yeah, so? Was he good?"

"I had nothing to compare him with."

"You do now."

Jess pulled down her visor and squinted in the sun that glared off the water on the left. "I honestly don't remember. I thought I loved him, I remember that. He made me feel . . . safe."

Ginny nodded and turned her head out the window. Feeling safe was something she could now relate to. She had felt so safe with Jake. Now, she felt so lost. "Richard is divorced," she said, "which means he is available."

"My God, Ginny, I haven't come here to find a man to sleep with. There are other things in life, you know."

Yeah, Ginny thought, *I know*. And it was a good thing that she did, because chances were she'd never sleep with any man again, because she didn't have the need. She shifted uncomfortably on the seat and realized what an unfamiliar feeling that was and how much it basically sucked.

They did not speak again until they pulled into the small, quaint place named Edgartown—with an *O*, which meant they could have a drink if they wanted. But Ginny didn't need a drink: she was simply grateful to be there.

According to the map, the *Vineyard Gazette* was located on a side street, around the corner from a bookstore Ginny recognized from that Bob Newhart sitcom, *George and Leo*, that she had watched so many times, remote and Tostitos close at hand.

"Take a right," Ginny directed.

Jess slowed the car and took a right. The newspaper office was straight ahead. She gave a small sigh and found a parking space nearby.

Beside her, Ginny stared at the old building. It was, of course, gray-shingled, because weren't they all? And it hugged the sidewalk and had a sign hanging out in front. "There it is," she said.

Jess did not say "Wow," or "Oh, God," or "Shit" or anything that Ginny might have said. She merely clicked off the ignition, turned to Ginny and said, "Wait here. This I have to do alone."

Ginny watched her go and realized with genuine delight that for a spoiled rich kid, Jess had turned out to have guts.

She had dressed in pale peach pants today with a matching short-sleeved cotton sweater and low-heeled calfskin shoes that now felt as if they'd been weighted with sailboat anchors and concrete soles.

Jess walked slowly along the brick walkway, her thoughts as floundering as her feet.

Richard.

What would he look like?

How would he react when he saw her?

Would he remember her?

Richard. The boy who had comforted her, the boy who had promised . . . had promised to love her forever, to take care of them, to be a family . . .

And now, he was there. On the other side of the rose-covered fence. At the end of the brick walk, inside the building, never expecting, never dreaming that his refuge on this island was about to end, that he was about to be exposed for who he really was and what he had really done.

She paused at the roses and touched the budding vines, trying to find the courage to keep walking, trying to find the strength to face what she must do.

We were children, she reminded herself. *We are not children anymore.*

She remembered how she'd felt the day she learned that Father had paid Richard's family off, that Richard had deserted her because his family wanted money. Now, she'd learned that even that had been deceit. They'd wanted the money, and they'd wanted her baby, too.

She closed her eyes, surprised that tears were there, that when she opened them again the sweet pink budding roses had blurred together as if they, too, had cried.

He and his lowlife family took the money and ran. Her father's words reverberated in her mind and flowed down to her feet, and she began to move again, propelled by anger, powered by scorn, determined to make this right.

Jess marched up to the front door of the *Vineyard Gazette.*

She opened the door and stepped into a low-ceilinged room. An older woman who sat at a desk behind the counter looked up pleasantly and smiled.

"May I help you?"

Jess twisted the emerald and diamond ring that dug into her finger. "Yes," she said so softly, she had to clear her throat and begin again. "Yes. I'd like to see Richard Bradley, please."

The woman smiled again. "Richard? I'm afraid he won't be back until next week sometime. He's off-island."

"Off-island?"

"He's doing research for a story out of Boston. The environmental control legislation . . ."

The woman continued speaking, but Jess had turned and moved out the door again, and did not hear what else she said.

Back at Mayfield House, Jess told Ginny she needed to rest. "Find somewhere and get some lunch," she suggested to her friend, who always seemed hungry. "I'm going to take a nap."

Ginny left her blessedly alone in the chintz-wallpapered room number seven.

Stretching out on the bed and staring up at the canopy, Jess tried to decide what to do. She had only planned to stay a few days, not until "sometime next week" when Richard would return. She could not stay that long. She had a business to run, though Carlo could most likely handle things without her. But there were the children: Maura and Travis. Then she remembered that they were old enough not to need her anymore.

The fact was that she could stay that long if she wanted to continue, if she needed to learn any more about the truth.

Rubbing a muscle that had knotted at the base of her neck, Jess wondered if it was right to confront Mr. Bradley about his daughter Melanie, the elementary school teacher who may or may not be almost thirty, who may or may not be hers.

Or maybe she should simply leave the island and forget any of this had ever happened.

She thought of Phillip, how he had longed to meet his birth mother, how he had yearned to know the truth.

Didn't Melanie—if Melanie were hers—deserve to know the truth?

Jess rolled onto her side, picked up the phone, and dialed Phillip's office in Manhattan. Maybe he would help her make the decision. Maybe he would tell her what to do.

A woman whose voice she didn't recognize put her through to him.

"Phillip," Jess said, "how's the new office?"

Just the sound of his warm laughter made Jess feel better already. He had, she realized, the same effect on her as Travis, as if Phillip, too, could be her son.

"We're still unpacking," he said. "I think the movers dropped most of my files somewhere on Fifth Avenue."

"You'll find them," Jess replied with a smile. "Besides, isn't that what your new secretary is for?"

"Between you and me, her looks far exceed her brains."

"I'm not sure you're supposed to admit things like that today."

"Sad, but true," he said. "But what about you? Are you home?"

"No. I'm on Martha's Vineyard."

The light, easy conversation ceased. Phillip paused. "And?"

"And, oh, Phillip." Without planning on it, Jess began to cry. She wished she could say something, anything, so he would not suspect.

"Jess? Are you all right?"

It was too late. She could not stop her tears or this embarrassing display. "I'm sorry, Phillip. I didn't mean . . ."

"Jess, what's going on?"

She told him. She told him about Richard's father, and the fact that Richard was off-island, and about the daughter Mr. Bradley called Melanie and that maybe she was hers.

She told him she didn't know what to do next. Then she apologized for crying.

"Don't apologize for how you feel," Phillip said with wisdom far beyond his years. "Is your friend with you? Ginny?"

"Yes, but she's going through her own problems right now. I had hoped this would be a good distraction for her, but I'm afraid I'm so confused . . ."

"Do you think you should talk to Richard's father?"

"Oh, Phillip, I don't know if I have the strength. He seems like a nice man. His other daughter, Karin, is rather strange, but he seems to genuinely care about his family. Especially Melanie. I don't know if I can upset him. I think this should be between Richard and me."

"I'm coming over," Phillip said.

"What?"

"I said I'm coming to the Vineyard. You're too emotionally involved, Jess. If you want to learn the answers, you're going to have to be direct. Or have someone who will be for you."

"But, Phillip . . ."

"I'll be there sometime this weekend. What time is the ferry?"

"I caught one out of Woods Hole at two-thirty. But I don't know the schedule. It's a holiday weekend . . . Memorial Day . . ."

"I'll try to make that one tomorrow. I'll call if anything changes."

"Phillip . . . thank you."

"No thanks required," he responded.

Jess hung up the phone, dried her tears, and was glad that she had called.

Phillip couldn't get out of the office fast enough. He knew Nicole would be angry: the semester had ended and she was on vacation until the summer session began next week. He had promised to take her to the Hamptons this weekend—their first official getaway without books or libraries or Phillip trotting off to meetings that Joseph had arranged.

That, of course, would be the best part—that Joseph already knew his brother and Nicole were going out of town this weekend, so Phillip wouldn't have to explain about Jess, about the Vineyard, and about how it was really none of Joseph's business what he chose to do off-hours.

Phillip grabbed his jacket and briefcase and left.

Surprisingly, a cab came quickly. Once inside, he gave the driver Nicole's address, then settled back for the stop-and-go ride across town. Several blocks down Lexington, Phillip had an idea: He could take Nicole to the Vineyard instead of the Hamptons. Surely she wouldn't mind; surely it wouldn't matter. And maybe they could salvage a romantic weekend after all. Maybe she would even help them find Jess's little girl.

The prospect was exciting—to share something more than sex and dinner and talk about exams and cases; to at last take her into his confidence and tell her about P.J. and how much she'd meant to him.

He looked out the taxi window and smiled, feeling that his life really was coming together and that perhaps Nicole would play a lasting role.

"I don't want to go to Martha's Vineyard," Nicole said. "I want to go to the Hamptons. You promised."

They were in her brick-walled loft. The worst part was, Phillip had told her. He had told her the truth about Jess; he had told her about P.J.; and he had told her how important it was to him to help his birth mother's friend. He had confided all of this to her, and it didn't seem to matter. She must not have understood.

"This means a lot to me, Nicole," he said again. "I thought you'd be excited."

"I was excited. About going to the Hamptons. Not about going off to help a woman find a long-lost baby."

"Excuse me," Phillip said, running his fingers through his hair. "I thought you wanted to be the big child-advocate attorney. I thought you cared about things like this."

Nicole shrugged and turned away. She moved to the bed and sat down on the mattress. Phillip looked around the huge square room, suddenly annoyed that there were no chairs, that the only places to sit were on the bed or the textbook-covered floor.

"I'm tired," she said, pulling off her T-shirt, revealing her small, dark-nippled breasts. Phillip turned his eyes toward the window; he did not want her lure of sex to interfere with what he had to do. "What you want sounds too much like work."

"But . . ." he protested, turning back in time to see her slide out of her jeans, leaving only her thin panties that were the color of orchids today. Lovely, lavender orchids, so soft, so . . .

"This is what you had that fight with Joseph about, isn't it?" She put a finger to her mouth, slowly licked it, then used it to trace a circle around her luscious, hardening nipple.

Phillip was smart enough to know when he was being manipulated. But nonetheless, his eyes were drawn to what Nicole was doing . . . and the stirrings had begun beneath his tightening undershorts. "Joseph and I don't agree on everything," he said lamely.

Her hand moved down between her legs to the silky, orchid patch. She gently moved the fabric to one side, revealing the tangled curls that glistened clean and wet and so inviting. And then she stroked herself, and Phillip started to step forward, longing to touch her for himself, to plunge his face into her sweet and ready warmth and taste her velvet on his tongue.

Suddenly, she pulled one leg upon the bed and grasped her knee with her arms. "If you don't want to take me to the Hamptons, I'll go with some other friends. I need a break, Phillip."

He wiped a trickle of sweat that somehow had formed on his forehead. "The Vineyard would be a break."

"While you're spending time with a menopausal woman dredging up her past?"

His heat began to cool. "That's not fair. You don't know Jess."

She rose from the bed and came close to him again, her scent within his space. She took his hands and slowly pressed them to her breasts. "I want to be with you, Phillip. I want you to make love to me all weekend."

His fingers felt the hardness of the mounds beneath them. He looked into her eyes. He felt the stir begin again. Nicole had never said such words . . . *make love to me all weekend.* Until now, she had taken sex for granted, had acted as if it were a ritual that needed to be performed. Gently, his hands began to roam her breasts. She arched her back and smiled.

"Besides," she whispered, "you don't owe that woman anything. You said yourself she's not a paying client."

His hands stopped. He pulled them away and stepped back from her. "I don't think you understand, Nicole. Jess means a lot to me. If it weren't for her, I never would have known my birth mother."

Nicole's eyes narrowed. "So on a scale of one to ten, she comes out a ten, and I'm somewhere down around a five." She turned back to the bed, grabbed her T-shirt and pulled it over her head.

"Is this what you're all about?" Phillip asked. "Your quest for helping children only matters if the almighty dollar is involved?" His anger flared. He paced the room. "God, Nicole, I thought you were different from my brother. I thought you cared about things other than money. I guess that was my mistake."

She laughed. He couldn't believe she laughed.

"Why do you have to take everything so damn seriously?

If one of us was wrong, I guess it must be me. I thought you wanted to spend time with me when I was available."

"When *you're* available," Phillip said, an unfamiliar frostiness creeping into his voice. "It's all about you, isn't it, Nicole? You want someone who will share your bed whenever *you* have the time. You want a half-assed relationship that will fit into your schedule. It's just like how you're always late. Have you ever showed up for one date on time? What is that? Some kind of control issue?" The words rushed from his mouth. He watched her anger rise, her chin raise, her jaw set.

"I think you'd better leave," she said.

"Fine," he replied, grabbing his briefcase. "Have a nice weekend."

Ginny knew there were other ways to get what one wanted without playing by the rules. After all, she'd spent a lifetime doing it until the last few years. Being nice should be reserved for the Jesses and Lisas of this screwed-up world. Or at least, for the kind of woman Jess was and Lisa had been before taking up with Brad.

She shook her head and glanced around the living room at Mayfield House. Now was not the time to be thinking of her daughter. Now was the time to think about this predicament with Jess and come up with a solution that would override the obstacles.

All around her, clocks ticked. She shifted awkwardly on the stiff sofa; she could think better if only she had a big bag of Tostitos.

In the old days, she would have used sex to approach Richard's father, to make him feel he was the hottest male in the universe. In the old days she would have flirted and strutted and made him pant, then enticed him into telling her everything she wanted to know.

The concept was intriguing, but when Ginny looked down at the bubble of her stomach under stretchy leggings, she reminded herself it wasn't as easy to flirt and strut when your gut was hanging out, and that the old days, like so many other things, were apparently long gone.

Still, she reasoned, Old Man Bradley was getting on, and probably hadn't done it for many years. Besides, she thought, maybe a little action would revive her lost libido.

A slow smile crept across her face. Ginny stood up and decided to go and find Richard Bryant/Bradley, Senior, in this mausoleum of a house. Maybe the results would be as beneficial to herself as they would be to Jess.

He wasn't in the house. He was in the backyard, sanding paint off a sailboat that was turned upside down on wooden horses.

"Nice day," Ginny commented.

"Be nicer once we can get this baby back in the water."

"I'm surprised you have time for sailing. This house must take a lot of work."

"Have to make time for the finer things in life. The tourists are going to come anyway. Got to leave room for a little fun. Put that in your research paper."

It took a brief moment for Ginny to realize what he was talking about. "My paper," she said, "right. Well, if you don't mind, there are a few other questions I'd like to ask."

He sanded slowly, then scratched his chin.

She stepped closer to him, brushed her hair behind one ear, and gave her once-famous Ginny pose: one hip out, one leg propped against the other. "Please?" she asked, thinking she'd give anything not to feel quite so ridiculous.

"Well, I guess. Don't ask me anything I don't want to answer, though." He eyed her empty hands. "You're not going to take notes?"

"I have an excellent memory."

"Okay, then. Shoot." He returned to sanding.

She stood up straight and congratulated herself that she still had it, even though it didn't feel as if she did. Her thoughts turned back to Jess. "You mentioned your other daughter is a teacher," she began boldly. "Did she leave the island to go to college?"

"Yep. Came back, though."

"Why?"

He shrugged. "Because it's home. It's where she lives."

"Is she your youngest?"

"Yep. She'll be thirty this year."

Thirty. Oh, shit, Ginny thought, *it's her. It's really her.* She stopped herself from asking if her birthday was in November. Instead, she assumed her Ginny-pose again. "Well, tell me then. What does a thirty-year-old—or anyone, for that matter—do for excitement on this island?"

Mr. Bradley laughed. "Well, Melanie loves her teaching. And she's married, too. Got a little girl who looks just like her."

Ginny took a step back. She hadn't expected that: a little girl, a little girl who was Jess's granddaughter. Ginny winced when she thought of Jess's reaction. More crying, she supposed. More of those *feelings.*

"And Karin has her sea glass," the old man continued. "I wish she had more."

"Karin's not married?"

"Nope." He did not elaborate, but Ginny noticed he rubbed harder with the sandpaper.

"In L.A., teaching and collecting old glass aren't considered terribly exciting."

He chuckled. "Maybe that's the problem with L.A. Folks here enjoy the simple life. Take tomorrow, for instance. Every year the folks of Tisbury get together for one big picnic. Our last hurrah before the tourists descend in masses."

"A picnic? With all the people from the town?" *A town picnic,* she thought. *Hold me back, Lord, I cannot take much more excitement.*

He set down his sandpaper and looked at Ginny. "Over at Tashmoo Pond. It's tradition on the island, like most everything else. Anyway, the inn is booked this weekend, but we have an inn-sitter come and take care of business. Wouldn't miss the picnic for all the scallops in the sound."

"I see," she said, turning away. And then, an idea came. Another of her "Ginny specials"—an idea that might get them into trouble, but there was nothing much to lose. "Well," she said, trying not to show her smile, "I'll let you get back to your work. I'll see you later." She strutted off, feeling his eyes on her backside, feeling mighty happy that they were. Not only that, but she'd really scored. A picnic at Tashmoo Pond, wherever the hell that was. Chances are, the old man's "daughter" Melanie would be there. And she'd probably even bring her little girl.

Ginny walked toward the house, rubbing her hands together, pleased that she still had it, the way to get what she needed from a man. She hoped that Jess had brought some old jeans and a sweatshirt to wear to Tashmoo Pond . . . something that hinted "townie" and didn't have Ann Taylor or St. John knit oozing from every seam.

Chapter 16

"We can't just crash a picnic," Jess had protested when Ginny told her of her plan.

"We won't exactly 'crash' it. We'll make Richard's father think we were out exploring and just 'happened' to come across it."

"I don't know, Ginny . . ."

"Look, do you want to get on with this or would you rather spend the next week holed up in that room, waiting for your darling Richard to return?" She suggested that Melanie might be there; she did not tell her about the little girl, the granddaughter Jess did not know she had. Even Ginny knew it would not be fair to raise Jess's hopes too high.

Yet finally she'd convinced Jess, and now the two of them stood on the roadside, dressed in jeans and "Vineyarders" sweatshirts that Ginny bought for them last night, peering down a grassy hill toward a small, duck-infested pond, where half a dozen rickety skiffs were rowed by kids in orange life vests, where picnic tables had been set close to the water's edge, where people milled and others sat in lawn chairs and on blankets, where accordion players strolled and played, where chatter and laughter mingled with aromas of sizzling charcoal grills. The islanders seemed to be enjoying their last hurrah.

"I feel like I'm watching someone else's family reunion," Jess said.

"Well, it could be yours. All we have to do is walk down the hill. Besides, that smell of hot dogs is mighty appealing. Maybe I can convince the old man to give us one or two."

"I don't know, Ginny . . ."

"Trust me, kid."

She saw them. They were standing on the knoll, looking down into the crowd, and she saw them, big as life.

And then she saw them walking. Slowly. With determination. The fat one waddled down the hill, followed by the other.

Karin leaned against a tall oak tree and marveled at how easily things fell into place when one simply planted a small seed and let nature do what nature did.

No one stopped them. Jess stayed close behind Ginny, trying to mask her embarrassment, trying to act as if they both belonged there, which of course they did not. It was not the first time she'd followed Ginny's lead; it was not the first time she'd stepped away from the so-predictable and into Ginny's world. She wrapped her hands in the hem of her too-large sweatshirt and admitted it was fun, in a Ginny sort of way.

"Hello. Good morning," she heard Ginny saying now as they passed among the people. "What a lovely day."

An old woman behind a makeshift booth was handing out free ice cream. "Chocolate, vanilla, or strawberry?" Ginny asked Jess.

"Forget it!" Jess whispered. "You're not going to get any." Fun or not, she could only go so far. And she would be content if this new adventure yielded only a glimpse of Melanie and nothing more.

"God, you're such a priss. Just like always."

"Just find Richard's father. Let's get this over with."

They walked past a horse-pulled wagon that kids were piling onto. "Ride?" asked a young man.

Jess poked Ginny in the back.

"Maybe later," Ginny replied, then turned around to Jess. "Let's walk down to the water. Maybe he's there."

Jess ambled after Ginny, remembering when they had all gone to the state fair together, four very pregnant girls trying to have a good time—eating cotton candy and playing games of chance, and forgetting all their problems if only for one day. She wondered if it had been that long since she'd smelled hamburgers cooking on a grill; she wondered if it had been that long since she'd felt like such a kid.

They stopped beside some tall cattails. "I should have paid attention to what he wore at breakfast," Ginny said. "We may never find him in this crowd."

As soon as she spoke the words, Jess noticed Richard's father, sitting at a picnic table, laughing with another man.

"There he is," she said. Immediately Jess regretted coming here. After all, this was not a state fair and they were no longer teenage girls.

But Ginny had followed her eyes to the table, and now it was too late. She marched forward.

"Mr. Bradley," she said, tossing back her hair and strutting her Ginny strut. "So this is where you hang out on Memorial Day."

"Ginny," he said with some surprise, and quickly stood. "What are you girls doing down here?"

"We were drawn by the music," Ginny said. "Don't worry," she added with a small smile, "we're not staying."

He stepped away from the table. "No? Not even if I cook you up a burger?"

"But this is a town picnic . . ." she protested, though not too much.

Richard's father shook his head. "No problem," he said, then added with a wink, "You'll be my guests. Now what'll it be? Burger with the works? How about some clam chowder? It's nice and fresh. . . . Millie Johnson made it. . . ."

"Well . . ." Ginny feigned a thin protest once again. "If you insist."

"I do. And I also insist you call me Dick."

Dick, Jess thought. *Leave it to Ginny to befriend one of those.*

"If you stay," Dick was saying, "maybe you'll get some good material for your research."

"Oh, believe me," Ginny responded, "I'm sure I will. And since you insist, I'll have a hamburger. With the works." She turned to Jess. "Jess?"

Jess shifted her eyes back to the crowd, wondering if the youngest Bradley, Melanie, was among the group. "No thank you, I'm not hungry."

"No burger?" Richard's father—Dick—asked. "We've got plenty. With Richard and Melanie not here, I've brought enough to feed an army."

If Jess were playing poker she'd have lost the hand for sure. She quickly turned her back, so Dick would not see the disappointment on her face.

"Your kids aren't here?" she heard Ginny ask.

"Only Karin. Richard's off-island, and Melanie's home with my poor little granddaughter, Sarah."

The air was filled with the sounds of laughing, squealing children, the chatter of adults, the clink of horseshoes on metal posts, and the off-key notes of accordions being played by men in overalls. The air was filled with sounds and yet they all seemed to have frozen—still and dead and hanging there, while the meaning of Dick Bradley's words sank in.

Jess turned back. "Sarah?" she asked.

His face glowed as much as she supposed a seventy-year-old, weatherbeaten face could glow. "She's a pistol, that one. Broke her leg on the school playground. Poor little thing. She's in a cast up to her hip."

Jess's cheeks were hot. Her heart began to ache, those butterflies from long ago returned to flutter in her stomach, in her arms and in her legs. "Sarah's your granddaughter?" she asked.

Ginny elbowed Jess. "Well, that's too bad," she said. "If we stay on this island any longer, maybe we'll get to meet the entire Bradley family."

"How long are you staying, anyway?" The question did not come from Richard's father. It came from Karin. Jess had not heard her approach, but she was standing there staring at them with curious, doubting eyes.

And suddenly Jess knew that Karin knew. The chill that ran through her was not from the chilly morning. It was not from the breeze that drifted off the water. It was from those eyes of Karin's, those eyes that told her that she knew. She knew who Jess was. And she knew what Jess was doing there.

Why haven't I heard from my mother? The garbled voice on the telephone came sharply to her mind. And every instinct or intuition Jess ever had now told her that the voice had belonged to Karin. Karin had made the call; Karin had written the letter.

But why?

She stared at Karin; her mouth was dry, her eyelids could not blink. And then Jess heard Ginny answer, "We're not sure how long we're staying."

"I need to know soon," Karin said. "It's Memorial Day weekend. I have to know when we can rent your rooms again."

"We'll let you know," Ginny replied, then turned back to Dick. "Now where's that burger? I'm starving."

Jess pulled her eyes away, yet still felt Karin staring, her eyes moving from Jess to Ginny, then back to Jess again. Finally, silently, she left the group, walking toward the water, walking along the shore, away from Jess and Ginny, away from the Memorial Day town picnic.

"She doesn't like us," Ginny said to Dick.

"Karin? She doesn't like anyone. She's happiest when she's walking on the beach, collecting that damn sea glass that she does nothing with."

After Ginny had her fill of burgers and two free ice cream cones, Jess persuaded her to leave the picnic. "Please," she whispered. "We're not going to find out anything else. Melanie isn't here."

Ginny relented, and they trudged back up the hill where Jess had parked the car.

On the way back to the inn, Jess had a sudden need to see the water, to feel the sun against her face and hear the soothing tide.

"I want to find a beach," she said to Ginny. "I need to look at the sea for a moment and think."

"Great. And me without a sand pail."

Jess smiled, then steered the car in the opposite direction from town. Soon they were surrounded by large, stately homes spaced far apart, homes that looked like they'd been there for half a century or more, houses that seemed empty now.

"They must belong to the summer mucky-mucks," Ginny said. "The city people with the big bucks." She turned to Jess. "Kind of looks like the sort of place you would have 'summered' as a kid, if your father ever talked to you."

"Very funny," Jess replied, glad that she could now be amused by the way that she'd been raised, that among so many other things, Ginny had taught her that life could have been much worse.

Ginny laughed. "When I was little my mother and I went to Revere Beach every summer for a week. We stayed at a boarding house and shared a bathroom with everyone else in the damn place."

"Except that time when you came here."

"Yeah. That was only once, though. Then she met the asshole she married and we never went anywhere else."

"Oh, right," Jess said. "I remember him."

Beside her, Ginny howled. It was good, Jess decided, that they could both accept the past.

They passed a group of tennis courts, a small, closed-up post office, and an equally deserted community hall. At the end of the road was a giant curve, a loop that continued past the huge, salt-faded houses. On the curve was a tall flagpole and two benches. Jess pulled to the side of the road and turned off the ignition.

"Let's get out and walk down to the water," she said.

Ginny groaned but opened her door.

The water was several feet below, its low tide lapping gently on the shore. Between them and the water was a sharp drop, covered mostly by tall sea grass, bending in the breeze.

"There's a path over there," Ginny said, pointing to a small road, leading off to the left. Beside the road was a sign that read, *Private Road. West Chop Association.*

"We can't go there, Ginny. It's private."

Ginny rolled her eyes and started toward the path.

Something caught Jess's eye. "Ginny," she said. "Wait."

She looked again, and saw what it was she thought she'd seen: a swish of red on the beach below; a swish of a red sarong that ambled barefoot in the sand, bending now and then, pulling the hair back from her eyes and looking off across the sound.

"It's Karin," Jess said.

"God, she's weird."

"It's more than that. I think she knows. I think she's the one who sent me the letter and made the call."

Ginny looked off to the beach. "Why would she?"

"That's what I intend to find out." Jess tucked her hands

inside her shirt once more, warding off the chill. "Come on, Ginny," she said. "Let's go back to the inn."

A woman they had not seen before—the inn-sitter, Jess assumed—greeted them at the door.

"Nice day for the picnic," the woman said.

"Picnic?" Ginny asked, as if to say "what picnic?" as if to pretend she'd never heard of it.

"Town picnic," the woman replied. "Everyone goes."

Not everyone, Jess wanted to say. Melanie wasn't there. Neither was her daughter, *my* granddaughter. Maybe.

Sarah. What a beautiful name.

"Well, it's nice that everyone goes," Ginny said aloofly, heading for the stairs. "I'm going to take a nap, Jess. I'm tired and I'm stuffed."

"Oh, that reminds me," the inn-sitter added. "I hope you don't mind. I let a guest into your room."

Ginny looked at Jess.

"Phillip?" Jess asked.

"She said you were expecting her."

"She?" Ginny asked.

The inn-sitter shrugged. "Like I said, I hope you don't mind. All our other rooms are booked. I had no where else to put her."

Ginny let out a huge sigh. "Come on, Jess. I think it's my turn to need you now."

Jess followed Ginny up the wide stairs and into room three, Ginny's room. There, on the corner of the non-canopy bed, sat Lisa. And she was alone.

"Where's Prince Charming?" Ginny asked without so much as a hello.

"Ginny . . ." Lisa began, her eyes wet with tears.

Jess backed away. "I think I'll leave you two alone. I'm going to walk down to the ferry in case Phillip arrives."

• • •

They stood and stared at one another, not unlike the way Morticia had stared at Jess and Ginny at the picnic, with steady, not-backing-down kind of eyes.

Ginny broke the stare and walked to the bureau where she tossed her room key on the top. In that sober, awkward moment, she regretted calling Lisa's parents from the airport; she regretted saying where she was.

"I thought you'd be glad to see me," Lisa said.

"Glad? It all depends."

"On whether Brad is with me?"

Ginny walked to a maple rocking chair tucked under a slanted eaves. She pulled it out and sat down, as far from Lisa as she could get, as if her daughter were contagious, as if the further she could be from her, the less she'd have to feel.

"He's not with me, Ginny."

Ginny cocked her head. "Do you mean he's not with you now, in this room, or he's not with you in the biblical sense?"

"I mean he got on a plane this morning and flew back to the Coast. He had his car shipped yesterday."

Ginny nodded and creaked the rockers, one rock forward, one rock back. "Fine. But you didn't answer my question."

"It's over between us, if that's what you mean."

Yes, of course, that was what she'd meant. She wondered if Lisa could see the relief flooding through her.

"I saw a lot of pictures of the two of you," Ginny said. "In the tabloids."

Lisa let out a pained snicker. "Every time we turned around another flashbulb popped."

"You're a star, Lisa. What did you expect?"

Lisa shrugged. "Brad liked it."

"I'm sure he did." Ginny wished she hadn't said that, but it was too late to take it back, too late to reach into the air between them and grab the words and take them back. She folded her hands on her lap. "So now you're here."

"I'm here for a reason, Ginny. We have to talk."

It was as if an invisible cloud descended upon the room. Or maybe it just descended across Ginny's heart. She didn't like what Lisa was about to say, and she knew it before Lisa said the words.

"He asked for money," Lisa said.

Ginny did not reply this time, proud of herself for holding back her tongue. She rocked again, forward, back.

"He asked for money. A lot of money. When I told him no, he got angry."

Ginny stopped rocking, tensing from the hurt that rimmed her daughter's eyes.

"Then he told me about you."

She gripped the seat of the chair. Her shoulders slumped. "Me?"

"About the two of you."

The stab was deep and slow, a long, dull saber piercing through Ginny's breast and inching downward through her body, bumping, bruising, wounding every nerve along the way. It hurt too much for her to answer. It hurt too much for her to cry.

Across the room, Lisa wrung her hands. "I guess I wasn't shocked. But I was disappointed that you . . . that Jake was still alive when you and Brad had the affair."

Ginny closed her eyes, deciding if this wasn't hell then at least it must be purgatory, where all her sins were going to hover for eternity.

The rockers creaked.

Two people in the room breathed.

Then Ginny heard what Lisa had just said. She opened her eyes and moved to the edge of her chair.

"The affair?" she asked. "What *affair*?"

"He told me, Ginny."

Ginny jumped up. She stomped to the corner of the bed

and shook a finger at Lisa's face. "It was *not* an *affair*, Lisa. I did *not* have an affair with Brad Edwards."

Lisa glared at her. "He said you shaved your pubic hair into a narrow strip."

Ginny backed away. She was going to be sick. She just knew she was going to be sick. She clutched her stomach. The taste of grilled hamburgers and chowder and too much ice cream backed up into her throat. "I was drunk one night," she said. "I was drunk and I let him screw me. I regretted it from the moment it happened."

Lisa turned her head away. Ginny could almost feel the sting of her tears. "It wasn't an affair?"

"I was drunk, Lisa. That's not an excuse, but it's reality." The bile settled down.

Her daughter was silent a moment. Then she turned to Ginny. "That's not what he's going to tell the tabloids."

Ginny felt herself go rigid.

"He said unless we give him half a million dollars, he's going to tell the tabloids everything. Everything, in his words. That he had an intense affair with his stepmother . . . the mother of Lisa Andrews."

Rage surged through her. "That fucking son of a bitch. He wouldn't dare."

"I think he will."

"It will ruin your career."

"Yes," Lisa quietly replied. "I believe that's his intent."

Ginny laughed a sick, disgusted laugh. "He'll get more than that, too. He'll also get revenge on me for getting Jake's estate." She clutched her hand against her stomach and wondered when—or if—her pain would ever end, and what the hell she'd ever done to deserve this kind of life.

On the way down to the ferry, Jess stopped at the Tisbury Inn. Luckily, they had a vacancy. She reserved a room for Phillip; he had not said how long he'd stay, so she booked it for two nights.

The late afternoon sun was being threatened by a slate-colored sky and a hint of fog. She stopped at the Black Dog Bakery and bought a corn muffin and a cup of tea, deciding that she must be hungry, though she didn't really feel it. Walking across to the ferry pier, she passed the lines of cars awaiting the next boat, sat down in a small gazebo by the water, and tried to figure out what she was feeling.

Despair, maybe. Emptiness. Confusion. And a hapless, hopeless sense that she would never know her daughter, the baby she gave up.

The baby who now had a baby of her own.

If Melanie was hers.

Opening the small white bag, Jess broke off a piece of muffin and slowly chewed. She washed it down with a swallow of tea, then stared out across the water toward Cape Cod on the horizon, toward the town of Falmouth, where Miss Taylor had once lived, and wondered why she couldn't leave well enough alone.

From the way Richard's father sounded, Melanie was happy. A young mother with a career she loved. What right did Jess have to step in and shake that up?

And then she thought of Ginny. And Lisa. And how the two of them had back-and-forth problems not unlike the ones Jess and Maura had. Not unlike the way the real world worked. And yet the bond between them hadn't yet unraveled.

A seagull landed on the floor of the gazebo, his black eyes shifting from the small white bag to Jess then back again, as though his X-ray vision knew that there was food inside. Just as she began to open the bag to feed the gull, a little bird landed on the bench across from her, and looked at her with pleading eyes.

She tossed a piece of muffin toward the little bird. The gull flapped its wings and flew up to the bench, startling the bird, scaring it away. It gobbled the morsel, then returned to the floor at Jess's feet.

"Scavenger," she said. "Couldn't you save some for the

little bird?" Angrily, she closed the bag. The seagull would get nothing else. She stared down at the beady black eyes that stared back at her. It struck her that the bilge-colored creature was only doing what it needed, that it was only fighting for survival. She thought of Maura and her need to fight with Jess about finding her other daughter. Maybe it was Maura's way of fighting for survival, struggling to retain her place within her mother's heart, fearful that she would be dislodged. Tears formed at the corners of Jess's eyes. She reached back into the bag, broke up the crumbs of muffin, and tossed them at her feet.

The blast of a ferry horn sounded. Jess looked up to see the massive iron beast pull into the dock. She rose and started to walk toward it just as the little bird returned. Quickly, she bent and scooped up some crumbs, and set them on the bench. The little bird descended. The gull did not seem to notice. Now both were fed, and both were satisfied.

Jess wiped her eyes and hurried to greet the boat.

The ride on the ferry had been queerly similar to Manhattan rush hour on the subway, the crowd of eager people jockeying for the best position while the vehicle lurched and lumbered its way toward their destination.

Phillip discreetly held his stomach as the boat bumped against the pier and wondered how anyone could possibly feel seasick on a forty-five minute trek across the water that wasn't even open ocean, more like a large lake with a tide. He stood in line, waiting for the chain to be removed from across the gangplank or whatever it was called, gripping the handle of his small bag that held only clean underwear, a different shirt, and running shorts in case he had the time. His mission, after all, would be quick: He would simply confront this Mr. Bradley, the way he had confronted William Larribee. They would learn the truth once and for all, and Jess could get on with her life. And he with his. If there was much of one remaining, now that Nicole apparently would not be in it.

A deckhand dressed in jeans removed the chain; the crowd jostled forward, Phillip among them, wedged between an Asian family with several cameras around their necks and a yuppie-looking couple with a black Labrador retriever on a bright red leash. As they herded down the walkway, he kept his gaze fixed on the yuppie woman, khaki shorts pressed neatly, a white T-shirt clean and neat, a visor cap set atop her blunt-cropped, blond-streaked hair. He watched her walk and tried not to envy the yuppie man, but could not help himself. He imagined their home, with light oak woodwork and gleaming floors and fat earthen jars holding clusters of tall flowers. It only made him seasick again.

They stepped down onto the pavement—onto land, thank God.

"Phillip!"

Phillip pulled his gaze away from the khaki shorts and looked up to see Jess approaching, her hair wispy in the breeze, her smile warm and friendly, the kind, sweet woman without whom he would never have met his mother.

"Jess," he said, accepting her gentle hug.

"Did you have any trouble getting across?"

"Not as long as I left my car there. In some town called Falmouth. I hope that's okay."

"It's fine. You won't need your car. Falmouth is where Miss Taylor lived."

"Ah, yes," he tried to say cheerfully, "the infamous Miss Taylor who's at the bottom of it all."

Jess laughed. She looked off toward a gazebo, blinked, then looked back at him. A look of fear now filled her eyes.

"What's wrong?" Phillip asked. He followed where her gaze had gone and saw that a woman was standing at the gazebo, a woman dressed in a white jersey and red sarong. "Who's that?"

"Karin," Jess said quietly. "Richard's sister." She steered Phillip from the area. "I think she knows why we're here, Phillip. I think she's the one who summoned me."

He smiled. "Are you sure you're not being paranoid?"

Jess gave a small, forced laugh. "You're right. I probably am."

He nodded, and they wove their way through the crowd and the cars and the black Labradors on leashes. He wondered if the black Lab was the official dog of the island.

"I'm sorry," Jess said, "but I left the car at the inn. I needed to walk."

"No problem. I sure could use a Coke, though. My stomach's a little queasy." He would never have admitted that to Nicole or, probably, to any other woman he'd dated. But Jess was so . . . motherly, despite her tiny frame, despite the fact that he towered over her and felt compelled to protect her. He felt he could tell her anything, much as how he had felt with P.J. He wondered if that was how most children felt with their mothers, then wondered why he never had with Jeanine Archambault, the woman who had raised him.

"The Black Dog Tavern's over here," Jess said. Phillip followed her through a maze of ancient-looking, weathered structures that looked more like shacks than buildings and were decorated with paint-worn buoys and wooden lobster traps. He shared his observation with Jess about the black dogs that he'd seen; they laughed again and he felt better now and so glad that he'd come, so glad that he had stood his ground and not caved in to Nicole.

Inside the restaurant, they were seated on a glassed-in porch that overlooked the water and the madness of the ferry. They ordered: Jess, tea and a salad; Phillip, a burger and large Coke.

"I'm not sure why you wanted to come," Jess said. "I'm so embarrassed that I broke down on the phone."

"I came because I wanted to," he responded. "If you'll

let me, I want to confront Mr. Bradley. I want to ask him directly about his daughter Melanie."

"Oh, Phillip, I'm not sure . . ."

"I think it's the only way we'll know, Jess."

"But if Melanie really is my daughter, wouldn't he lie? She's almost thirty years old. Why would he tell the truth now?"

"Maybe she already knows the truth."

Jess shook her head. "I wondered about that. But if she knows that Richard is her father, why would they have sneaked here from Connecticut? Why did they vanish from their hometown? Why did they change their name?"

"Because I expect your father demanded it. It was probably a stipulation of his payment." He put his hand over hers. "Please, Jess, let me ask him, and we can put a stop to this once and for all. No more waiting for elusive people to show up; no more wondering if this other daughter of his is out to get you."

"I'm not sure, Phillip. I need the night to think about it, okay?"

"Of course." He pulled back his hand and spread his napkin in his lap. "In the meantime, I'm famished."

"So are we," said a woman who appeared beside their table. "Can we join you?"

The woman looked vaguely familiar.

"You must be Phillip," she said. "Only a New York suit would show up on Martha's Vineyard in a tie."

"Phillip," Jess said, "this is my friend, Ginny."

"And this is my daughter, Lisa," Ginny said, stepping aside and gesturing to the young woman behind her.

He stood up quickly, his napkin sliding to the floor. "Nice to meet you," he said, loosening his tie with one hand, extending the other to Ginny, and having a difficult time pulling his eyes from her daughter, the most beautiful woman Phillip had ever seen.

Chapter 17

 They were growing in numbers.

Karin stood beside the bench outside the Black Dog Tavern and peered inside at the two women and the new ones: the young woman and the young man, looking almost as young as Melanie. She had no idea why so many had come, but she decided it could only work in her favor: more people usually resulted in greater chaos—you didn't have to live in a vacation spot to know that.

She also knew it was too late. She had started something that could not be stopped now, any more than tourists could be stopped from coming in summer or bits of sea glass could be stopped from eventually making it to shore.

Moving from the window, she tiptoed away, her adrenaline escalating with each barefooted step. Surely, she had not felt this alive with anticipation since those long-ago months of waiting for Brit. Now all she had to do was wait. The explosion, she knew, would come soon. It was time to prepare the ammunition.

•　•　•　•

"If you're such a hotshot attorney," Ginny said once they were seated, "tell me how to have someone killed and not be found out."

"I'll pretend I didn't hear that," Phillip said, sipping his Coke, still trying to keep his eyes off Lisa, off her tawny hair and topaz eyes, off her skin that looked as if it would feel like silk on his fingertips. He tried to stop himself from leaning across the table to see what scent she wore: Would it be lightly musky like Nicole's, or the aroma of vanilla, pure and clean and so inviting? "Besides," he added with a smile, "I'm a corporate attorney. I don't deal in criminal cases."

"Who are you planning to kill, Ginny?" Jess asked.

Ginny leaned back on her chair and stared off toward the water. "My stepson," she said without hesitation. "He's trying to blackmail us for half a million dollars."

Phillip nearly choked on his straw. "Blackmail?" For someone who spent his days and often his nights in the tedium of corporate law, the word "blackmail" seemed to be popping up with strange frequency.

"I guess it's the price one pays for stardom," Lisa said quietly, a touch of cynicism in the low, husky voice.

Stardom, Phillip thought, and then he recognized her. This was not merely Lisa, Ginny's daughter. This was Lisa Andrews, leading lady of *Devonshire Place,* one of the few things that made TV worth watching no matter how many briefs there were to write, no matter how many cases there were to read. He moved a little on his chair and tried to pretend it was no big deal that Lisa Andrews was sitting across from him.

Ginny shrugged. "I don't think Lisa has anything to do with it."

Of course she doesn't, Phillip wanted to say. Despite the caustic character she played, it was well publicized that Lisa Andrews was the epitome of niceness, a star without the hint of a chip on one of those smooth, lightly tanned shoulders so invitingly accented by the halter top she now wore. She wouldn't be involved with anyone unsavory.

"It's my own fault," Ginny continued. "Brad and I had a night of . . . shall we say, indiscretion. But it was years ago. Now he's threatening to lie to the world, turn it into an affair, and destroy Lisa's career."

"How would it destroy your career?" Jess asked Lisa.

Ginny answered for her daughter. "Because half the world already knows she's the one sleeping with Brad now."

Phillip took a huge bite of his burger to hide his disappointment and the fact that he was among the other half of the world who had not yet heard.

Lisa paled. "Ginny . . ."

"I know, I know. It's over. He's back in L.A. where he belongs. But it's not over for us. I'm afraid it's only just beginning."

Phillip cleared his throat and tried to sound professional. "Would it really ruin Lisa's career? It seems to me that today the more dirt people learn about celebrities, the more they pay attention to them. Why not let him go ahead and do it? Call his bluff. From what I understand, the average extortionist doesn't have the courage to go through with the threats."

"Brad isn't average about anything he does," Lisa replied.

Ginny laughed. "It would be bad enough if he told the truth. But he's always felt a need to be larger than life. To make everything much more grand—or more sordid— than it actually is. Or, in this case, was."

"Truth," Jess mused, picking at her salad. "Why is it that even honesty can get us into trouble?"

"Whoa," Ginny said. "I thought you were the poster child for truth, justice, and the American myth. For honesty at any cost and all that crap."

"I'm beginning to have my doubts. Phillip wants to challenge Richard's father—one on one—and force him to tell the truth."

"Hey," Ginny said, popping an onion ring into her mouth. "Maybe we could kill him, too." She chewed, swallowed, and added, "Then you could go and meet Melanie, I could go home and kill Brad, and we'd all have some godforsaken peace."

Phillip picked up a ketchup bottle and doused his hamburger. "I didn't hear that, either," he said.

Jess had promised to sleep on it and let Phillip know in the morning if she wanted him to confront Dick Bradley. But as she stood in the Mayfield House living room after breakfast, studying the ticking clocks on the walls, she was no closer to making a decision than she had been last night.

In her heart, she knew she'd rather wait and talk to Richard herself, but she couldn't be certain if that was because she felt it really was best or because a small spark within her longed to see him again—that same spark, no doubt, that was hell-bent on romanticizing, that same spark that had dreamed of his coming to Larchwood to rescue her, to carry her off on his stalwart white stallion to a land where they would live happily ever after.

She realized that maybe she should just act her age now and let Phillip handle it. After all, he had taken the time to come to the Vineyard. Ginny had, too. They had taken their time to try and help her—maybe she should simply let them and stop dragging this out.

If only she could just see Melanie once. If only she could see her, then she would know.

"By the looks of this map, I need to borrow your car," Ginny announced as she burst through the French doors into the room. "Lisa wants to do the tourist thing, and Dick insists we go out to the cliffs at Gay Head." She snickered a little and looked down at the map. "Gay Head. I'm not even going to wonder where they came up with that name."

Jess laughed. "Maybe you'll learn something."

"Yeah. Dick said it would help with my research if I learned about the island's history. The Indians and all that."

Looking at the map, Jess smiled. "You're not doing a research paper, Ginny."

"Hey, maybe I should. Maybe I should go to college. That's not a bad idea."

"To become what? What did you ever want besides being an actor?"

Ginny shrugged. "I don't know. I never had the chance to find out. My mother wanted me to be a teacher. She thought it was the most respected career a woman could have. Mom, we all know, was big on respect. But can you imagine, me, a teacher? What a hoot."

Jess tossed Ginny her car keys. "Take the car. Maybe you'll find your vocation out on those cliffs. Maybe you can go back to L.A. and teach the surfers about the East." Suddenly, Jess had an idea. She grabbed the map from Ginny's hand. "I want to see something," she said, and headed for a table made of driftwood and glass where she could spread out the map. "This is the whole island, right?"

"How do I know? Yeah. I guess."

Jess studied each small area until she found Tisbury/ Vineyard Haven. She bent closer and moved her finger across the paper, searching.

"What are you looking for?"

"Nothing special," she said. Then she saw it. She traced her finger down to the road where the Mayfield House was, then looked back again, implanting the route in her mind. Certainly, it was within walking distance, though probably all uphill. She handed the map back to Ginny.

"You have a crafty look in your eyes," Ginny said. "Are you planning to do something I know nothing about?"

Jess shook her head. "I wanted to see how far West Chop

is from here. I thought I'd take Phillip with me to find some of that sea glass Karin likes." It was, of course, a bit of a lie. But Jess had decided that maybe it was time to stop being so damn honest, so damn, get-you-nowhere honest.

"I'm sure picking up broken glass will be a truly scintillating experience for a thirty-year-old male," Ginny commented. "Just stay away from Morticia, all right? She's bad news if I've ever seen it."

"Not to worry," Jess replied. "I'll be careful."

Karin sat in her attic room, reviewing her plan, sifting a pile of sea glass through her fingers, letting the smooth, cool stones *ping-ping* onto the hardwood floor. One-two, three-four. Five-six, seven-eight.

Once she had planned to make a necklace for Mellie—a beautiful necklace that would reach to her waist and sparkle with all the colors of the sea. She had wanted to give it to her for her fourteenth birthday. But then Brit had not returned, and Karin's world fell apart, and Mellie was too old for handmade junk anyway, even though she would have pretended it was the prettiest thing she'd ever seen just because Karin had made it and Mellie felt sorry for her.

Nine-ten, eleven-twelve.

Karin wondered if Jess would have ever expected that a daughter of hers would wear glass instead of diamonds, pieces of old bottles instead of trinkets from Tiffany's.

Sighing, she dumped the rest of the glass on the bed and picked up the cigar box that held all that she needed— those things that she'd read dozens of times since she'd found them in the secret compartment of the old rolltop desk, buried away for what was surely meant to be forever, safe from Karin's wandering eyes.

They would have been, too, if she'd not been searching for a place for her sea glass, a place to hide her treasures away from the others, where only she would know where they were in case he came back to her. Then she could show him how much she had found, and they could save them together, a symbol of their love.

Just because he hadn't come back did not mean he wouldn't.

But he hadn't returned yet, and she'd found these instead. And now she knew them by heart.

"Dear Richard." She closed her eyes as she softly recited the words that had been written on thin, scented paper. "I miss you so much. Why haven't you come for me? Why haven't you come to take me away, so we can be a family with our baby?"

Karin clutched the cigar box closer to her chest. "The baby kicked inside me today. Just a little kick, but I'm sure that was it. Oh, Richard, it's so exciting! And yet I'm so frightened, because you're not here and I haven't heard anything and I hope you're all right."

She smiled and opened her eyes. Then she lifted the lid of the box and peered inside at the bundle of letters tied up in a ribbon.

"Your darling Richard survived," Karin said into the box. "Soon we'll know if he'll think it was worth it."

She picked up the sea glass again and dropped them to the floor. One-two, three-four.

Lisa wanted to talk to Ginny, mother-and-daughter, just the two of them. That had been apparent when Lisa said she wanted to make like a tourist and get away, away from the confines of the inn, away from Jess and Phillip and Jess's problems trying to find her daughter—the things that were keeping Ginny sane right now, were deflecting the pain from the fact that rotten son of a bitch Brad had told Lisa what she had done.

She hadn't wanted to come, but Lisa had mentioned it at breakfast and Dick had overheard and quickly produced a map just like the one Ginny had stolen off the table the other day but had to pretend she'd never seen.

"It's the island's biggest attraction," Dick had said. "Not to mention the purple and blue and pink shacks where the Indians sell their souvenirs."

So here they were, driving on a winding, narrow road where the trees on the sides were old and arthritic-looking and arched their gnarly limbs across the pavement, creating a leafy-green tunnel that was supposedly aimed toward a place called Gay Head that seemed to take as long to get to as Boston. Other than saying things like "Gee, isn't this pretty" and "Wow, it seems so remote," Lisa didn't have much to say after all.

Finally, the trees began to thin, the road began to straighten, and they could see water off to the left.

"Look," Lisa said, pointing ahead, "a lighthouse."

It was brick and it was ancient and it was just a lighthouse stuck up on a cliff. Nothing spectacular. Not worth the trip.

But Ginny said, "Yeah, wow," to keep Lisa happy. Then she drove up the hill and spotted the purple and blue and pink shacks that were littered with hand-painted signs that read *T-Shirts,* and *Jewelry,* and *Lobster Rolls,* and pulled into a parking space behind two giant tourist buses with Pennsylvania plates that must have been stuffed onto the ferry the way she now was into her jeans. All things considered, she was glad she had flown.

They got out of the car and climbed the hill along with the streams of camera-clad, T-shirted tourists. By the time they reached the top, Ginny was puffing and wishing she hadn't taken Dick Bradley's advice.

"Oh, wow," Lisa said, looking off to the right. "This is incredible."

Ginny stopped long enough to catch her breath and follow Lisa's gaze to the rust-colored cliffs that looked as if they'd been finger-painted with browns and coppers and hints of gold. She wondered if the Indians had done it as part of their masterful art of drumming up tourist dollars.

"Look!" Lisa exclaimed, like a ten-year-old kid. "A telescope! Do you have a quarter?" Ginny dug one from the bottom of her purse and handed it to her daughter, who darted toward a pole that had an instrument on top with two black eyeholes and looked more like the head of an alien than a telescope.

With an audible sigh, Ginny crossed the fenced landing and stood next to Lisa.

"Those are the Elizabeth Islands," Lisa said, her eyes fixed through the alien eyes, her finger pointing past the cliffs and over the water to a few dots of green on the horizon.

"That's nice," Ginny said. What else were you supposed to say? Until Jake, most of her sight-seeing had consisted of oohing and ahhing in dimly lit bars. She pulled a roll of Life Savers from the pocket of her denim shirt, popped two in her mouth, and brushed her windblown hair from her face. "Why did you really want to come up here, Lisa?"

"To see the cliffs." The hum of the contraption stopped, and a *click* told Ginny that Lisa's quarter had run out. Lisa stepped back. "I want to pay him off," she said, still looking out over the water.

"What?"

"I have enough money saved to pay Brad half of what he's asking. If you can come up with the other half, he'll leave us alone." She folded her arms against her waist.

"Over my dead body," Ginny replied. "To begin with, you've worked hard for that money. I won't have you using it for something that was my fault."

"Look, Ginny, I'm as much at fault as you are. I didn't tell you when I started seeing Brad because I knew you'd be upset."

Ginny couldn't argue with that. But Lisa was her daughter. Surely the parent should be more responsible than the child. She stared off toward those lumps called the Elizabeth Islands and wished with everything she had that Jake were there. Jake would have known what to say. Jake would have known what to do.

"I want to pay him, Ginny. I want this over with."

Her gaze dropped to the water, to the waves that broke and splayed their foam over the rocks below. "With people like Brad, it's never over," she said. "He uses sex as a power play to fulfill his greed."

A pair of seagulls glided across the sky.

"The sex was good," Lisa said quietly.

"With men like Brad it always is." She did not mention that a man like Brad, or any other man, would probably never be able to make sex good for Ginny again. She did not mention that her once unstoppable lust seemed to have been buried with Jake.

"Sex always gets in the way, doesn't it? It screws people up, wrecks friendships, and destroys families."

Ginny looked back to the horizon. "Yes," she replied. "Which is why I hate it."

Lisa nodded. "Me, too. Let's make a pact never to have sex again."

Ginny put her arm through her daughter's. "You're too young to say that. As for me, well, I have no interest in it anymore."

"Because of what happened with Brad?"

"No," she admitted. "Because Jake is gone."

They stood on the cliff for a long, long time, Ginny's arm locked through Lisa's, watching together the sun glinting off the copper cliffs and reflecting in the water below.

It was taking Jess longer to walk there than she'd expected. She had threaded her way through the side streets of Vineyard Haven: up Centre Street, crossing William, Franklin, and others, wondering all the way why she was doing this and what she planned to achieve.

"I just want to see her," she told herself over and over. "I just want one look at her in case I never have a chance to see her again."

She did not, however, know how she'd recognize Melanie. Part of her believed she'd know her on sight; that a mother would instinctively know the child to whom she'd given birth, by the way she walked, the way she sounded, the way she held her head.

The other part of her told herself she was nuts. If she didn't know Maura, would Jess instantly recognize her as her daughter?

The backs of her calves ached as she continued her climb. She tried not to think about Maura now. She tried not to wonder if Melanie would perhaps resemble Maura rather than herself, and, if she, like Maura, would think the past didn't matter and that Jess should get on with her life.

She kept walking. The huge old homes gave way to a newer, more middle-class neighborhood—small Cape Cod–style houses shingled in gray with white picket fences and narrow driveways made of bits of ground clam shells. The trees were more abundant: maples and oaks shaded the streets with their new spring green leaves. It was quieter here than in the center of town, quieter, and devoid of the scent of salt water, the dampness of the sea, and the claustrophobic crush of the tourists.

And then Jess heard laughter; the muted, high-pitched laughter of children at play. She looked up and saw it: the Tisbury Elementary School, an old brick building with tall windows and high concrete stairs, next to which was a large playground where shiny-haired, pink-cheeked children scrambled on jungle gyms and chased one another, some singing, some shouting, and all appearing to have fun.

Recess, Jess thought, standing still on the sidewalk, her memory drifting to the many times she had watched Chuck, Maura, and Travis at play with their friends. But none of these children were Chuck, Maura, or Travis: they were the children of strangers, island children. Scanning the happy, laughing faces, Jess wondered if this was the school where Melanie had come, if this was where she'd learned to read and write and laugh on the playground.

"Miss Gorman's class, line up for the cafeteria," came a

tinny voice from the end of a megaphone. "Line, up, line up, line up," the voice commanded.

Little feet scampered to the side of the building where a dark-haired woman in a long peasant dress—Miss Gorman, Jess presumed—began organizing her charges with a stern look and a lot of finger-pointing. Jess was glad that Miss Gorman was not Melanie: she would not have been pleased to have a daughter who'd turned into a sergeant.

Her eyes scanned the playground once more, searching the small children and grown-up monitors who stood nearby with watchful eyes. Among the half-dozen adults— five women, one man—no one resembled Maura, no one resembled Jess. There was a fat one, a tall one, and three in between, but none with wispy blond hair, none that made her instincts converge in her heart to whisper "This is her. She is Melanie. She is yours."

Just then one of the big metal doors on the building opened, and another band of children flooded onto the playground. Jess put her hand to her throat and strained to see, strained to pick out anyone who might be part of her.

And then she saw her.

She was a tiny little blond girl, so tiny that the crutches she awkwardly maneuvered seemed especially cumbersome, and the long white cast that encased her right leg seemed especially heavy.

"Sarah," Jess whispered into the air. She twisted the ring on her finger and tried to swallow past the rising lump in her throat, the lump that told her that Sarah, was, indeed, part of her, the lump that said she was her first grandchild, born to her first daughter.

She stepped toward the fence and clung to the metal. "My God," she said. "What a precious little child."

Slowly, Jess moved along the fence to get closer to Sarah. If she could hear her laughter, if she could see her eyes, she would not need anything more. She would not need to know Melanie, she would not need to hurt Richard, or interrupt their lives. She would not need to know who had sent the letter. She would need none of these things. If only she could get close enough to know for certain.

"Mommy!" The little girl's voice was so sudden, her word so startling, it took Jess a moment to realize it was not meant for her. She blinked, then pulled her eyes from Sarah and followed her gaze to the door of the building where a young woman stood, arms folded across her thin middle, long blond hair tied back in a neat ponytail.

"Honey," the young woman responded and hurried onto the playground toward the little girl with the crutches.

Jess watched in silence, certain her heart had stopped beating, certain she would never be able to move from this place again.

And then the little girl's mother was close enough for Jess to reach through the fencing and touch her shoulder, close enough for her to feel the warmth of her breath.

"How are you doing, honey?" the young woman asked.

"Okay. My armpits hurt."

The young woman bent down and gave the little girl a hug. Jess felt as if it were her arms around the child, felt as if it were her hands that were running through the wispy, light hair.

"The substitute teacher is here so we'll go home after lunch," the young woman whispered. "There's pizza today."

"I'm not real hungry."

The young woman kept her arm around the little girl. "Well, you don't have to eat, honey. But the doctor said you need naps this week. Maybe after your nap we'll bake cookies. Would you like that?"

"Chocolate chip?"

"If you want. And maybe we'll make some sugar cookies, too, and decorate them for Daddy."

"How will we decorate them?"

"Hmm. Let's see. Well, we could write 'Daddy' on one."

"On a big one?"

"Of course! And we can make another big one, just for you, and we'll make some pink frosting and write 'Sarah' across it."

Jess thought she was going to faint. She held fast to the fence to keep herself steady, to keep herself from sliding down to the ground. "My God," she wanted to shout. "My God, it is you! My baby, my daughter! It really is you!" But she held on tightly, afraid to let go, afraid to faint, or to fall, or afraid she might run though her feet seemed to be stuck to the sidewalk, her body unable to move.

"Do you want me to carry you into the cafeteria?" Melanie asked.

"I'm too big to be carried," the little girl replied. "I'm five, you know." She placed her crutches under her arms and limped toward the building, her mother guiding her with one gentle hand placed on her back.

Chapter 18

He was having an invigorating run this morning to clear the fog from his brain and help him plan his strategy for Jess. The man at the front desk of the Tisbury Inn had suggested he head toward West Chop where the hills weren't as "challenging," and where he could see the water from time to time through the trees.

As he passed a place called Owen Park, Phillip, indeed, could see the water off to the right, down a steep hill, to a harbor filled with boats whose masts looked like matchsticks lined up with precision against the blue, cloudless sky. It was so tranquil it had almost taken his mind off Nicole. It was so peaceful it had almost reminded him that there were other women in the world besides selfish, intense law students. Women like Lisa Andrews, as if she'd ever look at him twice.

He turned his head back to the road and picked up his pace, wondering what his mother would think of Lisa, and if Lisa would be comfortable at Jeanine Archambault's dining room table. Then he thought about Joseph—was Lisa the type of woman his brother would consider "sensible" for a Manhattan attorney who had recently moved uptown?

Uptown, he mused with a groan. Where the days were

filled with meetings and dinners and racquetball games, all
for the sake of a career. Inhaling the cool salt air, Phillip
wondered why every day couldn't be more like today, and
why life couldn't be as simple as it was here on the island.

Not that it was simple for Jess. Not that it could have
been simple for a family that had changed their name and
fled here, a family with a secret.

He kept his stride even as he jogged past the small library
and continued along Main Street, away from the center of
town, away from the houses that were set too close together
with little space left for yards. As he ran, he began to re-
hearse what to say to Mr. Bradley.

He thought he would begin, "I am an attorney retained
by Mrs. Randall," since the word "attorney" could still
evoke a hint of intimidation in some men and most
women. "I am investigating the criminal misconduct of a
Dr. William Larribee, and I have reason to believe you are
involved."

He wiped the sweat from his brow and smiled. "Criminal" was another intimidation-inducing word.

While Bradley was squirming, Phillip would pounce.
"My client has knowledge of a certain sum of two hundred
thousand dollars paid to you by her father in 1968," he
would say, careful not to mention the note for the fifty
thousand in Miss Taylor's things or the menacing letter and
call Jess had received. Those, after all, could be tied to the
Bradleys only through mere speculation, and it was too
early for Phillip to reveal all the cards in his very screwed-
up deck. "We believe there is a connection with Dr. Larribee's misconduct," he would continue, "and we believe
you were involved."

Brilliant, he thought, as he kept running. *Worthy of a
standing ovation at the Brief Room,* the beer-scented pub
where he'd spent too many hours as an eager law student.

He rehearsed his lines, deciding which gestures to use,
how he could come across firm and believable, authorita-
tive and . . . well, yes, intimidating. His brother would be

better at this, but Joseph wasn't here. Thank God, Joseph wasn't here to see what he was doing away from the firm.

He wondered if he would ever tell his mother about meeting the woman who had given birth to him. He envied Lisa her relationship with Ginny. She still had both her mothers, and they even conversed from opposite coasts. Maybe if P.J. had lived, he would have told Jeanine about her and they might have met. But P.J. had died, and there hadn't been any reason to tell Jeanine.

A few moments later, Phillip passed a small cemetery with centuries-old markers bearing names that were faded and worn. He felt a brief tug at his now-empty heart, a tug for P.J., the woman who had given him life.

Sweat trickled down his face—or was it tears? Phillip shook his head and again stepped up his pace.

The houses were getting bigger now. Off to the left was a thickly wooded area, with a crudely made sign reading, *West Chop Woods*. It looked like a fun place to explore, a place he might have brought Nicole if only she had come. He wondered if they would have made love in the woods, or if she would have preferred the dunes or the beach . . . then he wondered why he was thinking of her. She was out of his life. "They come, they go," he had said to Jess, though he'd hated it that it was so true.

He straightened his back and kept running, trying to force his thoughts back to Mr. Bradley, to the Perry Mason moment Phillip was going to orchestrate as soon as Jess gave him the go-ahead, as soon as Jess was ready to find out the truth, no matter what the cost.

He was heading into an area dense with tall pines, where huge homes stood off to the right—houses with magnificent vantage points overlooking the water, picture-postcard scenes to send to loved ones back home, if the loved ones knew you were there and you had nothing to hide. As he rounded the bend, Phillip spotted a tall flagpole and two park benches. Just as he was about to run by, he looked down onto the beach and saw a woman, the woman from last night. This time she padded along the sand in bare feet, a lonely-looking woman draped in a long skirt. Richard's sister. Karin.

I think she knows why we're here, Jess had said. *I think she's the one who summoned me.*

Phillip hesitated a moment, then thought, *What the hell.* It was a free country and it was a free beach.

He saw an opening in the dunes and jogged down a path toward the water.

"Good morning," he called out to the woman named Karin. "Beautiful morning."

She dropped something she had held in her hand. She looked up at him quickly and shielded her face against the sun.

"Brit?" she asked.

"No," Phillip replied, walking now, approaching her. "I'm Phillip."

He reached her and she stared at him. A veil of distance crossed over her eyes. "You're not Brit."

"No. My name is Phillip."

She turned her back and sifted sand through her toes. "Go away."

"Hey," he said, trying to sound gentle, "I'm sorry I'm not Brit. But it's still a beautiful morning, isn't it?"

Her back went rigid. Suddenly she snapped around. "Why don't you just do it and get it over with?" she hissed.

The venom in her eyes made him back off. He turned and walked away. So much for the brilliant, intimidating attorney and his standing ovation.

"I know who you are," she shouted after him.

Phillip stopped in the sand. He did not turn around.

"I know who you all are. But what's taking so long? There's no one left to protect, you know. No one at all."

He stood numb for a moment, then slowly he turned. But her figure was disappearing down the beach, her loose skirt flowing after her from the breeze that wafted off the water.

• • •

By the time he got back to Vineyard Haven, Phillip was tired and his brain was worn out. All the way back he had tried to sort Karin's words in his mind, tried to make sense of them, and tried to decide whether or not he should tell Jess. He also tried to figure out who the hell Brit was, but he had no idea.

Obviously, Jess had been right, and he had been wrong. Karin was the one who had sent the letter postmarked Vineyard Haven; the one who had made the call. That part was clear now. But he had no idea why. Other than she seemed a little bit crazy.

As he trotted down Main Street, he spotted Jess sitting on a bench on a grassy slope that rolled from the sidewalk down to the water. She was staring out at the boats that stood in the harbor.

"Jess," he called, slowing his pace until he reached her.

She had a smile for him, but it looked disconnected. "I tried your hotel," she said. "The man at the desk said you'd gone running."

"Yeah," Phillip replied, swiping his brow, "it's my addiction. Not much time for it in Manhattan."

"Or places to do it, I'd expect."

He started to sit next to her, but he was so sweaty, he decided against it. "If you want to wait here, I'll go grab a shower and we can get some lunch."

"Maybe," Jess said, "but I'm not terribly hungry."

He leaned against the bench. "You weren't hungry last night, either."

She smiled. "I know." That's when he noticed the red lines in her eyes and the fact that her eyelids were pink and swollen, as if she'd been crying a very long time. She turned her face back to the water. "I saw her," she said.

"Saw who?"

"Melanie. My daughter."

He pulled up one knee and rested his foot on the bench. "Jess, we still aren't sure . . ."

"She's my daughter, all right. And I saw my granddaughter, too. Sarah." Her words sounded like whispers as they floated in the air.

"Oh, God," Phillip said and sat down. "What happened?"

She told him. Between brave tears, she told him of the school. Of Melanie. Of the little girl with her leg in a cast. Phillip wanted to put his arm around her, to comfort her. But he was so sweaty it didn't seem right.

"I want to go home," Jess said suddenly. "I know what I needed to know. And now I want to go home."

"But we don't know for sure . . ."

"*I* know. In my heart, I know. That's all that matters. I've been sitting here thinking for over an hour. And that's what I've decided. I want to go home."

He looked into her eyes, pale and tired. She looked like she must have looked when she was a child, a little girl herself, tiny and in need. "Jess, what about Melanie? What about her right to know the truth?"

Jess swung her feet under the bench. "She's with her family," Jess said. "That should be enough."

"It wasn't enough for me," Phillip said. "I always wanted to know my real mother." Then he stood up. "I'm going to go take my shower."

Jess nodded. "And if you don't mind, I'm going to pass on lunch. I want to go back to Mayfield House and check on the ferry availabilities. Thank you for all you've done for me, Phillip. But the sooner I get off this island, the better."

"I'll come up there when I'm done," he said. "Promise you won't go anywhere until then?"

She smiled again. "I promise."

He couldn't believe Jess wanted to leave. After thirty years of wondering, she had at last found her daughter. He couldn't believe she didn't want to meet her, talk to her, find out if she was happy, and learn what had happened.

Not that they needed Sherlock Holmes to solve the island mystery.

He changed into a pair of jeans he had bought first thing this morning and a green Black Dog T-shirt. If he ran into Ginny, she could not make any more comments about his looking like a "suit."

He stood before the mirror, combing his hair, taming his cowlick, just as the telephone rang. *Jess,* he thought and moved between the twin beds to answer it.

"Phillip?" the voice asked, a voice deeper that Jess's, yet very much female.

"Yes?"

"It's Lisa, Phillip."

Lisa? He ran his hand through his freshly combed hair. "Hi," he said, stupidly.

"I left Ginny with Jess," she said. "But I hate eating alone. Have you had lunch?"

Lunch? With Lisa Andrews? "No. Not yet."

"I'm downstairs. I can get us a table at the sidewalk café."

"Sounds great," he said. "I'll be right down." He hung up the phone and felt himself begin to sweat all over again. He walked back to the mirror and stared at his cowlick. "You are such a geek," he said. "All she wants is someone to have lunch with. Nothing more." But as he tucked his wallet in his jeans, he left the room smiling, happy that at least Lisa Andrews had remembered his name.

"She couldn't get ferry reservations until tomorrow night," Lisa explained once Phillip had settled on the white metal folding chair out on the sidewalk.

He toyed with the straw in his glass of iced tea. "I'm glad," he said. "I'd like to see Jess give this a little more thought."

The waiter arrived with a salad for Lisa, a roast beef sandwich for Phillip. After he had gone, Phillip looked at her, trying to discreetly study her creamy complexion, wishing that she would look at him with those gorgeous topaz eyes. "Before you met Ginny," he asked, "did you ever wonder about her? Who she was? What she looked like?"

"Sure," Lisa said, and her eyes met his.

He took a huge bite of his sandwich and forced himself not to blush.

"My parents are nice people," Lisa continued. "Good people. But I always wondered where I came from, you know? I used to pretend I was a princess and that someday the queen would return for me and wisk me off to the castle where it was surrounded by green fields and big trees and horses and knights and didn't look a thing like New Jersey."

Phillip laughed so hard he nearly choked. "No wonder you're an actress," he said, regaining his composure.

Lisa smiled. "Yeah, well, I get that from Ginny. What about you? Did you always wonder?"

"Sometimes. I remember watching my brother, and I knew he and I were so different. He was so . . . straight-laced. I liked to be around people. I liked to paint. My birth mother was an artist, did you know that?"

Lisa shook her head. "I know that she died. I'm so sorry."

"Yeah, me too. At least I got to know her, though."

They ate in silence for a few moments.

"It's strange, isn't it? We probably were in bassinets next to one another," Phillip said.

"I thought you looked familiar," Lisa said with a smile.

Phillip returned the smile and took another bite. This time he did not look away.

"You have incredible green eyes," Lisa said.

"From my mother," he answered.

"I feel bad for Melanie," Lisa went on. "I mean, if she really is Jess's daughter, I bet she'd want to know."

"I wanted to confront Mr. Bradley. But Jess doesn't want me to."

"What about Melanie?"

"What about her?"

"Maybe we should confront her. Maybe if the two of us went, she'd be more responsive."

"What if she doesn't know she was adopted?"

"Maybe it's time she was told."

Phillip chewed slowly and considered Lisa's idea. Jess would probably be appalled. And he couldn't be certain, but such action seemed a lot like a breach of attorney-client privilege. But Lisa seemed determined. And he had to admit it would be nice to spend more time with her. Maybe there was a way he could come up with the right words to talk to Melanie—words that would not breach Jess's confidence. Maybe he could do it without being direct, and at least learn if she knew that the man who posed as her brother was really her father, and the man she called "Dad" was really her grandfather. If any of it were true. Maybe he could do it. If he were half the lawyer he pretended to be to himself.

"We could go to the school," he said to Lisa now. "Jess saw her there."

"Oh, yes!" Lisa exclaimed. "Let's go tomorrow, before Jess can leave."

She returned to her salad, and he to his sandwich, his thoughts spinning with what the right words to say to Melanie would be, and how he could prove to Lisa Andrews that he was a brilliant attorney, after all. He wondered if she would give him a standing ovation.

Ginny sat on the wide veranda at Mayfield House next to Dick Bradley, and tried to ignore Morticia, who kept swishing past them, cruising the front lawn as if she were the grass inspector checking for slugs. Jess had said she wanted to lie down; Lisa had gone into town, and there was nothing better to do. She decided she might as well spend a few minutes with the old man. Maybe she could dig up some more of her old man-enticing wiles and pry some information out of him about this kid called Melanie. Maybe Jess no longer cared, but she did. She'd always hated a script where the plot had no real ending.

"So you won't be leaving today after all," Dick said, tapping a copy of the *Vineyard Gazette* on his knee.

"There was room on the ferry for people, but no cars," she replied.

"Hmph. Damn ferry. They changed their reservation system last year and have the tourists all in an uproar."

"I don't care about the ferry. I'm flying."

"Do you have a flight yet?"

"No."

"Well, don't think that's going to be any easier."

"Christ, can't they decide if they want tourists here or not?"

Dick laughed and picked up a plate that sat beside him on the floor. It was layered with cookies—big, round, gooey-looking cookies. "Have one," he said. "Millie Johnson made them this morning."

"Millie Johnson? Isn't she the one who made the clam chowder at the picnic?"

"The very same."

"Don't tell me," Ginny said. "She's a widow lady with designs on you."

Dick laughed. "Hardly! She's a married woman whose husband got laid off and she cooks homemade soup for a couple of restaurants and sells her cookies all over town."

Ginny laughed in return.

"Besides," he said, "who'd want an old man like me?"

"You're not so old."

"I'm a grandfather! And I'll be seventy next year."

"So you're sixty-nine. My last husband wasn't much younger than that."

"What happened to him?"

Ginny picked up a cookie and tried not to smile. "He dropped dead," she said. There was silence for a moment, then both of them laughed.

"See?" Dick said. "Who'd want an old man like me?"

Ginny decided not to tell him that Jake, the old man, had been the best thing in her life, that he had plenty of life left in him himself and would still have if he hadn't dropped dead. She decided not to tell him because she decided he wouldn't understand. Instead, she thought about her mission. She tucked her swollen feet under her on the newly painted Adirondack chair and tried to look fascinated by his every move. *Flirting,* she thought, *is so much easier when you're young. And thin.* "You're not so old," she said. "Besides, didn't you say you have a daughter who's only twenty-nine?"

Out on the lawn, Morticia stopped strutting. She moved to the stairs and came up on the veranda.

Dick nodded. "Late-in-life baby for my wife, God rest her soul."

"Not so late today," Ginny said, ignoring Morticia. "Lots of women are having babies in their forties."

Dick shifted on his chair, obviously uncomfortable with the conversation. His eyes darted to his daughter, then back to Ginny. "My wife was dead by the time she was forty-five," he said.

So, Ginny thought. His kids had been young. She cast a quick glance at the woman who had probably raised Jess's baby . . . maybe as if she were her own. Was this the motivation behind it all? Was she pissed because she'd had to raise a kid she'd somehow just learned was really Jess and Richard's?

"Thank God for my kids," Dick continued. "After my wife died, they kept me going."

"And this inn," Ginny said. "I'm sure this was quite a burden."

"Oh, we didn't own it then. I just worked for old Mrs. Adams. She left it to me when she died."

So it was true. The two hundred thousand had not bought Mayfield House. But it had helped pay to get Melanie from greedy Miss Taylor. With a little help from Dr. Larribee. And probably that sleazeball Bud Wilson.

"We all worked for the old biddy," Morticia spoke up. "She left it to all of us."

"Right," Dick added. "Well, Karin here is the only one who still cares about it. Melanie and Richard both have their careers. . . ." His eyes drifted from the porch onto the lawn. He tapped the paper again. "He comes back tomorrow," he suddenly said. "I need to remember to have him help me with the gutters."

"What did you say?" Ginny asked.

"I said my son Richard is coming back tomorrow. He's been up in Boston. . . ."

"Oh, shit," Ginny said, standing up quickly. "That reminds me, I'd better check with the airlines about a flight back to L.A." There would be plenty of time to flirt with the old guy later, if it wound up to be necessary at all.

She quickly left the veranda and raced up the stairs to room number seven, looking for Jess.

Chapter 19

"What's the damn difference?" Ginny asked Jess. "We have to stay until tomorrow anyway. Even if Melanie doesn't know, even if you decide you don't want her to know, at least you'll find out the truth once and for all."

Jess rolled from her back onto her side and faced Ginny. She wondered why everything was always so clear-cut to her friend, as though she had been spared any pain in her life. "I thought you'd understand," she said quietly. "It hurts too much, Ginny. I am going to be grateful for all I have and not interfere in anyone else's life."

"You didn't feel that way five years ago when you wanted the reunion."

She closed her eyes. "Maybe I have finally learned something from that. Susan's son never wanted to meet her; Phillip got to meet P.J. only to have her die; and of the four of us, you . . . well, you're the only one who had a happy ending. Maybe I've decided that twenty-five percent of happiness is not worth seventy-five percent pain."

"You're an asshole," Ginny said.

"Yes, well, perhaps I am."

For a moment, Ginny said nothing. Jess opened her eyes

to see if she was still in the room. She was. She was standing by the window, looking down on the lawn.

"So because you're too damn sensitive," Ginny said, "you're going to let Morticia win."

"Stop calling her that, Ginny. Her name is Karin."

"Karin, Schmarin. Is that what's scaring you into leaving?"

"Karin has nothing to do with it. She's not scaring me at all. It's obvious she sent the letter and left me that message, but she hasn't done or said anything since we've been here."

"Well, I think she's a fruitcake."

"And I think what she is, is a lonely, troubled woman."

"Collecting that pathetic sea glass," Ginny continued. "Doesn't it bother you to think that she's the one who ended up raising Melanie when Dick's wife kicked the bucket? Doesn't it bother you that she's had such an influence over your kid's life?"

"Melanie seems fine, Ginny. She has a lovely daughter and a respectable job. If Karin raised her, maybe she didn't do such a bad job."

"Bullshit. She's a fruitcake. How come she never got married?"

"Maybe she was too busy taking care of my daughter."

"Well, why the big turnaround? Why is she blowing the whistle on her family now?"

Jess rolled back onto her back and stared at the canopy. "Oh, God, Ginny, I don't know. I'm only sorry I ever started this again."

Ginny walked back to the bed and sat on the edge. "You're forgetting one thing, Jess."

She closed her eyes again. "What?"

"You didn't start it."

"I could have ignored the letter and the call."

"What about Richard? Can you ignore him?"

Richard. The pain crept in around the corners of her eyes. An image of Melanie and Sarah on the playground came into her mind. A picture of young Richard—young, seventeen-year-old Richard—followed.

"Maybe you're afraid to see him," Ginny continued. "Maybe you're afraid you'll spit in his eyes, not that he wouldn't deserve it. You say you've learned a lot about pain, Jess. Well, I don't think you've even begun to learn it. You can't learn about pain until you feel it. Until, down to your bones, you feel it."

"I think I've felt quite enough in my lifetime."

"That's what I thought, too. Until Jake dropped dead." She paused a moment, her voice cracking a little. "Use Maura as an excuse if you want, but at least try to be honest with yourself."

Jess sighed and looked at her friend. Maybe Ginny was right. Maybe she was simply afraid of feeling any more pain.

"If you don't face this now, kid, you'll always wonder," Ginny said, then rose from the bed. "And I think you'll regret it for the rest of your life. But it's up to you. I'm going to take a walk downtown, buy some tacky souvenirs, and try to think of a way to convince my daughter not to give that scumbag stepson of mine a rotten cent." She headed for the door, then turned back. "Think about what I said, Jess. Life has no guarantees against pain. But as long as we're here, kid, we might as well grab whatever happiness we can."

What she needed to do was call Maura. Jess had not checked on the kids since she'd come to the Vineyard; it would be perfectly normal for her to call, say hello, and make sure they were okay. Her daughter would not think it strange. Her daughter would not read into the call that Jess was trying to ground herself once again, that she was trying to reassure herself that her life was fine without another daughter, and that anything else would simply be more complications—complications she and her family did not need. Hearing Maura's voice would do that for her.

First, however, she placed a call to her shop, where Carlo told her everything was fine, to enjoy herself, not to hurry back.

Then she hung up and dialed again.

Travis answered the phone.

"Hi, honey," Jess said, then a quick churn of her stomach reminded her that was how Melanie had addressed Sarah. *Hi, honey,* was what she had said to the sweet little girl with her leg in a cast. "It's Mom."

"Hey, Mom. What's happening? You having a good time?"

"Yes, dear. Martha's Vineyard is lovely. How are you doing? How's Maura?"

"We're okay. I've been working my tail off. I don't think I'll be a landscaper in my next career. Too hard."

Jess laughed. "You've never been afraid of a little hard work." Of all her children, Travis was the one who did not take their financial comfort for granted.

"I never had to rake bark chips before. When are you coming home?"

She tugged at the phone cord. "I'm not sure yet."

"Well, no rush on this end. Maura's not here half the time, and I'm teaching myself to cook."

An imaginary picture of a teenage-boy-ravaged kitchen flashed into her mind. "Cook?" she asked, trying not to sound too alarmed. "What are you cooking?"

"Chicken."

"Make sure you wash it well."

He groaned. "Don't let my freckles fool you. I'm not exactly an imbecile."

She laughed then asked, "What about Maura? Is she there?"

"I don't know. Let me check."

Before she could tell him to stop, never mind, he covered the receiver and shouted, "Hey, Maura! Mom's on the phone!" She took a deep breath and waited, hoping her voice would not betray what was really going on in her heart, that she really needed to talk to Maura, to remind herself of what was important in life.

"Maura!" Travis shouted again. Seconds passed. She must not be home. A wave of anxiety passed through Jess for needing her daughter too much. Then she heard a click on the line.

"Mom?" It was Maura.

Jess sat up straight. "Yes, honey. I just called to say hi."

"Where are you?"

Her eyes danced around the room as if she'd forgotten where she was. "I'm still here," she said quickly. "On Martha's Vineyard."

"Oh. Is your friend still there?"

"Ginny? Yes. We're having a good time."

"Oh." There was silence a moment. "Mom, what are you doing there?"

"I told you. Ginny recently lost her husband. I'm trying to help her . . ."

"Did you find your baby?" Her tone was sharp-edged as a razor.

Reality collided with fantasy again. Maura and Travis might be grounding for Jess, but they were not—could not be—her whole life. Sometimes, like now, Jess had feelings of her own. Feelings that she needed to address or that would haunt her forever.

"I figured out what you're doing, Mom," Maura continued. "Some lady named Loretta Taylor called yesterday. She wanted you to know she found out for sure that Mabel Adams was dead."

"Yes," Jess replied slowly, "I knew that."

"She mentioned the Vineyard. I told her you were there. She said you must have found your baby. Then she hung up."

Jess did not, could not, reply.

"Mom, I thought you were going to stop all this stuff."

"Honey . . ."

"It's not fair, you know. Not to me. Not to Travis."

Jess noted that Maura had not mentioned Chuck, as though her older brother were no longer a part of the family, just because he lived in Manhattan and was close to their father. Apparently, Maura's week in the islands had done little to reglue the bond between father and daughter after all.

"Honey, I'm not asking you to understand," Jess said. "Any more than you asked me to understand when you went on spring break with your father." She felt guilty for the silence that once again draped over the line. "I need to do this for myself, Maura. Please accept that. And please accept that it has nothing to do with you."

After a moment, Maura said, "I only wish you had been honest with us in the beginning. About the real reason for your trip."

"How would you have reacted?"

"I would have told you I hated what you were doing."

The veins in her head constricted more tightly. "And I would have tried to explain that we are all entitled to have some privacy, and some respect for our feelings," she said. "Perhaps you haven't learned that in one of your psychology classes yet."

"Okay, Mom," Maura replied brusquely. "I get the message."

Jess cleared her throat. "Well, then, I'll see you when I come home. We'll talk then, okay?"

After a heartbeat, Maura replied, "Sure, Mom. See you." She hung up the phone and left Jess sitting on the edge of the bed, receiver in hand, wondering if things could ever be the same between them again, yet filled with resolve that Ginny was right. Life had no guarantees against pain. And if Jess didn't get this over with once and for all, she would regret it for the rest of her life. She would stop acting so childish and she would go and meet Richard, and Maura would get over it or Maura would not.

• • •

Ginny bought a hand-knit sweater for Consuelo, a gold charm for Lisa—the map of Martha's Vineyard with a small diamond chip—and a tie-dyed, short dress for herself. The dress was a "trapeze," the politically correct nineties term for a "tent," that actually looked good on her, skating over her newly-formed lumps and bumps as if they weren't there at all. Not that she cared much how she looked, since—for once in her life—she wasn't looking for sex. But she had to admit the brief flirtation with Dick Bradley had set off *something*—nothing scintillating, maybe, but something that, well, that felt good. He had a generous smile and a warm laugh, and, what the hell, if Jess decided to stay another day or two, Ginny might as well take advantage of the opportunity to see if her libido would ever return. And maybe she could get him to tell her the truth about Melanie, about what really happened thirty years ago. After all, she thought, leaving the dress shop, men say things in the bedroom that they'd never say in the parlor—especially if the parlor was loaded with clocks ticking and tocking all over the place, reminding the male species that time was, indeed, marching on and their heart might give out before the top of the next hour.

As she headed for the bookstore—*Bunch of Grapes,* the sign read, which seemed fairly absurd for the name of a store on an island called the Vineyard in a town where no alcohol was allowed—she thought she heard her name being called from across the street. She looked over and there stood Phillip on the curb, waving his arm like he was hailing a cab.

"Ginny!" he shouted across the traffic-clogged one-way street. "Lisa's here. Come on over."

She didn't bother to go to the crosswalk. A guy in a pickup truck blasted his horn, but Ginny refrained from giving him the finger. She might have, if Lisa had not been within eyeshot. Lisa had learned enough about Ginny's character flaws in the past few days to last a lifetime and a half.

"So what's going on?" Phillip asked, pulling a folding chair out for Ginny to sit at their table. "Is everyone staying until tomorrow?"

Ginny dropped her bundles and plopped herself down on the chair, which wiggled and wobbled on the uneven bricks. "We don't have much choice. But I don't know what Jess intends to do. Old Man Bradley told me Richard is coming back tomorrow. I don't know if she's going to see him or not."

"Not see him?" Lisa asked. "Why would she not see him after all this?"

Ginny shrugged as a waitress appeared. "I'll have a burger and fries," she said, then looked down at her bags and thought about the tie-dyed trapeze that lay inside. "No, change that. I'll have a salad. With oil and vinegar on the side." She might not drop the twenty pounds that she'd gained since Jake died in one afternoon, but she damn well might feel more like flirting if she weren't such a water-retaining blob.

The waitress left. Ginny reached into her bag, pulled out a small box, and set it down beside Lisa's plate. "For you," Ginny said. "Happy Memorial Day."

Lisa's eyes lit up. She'd probably looked just like that when she was a kid, Ginny thought, at Christmas or on her birthday. Lisa's family had probably been big on presents, not like Ginny's mother, who'd never been able to afford much besides cigarettes and booze, though during the holidays they were packaged to look like they were tied in red bows.

Lifting the lid slowly, Lisa peeked inside. She took out the gold charm. "Oh, Ginny," she exclaimed, leaning over and kissing her cheek. "It's beautiful. Thank you."

Ginny shrugged. "I just wanted you to know . . . well, I'm glad you came." She did not add that what she was really glad about was that Brad was not here, that he was back in L.A.

"I wouldn't have missed it," she said, with a look in her eyes that told Ginny she knew exactly what Ginny had been thinking, and that it was okay. "I wish we could have done something to help Jess, though. She's such a nice woman."

"Well, it ain't over till the fat lady sings," Ginny said with a laugh. "Or until I do whatever it is I decide to do."

"Ginny," Phillip said, "Lisa and I have been thinking that maybe there is something she and I can do."

Ginny raised an eyebrow.

"We thought we could go to Melanie. Maybe if the two of us talked to her . . . we're the same age . . . we were both adopted . . ."

Without hesitation, Ginny shook her head. "I think Jess would shit if you ever did that."

"Why?" Lisa asked. "She walked into our lives and shocked the hell out of us. What's the difference?"

"The difference is . . ." Ginny began, then was distracted by that sensation of being stared at by someone.

Ginny turned her head. And there, on the opposite side of Main Street, stood Morticia. Watching.

"Shit." Ginny got to her feet. "I'm sick of this crap." She began to move just as Phillip jumped up and took hold of her arm.

"No, Ginny, please," he said. "Leave it alone."

"That woman is a freaking fruitcake."

"I know. But she's got some kind of problem. Leave her alone."

"You talked to her?"

"Only by accident. She thought I was someone named Brit. I tried to talk to her, but she blew me off."

Ginny stared at the woman who stared back at her and suddenly realized that despite what had or had not happened thirty years ago, Dick Bradley had had his share of heartache, and his share of pain. But so had Jess. And so had Ginny. And she was sick to death of all this dancing around, all this spying and sneaking and pretending to be who and what they were not. It was time to get on with the show, whether Jess liked it or not. Jess didn't have to confront Richard if she didn't want to, but Ginny for one was going to find out what had happened. And Jess was going to be told the truth. And then Ginny was going to go back to L.A. and have it out with Brad, once and for all. She straightened her back. "If you kids want to talk to Melanie, I won't talk you out of it." She looked down at the bag that held her new dress. "As for me, I've got a plan of my own."

It was long past time. Karin turned away from the trio at the café and started walking down Main Street, heading toward the only place she could ever find peace.

Tomorrow, she told herself over and over again. If they did not do anything by tomorrow, she'd take action herself.

Tomorrow.

Tomorrow.

She fixed her eyes on the ground and kept walking toward West Chop. Maybe today Brit would come back. If he'd never left in the first place, none of this would matter now. For if he had not left she'd have been married by now with kids of her own and it wouldn't have mattered a damn whether or not Daddy or Richard or anyone of them cared about her. It wouldn't matter who Mellie did or did not belong to. None of it would matter because she would have had Brit.

But maybe he would come back today. Maybe he would see her picking sea glass on the beach, the way they had picked it together. Maybe he would find a special stone, just for her. The way he had so long ago. Then she would string them together—no, not for Mellie, but for herself. She'd make a long stranded necklace and a bracelet to match and a crown of sea glass to wear in her hair. She'd wear it on her wedding day—the wedding between the Yank and the Brit that had taken so long to occur.

And she would be as beautiful as the girl in the *New York Times* clipping tucked under the ribbon tied around the letters to the young boy named Richard. She would be as beautiful as that long-ago photo, of that society girl named Jessica Bates Randall . . . the girl they had told her had not wanted her baby, but whose father had paid hers to raise it instead . . . the girl Karin had been led to believe had not wanted her baby, had not wanted Mellie at all.

And Karin had believed them. Until she had found the letters. Until she had sorted out the reality from the lies.

She lifted her gaze toward the clear island sky and felt the familiar ache in her heart that told her Brit would not come back today. Or tomorrow either, in fact.

Ginny and Lisa and Phillip had ganged up on Jess and forced her to go out for dinner with them. "A decent place," Ginny had demanded, "where we can put some much-needed nourishment into that withering body of yours." The truth was, Ginny had wanted to wear her new dress. The truth was, she wanted to look good when they returned to the inn after dinner. She wanted to look good because she was going to go through with her plan—come hell or high water or any other acts of God, if God would be so vindictive as to try to spoil her fun.

Phillip had found a place in Chilmark—the Red Cat, it was called—a funky place where the walls were lined with portraits of jazz greats and the food was gourmet-scrumptious.

But Ginny had been good. She'd stopped herself from cleaning her plate of lobster fra diablo and garlic mashed potatoes; she'd even passed up the chocolate cake with three layers of the fudgiest frosting she'd ever seen. Dick Bradley might be pushing seventy, but he wasn't blind. And if she was going to get him to get it up, she'd have to look—and feel—as sexy as possible. So she opted for decaf while the others pigged out on the cake, which helped boost her confidence, though it seemed to wane now, as she stood at the closed door of Dick Bradley's bedroom.

Shit, she thought. *I'm as nervous as a wedding-night virgin—if there is such a thing anymore.*

She popped a mint into her mouth, lifted her hand, and knocked.

There was no answer.

She looked over her shoulder to be sure Morticia wasn't snooping nearby. Then she sucked in her breath and screwed up her courage again. She knocked more loudly. For a moment, all she could hear was her heart beating.

Then she heard footsteps on the other side of the door.

"Go, girl," she said to herself.

Dick Bradley opened the door. He was wearing a plaid flannel robe that looked as if it had been hastily tied around his middle—a middle that was not too paunchy for a guy his age.

Ginny smiled. "Did I wake you?"

He ran his hand through his already tousled gray hair. "Not really."

Quickly, she placed one foot into the room before he was awake enough to realize she was there, before he came to enough of his senses to realize what she was doing. Or before she did.

"I need to ask you something." She stepped all the way inside now and put one hand on the door. "You don't mind, do you?"

He scowled a little. "Well . . . I guess not. What is it?"

"I was wondering," Ginny said, her voice as low as she could possibly make it, "how long has it been since you've been with a woman?" She closed the door behind her.

He scratched his chin and smiled. "Excuse me?" he asked.

She reached up and placed her hands on his shoulders, then ran them down the front of his chest, slipping her fingers inside the lapels of his robe, feeling the smooth, curly hairs on his skin. "I asked how long it has been since you've been with a woman." The touch of his flesh was warm on her fingers. The softness of his skin was surprising, as was the stir she felt somewhere inside.

"Ginny—" he began to protest.

She shushed him, then rose up on her toes and breathed into his ear. "I've wanted you from the first moment I saw you," she lied, but was uncomfortably aware that it might not be as much of a lie as she needed to believe.

His hands moved to her waist. "I don't think this is a good idea . . ."

"Don't you want me?" she whispered.

"That's not the point."

Her hands slid down to his not-too-paunchy belly. Deftly, she untied the belt of his robe. The flannel fell open; she looked down and saw he wore boxers. Loose, easy-to-get-into boxers. Without hesitation, she slipped her hand inside, down to the warm spot that lay below. Slowly, she rubbed his flesh. Slowly, ever so slowly, she felt it come to life.

Ginny withdrew her hand and, without speaking, raised her dress over her head. She picked up his hands and placed them on her breasts. She was surprised, and pleased, when her nipples stiffened under his touch. If she couldn't enjoy sex anymore, it was at least a good thing her partner wouldn't know the difference.

She returned her hand to his crotch. "Take me to bed," she commanded. "I need it even more than you."

Chapter 20

 When the morning sun spilled into Jess's room, she opened her eyes, surprised she had slept through the night. They'd had a lovely dinner; being with Lisa and Phillip was so enjoyable. Once or twice they made her feel old, for their youth and optimism for life was so untarnished, their eagerness to share and to learn and to do something productive with their lives was both admirable and enviable. Phillip and Lisa were definitely going to make their marks on the world.

She had listened to them and watched them, startled that this young woman and this young man had been born at the same time as Melanie—that they, like Melanie, were adults now, capable people, independent, intelligent human beings. It had made Jess sad that she did not know her own child, born at the same time as them—Melanie, with the sweet little daughter of her own.

Turning onto her side, she realized that maybe the reason she'd slept so well was because she had made a decision and she was going to stick with it. Sometime between the lamb chops with fresh mint and the caramelized pears drizzled with fudge sauce that Phillip had insisted Jess try, she knew what she had to do. And she was going to do it this morning. She was going to drive over to Edgartown. She was going to confront Richard, one on one, just the two of them. He was no longer going to cheat her out of knowing her child.

They had screwed most of the night. When Ginny woke up she noticed Dick was gone, probably off making breakfast for the guests of the inn. She wondered if they wondered where the smile on his face had come from.

She had to pee. She hauled herself from the bed and rubbed her aching thighs. *Out of practice,* she told herself. *Out of practice and out of shape.*

But Jesus, it had been good. She tipped back her head and laughed. Sixty-nine or a hundred and sixty-nine, a man was a man, and a man with a need could screw like the best of them. The hell with what the magazines said about age and impotence or the need for Viagra.

And best of all, she had *liked* it. She had liked all the things he did to her, and all the things she did to him. She had liked it, for chrissakes. Her libido had risen like the phoenix from the ashes, returned like the prodigal son, blasting her into orbit like the space shuttle on a hot, energy-driven mission.

Christ, it had been good. There had been no time to talk to Dick about Melanie, no time to pry information from him on what really had happened. There had been no time for her to think about Brad and about what she'd do once they left the island and she returned to the hideous realities of her life. There had not even been time to think about Jake. There had been no time because Ginny had been too busy feeling good, feeling alive. Finally, feeling alive.

She laughed again, shuddering the last throe of orgasm from her still-tingling body, and started to move toward the bathroom. That's when her lower back went *ping.*

She stopped. She froze. "Fuck," she said, reaching

around and pressing her hand against her spine. "Fuck. Shit."

She tried to take another step forward. Pain shot across her ass and down her leg. "Son of a bitch." She looked toward the bathroom and knew she'd never make it. It must have been ten feet away. She glanced back to the bed. The three steps to the mattress looked like a mile and a fucking half.

Ginny stood stupidly in place, a Rubens nude chiseled in stone. "Help," she cried softly. "Somebody help me."

Karin was juggling a stack of fresh linen to make up the guest rooms. She walked past her father's bedroom when she heard the small cry. She stopped in the hallway and listened. It sounded as if someone was calling for help. It sounded like a woman. And it sounded like it was coming from inside her father's room.

She stepped close to the door and pressed her ear against it.

"Somebody fucking help me," came the barely audible whimper.

Karin set down the linens and stared at the door. Who was in there? Who the hell was in her father's room? No one had any right . . .

She reached for the doorknob and threw open the door. There, in the middle of the floor stood that woman—the fat one—totally naked.

"What are you doing in here?" she shouted.

"I was sleepwalking, for chrissakes, and now I can't move."

"Why are you dragging this out? Why don't you come what you've come for and leave?"

"Because I can't, you asshole. I can't move. I've hurt my back."

"So what do you want from me?"

"Help me. Put me back on the fucking bed."

Karin took one step forward, then two. She glanced at her father's bed. The sheets were torn from the bottom of the mattress; the blanket was hanging off the side. And there, on the floor, was a woman's dress, rolled up in a ball and lying in a heap.

"You slept with my father," she snarled.

The woman laughed. "And to think I thought you were stupid as well as a fruitcake."

Karin marched over to her, leaned into Ginny's face, and slapped it. Hard. "How dare you," she screamed.

Ginny turned her head. "Look, Morticia, I'm in pain here and I really don't feel like getting into a catfight with you. Just help me back to bed or leave me here and get your father. I'm sure he'd be glad to do it."

Karin seethed. "You make me sick," she snarled again. "This was supposed to be easy. I only wanted to do the right thing. But now, you all make me sick." She turned on her bare heel and stomped from the room.

Ginny stayed standing for what seemed an eternity. Then slowly, she tried to move. With each inch, the pain assaulted her, searing every nerve from her waist down on the right side, stealing her breath, piercing her flesh.

"Fuck. Shit," she repeated over and over, until, at last she reached the bed. She gingerly tried to bend one way. It did not work. She tried the other way. A little more movement, enough to reach the mattress. She took in a deep breath, squeezed her eyes closed, and dropped onto the bed.

"*Fuck!*" she shrieked, as the pain shot through her again. Then she opened her eyes, stared at the ceiling, and felt her bladder let go all over the sheets.

He had thought about her all night. He had tossed and turned, trying to push Lisa from his mind, as he had been trying to do since they'd left the Red Cat, since Jess had dropped him off back at the Tisbury Inn, since the car had driven away, carrying the only woman he had ever been this nuts about away in the backseat.

He had tried to sleep, then paced the room, then sat at the chair by the window and watched the darkened Main Street and the locked-up shops all night. All damn night. And all he could think of was how long it would be until they met this morning, until they went on their mission to find Melanie, to tell her who they were and why they were there.

Phillip knew he had lost focus. He wasn't even sure if it was the right thing to do, if they should interfere with Jess's life without her knowledge. He knew he'd lost focus, but he didn't care. It was as if Lisa Andrews had gotten under his skin like the needle of an addict. And like an addict, he needed her there, no matter how much it would hurt when the high wore off, no matter how painful the withdrawal would be.

He looked at the clock and decided he might as well run this morning. It might return some energy to his body and some sense to his brain. But first, there was something else he had to do.

Phillip groaned. He had to call the office and let them know he wouldn't be back for another day . . . or two. He hoped Joseph would not be there. He wanted to hang on to this high as long as he could. And that might be hard to do if he had to explain to his big brother what the hell he was doing on Martha's Vineyard.

Unfortunately Joseph picked up the line. "Nicole is frantic over you," he said.

"Nicole? Frantic? I doubt it. She seemed perfectly happy to make alternate plans."

"Why are you doing this, Phillip?"

It was obvious from his tone that Nicole must have told him about Jess, and why he was here.

"Jess is a nice woman, Joseph. I know you can't understand this, but I feel as if I owe her."

"Please. Don't start that again."

"I'll be back in a couple of days."

"Have you called Nicole?"

"No."

"Don't be a fool, Phillip. She's the best thing that ever happened to you."

Not really, he wanted to say, but didn't want to argue with his brother.

"Besides," Joseph added, "her father is a very important man."

"I haven't been dating her father."

Joseph sighed. "Well, I guess you're going to do what you feel you have to. In the meantime, get it done quickly. I've got to go now. I'm playing racquetball with Ed Smith."

Racquetball. After he hung up, it occurred to Phillip that if he made up with Nicole and married her, he'd be playing racquetball for the rest of his life.

Karin could barely breathe. She leaned against the door of the linen room, her eyes wide, her breath shallow and quick. She could not believe that *that woman* had slept with her father. That woman who pretended to be Jess's friend, but who was about as much like Jess Randall as most Vineyarders were to Americans.

She sucked in another small breath and held the pile of sheets close against her chest.

That woman had slept with her father.

That woman who was only here because Karin had started it all, and was now probably trying to get to Karin's father to learn the truth about Mellie. . . .

She bit her lower lip and forced back the tears.

She wished they would all just go away.

Ginny and Lisa had not yet come down for breakfast. *Good*, Jess thought, sipping her coffee and glancing at the clock. She would have plenty of time to escape to Edgartown before having to explain to anyone where she was going.

She placed her napkin on the table and rose, excusing herself to the other guests. As she crossed the dining room, Dick Bradley entered carrying another pot.

"Fresh coffee," he announced to Jess with a wide, beaming smile.

She shook her head. "No, thanks. I think I'll go for a drive this morning. Get some salt air in my blood."

He nodded, the smile not leaving. "Be sure to go out to Gay Head. The cliffs are magnificent. . . ."

Jess slipped from the room, not caring to listen to a travelogue of the island. She had no intention of going to Gay Head. She was going to Edgartown.

It was another fucking hour before Dick returned to the bedroom to find Ginny sprawled on the mattress in her own pee, tears streaming down the sides of her face and running into her ears.

"What the hell?" he asked, the smile on his face turning to a frown.

"My back," she murmured, the pain so intense now she could barely hear her own voice. "I threw my back out. And I pissed the bed."

"Oh, my God," he said, moving to the bed and crouching beside her. "Don't worry, Ginny," he said, awkwardly wiping her tears, looking somewhat shy about seeing her in the daylight, naked as she was, and in his bed. "I think I can get you some painkillers. Maybe we can figure out how to get you turned somehow so I can give you clean sheets. . . . Oh, my God, did I do this to you?"

"No," she said, the pain easing a little as she smiled. "I believe I did it to myself. Sex at my age. Who did I think I was?"

He smiled back, patted her hand, and kissed her forehead. "I'll be right back," he whispered. "Don't go away."

"All the men in the whole fucking world, and I've got to find me a comedian."

She found Edgartown again without a problem. She found the *Vineyard Gazette*. She even found a parking space. Now if Jess could only find the courage to go in, she'd be able to get on with her life.

Drumming her fingers on the console, she rehearsed what she would say.

"Richard, it's me. Jess Bates."

It would take him a moment to recognize her. Then he would frown and say, "Jess. How did you find me?"

She would stand as tall as she could and look him squarely in the eyes. And then she would say, "I found you and I know about Melanie. Now I want you to tell me the truth."

It would be as simple as that.

If only she could do it.

Then she thought about Phillip again, and about Lisa. And about the child she had been cheated out of knowing, cheated out of loving. And quickly, before she changed her mind, she got out of the car. This time she did not linger at the roses on the fence. This time she marched up the walk, through the door, and up to the receptionist's desk.

"I'd like to see Richard Bradley, please," she said as clearly and as firmly as possible.

"Just a minute," the woman said. "I'll see if he's in. May I give him your name?"

Her name? If she told the woman her name, then Richard would know she was here. He'd know she was here and he'd have a chance to slip out the back door, slip from her life again.

"No," she said quickly, then tried to smile. "I'd rather surprise him."

The woman kept her eyes fixed on Jess as if she were a terrorist come to invade the twice-weekly-in-summer newspaper. She lifted the receiver of the phone and pushed in two buttons. "Mr. Bradley," she said, "there's a woman in reception to see you." He must have asked who it was, because the woman paused before answering, "She chose not to give her name."

Jess shifted on one foot and twisted the ring on her finger. Those old, familiar butterflies were back in her stomach as if she were a child again, about to recite a poem at Miss Winslow's school. *Of course you feel like a child,* she told herself. *The last time you saw Richard you were a child. . . .*

And then, from behind her, she heard footsteps descending the stairs. She knew they were his before she turned around. She didn't know how she knew, but she knew. Slowly, Jess turned around.

It had been thirty years. It had been thirty years, yet she would have known him anywhere. In his jeans and denim shirt, he looked no more like forty-seven than he did eighty-five. He looked so much younger than . . . Charles. He looked so much more content, and so youthful, as if he'd just delivered towels at the swim club and was coming to bring her a cherry Coke. His face looked as tanned as it always had in summer; his brown hair seemed lighter—thinner, perhaps, but it still had that way of catching the light that had always made Jess envious she'd not been born a brunette. And then there were his eyes. As blue as her own. As steady on hers as hers were on him.

"Jess," he said, before she had a chance to say what she'd intended to say. "My God. How long has it been?"

He knew perfectly well how long it had been. But for some reason, standing here in the reception area of the ancient colonial that housed the *Vineyard Gazette,* it didn't seem to matter.

"I didn't think you'd recognize me," she managed to say.

"Of course I do. I'd know you anywhere."

They stood for a moment, staring at one another, the receptionist, Jess sensed, staring at them.

"My God," he repeated. "What brings you to the Vineyard?"

She couldn't say what she wanted right here in the office, right here in front of this woman she didn't even know. "Could we go outside?"

He walked to the door and held it open for her. As she passed by him to the front walk, Jess was keenly aware of his height, his mass, his being. Richard. Her Richard. It really was him.

When the door closed behind him, Jess looked into his eyes once again. She tried to decide if Melanie looked more like her or like him. Him, perhaps. And perhaps Sarah looked more like Jess.

"So," he said, stuffing his hands into the pockets of his jeans. "What brings you to the Vineyard?"

She wondered if he knew he'd already asked her that. She wondered if he was as nervous as she was. She twisted her ring again and looked off toward the roses. "I've seen her," she blurted out.

The second he paused was long enough for Jess to know he knew what she meant. "Her?" he asked. "Who?"

"Melanie."

"My sister?"

"No. Melanie. Our daughter." *There,* she thought. She'd said it. She'd admitted it to Richard and to anyone within hearing distance of the sidewalk of the *Vineyard Gazette.*

"Maybe we'd better go somewhere and talk," he said. "Wait here a minute. I'll let Bertie know I'll be out."

She stood on the walk, half wondering if he'd have the nerve to slip away now, if he would be too afraid to face what he'd done. It was easier, she realized, to think about that, for right now Jess was unsure what she was feeling herself, unable to get past the butterflies to find out.

He came back.

"There's a little park around the corner," he said, guiding her elbow down the walk. "We can sit there and talk."

They walked down the street and turned onto Main, moving slowly through the early-summer people, past the bookstore and toward a small patch of green lawn where a few benches sat. He escorted her to one, and they sat down. They sat down and said nothing.

Then Jess spoke.

"I want to know what happened. I want to know everything."

In the heartbeats that followed, she sensed he was going to deny it, that he was going to insist Melanie was his sister and that he didn't know what she was talking about.

Instead, he said, "I'm the one who should be asking you what happened."

So he was going to be defensive. She almost laughed at herself for thinking that Richard was any different from Charles. "Excuse me, Richard," she said, with even greater conviction, "but my baby has been with you for almost thirty years. I never saw her, did you know that? Did you know they never even let me see her?" Then her throat choked closed, her eyes filled with tears, as she felt the picture of her romantic knight on his stalwart white stallion vanish from her heart, and her life, forever.

"But you didn't want to see her," he said. "You wanted nothing to do with her."

"Who told you that?"

"My father."

"Your father? What the hell did he know?"

Richard crossed one leg over his knee and rubbed the side of his sneaker. He dropped his head and lowered his voice. "Your father paid us a great deal of money."

"Two hundred thousand dollars, if I recall," Jess said.

"He said you wanted nothing to do with me or with our baby."

In the silence that followed, Jess did not hear the murmur of shoppers, the giggles of children, or the sounds of cars passing by on the street. She did not hear these things because in her mind, over and over, she could only hear the harsh echo of Richard's last words: *You wanted nothing to do with me or with our baby.*

And then she remembered Father on the day that he'd brought her to Larchwood Hall, when he stood in Miss Taylor's office writing out checks, pretending this was just one more business expense, and that his fifteen-year-old pregnant daughter was not in the room. When the house-mother left them alone, Jess wanted to talk to him. She wanted to tell him that she was sorry, that she loved Rich-ard and Richard loved her. And that Richard would make everything work out. She wanted to tell him, but he did not want to listen. He merely fumbled in his pocket for his pipe and tobacco pouch. Then he put the pipe in his mouth, buttoned his Burberry coat, said "Enough has been said," and left.

"My father," Jess said slowly now. "My father lied. I can't believe you believed him. I can't believe that the money had nothing to do with it."

"Jess, listen to me."

She jumped from the bench. "I *waited* for you, Richard. Night after night, I waited for you. You were supposed to come and get me. You took my father's money instead. You took my father's money, and then you took my baby." She spun on one heel. She noticed a small crowd of people who had gathered, who were looking in shop windows as if they weren't listening, as if they hadn't heard every word she'd just said. Without even telling Richard that he could go to hell, she marched through the park, up Main Street and back to her car.

It wasn't until she was speeding down the Beach Road back to Vineyard Haven that Jess was aware of what had just happened: Melanie was hers. Richard had confirmed it.

Chapter 21

 "Ginny, for God's sake, what happened?" Lisa cried, rushing into Dick Bradley's bedroom.

"Among other things, one of the most humiliating experiences of my life." At least Dick had managed, somehow, to get the bed changed and dress Ginny in one of his long denim shirts before alerting Lisa about her mother's whereabouts and her unfortunate demise. At least he hadn't turned out to be a creep more concerned with how things looked for him than with the pain Ginny was in.

"When did this happen? I was so tired last night I fell right to sleep when we came home. I didn't hear you come up to the room. . . ."

Ginny sighed, a movement that made the muscle go into another spasm. "You didn't hear me because I wasn't there."

Lisa looked at her a moment. "Oh," was all she said.

"I guess I have to take back everything I said out at Gay Head."

"About sex?"

"Well, it's obvious, isn't it?"

Lisa smiled. "I think what we need to worry about right now is what about your back. Can you move at all?"

For a kid of hers, Lisa wasn't half-bad. "Move?" Ginny asked. "I can barely breathe."

"Shouldn't we call a doctor?"

"Dick's taking care of it." She tried to wiggle her toes. The pain stopped her.

"Well, then," Lisa said, folding her arms, "I guess we'll have to extend our vacation."

"Try not to let it bother you so much."

"It doesn't," she said with a shrug. "Who knows? Maybe Phillip will stay, too."

Eyeing her daughter, Ginny replied, "And maybe we'll both have to take back what we said at Gay Head."

Lisa laughed. "Maybe not. All I know is he's meeting me in a while and we're going up to the school."

"To see her?"

"Hopefully."

Hopefully, yes. And hopefully, they'd make better progress than she had. "And then what?"

"And then, who knows. Maybe Phillip will figure out a way for us to kill Brad after all."

At first Jess was too blinded by pain, too ripped by her emotions to notice the Bronco that peeled into the May-field House parking lot behind her. But as she crossed the walk and heard a car door slam, instinctively, she turned around.

She wished she hadn't.

"Jess," Richard called out, rushing up the clamshell walk to her side. "Please. Listen to me."

She shook her head. "There's nothing I need to hear. I've heard enough."

She began to walk away; he pulled at her arm. "Jess. Please. You don't know the whole story."

Closing her eyes, she let the sun seep into her pores. But the warmth did little to soothe the hurt.

"I think we owe each other that, don't you?" Richard asked.

"I've never felt I owed you anything."

"I thought you did. Maybe I was wrong. Maybe I was too young and too stupid to think anything else."

"Richard. You're not making sense."

"Please, Jess. You've come this far. Please sit down and listen to me."

She opened her eyes and looked into his. They were troubled now, their blueness hazed with something Jess recognized. It was pain. It was hurt. And it was thirty not-quite-right years of keeping a secret that they never should have had to have kept. It was thirty years of knowing things were not at all what they seemed.

"All right," she said quietly.

He lead her to a long white swing that hung from a huge maple tree in the backyard. Jess sat down. Richard stood in front of her.

"I'm listening," she said.

He ran his hand through his brown, still-shining hair, and began. "We were kids, Jess."

She held her stomach where it hurt; it was true. She had only been fifteen, Richard seventeen. But Jess had not felt like a kid. She had felt like a grown woman, old enough to carry a child inside her, old enough to love. She did not answer.

"You were the rich kid; I was the poor kid," he continued. "I fell in love with you, but part of me knew it would never work. That our worlds were too different. That your father would never allow us to be together."

She pushed her feet against the ground. The swing began to creak. "Please, Richard, don't patronize me. You're making it sound very much like a clichéd B movie."

He shoved his hands in his pockets and looked at the ground, ignoring her remark. "When your father contacted my dad, Dad came to me right away. We may have been poor, but we were a close family."

Yes, she had known that. Richard's family was a real family. So like the family she longed to be part of. So unlike her own. She remembered now how that had added to the hurt, that she could not become part of a good, loving family, that he had robbed her of that opportunity, too.

"Anyway," he continued, "your father had said you never wanted to see me again, never wanted to hear from me. I was devastated." His voice faltered. He looked away for a moment, as if stalled by emotion, stopped by a tear. Then he cleared his throat and looked back at her. "He also said you wanted nothing to do with our baby."

It took all the strength she could find to stay seated on the swing, to not lunge straight at him and slap him and punch him and kick him until he bled. The only thing that held her back was that she wanted to see how far he would go, how big a tale he would weave to justify what they'd done.

"I believed it, Jess," he said. "I believed it because I'd always thought you were too good for me. I believed that you wouldn't want me, and you wouldn't want a baby that was half mine. Can you ever understand that?"

She pushed the swing again. Richard paced the ground.

"My parents were heartsick that you were pregnant," he went on. "They thought about the baby as my child, too— their grandchild. That's when, together, we came up with the plan."

"To steal my baby," she said quickly, spurting the anger she could no longer contain.

"No, Jess. Not to steal her. To take her and raise her as our own. To raise her as a Bradley. We changed our name; we moved to the island from Connecticut. I was so young we decided it would be best for the baby—for Melanie—if everyone thought she was my parents' child. If everyone thought she was my kid sister."

"And what did Melanie think? What has she thought all these years?"

He sucked in a small breath. "That she is my sister."

"Oh, God, Richard," was all Jess could say.

He fell to his knees and took her hands in his. "She's had a good life, Jess. A happy life. When my mother died, she was only five. But Karin took over the mother role. And she's been a good mother figure to Mellie. She sacrificed her own chance at happiness for Melanie."

"Karin is strange."

Again, he lowered his head. "I know. But it hasn't been easy for her. Mellie told me once that Karin had a boyfriend. But I never met him and I chose to ignore it. I guess I was afraid Karin would want her own life and I would have to take responsibility for . . . our little girl. So for much of Karin's unhappiness now, I blame myself."

Jess wanted, in that moment, to tell him about the letter, to tell him about the phone call his sister had made. She did not know what stopped her, but she thought it might be because she no longer saw Karin as a villain, but as a victim. A victim of her brother's sins and her parents' greed.

"What about the two hundred thousand dollars? The payoff my father gave you?"

He stood up and began to pace again. "Your father gave us that money to pay Miss Taylor for Melanie."

"As far as I understand, that only cost fifty thousand. What happened to the rest?"

Richard stood still. "I don't know where you've gotten your information, but the fifty thousand was a down payment. The rest went to her when Mellie was born. Part of the deal was that Miss Taylor arranged for us to come here, and she got Dad a job as a caretaker for Mabel Adams. Your father didn't 'pay us off,' Jess. He gave us the money so we could get the baby that was his grandchild. So she wouldn't be adopted by strangers."

She must have heard him wrong. "Father did what?" she asked.

"He gave us money so we could get Mellie," Richard repeated. "When I said that we came up with a plan *together* . . . well, it was really between my parents and your father. Other than that only Karin and I knew the truth.

"And Miss Taylor."

"I have no idea how much she did or did not know. I suspect all she cared about was the money."

Jess's head felt light, she was suddenly dizzy. She steadied her feet on the ground, trying to digest all Richard had said, wanting to believe him, yet not being quite able. "But it's all a lie, Richard. I wanted our baby. I wanted us . . . Father *knew* that . . ."

"I guess he thought we were too young," Richard said. "I suppose he only did what he thought was right for you."

Father, she thought. How little she'd known him. She raised her chin and looked at Richard. "And now Melanie has a child," she said. "Our grandchild, Richard. Yours and mine."

"Yes. And she's pregnant again. There's another baby on the way."

Jess clutched her stomach. "Oh, God, Richard. How can you do this? How can you keep pretending?"

"I have to, Jess. Melanie is, well, she's sweet and she's gentle, and she's so much like you. But Karin and I made a promise to my mother on the day she died that Melanie would never know the truth about her birth. Melanie can't find out now, Jess. It's too late, and it wouldn't be fair."

And in that instant, with those words, Jess knew that Richard was right.

Phillip walked up the hill with Lisa by his side, headed in the direction of the West Tisbury School. He supposed he should feel guilty about Nicole, but decided there would be time enough to deal with that when he returned to New

York, when he went back to the real world where mothers and brothers had expectations of you and where big-time television stars didn't walk next to you on back streets of the Vineyard.

"I think we should start by coming right to the point," Lisa said. "I think we should ask her if she knows she was adopted."

Phillip shook his head. "She's not like us, Lisa. Melanie wasn't adopted, remember?"

Lisa frowned, the lightest little wrinkle carving itself across her forehead. "Oh. You're right. Then what should we say? We can't just come out and ask if she knows that her brother is really her father."

"Maybe we should just introduce ourselves. Then tell her we're there to talk with her about a baby scam that happened in the sixties. Lead into it a little more gently."

Lisa smiled. "I'm not great at being gentle. I guess I get that from my mother."

Phillip laughed. "She's a character, you know that?"

"Yeah. And right now I'd give anything to fix this mess I've made for her with Brad. If you have any ideas, I'd love to hear them."

He did not want to tell her the best idea he'd come up with was to fly to L.A., hunt down the jerk, and push his red Porsche off the side of a cliff. "Well, I know you can't give Brad any money. Once you start, he'll never stop asking for more. Can't you go to the police?"

"And risk having it leaked to the tabloids?"

"Oh. Right. What about Ginny? What does she want to do?"

"Simple. Kill him."

"And you?"

Lisa closed her eyes. "I only want it to end. I'm so ashamed of myself for getting involved with him. He's not even my type. He's flamboyant and crass. I guess I was just needy. And he was there."

In that moment, she was no longer a Hollywood star.

She was frightened and hurting, a plain old all-American girl in shorts and a T-shirt who had trusted the wrong man and was paying too steep a price. Phillip gently put his arm on her shoulders. "It'll be okay, Lisa," he said. "We'll figure something out." He didn't know what, and he didn't know how, but he was determined to help. The hell with the expectations that awaited him at home.

They walked for another few minutes in silence, then Lisa pointed up ahead. "There it is," she said. "That must be the school."

He smiled and dropped his arm from her shoulders, musing at his entanglements with his birth mother's friends and wondering if P.J. would be walking beside them if she were still alive. Then he decided that maybe she was here; maybe it was her spirit that had been encouraging him all along.

"Should we just go in the front door?" Lisa asked.

"Follow me," Phillip said. With renewed spirit, he climbed the stairs.

The school was not at all like the one Phillip had gone to in Fairfield—the shiny, bright, new school with sparkling windows and pristine corridors befitting the inflated tax dollars contributed by the community. Lisa, however, said it was a lot like what she grew up with in her New Jersey town. Old. A little too dark. With echoes in the hallways of too many children of too many generations.

Their first stop was the office.

"We need to speak with Melanie . . ." Phillip stopped, realizing he did not know her married name. "Gosh," he said to the weather-worn woman who stood at the counter, "I've forgotten her married name. Bradley was her maiden name. She has a daughter named Sarah." He tried to smile as he spoke, tried not to look as if he was being clandestine.

"Melanie Galloway," the woman said. "She's teaching her class right now. I'm afraid she can't be disturbed."

Lisa stepped forward. "If you could just tell us what room she's in, we could wait in the hall."

The woman shook her head. "Sorry. No civilians are allowed to wander the halls. This is a school. We have children to protect."

Phillip wondered if the woman was a weekend warrior with the National Guard. "We're old friends from college," he lied, subtly taking Lisa's hand and trying not to be distracted by her smooth, warm touch. "We're honeymooning on the island and we'd really love to see Melanie."

The woman scowled. "If you want to wait in the office, I could send her a message to let her know you're here. She's only teaching half days this week on account of her daughter broke her leg. Her class will be over in twenty minutes."

Phillip looked at Lisa. Lisa nodded.

"Just give me your names," the woman said, pen poised over a pad.

"Our names?" Phillip asked.

Over half glasses, the woman peered at them. "I presume you have names."

Lisa laughed. "We really planned to surprise her. Maybe we'll just wait outside on the steps."

"It's up to you. You'll know her when you see her. Melanie Galloway hasn't changed since she came here as a student herself."

Phillip did not mention that unless she hadn't changed from when she was in the hospital nursery, chances were they would have absolutely no idea what she looked like.

Outside on the stairs, Lisa sat on the concrete and put her face in her hands. "This is hopeless," she said. "We'll never recognize her."

"Yes we will."

"How? Do you think she looks like Jess?"

"It doesn't matter. We'll just look for a woman our age with a little girl on crutches. There can't be too many of them, can there?"

Lisa smiled up at him. "You are really quite brilliant, Counselor."

He turned his head so she wouldn't see him redden. He did not tell her that that was how Jess had spotted Melanie; better that she think he was brilliant. He smiled up at the cloudless day and wished he could capture this feeling and hold on to it forever, wished he could reach out and hug P.J. right now and tell her how grateful he was to have been born.

"Did you ever wonder about your father?" Lisa asked suddenly.

"My birth father?"

"Well. Yes."

Looking back to the sky, he answered, "P.J. told me about him, that he was a boy she'd dated in college, that he wouldn't admit he was . . . responsible." He smiled at the memory of that sunny day when they'd sat in Central Park and P.J. told him about Frank. He smiled because he knew that her words were enough, that Phillip did not need to know the man. He turned to Lisa now and asked, "What about you?"

She laughed. "Mine is a long story for a different day. I was thinking how nice it will be for Melanie. To know both her parents."

Phillip nodded just as the large door opened and children began scurrying down the stairs. Lisa stood up and moved next to him: together they scanned the heads for a little girl on crutches, for a mother protectively helping her child.

But among the young faces and old faces of the students and teachers, there were no kids on crutches, no legs sealed in plaster.

And then they stopped coming. The door closed behind the last of the crowd. And Phillip stood staring at Lisa, and Lisa at Phillip.

"Maybe her daughter didn't come to school today," Lisa said. "Maybe she walked right past us and we didn't even know it."

"Maybe," Phillip replied, feeling less brilliant than he had in ages, and embarrassed that Lisa had witnessed his failure.

She couldn't let them do it. From across the street, Karin stood behind a thick-trunked old oak tree and watched the two of them scan the crowd, no doubt looking for Melanie, no doubt looking for Sarah.

But it was not the right way. Melanie needed to learn this from Jess, to learn it from Richard. Not from a couple of kids, whoever they were. Not from a woman named Ginny who was trying to use sex to lure the truth out of a lonely old man. No, Mellie should not learn this from them. Jess and Richard would be kinder, more gentle. It would hurt Mellie less.

She smiled now at how clever she'd been. As soon as she'd realized what these two kids were up to, she'd called the school office and told May Weston, the receptionist, to have Melanie get Sarah and wait for Karin in the school cafeteria, that Karin wanted to see them, that they should not leave the building until she arrived. As always, Mellie would do whatever Karin asked.

And thank God May Weston ruled the school—and had since practically the turn of the last century—like a secret service agent. Thank God May Weston was an islander, and despised the tourists as much as Karin did.

She leaned against the tree and waited and watched, until at last the pair gave up and started back down the road. Then she crossed the road and headed into the school. She'd have to remember to bring May some sea glass the next time she was around. Just as soon as all these damn people left this damn island and life was back to whatever was normal. She would have to find a way now to hurry that along.

"If you're worried about leaving me here with Dick Bradley, don't be," Ginny said to Jess. "I'm in the best hands I could ask for unless they were Jake's, and that's pretty impossible, so I might as well be grateful for what I've got."

Jess walked to the window of the room where Ginny lay prone, unable to move more than her lips. "I can't believe this has happened to you," she said.

"I can't believe a lot of things," Ginny said. "Like I can't believe what you're telling me about Melanie and about Richard, and that you're actually going to leave here and do as he wishes."

"I don't have much choice, Ginny. I don't want to ruin Melanie's life. Or Richard's either, for that matter."

"So they hold all the cards, is that it? Shit, kid. I thought you stopped letting people dictate your life when you got rid of your husband."

"You talk as if you're any better. You still haven't come up with a plan to take care of this mess with your stepson, other than deciding he should be killed."

"I've changed my mind about that," Ginny said. "I decided to have him throw his back out instead. I think it's more painful." She groaned and squinted her eyes. "Those damn pills Dick's doctor gave me only last half the time they're supposed to."

Jess went back to the bed. "Oh, Ginny, I'm so sorry. I'm being so selfish and you're in so much pain."

"No problem, kid. But even though I think you're being a jerk for not wanting to meet Melanie, for not wanting her to know the truth, I really don't want you to hang around on account of me. I may be here a while."

"I've seen her," Jess said. "I've seen her and I've seen my granddaughter, and now I know what happened. It's really hard to believe that Father did this—well, I suppose to protect me. It's really hard to believe he cared enough about the baby to be sure she had a good life." She twisted her emerald and diamond ring and tried to smile. It's hard to believe, but I'm working on it."

"And dear Daddy is dead, so you can't ask him."

"No. But I can be happy, Ginny, if I choose to be. Until a few months ago, I thought my baby was dead. Now I know better, and now that has to be enough."

She told Ginny she'd bring her some tea later, after she'd had a nap. She'd wait until Phillip and Lisa came back from wherever they'd gone off to, then tell them she would catch the seven-thirty ferry out of Oak Bluffs. It was time to get back to her life: to her business and to the family that truly was hers.

An hour or so later, Jess was awakened by a rustling at the door of room number seven. She looked down and saw a pale pink envelope on the floor. She pulled herself from the bed, yawned, and bent down to pick it up. Walking toward the window, she rubbed her eyes. Then she caught her breath, and rubbed them again. But the recognition was quick: an instant flashback.

Printed on the envelope was the name *Richard Bryant*, followed by an address in Connecticut. She did not have to wonder what the envelope was, because she knew it was one she had addressed herself—a letter sent three decades ago—one of the letters that had gone unanswered.

She bit down on her lip and with trembling hands, opened the envelope that had already been unsealed.

But her letter to Richard was not inside: instead was a note, hand-scrawled in black ink.

Meet me after dinner in the West Chop Woods, it read. *Take the entrance off Main Street. Follow the markings for the red trail. Come alone. Tell no one. We have so much more to discuss.* It was signed simply, *Richard.*

Chapter 22

"I thought she wanted to leave tonight," Phillip said to Ginny as he and Lisa stood in a man's bedroom where Ginny had apparently spent an interesting night and a very painful day after. It was already late afternoon: Phillip and Lisa had spent the rest of the day walking—along the water by the harbor, past the pier and the West Chop lighthouse, clear around to Tashmoo Pond. They had walked and talked and walked and didn't talk. Phillip had savored every moment, trying to freeze each word from her mouth, each movement of her body into his memory. He did not know why.

"She made reservations on the seven-thirty ferry," Ginny said. "I have no idea where she is. How did you two make out?"

"We didn't," Lisa said. "Melanie wasn't there."

Ginny nodded. "Maybe it's just as well."

"Yeah." Phillip glanced at his watch. "Well, I guess I'd better get down to the Tisbury Inn and pack my bag," he said. "When Jess comes back, tell her I'll be ready." He looked at his shoes—*Damn*, he thought, *why am I looking at my shoes?*—then he pulled his eyes up to Lisa. "Well," he said. "It was nice meeting you."

Lisa nodded. "You, too, Counselor."

He shuffled his feet a moment, then moved from one bedpost to another. "I hope your back gets better, Ginny."

"Yeah. Me, too."

He put his hands in his pockets. "Well, then. I guess this is good-bye."

"If you're ever in L.A. . . ." Lisa said.

He smiled. "Yeah. I'll call." Then he took a deep breath, let it out slowly, and turned and left the room.

"You've gotten to him," Ginny said.

Lisa laughed. "What are you talking about?"

"Phillip. He's crazy about you."

"Well. He's nice."

"So are you. You deserve someone like that, Lisa. Not someone like Brad. Not another jerk."

Lisa crossed the room and sat on the edge of the bed. "Phillip lives three thousand miles away, Mother. And we both have demanding careers. I doubt there's much hope."

Ginny raised an eyebrow. "Then you do like him?"

She closed her eyes. "I told you. He's nice."

Ginny put her hand on Lisa's arm. "Look, kid, we all know I don't have the best track record when it comes to men. But one thing I do know is that when you find yourself someone decent, don't lose him. There are too damn few of them in the world."

Lisa looked around the room. "Is that what you've found here with Dick Bradley? A decent man?"

"Hey," Ginny laughed. "He's a good nurse. Right now, that's all I need."

"Did someone call for the nurse?" Dick asked as he entered the room carrying a tray with a teapot, two mugs, and a plateful of cookies.

"Now that's what I call good medicine," Ginny said, eyeing the cookies. She tried to prop herself up; the pain stabbed her back. It was not as bad as it had been, but it stabbed her nonetheless. "Shit," she said.

Dick set down the tray and rearranged Ginny's pillows. She was able to half sit, half lie and the pain was not as bad.

"In another hour you can have two more pills," he said.

"Yeah. Right. And the damn pain started again an hour ago."

"If you're not better by tomorrow, there's a holistic healer on the island I can call."

"Great," Ginny said, taking a cookie. "Just what I need is a voodoo doctor hovering over me."

Lisa smiled. "Ginny has never been one to want help from anyone."

"Well, she's got to have it now. By the way, have you seen your friend? I thought she was checking out today. Karin wants to know if she can rent the room out."

Ginny frowned. "Jess? I don't know where she is. I haven't seen her since she went to take a nap. She must have gone for a walk."

"I'll go check on her," Lisa offered.

"Take your time. It looks like Dick and I are going to have a tea party. Ah. A little afternoon delight."

Dick blushed and Lisa laughed. "I'll be back later," she said.

"Oh, Lisa?" Ginny called. "You might want to look for Jess at the Tisbury Inn," she said with a wink.

"The Tisbury Inn? But Phillip is there. . . ."

Ginny turned to Dick. "Sometimes my daughter is so intelligent it is truly heart-stopping."

"Ginny!" Lisa cried.

"Like I said, you might want to try the Tisbury Inn."

It took Phillip only three minutes to pack. He had crumpled his tie and folded his suit and decided to wear the

Black Dog T-shirt and jeans. They were comfortable. They felt more real.

After zipping his bag, he looked around the room, then sat in the chair by the window. He gazed two flights down, out onto Main Street, not really seeing the crowds on the sidewalks and the slow stream of cars that jockeyed for parking spaces. To him now, it all looked fuzzy and out of sync, people going about their lives, whether happy or sad, but going about their lives.

He did not want to go back to New York. He did not want to go back to Joseph and Nicole and racquetball or even the new uptown office. He wanted to stay here on the island; he wanted to run in the mornings on the quiet, dewy streets, he wanted to sit side by side with Lisa on the beach looking off at the sunrise and the sunset and everything in between. No, he did not want to go back.

He folded his hands and looked down at his city manicure—the clean, neatly trimmed nails of a corporate attorney, the soft, pale skin that had not spent enough time in the outdoors, was not accustomed to rugged, hard work, honest work, like sanding a boat bottom or chopping wood for the winter. He thought about Dick Bradley, nearly forty years older than himself, yet probably in better shape, despite Phillip's running, despite his attempts at physical fitness. There was nothing, he supposed, as healthy as doing things naturally, as breathing the fresh salt air as you worked, instead of the air in a sweaty gym.

He wondered how fresh the air was in L.A., and if the smog was thinner up in the canyon where Ginny lived. Then he realized his thoughts were drifting back to Lisa. He got up, shook his head, picked up his bag, and decided to wait for Jess at the sidewalk café.

Just as he turned the knob to open the door, a knock came from the other side. *Jess,* he thought quickly, opening the door.

But it was not Jess. It was Lisa.

"Hi," she said.

He went mute for a moment. "Hi," he finally answered. "I thought you were Jess."

"No," she said. "I'm Lisa."

He smiled. "Yeah. I know."

"May I come in?"

"In? Yeah. Sure." He stepped out of the way, set down his bag, and closed the door. "Did you find Jess?"

She shook her head.

"I wonder where she went," he said, though what he really wondered was why Lisa was here, and what he was supposed to do next.

She went to the window and looked out. "Nice view," she said.

"Main Street," Phillip answered, as if it wasn't obvious.

"Phillip—"

"Lisa—"

They laughed.

"Phillip, I hate to see you leave," she said. "I have the oddest feeling that I'll never see you again."

A strange, light feeling rose in his stomach. "Well, there are worse fates, I suppose."

She walked over to him. She stood close. He inhaled her scent—clean, fresh. *God,* he wondered, *why am I such a sucker for the way a woman smells?*

"Phillip. I don't think you understand." Her voice was low and deep, a sensuous voice like he had never heard. "I like you a lot," she said, lowering those magnificent topaz eyes so he could not see them.

Without thinking, Phillip put his hand under her chin, then lifted it to see those eyes. And when they looked back at him, he slowly bent down and kissed her, kissed her smooth, full lips, tasting her cleanness, her freshness. Then he put his arms around her and kissed her again, more deeply this time, more urgently, as passion quickly rose within him, as every nerve in his body stirred and sparked, as every minute of every day of his life before this and after dissolved on the wings of the moment, this moment, the only moment in the world, or in life, that mattered.

"Oh, God, Lisa," he moaned. "I want you so badly."

And then he felt her arms around his back, caressing him gently, then firmly, her long, strong fingers gripping his flesh with ache and need.

"Yes," she whispered. "Yes."

He scooped her from the floor and buried his face in her hair, her silky, vanilla-scented hair. Then he paused. "I . . ." he hesitated, "I don't have any . . . protection."

Lisa smiled. "I do. In my purse."

"I wasn't planning . . ."

"Me either. But Ginny has always insisted . . . just in case."

"Because it's the nineties . . ."

"And other reasons."

"So there won't be more like us in the world?"

"Right. Not that we're so bad."

"No," he said, and carried her to the bed. "Not that we're so bad."

Then he lay her on the bed and slowly began to unbutton her blouse.

The sign on the side of the road was so small that Jess nearly missed it. *West Chop Woods*, it read. *Sheriff's Preservation Trust.*

She had walked from the inn; it was further than it had looked on the map. It was also less inviting than she had expected. It was merely a dirt path leading from the roadside into a thicket of tall trees. Why Richard had wanted to meet her here was puzzling. Yet he must have a reason. Maybe there was a special place on the red trail. Her heart beat softly. Maybe he was going to bring Melanie here to meet her, away from his father and sister, away from people whom he might not want to have know.

She stepped onto the path and began walking. A few feet

into the woods was a signpost that held a rustic-looking map hand-painted onto a small board. Jess moved close to it: the woods were depicted, along with four distinct trails. Blue. Green. Orange. Red. She followed her finger along the red trail, then looked for an indication of where it began. Off to her right she saw it: a small red arrow was staked into the ground.

Wishing she'd worn something other than the damn calfskin shoes, she gingerly began following the trail, eager to meet Richard, eager to know what he was planning to do.

She had to walk slowly. The trail was narrow, the uneven ground blanketed with roots and twigs and rotted leaves and pine needles. She stepped over acorns and threaded her way along the path, following the markers of red arrows, wondering with each step what was going to happen, uneasy that the woods seemed to grow more dense with each turn of the trail, and that the sun was no longer able to peek through the tall pines that surrounded her.

She thought about turning back. Soon, Jess knew, it would be dusk. Getting out of the woods would be difficult. Yet Richard . . . Richard was waiting. He had sent the note in the envelope of one of her letters—he could have written it on anything, but he'd chosen that to show her . . . what? That he had kept her letters all these years?

As she continued her cautious trek, Jess began to fantasize that Richard was waiting in a clearing, a beautiful, pine-needle-covered clearing, that he had a soft spread laid on the ground, a wicker hamper of cheese and fruit, a bottle of wine. She dreamed that he would tell her how much he loved her, how he always had, and always would. As she felt these thoughts and dreamed these dreams, Jess felt like that fifteen-year-old little girl once again, waiting for him at the window of Larchwood Hall, waiting for the boy who had not come then, but perhaps would come to her now.

"I've been such a fool," he would say. Then she would

sip wine and he would sip wine and he would kiss her as she had never been kissed in thirty years, a kiss of love—real, true love.

She tripped on a root, but quickly regained her balance and kept walking. Another fork in the trail: the red arrow pointed right. She stepped over a log and followed the path. Then, just as the trail began to straighten, Jess felt the ground go out from beneath her. Her right foot snapped as she went down into a hole, a shallow, ragged hole. "Damn!" she shouted.

She tried to get up but her leg would not move. She cried out in pain. "Richard!" she called. "Help!"

The trees swirled above her, the air grew quite still, and a sudden thought cut through her pain: If Richard had saved her letters all these years, then he must have read them back then; he must have known how much she wanted their baby; he must have known her father was lying.

She did not want to close her eyes: she wanted to sort out the confusion, to sort out the agony. But the pain that crawled up her leg was stronger than her will. Then, just before she passed out, Jess saw a flash of orange fabric float through the woods, heading away from her.

He had forgotten about Jess. Phillip sat upright, pushed back the sheets and looked at the clock. Seven-ten.

"God," he said, "I fell asleep." Not that it was surprising. Lisa had unleashed a passion in him that Phillip had never known, a passion that left him feeling weak, drained, and more incredibly out-of-breath-kind-of-lucky than he'd ever felt in his life. He ran his hands through his hair and tried to wake up. Then he felt her fingernails skate down his naked back. "You are so irresistible . . ." he said, turning to Lisa and tracing his hand over her flesh.

He kissed her softly, his passion rising again.

"Phillip," she whispered. "Oh, Phillip . . ."

He stopped. "I have to meet Jess."

She raked her fingers through his hair. "I know. I know."

He lingered a moment longer, studying her body, wanting to remember every inch, every soft curve and every gentle fold. "Oh, God," he said, then rolled onto his side and got up. "I hate this."

"Me, too."

He walked to the window and looked out. "I wonder why the desk didn't call. I wonder where she is."

"Call the inn," Lisa suggested.

He did. Jess was not there: she had not yet returned. He checked downstairs. She had not called, had not left any message.

He pulled on his jeans and scratched his head. On the other side of the bed, Lisa dressed. "I don't understand," he said. "She wanted to leave at seven-thirty. It's almost that now." He looked out the window again. "And it's practically dark out. Where the hell is she?"

Lisa combed her hair and repaired her smudged makeup. "I think we'd better go find her."

Phillip nodded, sadness filling him. He would probably never see Lisa again.

"I'm glad you came to see me," he said.

She reached her arm around his neck and kissed him in reply. He put his arms around her and pulled her body into his.

Karin raced down to the beach, her sarong flying behind her, her heart beating like an Indian drum through the light fabric of her T-shirt. She dropped onto the sand, threw back her head, and wailed a loud, lowly wail into the wind and the graying sky.

It wasn't supposed to have happened this way. Yes, she had wanted revenge. Revenge against this woman called Jess who had lived the life of a socialite lady while Karin raised the daughter she'd thought Jess had not wanted . . . while Karin sacrificed the love of the only man she'd ever loved because somehow Mellie had become her responsibility, her unexpected lot in her unimportant life.

But she loved Mellie, really she did. She did not regret raising her. What she hated was what a fool she had felt like when she'd learned the truth. How she had felt used. How she had felt betrayed.

But now something had happened to Jess. Karin dug her fingers into the bits of shells and stone and stinging grains of West Chop Beach. She pulled her hands to her face and drew her palms down her cheeks, grinding the roughness into her flesh, hoping the pain would erase what had happened.

"It isn't my fault!" she sobbed.

But she knew that it was.

She had wanted to tell Jess to get off the island. To take her friends and leave, to say that Jess had no business there after all, and that her fat California friend had no business sleeping with Karin's father. She had wanted to tell her, but then Jess tripped and fell. Karin had seen it happen. She knew right away someone would blame her. So she had circled back and watched. She had seen Jess pass out.

An ache clutched her stomach now, and Karin fell forward, her hair splaying onto the sand, her tears dripping onto the beach. She knew what she needed to do.

She had to find Richard and tell him what happened. Because fair or not, Jess was Mellie's real mother, and Jess had been innocent—a victim of society, a victim of life. She had also been the woman Richard had once loved, and the mother Mellie would have, if she had but known.

And if there was one thing Karin knew, it was what pain felt like, what the tear of deep-cutting pain felt like. She had felt it when Brit's letters started coming back marked "unknown." She had felt it that first summer when he did not return. That summer, and every summer thereafter.

No matter how, no matter why, Karin could not stand to bring either Mellie or Richard the kind of pain she had known.

She rocked back and forth on her knees in the sand, wondered how badly Jess was hurt, and if she was going to die.

"Her car is still here," Dick said to Ginny. He was standing at the foot of the bed, looking helpless and perplexed.

Ginny frowned, wishing she could get out of bed. "I can't imagine what's happened to her." She chewed the inside of her mouth, then realized it was time. The game was over; the jig was up. : "Dick, where is your son?"

"I don't know. Why?"

"He may know where Jess is."

"How would he know? He doesn't know Jess."

Ginny looked at Dick, hating what she was about to do to this decent, gentle man. "Richard knows Jess," she finally said. "She knew him thirty years ago."

The weathered, tanned complexion of Dick Bradley didn't change right away. Then a slow recognition passed over his face. He paled. "Jess," he said. "Jessica. Oh, my God."

"Yeah," Ginny said. "Oh, your God." She tried to hoist herself up again, but failed. "But right now the only important thing is that we've got to find her."

Dick did not respond. He stood and stared at Ginny.

"Call your son," Ginny demanded. "And call him right now." Dick pulled himself from the edge of the bed and started to cross the room.

"And while you're at it," Ginny called after him, "you'd better check on the whereabouts of your daughter Karin, too. I think she knows who Jess is and why we're here."

"She does," Phillip confirmed, as he and Lisa entered from the hall.

Dick hesitated, then slowly left the room, now looking every bit of his sixty-nine years and maybe a dozen or so more.

•   •   •

"Maybe you shouldn't have told him." Phillip paced from one end of the room to the other, then back again. "If he calls Richard now, it will give him a chance to—"

"To what?" Ginny asked. "Escape? We're on a friggin' island. It's not as if he can get away any too quickly. The ferries are booked, remember?"

Phillip wrung his hands. In spite of the relief he had felt with Lisa, in spite of the ways she had relaxed every muscle in his body, he was now tense, rigid with fear. If only he hadn't gone off today, walking with Lisa, maybe this wouldn't have happened. Maybe he would have seen Jess and . . . oh, hell. If only he hadn't been so damn selfish, none of this would be happening. "I think we should call the police," he said.

"Christ, is that all you ever want?" Ginny asked. "Call the police on Brad, now call the police on Jess. I don't know how to tell you this, Mr. Attorney, but the police can't solve all your problems."

"Well, we have to do something," Phillip said.

Just then Dick returned to the room. "I tried phoning Richard," he said. "He's left the office for the day. And he's not home."

"Great," Ginny said. "What about Karin?"

"She's not here."

A moment passed in which no one spoke.

"I'm going to the police," Dick finally said. "The chief is a friend of mine. Maybe they can help."

After he'd gone again, Ginny looked at Phillip. "There's someone else you need to try and find."

He nodded. "Melanie." He turned to Lisa. "Do you want to come with me?"

Ginny lay on the bed, helpless and hopeless and pissed that Jess had disappeared.

If she had been the one to vanish without a trace, it wouldn't have mattered. Ginny knew—had always known—how to take care of herself. But she feared that even age and heartache and the experience of life had not hardened Jess enough and taught her how to survive when—if—the going really got tough. Jess had been a princess of a child, born gagging on a silver spoon, into a world where money could take care of problems. Money, not guts. Not real, run-for-your-life guts.

She fiddled on the nightstand for another pill. Maybe if the pain eased, she'd be able to think more clearly, she'd be able to figure out what the hell she could do. Jess had saved her life once, so long ago. Jess had saved her life, and now Ginny couldn't even get out of a friggin' bed to try to save hers.

Life, she thought, downing the pill, *continues to suck.*

Moments or hours later—she did not know which— Ginny was awakened by the sound of footsteps in the room. She opened her eyes; it had grown dark. At the foot of the bed, silhouetted in the night, was the figure of a man.

"Dick?" she asked, but he looked too tall to be Dick. "Phillip? Did you find her?"

The figure moved closer. "Well, well," the voice said. "Imagine this. Me, finding Mommie dearest in bed."

A chill surged from her brain to her heart to her aching spine. "Brad," she hissed. "What the hell are you doing here?"

Chapter 23

 "I came for my money."

Ginny struggled to prop herself on her elbows. Lying flat on her back felt too defenseless: it was not a feeling she wanted around her stepson. "There is no money for you, Brad."

The silhouette moved closer to the bed. Ginny winced and drew up her knees.

"I want the five hundred thousand. Or your daughter—and you—will be plastered across every tabloid from here to Djakarta."

She glanced around the semidarkness of the room. There was nothing she could reach—the lamp was too far away, and there was no baseball bat . . . no gun . . . that she could use for a weapon, or at least a deterrent. No scissors, as Jess had used on her stepfather.

Her body broke into a shit-scared sweat, and she tried not to think about that other night . . . that night when that asshole had stood over her, struggling to rape her, until Jess arrived, until Jess stabbed the worthless, waste-of-a-life from him.

But now, Jess was nowhere around, having disappeared

somewhere among the fishermen and the tourists on Martha's Vineyard.

She tried to chill down her sweat. "You're not going to get away with it, Brad. I'll have you arrested for extortion."

"Extortion? That's quite a fancy word. And I thought your vocabulary was limited to four-letter ones."

"Fuck you, Brad."

"Ah. Now that's more like it. And for your information, Mommie, if when you say 'extortion' you're thinking of blackmail, forget it. You've got my father's money, and I deserve it."

"He didn't think so."

Brad stepped closer. "Only because you influenced him."

Ginny laughed. "You are such a loser, Brad." She tried to sound tough, tried to sound in control. She only hoped he did not realize that she could barely move.

And then he moved toward her, bent down and put his face near hers. His breath was hot on her skin. "Maybe I should just fuck you now. Like old times. What d'ya say?"

A rush of anger overrode her pain. Ginny shot out her feet and thrust them into his groin. He fell back, the shouts of his agony merging with the pain-screams of hers. She got off the bed, grabbed for the lamp, and whacked him over the head once, twice, three times.

He was silent.

Ginny straightened her back. The pain was still there. Still there, but more tolerable. She hobbled to the doorway. She had to get out fast. Before he came to. Before he came at her again. Limping down the hall, feeling her way toward the staircase, she hoped—she prayed—she could get to her room, and her clothes, before Brad woke up. She tried not to consider that she might have killed him.

Somehow, she made it up the stairs. Then she thought she heard footsteps behind her.

God help me, she thought. She reached a doorway. She ducked inside and quickly locked the door behind her. Snapping on the light, she realized where she was: it was not the room she had shared with Lisa these past days. It was Jess's room. Room number seven, where the suitcases still sat in the corner, where . . . the door had been unlocked.

Trying not to think of that now, Ginny wobbled toward the nightstand, picked up the phone, and called the police.

"There's an intruder at Mayfield House," she said quickly. "I slugged him with a lamp. He's either out cold or he's dead." While she talked, she noticed a pale pink envelope that lay on the floor, partially hidden by the corner of the bed.

"Just get over here, fast," she barked at the policeman. "He's in a first-floor bedroom—it's in the back."

She hung up the phone, her heart beating wildly. If only she could get to her room . . . if only she could get to her clothes. Her back throbbed. She rubbed it.

She sat on the edge of the bed in Jess's room and decided to wait for the police.

Her eyes fell on the envelope once again. She pushed her foot toward the note, curled her toes around the edge, and lifted it to her hand.

It was addressed to Richard Bryant.

Frowning, Ginny took out the note that was inside: *West Chop Woods . . . red trail . . . Richard.*

So that was where Jess had gone. Somewhere called the West Chop Woods. The red trail. To meet Richard.

But where the hell was West Chop Woods? She had no idea what she'd done with the map. She supposed she could find someone—on the street, in a store—someone who would know where it was.

But first, she had to get dressed.

Just then sirens wailed in the night. And Ginny knew she had to move fast before the police arrived and she lost any more time. Because Ginny knew where Jess was, and she knew—bad back or not—that she had to get to her.

• • •

Melanie and Bob Galloway lived on Tea Lane in Chilmark, according to the "Island Book"—a telephone directory and island information bible—that Lisa had taken from the living room at Mayfield House. While she had been doing that, Phillip had broken into Jess's room, quickly rummaged through her things, and found her car keys in her purse.

Now, Phillip pushed down on the accelerator as they turned off North Road and onto Tea Lane.

"I hope this is her," Lisa said from the seat next to him.

"It has to be," Phillip said. "There were only five Galloways listed in the Vineyard. And only one Melanie." He slowed the car and began rubbernecking at the mailboxes. "What I can't understand is that if Jess intended to come out here, how'd she get here?"

"We can't be sure she is here, Phillip."

For a few moments they were silent. "Let's hope she is."

Neither of them elaborated. But Phillip held fast to the hope that maybe Richard had picked up Jess, that maybe, together, they had driven out here so Jess could meet Melanie, so the truth would be in the open once and for all. Perhaps Richard had agreed to let her meet Sarah, too. The little girl in the plaster cast who Jess had said looked so much like her.

He hoped these things, but something deep down inside him warned Phillip not to count on it.

"There it is." Lisa pointed to a mailbox in the shape of a mallard duck. *Galloway* was stenciled on the side.

Squinting in the darkness, Phillip could not see a house from the road. He took a deep breath. "Well, here goes nothing," he said, then turned the car into a narrow, tree-lined, dirt-packed driveway—a winding driveway with two well-worn ruts. It was difficult to see. There were no lampposts, only a bit of crescent moonlight filtered through the trees.

"How can anyone like it out here?" Lisa whispered. "It's so isolated."

Just then something black and moving was caught in the headlights of the car. Black and moving, black and furry. With a long white stripe that snaked down its back.

"A skunk!" Lisa shrieked.

Phillip flipped the high beams off then on again. The skunk looked up at the car, turned, and waddled into the trees.

"I don't like this," Lisa said.

"You're just a city girl."

"And you're not?"

"Nope. I'm a city boy."

"Very funny."

Phillip didn't want to admit that he thought this was no place for human beings to live. Skunks, maybe. People, no way.

The driveway curved left. Phillip followed it. Abruptly, it ended. Phillip stopped the car just behind a four-wheel-drive brown Bronco with "Cape Cod & the Islands" Massachusetts license plates. The vehicle was parked near what appeared to be a front sidewalk, beyond which sat a small, square house with neat white shutters and the now-familiar gray, weathered shingles. Phillip could see that the front door was painted a cheerful red; rows of red geraniums filled window boxes. And the four many-paned windows on the face of the house—two to the left of the door, two to the right—glowed with lights from within.

"It looks nice," Lisa said. "Homey."

"I thought you said it was isolated."

"It is. But it's homey."

"I wonder if Richard drives a Bronco."

"I guess there's only one way to know for sure."

Phillip looked over at Lisa, who was looking at the house. "This is the right thing to do," he asked, "isn't it?"

She turned her head to him. "I have no idea."

He smiled at her frankness. "Come on." He opened his door. "Let's get it over with."

They were halfway up the walk when the red front door

opened. A man with a neatly groomed beard and a T-shirt marked *Menemsha Blues* called out to them.

"You folks lost?"

"Don't think so," Phillip responded, but said no more until they reached the bottom of the three-step stairs. "You must be Bob Galloway."

"That's me." He did not look much older than Phillip and Lisa.

"Is your wife home?" Lisa asked. "Melanie?"

Bob Galloway folded his well-muscled arms. "What's this about?"

"We're friends of the Bradleys," Phillip said, improvising as he spoke. "We'd like to speak with Melanie if she's here."

Bob Galloway eyed them a moment longer, then went back into the house without closing the door. Through the doorway Phillip could see a small, tidy living room with a fireplace against one wall. Next to it was a child's table and two chairs, a plaid sofa, and a small rocking horse; across the room stood two small bookcases, the bottom shelves of which were overstuffed with books, the top shelves with pictures—family pictures, perhaps—in oval and rectangular frames. From within came the aroma of beef stew or meatloaf, reminding Phillip that he hadn't eaten tonight, not that it mattered, because who needed food when . . .

A young woman in a long gingham dress appeared at the door. Behind her was Bob Galloway. "I'm Melanie," she said. Somewhere, far beyond the pines, an island night-critter howled a slow, muted howl. Phillip cleared his throat and introduced himself and Lisa. "We're looking for a woman named Jess Randall," he said. "Her name used to be Jessica Bates. Have you seen her?" He looked for recognition in Melanie's eyes—a quick flash, perhaps, or a knowing blink. There was none. Instead, she looked from Phillip to Lisa then back to Phillip again.

"No," she replied. "I don't know anyone by that name." Her eyes drifted back to Lisa. "Aren't you Lisa Andrews from *Devonshire Place*?"

Lisa took Phillip's arm. "Yes."

"Gosh, we watch your show all the time. . . ."

Nervously rubbing the skin of Phillip's arm, Lisa smiled weakly. Phillip realized it was the first time he'd been with her when she'd been recognized. He wondered if it bothered her; he decided that it did, and found her vulnerability endearing.

"Thank you," Lisa said. "You're sure you don't know a woman named Jessica Bates or Jess Randall?"

Melanie shook her head. "Sorry," she said.

Phillip believed her. He also believed that Melanie Galloway had a quiet life, a life in which she seemed to belong. And that they had no right to step in and try and change that.

Stones and twigs scraped her cheek. Jess opened her eyes. It was dark. She pushed a dead leaf from her face, and moaned.

There was no response in the night-dark woods. Only an eerie stillness, where no birds sang, no seagulls screeched. Nothing but stillness and a thin mist of fog that clung to the air like spun angel hair and prickled her skin with its touch.

Her foot throbbed. Slowly, she managed to sit up. She touched where it hurt. Her ankle had swollen over the side of her shoe, had puffed out like a balloon valance in a lady's boudoir. "Owwwwwwwww," she cried. Her head began to hurt and she began to shiver. She rubbed her hands against her arms, trying to brush the pine needles and pieces of decaying leaves from the sleeves of her sweater.

The ground was damp beneath her. She put down her hands and tried to stand. But her ankle couldn't take her weight. She slumped back to the ground.

"Help," she called quietly, knowing there was no one or nothing to hear her. No one but the animals that played in the night, nothing but the mysteries that danced in the shadows.

She wondered why Richard had not come. She wondered about the envelope and if he had tricked her. She wondered if the orange bit of fabric had belonged to Karin, and, if so, what she'd been doing here. She wondered if she was going to die here in the middle of the woods on an island in the middle of the sea. If she would die before ever seeing her children again—Chuck, Maura, Travis. Her children—the ones she had nurtured and loved and raised to become the young adults they were, the sometimes-spoiled, sometimes-unappreciative young adults whom she did not doubt did love her. She wondered if they'd miss her if she died here in these woods.

Then she thought about Maura, and how unfair this really had been to her. Once, Maura had been Jess's only daughter. Now she was faced with competing with an un-named, unknown, "other" daughter. No matter how many psychology classes Maura took, or how many case studies she researched, Maura would, perhaps, never be able to be objective about this situation: about Melanie and Sarah and Richard, the man Jess once loved.

And now, Jess's last hope that she might know her first child had been shattered, her last effort thwarted. And all she wanted to do was go home. She wanted to try and come to terms with what Father had done—that, despite his inability to show his true feelings, he had cared enough about Jess to take care of her baby in, she supposed, the way he had deemed best. She wanted to have a chance to try and come to terms with that. She did not want to die here in the woods. And, more than anything, she wanted to go home.

Instead, she remained motionless on the ground, wondering how long she would survive, and how long it would take before someone found her body. She dropped her head and lowered her eyes. She let the tears roll down her cheeks, just as, in the forest, it began to rain.

• • •

She was going to find the son of a bitch and kill him. If she'd done it to Brad, surely Ginny was perfectly capable of wasting this jackass named Richard.

Richard, she thought, jamming Dick's pickup truck into gear and heading toward the center of town. If she'd heard his name once she'd heard it a trillion-too-many times thirty years ago. "Richard is coming for me, you'll see," a young Jess had told them over and over. Well, Richard had not come. He'd come here instead. Not that Ginny blamed him. The Vineyard was far nicer than Larchwood Hall. And Mayfield House was definitely more upscale than the cold-water flat he and Jess would have had to live in with their baby if he'd married her and her father had cut off her cash.

But just like three decades ago, *Richard* was up to no good. He could give Jess any load of crap that he wanted, but his actions spoke volumes. And right now, the story didn't look much different than when he bailed out on her three decades ago.

She could kill the son of a bitch for screwing up Jess's mind again.

Rumbling along Main Street in the old Ford, Ginny rolled down the window. The sidewalks, of course, had been proverbially rolled up and packed away with the day's leftover saltwater taffy; it was after all, ten o'clock in Vineyard Haven and the tourists were expected to be snuggly tucked in their overpriced rooms at the overpriced bed-and-breakfasts. And as if that wasn't bad enough, Ginny thought as she flipped on the wipers, now it was fucking raining.

At least Dick had left the old pickup in the garage at the inn. At least he'd left the keys in the ignition. She tried to be grateful for such a small mercy, but all she really cared about was that her back was still killing her and she had to find Jess.

"Hey!" she shouted out the window at a yellow-slicker-clad figure that walked on the sidewalk. "Where's West Chop Woods?" The figure pretended it didn't hear her and scurried along, ducking into a dark doorway. "Asshole," Ginny muttered, swinging the truck up Spring Street to circle around and go back to the beginning of Main. If nothing else, she could stop at the Tisbury Inn. Someone had to be there. Someone with a brain.

Someone was there. A few minutes later, limping with pain and soggy from the rain that soaked through the nylon sweatsuit she'd managed to change into before the cops found her, Ginny hobbled up to the desk. "I'm trying to find West Chop Woods," she said. "Where the hell is it?"

The man at the counter smiled. "A little inclement for camping, isn't it?"

She grabbed the edge of the counter and leaned forward, ignoring the sharp pull in her back. "Just tell me where the fuck it is. Someone's life depends on it."

Whether he was intimidated by the rain-drenched woman who had not showered or put on makeup in two days, or whether he wanted to get her out of the lobby, Ginny didn't know or care. He quickly gave her directions to the woods. And she was out of there as fast as her aching back could carry her.

On and off, Jess dozed. As the rain came down harder the woods became noisier; the plop of the drops grew fiercer and firmer; the leaves and the branches and the solid, hard-packed earth grew wetter and wetter.

At some point, she had stopped crying. Now, when she was awake, Jess simply stared into the night.

Once, she had tried to drag her body along the path. But the roots and the ruts poked and dug at her stomach. So she had lain still once more, crying then staring then dozing a little, wondering why God had let this happen to her, and why it was taking so long for Him to simply let her have her last breath then quietly die.

She thought about something she's read long ago—maybe it had been in Sedona, where, if Maura had gone, things now might have been different. It was an Indian spiritual belief that we were all put here for a special reason, to work out unresolved issues from our past lives. If it were true, she wondered if she would wake up and be someone else, and if she would ever know if Chuck and Maura and Travis had grown into happy adults, and if Melanie had ever learned the truth of her birth.

Not, of course, that it would matter, for she would be dead.

"Jess!"

A name that sounded like hers drifted through the rain. Jess smiled. Now the raindrops were beginning to talk to her, she thought. She wondered if she would lose all of her mind before God gave her that last breath.

"Jess! Are you here?"

Jess blinked. She sucked in her breath and grew very still. She listened.

"Jess!"

The voice was louder now. More clear.

"Jess! It's Ginny!"

Jess put her hands to her face and let her tears flow. *Ginny. Ginny is here.* "Ginny!" she cried softly. "I'm over here! I can't walk."

"Over *here*? Over *where*?"

"I don't know. I fell in a hole . . ." Her words were mixed with her tears.

"Keep talking," Ginny said. "I'll find you."

"I can't . . . I don't know what to say . . ."

"Tell me what a fucking wonderful friend I am to find you in the rain when I can hardly walk either and you've scared the shit out of all of us."

"All of who?"

"Me. Lisa. Phillip. Dick."

Footsteps crunched close to Jess's side.

"Ginny," she said quietly, "if you keep walking, you're going to trip over me."

"Fuck," Ginny said.

They were silent a moment, rain drenching them both.

"Well," Ginny said, "what the hell happened to you?"

"I told you. I fell in a hole. I think I broke my foot. I can't walk."

"Where's Richard?"

"He never showed up."

"That figures."

Jess hung her head. "Ginny, please . . ."

"Well, I don't know how the hell we're going to get you out of here. I can't exactly sling you over my back."

"Maybe I should wait here and you should get help."

"It's raining."

"I've been here since before dark. Another half hour won't kill me."

Ginny stood still a moment, pondering a solution. Then the sounds of crunching and tromping echoed through the woods.

Jess's heart began to beat quickly. "Oh, God, Ginny, what's that?"

"Do I look like a Boy Scout?"

"Maybe it's a bear. Or a . . ."

"Jess?" The word was called out so clearly and loudly that it startled them both. "Jess? Are you here?"

Ginny reached out and grabbed Jess's wrist. She put her finger to her lips to shush her.

Jess frowned and pulled her arm from Ginny's grasp. "Richard!" she replied. "I'm over here!"

Ginny rolled her eyes and wondered how Jess could be so stupid as to let the man who'd left her here to rot come back and try it again.

Chapter 24

"Karin will be here in a minute," Richard said to Jess, pulling up a chair and sitting beside Jess's hospital bed, where she lay with her broken foot in a white cast, elevated, as the doctors had ordered.

Ginny stood on the other side of the bed, gripping the metal rail to keep herself steady, to keep her back the only way it did not hurt: straight. "What does your fruitcake sister have to do with this?" Ginny asked.

Jess gave her a look that said *Shut up*, but Ginny ignored it. Just because Karin/Morticia had finally gone to Richard and told him what had happened to Jess in the woods did not mean Ginny trusted her—or him.

Richard sat back in the chair. "She didn't mean any harm. She only wanted to get Jess to leave. To get you all to leave."

"She wrote the note about meeting me in the woods," Jess said to Ginny. "She signed Richard's name."

"So it was her all along," Ginny replied. "It was Karin who sent you that first note. Who made the call."

Jess and Richard both nodded.

"So why the hell does she want us to leave now? And why the sneaking around in the woods?"

"I expect she didn't want anyone to see us together," Jess said. "I think she changed her mind about wanting me to meet Melanie."

Richard closed his eyes. "If only I'd had some idea of how deeply troubled Karin has been all these years."

Ginny snorted. "Collecting sea glass in her spare time? Wasn't that a clue?"

"I never thought . . . " he said, dropping his face into his hands. "Oh, God, I just didn't know . . . "

Jess reached out her hand and touched Richard's arm. "Richard," she asked, "I'm still a little confused. First of all, why did Karin do it? After all this time, why did she choose now to get in touch with me? And another thing . . . she put the note in an envelope I had written to you, Richard. One of the letters I'd sent you when I was at Larchwood. What was she doing with that? How did she get it?"

"Don't ask him," came a voice from the doorway, "he never even saw those letters." Karin walked into the room wearing an orange sarong—the same color orange as the flash of fabric Jess had seen in the woods. She carried what looked like an old cigar box. "I'm sorry about your foot, Jess. I never intended for you to get hurt . . ."

"What letters, Karin?" Richard interrupted then shot a glance at Jess. "You wrote me letters while you were at Larchwood?"

Ginny groaned. "Letters isn't the word for it. Every damn day, where was Jess? Curled up on her bed with that scented stationery . . ."

Taking Jess's hand, Richard said, "I never got any letters, Jess. I had no idea. . . ."

"Of course you didn't," Karin said, holding out the cigar box. "They were all forwarded to Jess's father."

Even Ginny was lost now. But Richard took the box from his sister and opened it. Then he removed a stack of pink envelopes, tied with a ribbon.

"There's a newspaper clipping there, too," Karin said. "From Jess's wedding. That's how I found out her married name. That's how I was able to track her down in Greenwich."

"I don't understand," Jess said, staring at the stack of old letters. "Where did you get these?"

Karin laughed, but it was a laugh of neither amusement nor joy; it was a sad, melancholy laugh that sent a wave of compassion through Ginny that she did not know she possessed. "I found everything in a secret compartment of an old rolltop desk," she said.

With a frown, Richard asked, "What old rolltop desk?"

"The one I bought a few years ago at that yard sale."

Richard shook his head. "Wait a minute. You bought a desk at a yard sale and it had my letters inside? That doesn't make sense, Karin."

"Yes, it does," she replied. "I bought it from the people who owned one of the big houses in West Chop. The house I cleaned every summer when I was young. The house that was rented to a man who called himself Harold Dixon."

Ginny leaned gingerly against the wall, trying to decipher what was being said. She glanced at Jess, who seemed as puzzled as Richard. Then Karin continued.

"All along I knew it was foolish," Karin said, her eyes taking on a faraway look, "to fall in love with a summer person. But he was so handsome and kind to me. And he did not mind when mother died and I could not go away with him because of Mellie. He did not mind. He just kept coming every summer and loving us both—Mellie and me. I didn't know his name was not Harold Dixon. I did not know his real name was Gerald Bates."

The room grew still. The air grew heavy. And then Ginny figured out what Karin was saying. At about the same time as Jess did.

"My father?" she asked. "Was it Father?"

"I called him Brit and he called me Yank," Karin said. "I did not think that he would lie to me."

Jess turned as pale as the too-often bleached hospital sheets. "No . . ." she began to protest.

"Yes," Karin said, tears filling her eyes. "And he loved me, really he did. At first I guess he came only to see Mellie. To watch her grow up. To make sure she was safe. I don't think he planned to fall in love with me. But he did. Really he did." In the silence Karin toyed with the sea glass pendant around her neck. "But then he didn't come back," she continued. "He never came back and all these years later those people had the yard sale and oh, how I wanted that desk. It's where he used to work in the study when he was on the island. I wanted it to remind me of him. It wasn't until I was looking for a place to keep the best of my sea glass that I came across the secret compartment. It wasn't until then that I knew who he was."

"That he was Jess's father . . ." Richard said.

Karin nodded. "And Melanie's grandfather. I don't know why he had those letters here. Maybe he planned to give them to you, Richard."

"But how the hell did he get them?" Ginny asked. "Jess wrote them to Richard. She mailed them. More than once I saw her . . ." And then an idea came into her mind. "Oh, shit," she said.

"They were all in a big envelope addressed to Jess's father," Karin said. "That was when I realized that the man I knew as Harold Dixon was really Gerald Bates. I got so angry I threw the big envelope away, but the return address was from—"

"Bud Wilson," Ginny interrupted. The scum of a sheriff—who was also the postmaster.

"Right," Karin answered. "That was the name."

"He never sent your letters through, Jess," Ginny said.

Jess's eyes were glazed, as if she were sleepwalking. "Father probably paid him not to," she said.

"Your father must have cared a lot about you," Karin said. "A long time ago I thought . . ." She stammered a little, blinked, then looked out the window. "I thought he cared about me, too. But I haven't seen him in so many years. . . ."

Slowly, Jess began to speak. "How many years?" she asked.

"Not since the summer of 1982. My letters after that all were returned."

Jess turned her face away from Karin. "He died that October."

If the air had been heavy before in the room, now it was stagnant, unmoving, as if someone had pushed the Pause button on the remote. Then Karin lowered her eyes and looked down at the floor. "So he did love me," she said. "He didn't leave me. He died."

"He died," Jess confirmed.

"Oh," she replied, taking hold once again of the pendant she wore on a chain around her neck.

"I never knew he came to the Vineyard," Jess said quietly.

"Twelve years," Karin said. "Twelve summers."

"And he watched my daughter grow up."

"Yes. He was a good man, Jess. He loved us—Mellie and me. In his own very proper, sort of British way." She rubbed the sea glass and closed her eyes. "I called him Brit, you know . . . and the called me Yank. . . ." And then she drifted into a world of memories where only she had been.

"I don't understand why you didn't tell Melanie," Lisa said to Phillip, as Phillip parked Jess's car in the hospital parking lot.

He turned off the ignition and smiled at Lisa. "Because she's not like us, Lisa. Melanie has a good life. She's not single and adrift and doing things she's not comfortable doing. She's being herself, or at least she seems to be."

"What are you talking about?"

"I'm talking about how I hate being a corporate lawyer. Maybe it's because I was adopted. Maybe that has nothing to do with it. But the bottom line is, Melanie seems genuinely happy. We have no right to screw that up, just because our lives are a little disjointed."

"*Our* lives? Excuse me, Counselor, but I think you should speak for yourself. My life is perfectly happy. I am a Hollywood *star*, in case you hadn't noticed."

He threw her a look. "I noticed. And I also think maybe you're not always happy in the role of a star."

"You don't know what you're talking about."

"You're nice, Lisa. You're a good person. What really happened between you and Brad? I'm sorry, but I don't buy that story that after a whirlwind courtship he suddenly woke up one day and decided to blackmail you and Ginny."

She stared out the window, but didn't respond. Phillip reached across the console and put his hand on hers. "Lisa, I like you a lot. I may even be in love with you, whatever that means. But I think before you go back to L.A., and continue to do whatever it is you do, you should take a look at a few things. Or you'll wind up with another Brad Edwards and another disaster."

Those beautiful, irresistible topaz eyes began to water. Phillip wanted to shoot himself for hurting her feelings. But he felt he had spoken the truth, and if there was ever to be anything more between him and Lisa, he knew she had to be honest with herself. Only then would she be able to be honest with him.

"You're right," she said softly. "There was more to the story."

Rain pelted the windshield. Phillip took her hand in his. "I'm listening."

"Brad was planning to take Ginny to court over Jake's estate. He asked me for money to pay his attorneys. I couldn't do it. I knew Jake well enough to know he must have had his reasons for doing what he did. I tried to tell Brad there was no way Ginny would have been able to convince Jake to do anything. My mother loved him. He saved her life, in a sense. He was, I think, perhaps the first man in her life she ended up not using. If he wanted her to have his money, then he really wanted it. I also knew she had tried to convince him not to do it. But he had refused."

"So when you wouldn't give Brad the money to fight Ginny, he came up with the blackmail plan."

"Yes," she said. "And that's when I knew for certain that he didn't really . . . love me. He was only using me to get what he wanted. Just as Ginny tried to tell me."

"So you threw him out?"

"What else could I do? He was asking me to choose between him and Ginny. I'd spent twenty-five years not even knowing who she was. Sure, she's a little . . . different. But I love her, Phillip. She's my mother."

Phillip picked up her hand and held it to his lips. "You see?" he said. "You are a good person."

"But I don't care what you say, I do love acting."

"Acting, maybe. But being a star?"

She smiled. "No. Actually, I hate that part. I hate seeing my picture on the covers of magazines. I hate people recognizing my face."

Phillip smiled. "I knew it! You're simply too . . . *emotional* to like all that false surface stuff."

She slid over the console and took his face in her hands. "And just how do you know that I'm too emotional?"

Phillip smoothed the hair from her forehead; he wiped the tears from her cheeks. Then he kissed her slowly, deeply, warmly. And she kissed him back, their tongues touching lightly at first, then more urgently, the fire igniting, the passion rising.

"See what I mean?" Phillip said, breaking away. "Did you forget we're sitting in a parking lot at a hospital emergency room?"

"Yes," Lisa said almost shyly. "I seem to forget a lot of things when you're around."

"Hmm. Well, I'll have to decide what to do about that some other time. Right now, I really do want to see Jess."

"Okay," Lisa replied. "But no matter how long we stay

here, I want you to know I'm going to be sleeping with you tonight."

The grin that spread across Phillip's face he felt clear down to his toes.

Unfortunately, Brad survived.

Dick had arrived at the hospital and told Ginny the grim news: Her stepson had a nasty concussion, but was awake, alert, and being monitored down the hall from Jess's room.

After Phillip and Lisa had said "How are you feeling?" to Jess and "My God, Karin was behind all this?" Phillip turned to Ginny. She had not commented that the whole time they'd been in there, he'd been holding Lisa's hand.

"I think we should confront Brad together," he said. "And now seems as good a time as any."

Ginny frowned. "Everyone around here seems to forget that I was the first one in pain. And no one seems to care that right now my back is throbbing like an abscessed tooth."

"Would you like me to arrange for a bed for you?" Dick asked.

"Are you crazy? Hospitals scare the shit out of me."

"Then let's at least do something positive," Phillip said. "Come with us to see Brad. I'll do all the talking."

Ginny moved her gaze from Jess in the bed to Richard by her side to Dick to Phillip to Lisa. She did not look at Karin.

"Please, Mom," Lisa said. "I think Phillip is right. Let's get this over with."

"As for us," Dick said, putting an arm around Karin, "I think we should leave Richard and Jess alone. They must have a few things to talk about."

Ginny knew she was being railroaded, but didn't seem to have any control over it. "All right," she reluctantly agreed. "I'll go and see Brad. But I can't guarantee that this time I won't kill him for sure."

• • •

"The doctor said he only needs to keep you overnight," Richard said to Jess once everyone had left the room.

She nodded. The pain in her foot now had been replaced by a grogginess she couldn't shake, but the damp chill that had invaded her body out there in the woods had finally been warmed by the soft flannel sheets the nurse had put on the bed and by the presence of people, the renewal of life. "I'm so tired," she said, closing her eyes. "And I can't believe that Father and Karin were lovers."

"I knew Karin had someone, but I had no idea it was your father. I never saw him here," Richard said.

"You only saw him once anyway."

"At your mother's funeral."

"The day . . ."

"In the backseat . . ." Richard ran his hand through his hair. "God, how Karin loved it when he came each summer. She was a different person then—so happy and alive."

Jess listened to the soft rhythm of Richard's voice, trying to imagine her father with Karin, remembering the months that she herself did not—had not wanted to—see Father, because she'd thought he had never loved her . . . when all along he'd been here, loving Richard's sister, loving Jess's baby. Capable of loving, in his own private way.

Richard squeezed her hand now. "You're tired," he said. "I think we can wait until tomorrow to have our talk."

Slowly, she stirred. "I thought everything had been said. I told you I'm not going to pursue this with Melanie." She rested a moment, then added, "If you think it's best that she doesn't know about me—about us—then I won't interfere. I care about her happiness, Richard. I don't want to upset that." A wave of sleepiness came over her.

"We'll talk tomorrow," she heard Richard say as she drifted away, finally safe and warm.

• • •

"Blackmail is a felony," Phillip said to the man in the bed, who was wearing a turban of bandages. "If you persist in this charade, I'll be sure you are sent away for a very, very long time. And from what I understand, prison is not very pleasant for guys who look like you."

Brad did not answer.

"Don't think he can't do it," Ginny said. "Phillip is not only a good friend of mine, but he has friends in high places."

Ginny, of course, did not know what she was talking about, but Phillip admired her chutzpah at calling Brad's bluff. He only hoped Brad had never heard of the likes of Nicole's father—or his West Coast counterparts, who probably dealt not in divorce but in other legal forms of deceit. *Nicole* . . . Phillip wondered what he'd ever seen in the self-centered law student. No matter what happened next, he was lucky to have been saved from a life with her.

He turned back to Brad. "What we're doing is giving you a break," he said. "Technically, we could bring you up on charges right now. Attempted extortion. That would be good for at least a few years." He knew he was shooting in the dark; it had been too many years now since he'd had a class in criminal law. But Brad had no way of knowing that.

Finally, Brad spoke. "You can't prove a fucking thing."

Phillip smiled. "That's where you're wrong. You did try to assault Mrs. Edwards."

Brad struggled to sit up. He flopped back down on the pillow and raised his fist. "She's the one who attacked me!"

"That's funny," Phillip said, "that's not how Ginny remembers it, is it, Ginny?"

Ginny leveled her eyes on her stepson. "He tried to rape me," she said.

"Bullshit!" Brad shrieked.

"I'm sure a jury would see things differently," Phillip said. "After all, you do not exactly have a clean record in a court of law."

Brad started to say something, then he gave up.

"If I were you," Phillip continued, "I'd cut my losses. File bankruptcy, if you have to. And sell the red Porsche. It might appease the IRS for a while. Make a new start, Brad. And, for once, try and do something constructive."

He put one arm around Lisa, another around Ginny, feeling a bit like a comic book hero, but sometimes comic book heroes were called for. "And whatever you do, stay the hell away from them." He escorted the ladies toward the door in a purposefully dramatic exit. "Or you'll regret it until the day you die."

In the hallway, out of Brad's sight, Phillip moved to loosen his tie, then remembered he wasn't wearing a tie. Ginny high-fived him and gave him a huge hug. Lisa kissed him smack on the lips. Phillip Archambault would not have traded this moment for all the McGinnis and Smiths in the world.

"I'm okay, honey," Jess said into the phone to Maura. "I have a small break in my foot, but I'll be okay." She closed her eyes and half listened as her daughter said things like, "How did it happen?" and "Are you sure you're all right, Mom?" and "Do you want Travis and me to come there?"

"I'm okay, honey," Jess repeated. And she *was* okay. She had felt Richard kiss her forehead just before he left; she had heard him whisper, "I'm so sorry, Jess. I'm so sorry for everything." Jess had realized then that maybe that was all she needed. Or, at least, that it was enough. Enough for her to get on with her life. She had seen her daughter; she knew she was alive, happy, and healthy. She had seen her grand-daughter, the little girl who looked so much like her. Jess had seen them and now she knew. It was enough, and it was so much more than she'd had.

"Did you find her, Mom?" Maura was suddenly saying.

"Find her?" Jess asked.

"Your . . . daughter. Is she there?" Her voice sounded so childlike, so unsure, almost frightened. Jess knew that she had been right: Maura had felt threatened, afraid that her life was going to change, that she would lose that special place in her mother's heart, that there wasn't room for more than her. Jess knew she would have to work very hard to erase that fear; and she knew that every tenuous, difficult moment would be worth it.

She smiled. "Yes, honey, I did see her. But no, she's not here now. She has a little girl. A little girl who looks a lot like you did."

Maura paused a moment. "Really?" she asked.

"She's so cute," Jess went on. "And Melanie seems so happy."

There was hesitation again. "That's nice."

"It is nice, Maura. It's what I needed to know. I'll be home in a few days, and we can talk about it more if you'd like."

"Yes, Mom. I think I'd like that a lot."

At least Ginny could move without shrieking in pain. She sat on the veranda in a chair next to Dick. Morticia was nowhere to be seen.

"She's probably out at West Chop," Dick said, "looking for sea glass."

"She needs help, Dick," Ginny said, and was surprised to realize that she meant it.

"I know. I've ignored it for years. Now I'm going to encourage her to get some. She's only forty-nine. She still has the rest of her life to live." He turned to face Ginny. "What about you, Ginny? What are you going to do with the rest of yours?"

"Well, I probably won't go back to eating Tostitos and watching TV. I don't know what I'll do. I'm too old to act and I was lousy at it anyway."

"But you're going back to L.A.?"

"Well, sure. That's where I live."

"I was hoping I could convince you to stay here."

"You want me to live on a freaking island?"

"There are worse fates."

She felt a twinge in her back. She remembered how kind he had been. How kind he had been to nurse her in her pain; how great he had been as a lover, a partner, breaking through the sex block she had, making her feel special again.

"I don't know, Dick. I think that right now I need to go home and put things back together. I still miss my husband, you know. No offense."

"None taken."

"And I need to make some decisions about his business, which, believe it or not, I'm actually thinking of keeping and running myself."

Dick let out a hearty laugh. "I'm sure you'd be great. You'd show those Hollywood types a thing or two."

Ginny grinned, not realizing until now that maybe she really should do that, and maybe she would really be great.

Dick reached over and patted her hand. "But you'll need a vacation from time to time. And this 'freaking' island isn't going anywhere for a few thousand more years until the beach erosion wins the battle with the environmentalists and it drops it into the sea. Until then, I'll probably be here, too."

Ginny smiled.

Chapter 25

 Jess adjusted the crutches under her arms and hopped into the dining room at Mayfield House. She was the first one there; Richard had asked that they all meet there at one o'clock.

Thankfully, her discharge from the hospital had not taken long. Phillip had been waiting for her: Phillip, her new caretaker, it seemed. Jess smiled as she leaned her crutches against the sideboard and sat down at the long mahogany table. She was lucky to have him in her life. If only P.J. could have witnessed Phillip's wonderful, sensitive spirit and his bright, eager soul. At least P.J. had known her son for a few months; at least she had not died without seeing him.

"Jess," Phillip said now, as he entered the dining room. "Lisa will be right down. Ginny said it might take her a little longer. She's upstairs shouting something about being crippled and wondering if she'll be able to get handicapped plates for her car."

Jess laughed. "I guess she moved around too much yesterday."

"She should have let the hospital doctor check her out."

"Ginny likes to do things her way. In case you hadn't noticed."

Phillip smiled and took a seat next to Jess. "I wonder what Richard is planning to do."

"I don't know. Maybe he wants to give us complimentary ferry tickets so we'll leave as soon as possible."

Running his hand along the table's smooth edge, Phillip asked, "You still care about him, don't you?"

Jess didn't know what to say. How did one explain to an almost-thirty-year-old man that life doesn't always live up to your expectations, and that dreams are sometimes better left as just dreams? Then she thought about Phillip and the struggles he'd had, and she realized that perhaps he already knew.

She rested her hand on his. "Part of me will always love Richard," she said. "For the time that we had, for the love that we shared. But that was a long time ago, Phillip. And now I know it's time to go."

"I agree," Ginny spoke from the doorway, interrupting their moment. "But I figure I won't be out of here until sometime around the turn of the freaking century."

Ginny limped into the room, leaning on Dick. Jess smiled at the concept of Ginny leaning on *anyone*.

Lisa entered behind them and went directly to sit on Phillip's other side.

And then Richard came in. "Well," he said, "I see you're all here."

She blinked and looked up at the man whom, yes, a part of her always would love.

"As requested," Ginny said, sitting stiffly on the hard chair that Dick had pulled out for her.

Richard nodded and turned his head back toward the door. "Karin?" he asked. "Come on in."

Today her sarong was purple, her T-shirt, blue. Karin drifted into the room and sat close to Richard, and Jess tried not to stare, tried not to imagine Father with her, summertime lovers for so many years.

Around the table, no one spoke. Then Dick cleared his throat. "Before Richard begins, I'd like everyone to know that Karin has agreed to go into therapy. In fact, we're going together. I think this family could use a little counseling after . . . well, after all we've been through."

Jess held back her smile. *Therapy,* she thought, remembering the valuable hours and years spent in poorly decorated offices, working to find a sense of herself and a balance with her children. She had first expected perfection; she had quickly realized it was not possible. Progress was the key. And still, today, they progressed.

"But first we're going to start with a little old-fashioned honesty," Richard was saying. "We're going to clear out the cobwebs of the past and accept where it takes us from here."

Jess did not know what he meant. Then she heard the front door open, the soft banging of the screen behind it. And before she could say anything—before anyone could— Melanie walked into the room.

Jess sat perfectly still. Phillip reached under the table and took her hand.

"Richard," Melanie said. "Sorry we're late. We got tied up in traffic. I can't believe it's so heavy, and it's only the beginning of June."

The tall windows in the room were wide open. A slight breeze drifted in from the ocean. And yet Jess could not seem to catch her breath, could not seem to find any air.

Her voice, Jess thought. Her voice was so soft; her voice was so sweet. It was not like Maura's. Was it like . . . hers?

"Mellie," he said, "I'm glad you made it. Have a seat."

She looked around at the room full of strangers, then sat, with confidence, next to Dick, the man who she thought was her father.

Without hesitation, Richard began. "Mellie," he said, "we're all here to tell you a story . . . a story that's going to surprise you, shock you, and probably totally piss you off."

Jess lowered her head and listened.

"A long time ago," Richard said, "I fell in love with a young girl named Jess."

No one interrupted while he talked. Not a bird chirped outside. Not a buoy bell clanged. When Richard reached the part about coming to the island, about leaving Jess alone at a home for unwed mothers, gentle tears dropped into Jess's lap. She did not dare look at Ginny. She had an odd feeling that Ginny, too, might be shedding a tear, or at least holding one back.

And then the real honesty came. "Jess had the baby, Mellie," he said. "And that baby was you. Your grandfather gave us the money so you could come live with us. So you would always have 'family.' "

He paused, as if unable to go on. Jess looked up and saw him walk to the window, fix his gaze outside to the lawn, and run his hands through his hair.

Melanie did not speak.

Jess forced herself to turn her head, to look at her daughter. "I am Jess," she said. "I am your birth mother."

Dick put his arm around Melanie. "Oh, honey, we loved you so much. We didn't think Jess wanted you. We didn't know that she'd had no choice: that her father had forced her to give you up."

"But . . ." Melanie said.

"We did it for you. We wanted you to be with your family, not with some strangers . . . oh, honey," Dick continued, "can you ever forgive us for not telling you the truth?"

Melanie smiled, an odd reaction, Jess thought. "But don't you see?" she asked. "I've known all along."

The room was silent.

Karin rose from her chair and padded to the fireplace at the far end of the room.

"Mother told me, Daddy," she said to Dick. "Mother

told me all about it before she died. She made me promise never to let you know that she had. She told me about the money. It was two hundred thousand dollars, wasn't it? She told me how you used it to pay off the woman at the home, how you used it so you could have me and raise me as your own."

Richard began to laugh. "I can't believe this."

Melanie looked at Jess, her face wide in a smile. "So," she said. "You're my birth mother."

"Yes," Jess replied.

Melanie rose and moved to the other side of the table where Jess sat. She leaned down and hugged her, her thin yet strong arms enveloping her mother, her sweetness closing around Jess like a long-awaited treasure, a gift from above. "I've waited a very long time to meet you," she said. "Thank you for being so brave to come here."

Jess's tears came again. "Oh," she cried, "I'm not very brave at all. I'm just stubborn, I guess. Stubborn and a little bit foolish sometimes."

"We won't tell that to your granddaughter. Would you like to meet her?"

Jess nodded, unable to speak through her tears.

Melanie disappeared for a moment, then returned with the little girl on crutches, the little girl with wispy blond hair and rosy pink cheeks who looked so much like Jess, who focused her wide blue eyes on Jess now and clearly asked, "Are you my grandma?"

Jess could only nod. The little girl maneuvered her crutches over to Jess and gave her a hug. She smelled fresh and clean, like she'd just had a bath, and her skin was warm and soft, so soft, so little-girl soft. "My name's Sarah," she said.

"Sarah," Jess said. "It's so wonderful to meet you."

"Why are you crying?" Sarah asked. "Is it because you have to use those crutches? Don't cry about that. I can show you how they work."

Jess wiped her tears and laughed. Across the table, Ginny

stood up stiffly and cleared her throat. "Well, kids," she said to Lisa and Phillip, "I think this party can do with one less handicapped person. Let's leave them to their family reunion, okay?"

Phillip and Lisa rose and left the room with Ginny. But not before Jess saw the tears that filled Ginny's eyes.

He felt really good. Really good about himself, and really good about his decision.

"I'm going back to New York," Phillip told Lisa and Ginny as they sat on the verandah. "It's time."

"Are you ever going to tell your mother about P.J.?" Lisa asked.

He shook his head. "No. I think it's best to leave it alone." Then he smiled. "I am, however, going to tell her she can stop selecting women for me."

Lisa smiled.

"And I'm going to do something else," he continued. "I'm going to tell my brother that I no longer want to be a corporate attorney." He took Lisa's hand and studied her perfect, fine fingers.

"What are you going to do?" Ginny asked. "Be a bum?"

"Actually, I was thinking about teaching law. Spending hours in the library. I'm really much better at research than I am at practicing. Besides, it would give me time to run. I love to run, and I never do enough of it."

"Manhattan is an awful place to run," Lisa said. "All those buses and cars and taxicabs."

"I know. Which is why I was thinking of moving out to L.A."

Lisa squeezed his hand. "Then I think it's a perfectly marvelous idea."

EPILOGUE

The August sun sizzled off the water and burned her face. Jess reached in her handbag for more sunscreen, but Maura stopped her and handed her a different bottle.

"Try this, Mom," she said. "I like it better than the stuff you've always bought."

Jess smiled and squeezed out a small dot of white lotion. She did not mention that she was beginning to realize that maybe she did not have all the answers: that maybe her children really did have sensible, grown-up minds of their own. She wondered if this was the beginning of another passage of life, then realized it didn't really matter. They would live their own lives, have their own joys, feel their own pain. Whatever she did now, beyond being there for them, didn't matter.

What really mattered was that Maura and Travis were with her right now, on the ferry bound for the Vineyard. What mattered was that they were eager to meet their half sister, Melanie, eager to meet their niece, Sarah. It did not even matter that Chuck had refused to come, refused to be part of his mother's "other life," as Charles so often referred to her past.

What mattered was that they were a family, and that though the definition of the word perhaps had shifted, family was still family if you felt it in your heart.

She rubbed the sunscreen into her cheeks now and thought about Amy—the little girl who, for five years, she'd thought had been hers. After returning from the Vineyard, Jess had gone to the Hawthornes and told them that Melanie had been her baby, that Amy had not. And yet Jess knew that a small part of her would always grieve for Amy—the child whose life had been cut too short, the child whose birth mother had been deceived into believing she had died and never existed, the child who had been wanted and nurtured and loved by her wonderful adoptive parents.

As Melanie had been.

As Phillip had been.

As Lisa had been.

"My friends can't believe you know Lisa Andrews's mother," Travis had said over and over in the car on the way to Woods Hole. Jess had teased him and asked if he thought that might give him special status at Yale. Indeed, she did know Lisa Andrews's mother, and knew her well.

She leaned against the railing and looked off to the coastline of the Vineyard, wondering if Ginny was truly happy, and suspecting that, at last, she was. It had taken another couple of weeks for Ginny's back to heal, then she had returned to L.A. A few days ago she'd called Jess to report that business—Jake's business, *her* business now—was kind of a hoot and that she probably should have done something like this years ago. She also told Jess that Phillip had arrived, and that he and Lisa had become glued at the "hips, lips, and every other part in between."

She added that Jess might want to start looking for a dress . . . that it looked as if there would be a wedding in the "family" soon . . . and "Hell, probably grandchildren won't be far behind." She also said she didn't think it would take too much convincing for Lisa and Phillip to have the ceremony on Martha's Vineyard, maybe even on the beach in West Chop. She hoped Dick would help make the arrangements.

Jess had smiled and thought about P.J., and how happy she'd have been at the way things had turned out.

She folded her arms around herself now and watched West Chop coming more clearly into view. As for herself, she still was unsure what would happen next. She only knew that Richard had called, that he'd invited her and the children to spend the month of August on the island.

Whatever it brought, Jess knew it would be fine. She felt so much stronger now than she ever had in her life: strong enough to let Carlo and her other assistants take over her business for an entire month and not worry that it would fall into ruin; strong enough to no longer hide from Charles or from the friends they'd once had, friends who now hired her as they hired their maids. None of that mattered any longer, for Jess was Jess, and Jess was complete.

"Passengers, return to your vehicles for docking," said a voice over the speaker on the top deck of the ferry.

Jess gathered her purse, and two of her children, and, with a wide smile and a warm feeling inside, she walked down the stairs to the hold of the ship, and waited for whatever was going to happen next.

Karin sat at the antique rolltop desk in her attic bedroom at Mayfield House, holding the note that had come in the mail.

It was written on pale pink paper—not scented, though, not like the paper of the fifteen-year-old girl who had written so many letters to Richard from Larchwood Hall, letters that Richard at last had in his possession, to do with whatever he wanted. He said he might give them to Mellie, so she would know how much she'd always been loved, so she would know her grandfather Bates—Brit—had saved them for her.

Then Karin turned her thoughts back to the note that she held in her hand, and slowly, she read it again.

> *Dear Karin,*
> *There are so many things I could say to you now,*
> *but I'm afraid I cannot find the words. You have*
> *changed my life in so many ways; I look forward to*

knowing you better, to sharing some memories and making some new ones.

But for now, I simply can only say thank you. Thank you for helping Melanie become the wonderful young woman that she is; thank you for having loved my father when I was unable; and, most of all, thank you for having the courage to help me make my family complete.

Thank you, Karin. From the bottom of my mended heart.

It was signed, "With much love, from Jess."

She held it a moment, then felt herself smile. Then she folded the letter, put it back in the envelope, and tucked it inside the secret compartment of the old rolltop desk—right next to the prettiest, most special sea glass that she'd ever found on the beach.

In *Tides of the Heart*—her sixth novel from Bantam Books—Jean Stone recreates the characters of her first book, *Sins of Innocence,* and transports them around her favorite New England locales, including the celebrated island of Martha's Vineyard. A former advertising copywriter, Ms. Stone is now an adjunct writing instructor at American International College in Springfield, Massachusetts, and is working on her next novel.

Sizzling Romance from One of the World's Hottest Pens

SANDRA BROWN

New York Times bestselling author

Deborah Smith

*"A uniquely significant voice
in contemporary fiction."*

—Romantic Times

Silk and Stone　　　___29689-2　$5.99/$6.99 in Canada

Blue Willow　　　___29690-6　$5.99/$7.99

Miracle　　　___29107-6　$5.99/$7.99

A Place to Call Home　　　___57813-8　$6.50/$8.99

When Venus Fell　　　___11143-4　$23.95/$29.95

Ask for these books at your local bookstore or use this page to order.

Please send me the books I have checked above. I am enclosing $____ (add $2.50 to cover postage and handling). Send check or money order, no cash or C.O.D.'s, please.

Name _____

Address _____

City/State/Zip _____

Send order to: Bantam Books, Dept. FN72, 2451 S. Wolf Rd., Des Plaines, IL 60018
Allow four to six weeks for delivery.

Prices and availability subject to change without notice.　　　FN 72 11/98